THE METHUSELAH PARADOX

BY

EJ JACKSON

The Methuselah Paradox
Copyright EJ Jackson 2016
Published by Neon Sky Books

Neon Sky Books
admin@neonskybooks.com

Publisher's Note: This is a work of fiction. Names, characters, places, and incidents are a product of the author's imagination. Locales and public names are sometimes used for atmospheric purposes. Any resemblance to actual people, living or dead, or to businesses, companies, events, institutions, or locales is completely coincidental.

The Methuselah Paradox/ EJ Jackson. – 1st ed.

DEDICATION

For Graham

ACKNOWLEDGMENTS

'The Methuselah Paradox' has been a few years in the writing and I owe many people heartfelt thanks for their help along the way:

Thank you to Barbara Rogan and Eloise Miller for their encouragement and advice; Sue Thomason for her invaluable and detailed feedback on the very early drafts; my fellow writers on the Faber Academy 'How to Write a Novel Online' course, and The Writer's Workshop 'Self-editing your Novel' course; Marit for her help with London Underground travel for 'The Journey', the short story which led to 'The Methuselah Paradox'; Gary Curtis and Ben Lee for feedback; Dr. Carl Fratter FRCPath for his patience with my many questions about gene therapy – any errors are, of course, entirely mine; Mel Wilkins for extensive feedback for the manuscript and her help with the book trailer; Richard Oliver, Simon Bugg and Amelia Sefton for bringing the three main characters to life for the trailer; Sue Turner of www.elephantinscarlet.co.uk for recording and editing the trailer, and all these lovely people who helped to fund it:

Jean Thomson, Mark Bennett, Sue Thomason, Sam Jackson, Marit Røkeburg, Pamela Walton, Dawn Cockcroft, Thomas Walton, Gary Curtis, Alison Jane Reid, and Thomas Nightingale; Matthew Thomason for his haunting theme music; Catherine Archer-Wills for trailer artwork and Rachel Lawston for the book cover. Thank you too, to my husband Graham for his unfailing support.

And of course, thank you to you, dear reader!

Elaine Jackson

PART ONE: MANCHESTER, 2267

PROLOGUE:
UNITED ENGLAND POLICE AUTHORITY

'Interview suspended - this is a waste of time, Jim. File the report - let's get back out there.' Lounging in the corner across from his partner, Neil Sanchez's face was a study in disappointment – in the case, their lack of progress, and almost certainly in the badly-lit cupboard optimistically described as 'office space'.

James Moran shook his head. 'He'll talk – he just needs the right incentive.' He reached across the table, his hand breaking through the holographic image of the man in the holding cell three floors below them, and retrieved his ID card from the two-way HoloVu. The prisoner's image flickered and faded as Moran stood up, sliding the card into its usual position in the clear breast pocket of his police issue jacket. 'I'm going down there.'

Sanchez made it across the room in two easy strides and grabbed Moran's arm, his hand sliding off the black protective coating of his colleague's uniform. 'No way – you'll lose us the convic for sure – remember the last time…?'

Moran snorted. 'That was inevitable - nothing to do with what we did or didn't do.' He snatched his helmet from the table and punched the exit plate on the wall beside him. 'I'm not letting this one go,' he threw over his shoulder as he stepped into the corridor.

Sanchez rolled his eyes. 'Here we go again....' He gathered up his own helmet and followed his partner along the corridor and into the outer office.

'Who upset him?' Felice swiveled in her chair to follow Moran's progress.

'Don't ask,' Sanchez sighed. 'You didn't see us, Felice, okay?'

'Okay....' Felice shrugged. 'But CamVu will log it just the same. Can't you control him?'

'Me? Control Jim Moran? You're kidding. Besides, you know nothing will come of it.' He jerked his head upwards. 'Upstairs have more important things to worry about – I hope.'

'That's gonna look bad on your record,' Sanchez muttered as the black and silver patrol vehicle eased silently out onto the highway. The stabilizing fins did little to counteract the bumpy ride as it skimmed the weed-and-debris strewn surface on a cushion of compressed air, leaves and other detritus swirling in their wake. Like everything else they used, the vehicle was months overdue for a service.

Moran grunted. 'And the woman and child? It's a result, Neil – that's all I care about – and it's the only thing that matters at the end of the day.'

'We haven't got them yet. They'll have your badge if we lose him...'

Moran nodded at the heads-up display, where two red indicators had begun to flash. 'Now we do.' He flexed his palm, activating the built-in communications link to HQ. 'Moran, UEPA1443 – send a Victim Recovery Unit to co-ordinates...'

'Where the hell did you get a working tracker? On second thoughts, don't tell me...I'm not sure I want to know.'

Moran gave a tight grin. 'You don't.'

* * *

The overhead lights in DCI Walker's tenth floor office caught and reflected off the lenses of his spectacles – a ridiculous affectation in

Moran's opinion, with retinal stem cell rejuvenation the usual treatment for myopia. But Walker, for all his foibles, was a decent enough supervisor.

'Good result, James. Now take some down time – I'll block your access if I see you back here within forty-eight hours.' Walker's image flickered as the lift carrying Moran descended. 'Any word from the hospital?'

Moran shook his head. 'I'm headed over there now.'

'Good. Remember what I said – you're owed time out, so if you need to bring your vacation forward...'

'I'm better working, sir.'

'Your call. I'll see you the day after tomorrow.'

* * *

'I am so sorry, Mr. Moran.'

Odd, how five words could shatter a world. In truth, they were hardly necessary – the expression on Ballard's face was more than enough. The consultant carried on talking, but Moran tuned him out – just as he had when Cassie first got her diagnosis. He felt Ballard's hand on his arm and shook it off, taking a step away to put space between them. Moran didn't want the man's sympathy – he wanted him to say it had been a mistake, that his thirteen-year-old daughter was not going to die after all... but it wasn't going to happen. He took a deep breath, and let it out slowly, pushing his anger down.

'How long?'

Ballard didn't shrug –that wasn't his way– but he might as well have done. 'Difficult to say. Days, perhaps – certainly no more than a week. I'm...'

'Sorry. Yes, you said. Can I see her?'

'Of course. They're about to change the IV. Her veins are collapsing... it might take a few minutes. Perhaps there's someone you'd like to call....?'

Moran thought about the families to whom he had delivered the worst news imaginable, and knew how it went: shock. Disbelief.

Then, a shake of the head, a refusal to acknowledge the truth, followed by anger. *I'm sorry.* How many times had he uttered those same words, and been glad to hand over to victim support, relieved that he wouldn't have to witness the fallout? Telling his ex-wife that the one good thing to come out of their union would soon follow the majority of her peers...he didn't want to make that call. At least not until he'd seen Cassie.

'Later. I'd like to see her now, Doctor.'

At first, the room looked just as it had nine hours ago. He'd been on shift since then –and had managed one happy ending, while part of his mind had been here, in this room, with Cassie.

But now something was missing. Moran stood by the bed, and touched the pale hand of his only child. Cassie's chest – not yet filled out, marking her out as almost but not quite the woman she would never become - rose and fell in shallow movements, barely stirring the covers. The sunken face and waxy pallor told their own story. Cassie's eyes, naked without the dark lashes of which she had been so proud, were closed, her presence all but gone.

'Cassie...' he knew she couldn't hear him now, but he needed to say her name.

'She can't hear you.' Ballard had followed him into the small room.

Moran spun, his anger rushing to the surface.

'I'd like some privacy!' He knew his tone was bordering on rude, that he was being unfair, but he couldn't find it in himself to mind. It wasn't Ballard's daughter lying comatose. Did he even *have* a daughter? Moran neither knew nor cared.

'Of course.' Ballard must have seen this a thousand times before – more, perhaps. He bowed his head in apology and left the room.

Moran heard the soft sigh as the door closed and waited for the tears to come. But his eyes remained dry, and his pulse gradually slowed. The anger - and with it the urge to rage against the unfairness of it all - receded. He couldn't cry, not yet. He pulled up a chair and sat, covering Cassie's left hand with his own. It felt small, and cold.

* * *

Half an hour later Moran stepped out into a world that would care little for his pain; after all, his was just one sad story amongst billions.

He leaned against the low wall overlooking the memorial park, the warm spring breeze ruffling his silver hair. It carried with it the scent of new life, and he stared bleakly at the sea of force-grown poppies, their delicate petals fluttering as the air moved across them. Each bloom marked a life lost, and tomorrow, perhaps the day after, another would be added. He swallowed hard, and reached into his pocket for his Cell. It was an outmoded form of communication, and parts were -like everything else- hard to come by; but unlike Walker's spectacles, there was a practical reason for using it – Moran preferred his private communications to be off the grid, not subject to UEPA's CommScan facility. He turned the tiny device over and over, his fingers stumbling as he put off making off the call, delaying the moment when he would have to relinquish control.

Vita, as always, would be practical. She would cancel her engagements, and even though they were no longer co-habiting, would call the UEPA to log extra downtime for Moran, because he hadn't even thought to, despite promising Walker that he would; and she, knowing him of old, would know he hadn't. Moran had not told anyone but Walker where he was going, unable to face the sympathy of his colleagues, many of whom were also bereaved parents; but Sanchez would guess, word would get around. Vita, who still had access to the apartment – he hadn't yet got around to deleting her fingerprint from the lock- would turn up with a change of clothes for them both. Life would be divided into Before and After.

He sucked in a lungful of air, and hit 'V'. His ex-wife picked up straight away, almost as if she had been waiting for him to call.

'James?'

'It's time.' His voice caught.

'Darling…'

'Don't.'

'I'll be with you in thirty minutes.'

Turning away from the poppy memorial, Moran pocketed the cell and almost collided with a man standing on the path. He took a step sideways. The man countered.

'James Moran?'

'Who wants to know?' *Not now.*

The man blocking his way to Cassie was thin to the point of emaciation. An informant? Moran didn't recognise him.

'Mr. Gilling sends his condolences.'

Moran took a deep breath. *She isn't even dead yet...* 'I'll tell you and your employer again, I'm not looking for work. I *have* work. I also have...' Gilling had been pressuring Moran to interview for a post for weeks now, but Moran was no scientist, and he wasn't interested in security work, which would surely be all that Gilling would have to offer a man of Moran's career background.

'...a daughter who is dying. Yes, we know, Mr. Moran. It's precisely why he wants to speak with you.'

'If you know that, then you know that now is *not* the time.' Moran tried to walk around Gilling's flunky, but once more the man blocked him. Moran's fists clenched. It would be the work of a moment to deck him, and to hell with the consequences. What did anything matter now?

'Now is *precisely* the time. We haven't been entirely open with you, James, but if your daughter is to have any...'

'Don't talk to me about my daughter!' The anger was back, and with it an urge to do the man some damage.

'Do you *want* your daughter to die? There may be an alternative.'

Moran stared at him.

'What do you mean?' If Gilling's man was talking about cryogenic suspension, he could forget it – Moran had already checked it out. His and Vita's salaries combined wouldn't be anywhere near enough to pay for it, and there was no guarantee it would save Cassie.

'Please, just come with me – it won't take long.'

Moran shook his head. 'My daughter...' his voice broke. 'my daughter may have hours to live, and *you* ...'

'I understand. But if you will spare just thirty minutes... you *will* want to hear this.'

Moran doubted it. But it was a fact that Cassie was no longer aware of anything around her, and it would be at least thirty minutes before Vita got here, more if the traffic was bad. Did he want to sacrifice a last opportunity to be alone with his daughter on a fool's errand? Gilling's men were nothing if persistent – calls to his private line, e-mail... he had considered taking out a restraining order, hadn't got around to it. Besides, what reason could he give –that someone called Gilling was trying to headhunt him? Hardly just cause. This was the first time one had shown up in person.

'You asked if I wanted to save Cassie's life. You must know that's impossible.'

The thin man almost smiled. 'I know no such thing. Just *thirty minutes*, Mr. Moran.'

* * *

True to his word, Gilling's aide -who introduced himself as Zachary Lang - had brought Moran to the outskirts of the city in a little under eight minutes. He had almost certainly violated several traffic laws in the process, but seemed neither to notice or care, handling the aged but well-maintained vehicle with consummate ease. Moran wondered if Lang – or his boss- might have contacts in Traffic – it was amazing that the man still had a license.

Helmshore Inc. was housed in a building which, if the shabby exterior was any guide, had to go back at least three centuries. Sited half a mile up a hill and off the main highway along an unmade road, the once bright brickwork of the three-story construction was now neglected and crumbling, the grounds around it almost overrun by weeds. If Moran had ever had cause to pass it on the road, he might have assumed it abandoned – which could be intentional. What kind of outfit was Gilling running here?

Security appeared to be minimal, which confirmed Moran's suspicion – very few people had to be aware that the building was in use.

What kind of work was being carried out here, and why site it out of the city? Medical research attracted huge funding, especially since the cancer pandemic. Whatever kind of outfit Gilling ran, Moran doubted it was legitimate.

Lang parked in a bay adjacent to the entrance. He had barely spoken during the short journey, deflecting Moran's questions with a curt 'I'm not at liberty to answer.' Now he pressed a forefinger to the entry scanner and silently held the door open for Moran to enter ahead of him.

After Moran and Lang had climbed two flights of stairs – no elevator in sight- Anton Gilling stepped forward to grasp Moran's hand. He was tall and almost as thin as Lang, with a thatch of unruly black hair bisected by a silver stripe, and wearing tweeds under a shabby white coat. He looked to be in his thirties, but his bearing and the calculating eyes told Moran that Gilling had to be twice, perhaps three times that age. He looked every inch the scientist – his calling immediately obvious from his quirky dress sense and the racked equipment surrounding them.

'I'm Anton Gilling. Welcome to my workshop, James. I had begun to think we might never meet.'

Moran bristled at the familiarity, pulling his hand out of Gilling's. 'Please make this quick, Mr. Gilling – I don't have much time.'

Gilling smiled. 'That's where you're wrong, James. Isn't he, Zachary?'

Lang nodded. He had taken up a position beside Gilling which Moran immediately recognised – protector, perhaps even a colleague, but certainly more than the lackey Moran had taken him for.

'Please take a seat. Would you like some refreshment? Tea, perhaps, or black market coffee…?'

Moran shook his head. 'I don't need to sit down, Mr. Gilling, and I didn't come to socialize. What can you do for Cassie?' Every fibre of his being was urging him to ditch this ridiculous charade and head back to his daughter. *If she dies and I'm not there…*

'Have you heard of the King-Gilling theory?'

Moran shook his head. 'What has this to do with saving my daughter's life?'

'Look around you, James. What do you see?'

The interior of the building was in direct contrast to the exterior – money had been spent here. The entire top floor of the three-story building housed what appeared to be a state-of-the-art laboratory.

In the centre of the lab stood a small coffin-shaped booth encased in what looked like dull stainless steel. Thick cables coiled around it, snaking away beneath the floor. A surgical trolley seat stood nearby, and as Gilling led him closer, Moran saw a tray bearing syringes and phials attached to one armrest. He frowned, recognising a subcutaneous LI -learning implant, and what looked like a child-safe locator chip.

'What is this – some kind of experimental therapy? Because if you think I'm going to let you…'

Gilling held up a large hand. 'This isn't experimental therapy, James,' he said, his affable manner fading, replaced by something colder and more calculating. 'This is a far more direct intervention.'

'Then what is it? I don't have time for games.'

'Of course you don't. Your daughter is dying, and you want to know how we can save her. But we won't be involved, James - we will help *you* to save young Cassie's life.'

Moran glanced impatiently at his watch. 'You have five minutes, then I'm leaving.'

Gilling, ignoring Moran's hostility, put a firm but gentle hand on his shoulder and turned him towards the booth.

'What do you think this is, James?'

'Some kind of… irradiation booth?' He'd heard of such treatments – the radiation killed the cancer cells – but it damaged other cells too. The practice had been abandoned a century ago, then revived with the onset of the cancer pandemic. He and Vita had declined it for Cassie because they'd heard of no long-term survivors.

Gilling smiled. 'No. It's a time machine.'

Moran turned on his heel. 'I've heard enough.'

Gilling's hand shot out, grabbing Moran's arm in a vice-like grip which stopped him in his tracks.

'You've heard of the Methuselah program, I'm sure.'

Moran realised that Lang had circled around to cut off his escape route. What the hell were they playing at?

'Of course I have. It's a bloody disaster.' Not just for him, and Vita and Cassie – but for the whole of mankind. What were the latest figures – the estimated extinction of humanity within two generations?

Gilling nodded.

'Yes, it is. Now try to imagine if someone could go back in time to prevent the program from being implemented…so that the cancer pandemic never happens.'

He'd heard enough. 'Suppose you let me get back to my daughter, Gilling, and you think about joining the real world?' Moran pushed Gilling's arm away and headed for the door. Lang stepped in front of him, and Moran balled his fists, making his intentions clear. He side-stepped Lang and kept walking. Lang kept pace with him.

'We've had the capability to time travel for a hundred years, James,' Gilling continued, walking with him. 'We just had no way of working out when we would arrive, or how to return. Now we do.'

Moran reached the door, and turned to face the two men.

'You're not seriously expecting me to believe…' he followed the movement of Gilling's hand as the scientist reached into his pocket, and – a classic, stupid mistake- took his eyes off Lang. The sting of the hypodermic on the side of his neck was his punishment. He pushed Lang away, but it was too late –the cool liquid was already moving through his veins. His vision began to blur.

'I'm sorry it has to happen this way, James. Look, we don't have much time. When you wake up, you will still be in Manchester, but in the early twenty-first century. You'll have a data implant under your scalp - it will feed all the relevant data you're likely to need, and you'll have a transponder in your wrist so that we can retrieve you when your mission is complete. Stop the program from being implemented, Moran – by whatever means necessary. Do that, and Cassie will still be alive when you return. Do you understand?'

'You're mad…' Moran's knees finally gave way. He felt Gilling and Lang catch him and tried to pull free, but his muscles were no longer responding. He lay on the floor, helpless, as the two men crouched over him. Whatever had been in the syringe had all but paralyzed him – he couldn't lift a finger to save himself. He felt someone – Lang, he thought- lift his arm, turning it over to expose his wrist.

'No….' Moran barely felt the sting of the hypo gun as it pushed the tiny transponder under the skin of his wrist, or a similar sensation as the implant slid under the skin behind his left ear. 'Why … me?' He couldn't see them properly now – they were fuzzy shapes moving above him, nothing more.

'Don't fight it, Moran,' Gilling's voice sounded far away. 'Think of Cassie – you're doing this for her…'

As Gilling and Lang hauled him to his feet, Moran blacked out.

PART TWO: MANCHESTER, 1979

2: MANCHESTER, 2RD MAY 1979

Moran blinked, inhaled sharply, and coughed as dust irritated his throat. A dull headache throbbed in time with his heartbeat. His left hand felt as if it might be on fire. Had he been injured on duty? No, he'd been to the hospital… He opened his eyes to a faded pattern of flowers and interwoven stems in grubby yellow. What the hell…?

Pulling himself upright, Moran ignored mounting nausea and looked around. His surroundings felt vaguely familiar, but something was off…. he closed his eyes and took a long, deep breath, calming and centering himself. Then he opened them again.

The room was large, empty apart from a few pieces of furniture covered by dust sheets. It took a moment or two for Moran to recognise the tray ceiling and arched windows – he was still in Gilling's lab. But where the hell was the equipment?

Out of habit, Moran clenched his left fist to call for assistance, and gasped as pain ripped through his hand and up his arm. The hand itself had been coated in flesh-coloured WoundWrap, and the cause of his pain was immediately obvious – Gilling – or Lang- had surgically removed his Link. Not only was he now unable to raise the Department, but they would have no way of tracking him. He ran his finger over a small, raised and slightly red lump under the skin of his wrist – the transponder; his route home if Gilling was to be believed. He found a similar bump behind his left ear – the implant.

It was at this point Moran realised that he was no longer wearing his police issue uniform. These clothes were unfamiliar in both texture and appearance: dark brown trousers in an unfamiliar ribbed fabric, a thin black sweater in a soft acrylic material, and a black faux leather jacket. Black ankle boots -in real leather, he realised as he scrambled to his feet and heard the material creak - completed his ensemble.

Holding the faded yellow couch for support, Moran waited until the room stopped spinning around him. So had he really time-travelled? It seemed unlikely, but the room's transformation.... He tried to remember what Gilling had told him as he was going under; the mid-twenty-first century, he'd said.

Releasing his hold on the couch, Moran patted his pockets, and found a slim leather wallet, of the kind that few people used any more. In it, he found a small blue plastic card, similar to the keycards which had once been common as a means of entry to one's home, school, car, place of work... except this one had no personal identification other than his name, J Moran, followed by a row of numbers – six numbers in pairs of two, followed by a longer number. No fingerprint, no retina map. On the back, he recognised his own signature (obviously forged, or a damn good facsimile) and another series of numbers. 'Midshire Bank', he read aloud.

In addition to the bank card, the wallet contained a photographic likeness of himself on another card, this time coloured pink. It appeared to be an authority to drive vehicles. The card also carried a white flag with a red cross bisecting it, which Moran did recognise as the Independent UK flag of 2018. He also found five rectangular pieces of thin, flexible plastic bearing an artist's interpretation of a face he recognised – King William V. Each sheet bore the words 'Twenty Pounds' and Moran realised that he was holding banknotes – a form of currency which no longer existed in his own time. He would have to look after them – without them he might be unable to eat, find accommodation or even travel.

Moran shook his head, groaning as the nausea returned. What of Cassie? Was she still alive? What happened when Vita got to the hospital and he was nowhere to be found? How had he allowed himself to be taken away from his family? Finally, after the anger, the tears came.

* * *

Still suffering from the effects of the sedative – he wasn't normally a 'crier'- Moran slowly explored the rest of the house for anything that might prove useful, but found nothing. The last occupant of the house had been elderly and perhaps partially bed-ridden, if the various mobility aids gathering dust in almost every ground floor room were any indication. The tattered remains of blue and white crime scene tape – showing clear signs of rodent activity - lay scattered around the kitchen. Moran assumed a death to have taken place, but if the absence of further police intervention was anything to go by, it seemed to have been from natural causes.

Gilling had committed a crime, of that there was no doubt – the abduction of a serving officer in the UEPA would carry a detention sentence of at least five years. But as far as Moran was concerned, Gilling's real crime had been to take him away from his daughter. It was time to get out of here: he had a job to do, and then he could get back to Cassie.

* * *

Afterwards, Moran couldn't remember if it had been the stench, or perhaps the noise, which finally pulled him from the depths of unconsciousness. A mixture of rotting vegetation and decomposing meat with an underlying metallic tang he couldn't place, it caught at the back of his throat, making him want to retch. A rumbling and grinding sound from somewhere close by made the ground beneath him vibrate at a pitch that set his teeth on edge.

The proximity of the face looming over him - the man's expression as startled as his own must be - sent Moran flinching backwards to hit the back of his head on a cold, rough surface. Another wave of nausea washed over him. His joints felt stiff, his extremities numb with cold. How long had he been lying there?

The man coughed and spat onto the ground, narrowly missing Moran's leg. 'Bloody 'ell mate, ah thought you were a goner!' The craggy face turned away as he addressed someone out of Moran's eye line. 'Soakay Gaz– it's just some bloody wino…'

The man wasn't young – to Moran's eyes, accustomed to a different population demographic where the majority of the population appeared to be in their prime, he seemed impossibly ancient. Short and wiry in stature, a sprinkling of grey stubble peppered the sagging jowls, and the man's ruddy face was lined, prematurely wrinkled by exposure to the elements. A thin paper stick protruded from chapped lips barely covering an orthodontist's shame. He made an impatient sound and extended a hand encased in an oversized and filthy industrial glove. Startled, and unable to even begin to guess how old the man might be, Moran simply stared at him.

'Give us yer and, man – you gotta move, less you wanna end up under the effin cart!'

The man's dialect was not one Moran recognised, and it took him a moment -with the aid of Gilling's implant- to decipher the mangled vowels as originating in Newcastle. Wordlessly, he let the man pull him to his feet. He was stronger than he looked.

Moran's head felt as taut as a drum, the world around him a painful cacophony of unfamiliar sounds. The feeling faded, and he began to identify individual elements: a constant background hum he couldn't place, a regular, jarring clank of metal on metal, snatches of music, a dog barking – and voices. Happy, workaday voices: laughter, someone whistling. A background of city sounds which seemed at once both familiar and alien.

'What…?' his throat felt dry and he coughed, hating every lungful of the tainted air. The man ignored Moran's abortive question, and addressed the sky, rolling his eyes in dramatic fashion.

'Jeezus, he don't even know what 'e's doin' 'ere….' The man spat again. 'Sleepin' it off, I'd say! C'mon man, move yer bloody arse!'

With an impatient grunt, he grabbed Moran's arm and hauled him sideways. 'Christ on a bike, you still effin' drunk, or what?'

Moran saw that he – and his unlikely rescuer- had been in the direct path of a large vehicle; it was reversing steadily along the narrow street towards them, and now Moran understood the reason for the stench of decomposing organic matter: he had been lying next to a garbage dumpster, and it was collection day.

The truck shuddered to a halt less than a metre away from the two men, air escaping from the braking system with a shriek as the combustion engine (the source of the metallic tang in the air, Moran realised) revved and a pickup arm swung down to lock onto the dumpster. Moran turned to face the wall and leaned against it, retching as an overwhelming stink of decomposing matter filled the small space between the red brick buildings. The slight tingle in the underside of his left wrist as the transponder responded to his movement was small comfort as he finally remembered where – and more importantly *when-* he was.

3: MANCHESTER, MAY 1979

When Moran had tried to use the banknotes to board a bus after walking for almost thirty minutes to a village post office, he realised he had arrived four decades too early. The banknotes brought only a blank stare.

'I ain't takin' that, mate. Got any coin? Sorry – no money, no ride.'

Only the timely intervention of a middle-aged man in a vehicle which had clearly seen better days had saved him from a long walk back to the empty house and a night without food or water.

'Got that 'flu bug, mate? I've already had it so I don't mind giving you a ride. Anywhere you want to go in particular, like, or shall I just let you off on Chorlton Street? I'm off to railway station to collect the missus, she's been away to her sister's for nigh on a fortnight, been took poorly. Cancer.'

'That will do just fine,' Moran rasped – and he did indeed feel as if he might be coming down with a virus – was this how his immune system was going to cope with the twenty-first century, or simply the after-effects of his journey through time?

Thanking the driver for his kindness, Moran stood on the corner of Chorlton Street and took stock. He was effectively penniless and he badly needed to find somewhere to rest; he had thrown up twice already during the walk to the post office, and now had a headache like none he'd experienced before. What options would be available to a man with no money? Well, he wouldn't find them standing here...

A moment of dizziness made him pause outside a small store selling periodicals and candies, where a flyer in the window advertising a 'homeless hostel' on Downing Street caught his eye. He memorized the simple directions, and set off.

The stench of vehicle emissions made Moran's nausea worse – the air was full of it. So different to his own time, where hydro-fueled transport at least kept the air clean, and the traffic noise to a minimum. How did they bear this endless cacophony?

The small wound behind his left ear where the implant now sat under his skin had begun to throb painfully in time with his pulse – it was too soon for infection, surely? But he had no idea how long he might have lain unconscious at the house...or how many hours might have passed in his own time. It hurt to think of Cassie breathing her last without him. But Gilling had promised she would still be alive on his return... could he believe him?

The journey took Moran a good ten minutes. The 'no questions asked' attitude of the staff and the simple folding bed with thin blankets in a room hardly bigger than a cupboard was all he needed; his explanation that he was sick and had been mugged on his arrival in the city waved away with 'we don't judge, we're just here to help.' Moran thanked the man and lay down on the bed fully clothed. He was asleep within seconds.

4: MANCHESTER, 8TH MAY

Dorothy Hammond carefully applied more foundation, working it in until the bruise was barely visible; it would be hard to see, unless you knew it was there. She took a last look around the bedroom she had shared with Ray for the last eleven years, smoothed down her skirt, and walked out, closing the door softly behind her. On the narrow landing, she took a deep breath, forced her facial muscles into a smile, and poked her head around Ian's door.

'Are you ready, love?' Bless him, he would have no idea that today's visit would be the last to this school dentist, or that he wouldn't be going to Tim's birthday party tomorrow… but it couldn't be helped, and he'd soon make new friends, wouldn't he?

Ian looked up, his expression pensive. 'I s'pose so…' Like most kids his age (and older – Ray would never admit that he was petrified of the drill, but had a mouthful of grey teeth to prove it) her son didn't much like going to the school dentist.

'Come on then – I'll treat you to a bun in Woollies afterwards, before we get your pressie for Tim.' Her tone sounded false, but Ian's face cleared, and he smiled.

'Okay, Mum. Do I have to go back to school, after?'

Dorothy pretended to consider the question, and then shook her head. 'We'll both of us bunk off, shall we?'

Ian ran down the stairs ahead of her, and Dorothy shut the door on her son's room. It was a shame they wouldn't be able to take all his toys, but there wouldn't be room in the suitcase. She hoped he would accept it, not make a fuss.

Dorothy had been putting a bit by each week since Christmas, and had finally saved enough from her job in the kitchen at Woolworths to buy a new suitcase. It had to be new, because she had been petrified that Ray might notice if she took the battered one sitting on top of their wardrobe. The new case was in the cleaning cupboard at work, hidden amongst the buckets, mops and tubs of disinfectant with the aid of her colleague and good friend Gloria. Dorothy had been adding clothes to it in dribs and drabs over the past few weeks, so Ray wouldn't see anything was missing. Not that he would probably notice anyway – if it didn't directly concern him, he wasn't interested. Ian, typical boy that he was, would also probably never realise that he was missing a pair of trousers here or a t-shirt or jumper there. Dorothy's sister Hilda, who lived in Coventry and had never liked Ray, had offered to take them in until Dorothy could find somewhere more permanent.

'Don't worry about clothes for the lad,' she'd tried to reassure Dorothy. 'Stephen has grown that fast this past year, his casts-off are almost as good as new. They'll do for your lad until you get yourself on your feet.' Hilda had even put in a good word for her with the manager of the laundry where she worked, so there was the possibility of a job waiting for Dorothy if she wanted it. She'd need it, that was certain.

As she pulled the scuffed front door of the council flat shut behind them, Dorothy resisted the temptation to drop the key back through the letterbox – there'd be no going back after that, would there? But Ray would see it as soon as he got in, and Dorothy needed the hours he'd be sleeping after his shift to make her getaway. She had left him his tea on the side, wrapped in foil and with instructions on what oven setting to use and for how long the pie should bake. A pan of potatoes sat in water on the hob, and a note propped up against a tin of marrowfat peas (written and re-written many times that morning as she had struggled to find the right words) told Ray why she couldn't be there to get his tea on. She had apologised, explaining in a shaky hand that her sister wasn't well and that she was going to take Ian to the dentist and then get the train to Coventry, to make sure Hilda was all right. It would be a trip out for Ian, who didn't often see his auntie and cousin Stephen. Ray wouldn't like it, of course. But if she went home again he would no doubt add another bruise to the multitude already colouring her body, waiting until he thought she was relaxed –as if she ever was- before dishing out his punishment… This time, he wouldn't get the chance.

* * *

The first two days of Moran's life in 1979 had passed in a confused blur. He slept, drank a little water, took half of a small bowl of soup when it was offered, and slept again. At some point he overheard voices discussing whether he should be in hospital. He had enough wits about him to mumble 'No hospitals' before blacking out once more.

When he woke on the third day, it was to emerge from a muddled dream in which Gilling had been most insistent that he go to a store called Woolworths at Piccadilly Gardens on 8th May no later than one pm, and find a Peter King. Who Peter King might be, and why Moran needed to meet him, he had no idea, but at least it was proof that the implant was working.

Feeling stronger after a filling (if unhealthy but surprisingly tasty) breakfast of fried food, Moran asked for directions to Piccadilly Gardens. It was not far from the hostel, and Moran followed them without undue difficulty. His ability to understand the various local accents seemed to have improved whilst he had slept, and he guessed the implant might have something to do with it. He had been told very little about its capabilities -there hadn't been time- but he could make reasonable deductions, and sleep-enhanced learning was nothing new. What did puzzle him was that Gilling had given him papers which wouldn't be valid for another forty years, yet the implanted message -and the clothing, which was in a style consistent with what other men were wearing- indicated that he had known that Moran would find himself in the nineteen-seventies. Moran didn't like the direction his thoughts were heading.

Within seconds of taking up position outside the department store, the implant quietly informed him in Gilling's voice that the thin, curly-haired individual in a fawn duffel coat who had just walked past him into the building was Peter King, who would one day contribute quite significantly towards the development of the technology which had brought Moran to this place and time. It then, in slightly more urgent tones, advised Moran that this branch of Woolworths would shortly be engulfed in fire.

Was *this* why he had arrived three decades too early? But that didn't make sense – for Moran to have arrived here, King *couldn't* have perished in the fire, could he? Unless… perhaps Moran's presence was the *reason* King had lived, and had enabled Gilling to create the time machine in the first place.

Moran let a woman and her young son go past him, and followed them into the store. The woman, he noted, bore the anxious look of someone accustomed to fear – a victim of domestic violence, no doubt. Once a copper, always a copper…

* * *

'Are you getting Tim a card and all, love?'

Ian shrugged as he followed his mother into the store. 'I don't know if I've enough money, mum.'

'Ah, you should…' Dorothy Hammond paused, and looked at her watch. They'd been in the Dental surgery much longer than expected and time was pressing. Glo would be going off shift in half an hour, and then she'd be scuppered, wouldn't she?

'We'd better get a shift on.' She'd had to swap a day with Joyce because of Ian's appointment, saying that Ian wouldn't go if she didn't take him, which wasn't far from the truth. Besides, at eight -nearly nine- he was still a bit young to be running around the city on his own. No-one had questioned her, and only Glo and Dorothy herself knew that this would be her last day in Manchester.

She tried not to think about the job she was chucking away. She wouldn't miss the work, but she *would* miss the friends she'd made at Woollies, as they all called it, and the money.

'Ian, love, I just need to have a word with Auntie Gloria – I'll take you to the toys, you'll stay right there and pick your card and pressie for Tim. I'll just be a minute or two. Okay?'

'Okay, Mum.' Ian wasn't worried – he wasn't a baby anymore, and in any case he and Tim often came here on their own on a Saturday afternoon, when his mum thought he was at Tim's, and Tim's mum thought he was at Ian's. Armed with a pilfered schoolbook and a stubby pencil, they would update their league table of most coveted 'Star Wars' toys, working out how long it might take them to save up for this or that model. Their aim was to get the whole set, but it would take a very special kind of windfall to do that. Didn't stop them hoping, though.

* * *

Gloria's face shone with perspiration, but she grinned as Dorothy stuck her head around the kitchen door. The odour of cooked food turned Dorothy's stomach.

'So you're definitely going, then? Thought you might've changed your mind…. I don't mind telling you, Dotty, I've been that much on edge this morning, it's a wonder nothing's got burned…' Gloria wiped her hands on her apron, and called across to a woman at the serving hatch. 'Just nipping to the ladies, Bet, I'll be two minutes.'

'Too right I'm going,' Dorothy said as they hurried to the storeroom. 'I've left him a note – there's no going back now. Oh, you'd better have this.' She fumbled in her pocket for an envelope. Gloria took it, her dark eyes sad. Addressed to their manager, it was Dorothy's letter of resignation, which Gloria had helped her to write.

'You told *him* you were leaving?' Gloria tucked the envelope into her apron pocket, and pulled out a bunch of keys as they approached the locked storeroom.

'No – I told him I had to go to our Hilda's. It'll buy me some time. In any case he won't check, not for a while – he can't abide her, and she's not got a phone.'

Gloria nodded. 'Well, I've said it before, I'll miss you, love – but you're doing the right thing. What about your lad?'

'He doesn't know yet. I've left him looking at the toys… I hope he won't kick up a fuss.' She chewed her lip. 'I couldn't leave him, Glo.'

'Of course you couldn't. And he won't fuss… but even if he does, when he gets older he'll understand. He'll probably thank you for it.'

Dorothy took the suitcase from her friend. She swallowed hard, her voice thick with emotion.

'Yeah… Thanks for everything, Glo. You've been a good friend. When we're settled, I'll be in touch.'

'You do that.' They both knew it was unlikely - Gloria worked three days a week at Woolworths, and she also had a cleaning job in the evenings. She and husband Sidney didn't have a car, and unless Dorothy came to see her… well, she might just do that, Dorothy thought, but not for a good long while. The risk of running into Ray, or someone who might get word to him, would be too great.

Dorothy was just one flight away from the ground floor when she heard the first shout from above, and the sound of hurrying feet on the stairs heading her way.

'Fire!'

A tidal wave of people began to push past her, intent on reaching the ground floor, and safety. Their clothes carried a whiff of bitter smoke.

'Ian…' caught in the crossflow of people from above and those emerging from the first floor, Dorothy staggered. Her foot caught on the heel of a man who had just passed her, his hand firmly clasped around the upper arm of a youth in a duffle coat. Unbalanced by the case, she could do nothing to save herself. A flash of started faces, legs, and then the floor rushed up to meet her. A sharp blow to the side of her head as she hit the bottom step turned Dorothy's world black.

Ian had finally found a good card – it wasn't *too* babyish, and had spaceships on the front which, although they weren't from 'Star Wars', at least looked as if they *could* be, if you squinted and looked sideways at them. Then he realised his mum had forgotten to give him the extra money for the card, so he only had enough in his pocket to pay for the Millennium Falcon. The card didn't matter, he decided. He put it back, and as he turned away, was almost knocked over as someone barged past him. The Millennium Falcon slipped from his grasp and hit the floor – and although it was packed in plastic, Ian heard the crack as something broke. His heart sank – it had been the last one on the shelf.

'Oi!' The word slipped out before Ian could stop it, and he flinched as the culprit, a man who didn't look very old but had silver hair, stopped and turned to look at him. Pale green eyes bored into Ian's, then the man turned and hurried away. He didn't even say 'sorry'.

Ian bent to pick up the Falcon. He couldn't tell what was broken, but something was rattling about inside – he couldn't give it to Tim now. He'd have to go back and choose something else. If he was quick, hopefully no-one would see him put it back on the shelf.

As he headed back to the toy shelves, Ian saw that the man who had knocked into him hadn't gone far –he was talking urgently to a younger man in a duffle coat. They didn't seem to be friends – the silver-haired man had just snatched a card out of the other man's hand and shoved it back on the shelf – in the wrong place, Ian saw; it was a 'Happy Birthday Mum' card and he'd put it back in the 'Dad' section- and now he grabbed hold of the young man's arm. He tried to pull free, but Mr. Silver Hair wasn't letting go.

'Come with me – now!' he said, and turned and began to walk back towards Ian, the younger man in tow.

'What d'you think you're doing, man? You can't just…'

'I'm saving your life. Hurry!'

They pushed past Ian – who flattened himself against the display – and hurried towards the stairs.

'You're a bugger, you are!' Ian shouted after them, half-expecting the silver-haired man to come back and give him a good hiding for swearing at him, but it was as if he hadn't even heard – with the other man still protesting, the pair disappeared down the stairs.

Annoyed about Tim's present and the rude man, Ian hurried back to the toy section, keeping an eye out for his mum. If she was talking to Auntie Gloria – who wasn't really an Auntie- she had probably forgotten the time. Sometimes he'd be stood for ages, getting bored and fidgety as they yammered on. It was much better when he and Tim came by themselves, really.

He had almost decided on a Boba Fett action figure – he knew Tim didn't have that one, and it would even leave him money for a card - when he heard the first scream.

* * *

Afterwards, they told Ian that his Mum must have must been looking for him, and that she might have been overcome by the smoke. They told him that someone would fetch his father, and they would tell his father when they found her. They didn't say the words 'dead body' but Ian knew that was what they meant. He couldn't re-member crying, but his cheeks were sore and his nose was all bunged up, so he must have, mustn't he?

'She won't have known much about it, lad', the policeman who gave him a glass of orange juice said, as they sat in the station waiting for Ian's dad to collect him. Ian didn't believe him. His mum always knew a lot about everything, even when his dad told her she didn't know what she was talking about.

Ian thought about the man with silver hair again. He was sure he'd seen him before, when he and his mum first got to Woollies – he remembered him because he looked a bit like Colonel White in 'Cap-tain Scarlet', although he wasn't as old… Ian remembered Colonel White telling the other man that he was saving his life. So how come he knew about the fire before anyone else, unless he'd started it? Ian had tried to tell the policeman about him, but the man wasn't really listening; he was too busy talking to other policemen on his radio, trying to find out if Dorothy Hammond and Shirley Wilkins were among the casualties. Ian only worked out that the policeman's name was Wilkins when a crackly message came back:

'Just seen your missus in the crowd, Wilky. She's safe.'

But no word ever came about Ian's mum.

MANCHESTER, 8 MAY

'Mum! Mum! Where are you?'

The boy was a mess, tears and soot streaking his face.

Moran had good facial recognition skills, and was certain it was the same boy he had followed into the store with his mother; the woman with haunted eyes, who had tripped and fallen on the staircase. Moran had almost knocked the boy over getting to King, and the youngster had retaliated with a spirited curse.

He stopped, turned on his heel, and crouched down in front of the child, who turned wet, hopeful eyes on him.

''ave you seen me mum? She were inside, but I can't find 'er...'

Moran hesitated. *Don't get involved.* King had run off once they reached street level, too shaken by his close shave to even ask Moran how he knew about the fire -or to thank him- and Moran should have left, too. Instead he had found himself helping shocked survivors from the building until the emergency services arrived to take over. Moran had been unable to walk away from the tragedy unfolding around him, even though common sense told him that his involvement might change the course of history.

'I'm sorry, son...' If she hadn't got out, might it have been Moran's fault? If he hadn't been there, she might not have tripped... he hadn't seen the boy's mother emerge, but there were so many people milling about that she could have. He hoped so.

The boy's face crumpled. 'Can...can you find 'er for me, please? Her name's Dorothy 'ammond...'

Moran shook his head and stood up. It had been a mistake to stop. 'I haven't seen her.' He began to turn away, hesitating as the boy suddenly darted past him.

'Mister Wrigley!'

Moran turned to see an overweight man hurrying towards them, necktie askew and his florid face shining with sweat.

'Young Master Hammond, what...shouldn't you be in school? Ah, never mind, never mind – are you alright, son? Is your Mother not with you?'

Ian burst into tears and Wrigley gave Moran a hard look. 'Is this man bothering you?'

Ian shook his head. 'I can't find mum - she was s'posed to come back, but she didn't and, and he, he said he was sorry....'

Moran had lingered for far too long. He turned and walked away. Behind him, the child's explanation and Wrigley's responses faded into the background.

PART THREE: 1990-1991

5: LONDON, DECEMBER 1990

Moran stared glumly out at the passing view, his breath misting the glass. Snow – almost unheard of in his own time – had quickly ceased to be a novelty after only a few winters in Manchester. Falling prey to an influenza virus on his first day in the capital ensured that he spent the next few days in his hotel room, gripped by alternating fever and chills. Merry Christmas… New Year's Eve saw him determined to salvage something of the trip, but now all he wanted was to return to the haven of his room.

Driven by a viscous and biting north wind, snow was drifting sideways across the road in front of the bus, muffling the world. Moran fought the urge to close his eyes, the alcohol that he had consumed earlier conspiring with the influenza medication, the movement of the vehicle and the purr of its engine to create a relaxing, almost soporific effect. Only the frequent stops as passengers got on and off and the gust of cold air which hit him each time the doors opened kept him from falling deeply asleep.

As five minutes turned into ten and then fifteen, the bus began to struggle for traction, wheels slipping despite the vehicle's not inconsiderable weight. The ground was cold after a month of hard frosts; an icy weather front had enveloped the whole country, and the transport authorities were advising people not to travel unless absolutely necessary.

Although a decade in the past had enabled Moran's immune system to build up some resistance to viruses that had not been around in his own time, they still hit him harder than the people around him. A few days after the onset of influenza, he still felt weak and light-headed. Over-the-counter medication had helped, but coming out today had been a mistake. Leaving Manchester had seemed like a good idea at the time...a change of scene, a chance to visit the city where his parents would one day be born...Moran's parents had died when he was just two years old and the use of EMP weapons in both Eurasian conflicts had ensured that no data about their lives was available to the young Moran. His decision to join the UEPA following the injury that forced him to retire early from the European Armed Forces had partly been driven by the idea that police records might yield more information – they hadn't.

After ten years of silence, no further word from Gilling following King's rescue, and no indication that the implant was even still functioning, it all seemed hopeless. Moran could wait for science to catch up – he had no other choice, in fact – but what chance did he really have of finding the people responsible for unleashing the Methuselah gene on an unsuspecting world? He wasn't a scientist; he didn't move in the right circles. Why the hell had Gilling even chosen him?

With each passing year, and with no-one he could confide in, Moran's belief that his mission was doomed had grown. Depression had sunk in. It became more and more difficult to believe that he would ever see Cassie -or Vita- again. He felt trapped, completely helpless, and he did not like the unfamiliar feeling. He was accustomed to having at least some control over his own fate.

He had even begun to wonder if his former life might not simply be a dream, some kind of delusion... He had seen homeless men and women on the streets of Manchester, their minds gone, talking to people who didn't exist except in their own fevered imaginations. Would that be him, one day?

Without even a photograph of Cassie, his daughter's features had begun to fade in Moran's memory. He could, if he concentrated very hard, just about recall her voice, but the fear that one day he might lose even that felt very real. For a while after his arrival in the past, he had found himself looking for her face in crowds. He was, in a very real sense, bereaved.

What would happen to Cassie if he were to die here? Would she never be born? Moran had to keep reminding himself that everything in his own 'past' had yet to happen as far as this era was concerned... Even though his continued presence here was (probably) proof that saving King had worked, because the future which had spawned Moran must still exist, mustn't it? He didn't understand the mechanics of time travel... This, he thought bitterly, was why he had become a soldier and then a detective, not a scientist. Stranded in the past, what other events might his presence here change, or set in motion? Was that, in fact, the whole point?

Since arriving in 1979, Moran had read - and struggled to understand - all that he could find about the nature of time travel and paradoxes. The dry, scientific papers – just like the medical journals he also perused whenever he could - were difficult to get hold of for those who didn't move in the right circles - academia. And when he did manage it, reading them made his head ache and for the most part left him none the wiser. Even a popular science book by a renowned academic of the time, Professor Steven Hawking, didn't help. Some days, the idea that he might inadvertently do something to prevent Cassie from even being born terrified Moran, making him afraid to leave the soulless room he rented from a largely absentee landlord. Another day he might doubt his ability to change anything at all.

It now seemed obvious to Moran that Gilling had always intended to send him to 1979, and that he had intentionally stranded him in the past. Perhaps Moran had always been here to save the young Peter King, so that King could complete his early work on the time travel theory; without him, would the technology have been available to send Moran back in time? Might it have been a self-fulfilling prophecy ... Moran's timely arrival and stated intention giving King inspiration? A clever mind like King's would realise that Moran was unlikely to have started the fire, so the only inference he could draw would be that Moran must have had advance knowledge of the fire which could have ended King's life.

Saving one man's life might be a relatively simple matter, if you knew the future and could be in the right place at the right time. But to stop a scientific discovery from being made without knowing which individuals might be involved … that was altogether more difficult, particularly if, like Moran, you didn't move in the right circles. It didn't make sense.

The laboring work Moran had taken on in order to feed, clothe and house himself was dull and repetitive, but it was cash in hand, and often required little in the way of identity validation. Better still, his co-workers were members of a transient population – no-one would notice that he wasn't ageing at the same rate as everyone else. He changed his first name from time to time – John, Jack, Jim, James were interchangeable- and coloured his hair; sometimes brown, sometimes black, sometimes letting it grow out to reveal his natural silver, or keeping it military-short. People were, for the most part, unobservant, and it was easy enough to move on should anyone become curious.

Each May 8th, he remembered the small boy crying outside the burning department store, and wondered if his mother had ever been found. Now just as then, he was certain that she had been the same woman who had fallen in the stairwell… would she have been injured anyway, or would she have made it out if Moran hadn't been in the way? He had made a point of checking the newspapers for the names of the dead, and Dorothy Hammond had not been among them. He had been afraid to investigate further – far safer to assume that mother and son had been reunited.

So why hadn't Gilling been upfront with him right from the start, why kidnap and drug him? Would Moran have believed any of it? He'd been given no opportunity to agree to anything, which could only mean that Gilling either didn't expect him to agree, he didn't care either way, or the whole thing about being able to save Cassie had been a lie. Round and around it went in his head, year in, year out.

Well, he had saved King, and eleven years later, Moran was still waiting... The implant had fallen silent following the Woolworths fire and Moran had wondered then if the device might be faulty; there was simply no way to tell. He would have to wait; either until it started working again, or Gilling decided to recall him. If he ever did.

In the meantime, Moran intended to do whatever was necessary to save Cassie's life. But if the implant *was* faulty, how would he ever find his targets, the person or people who had created the Methuselah gene? He had no idea if they would be male or female, or even how many might be involved. Even assuming that he could identify them, how would he ever get close enough to eliminate them?

Moran decided that it would be safer to assume there must be several; he knew enough to realise that scientists rarely worked completely in isolation. So many people could have had a hand in the creation of the gene therapy. Some might play small roles, and would not be missed if they didn't turn in for work one morning; theoretically, and assuming he could get away with it, he could take dozens of them out and still not change a single thing. Others – the control figures – *would* matter. Their deaths would make a difference, provided he could get away with it more than once. Given that forensic science was advancing all the time, this seemed unlikely. And whilst he waited for gene therapy to become possible, what was he to do with himself?

He had briefly considered applying to the police force, but that might well involve giving blood samples and undergoing other medical tests, and even if it didn't, how well would his false background hold up under scrutiny? Not to mention his inability to age at the same speed as the people with whom he'd be working... no, it was impossible. And so he continued as a manual labourer, made a few investments, and worked all the hours he could because he couldn't bear to be idle. His bank balance grew, and he opened several accounts, spreading funds around to avoid unwanted attention.

He had hidden the identity documents provided by Gilling, and using his own knowledge of the criminal mind, had sourced replacements in various names, almost always keeping his own surname in the hope that doing so might serve as a flag should Gilling be looking for evidence of his presence in whatever records might survive the Eurasian wars and the data-wipe.

Moran had needed to prove that he could handle himself on more than one occasion during his quest for forged documents; a risky business, because he could not afford to be hospitalized. Automatic gene typing at birth was still several decades off, he guessed - but it was safer to assume that his altered genome might still be discovered were he to fall into the hands of contemporary physicians. Such a discovery could bring the discovery of the Methuselah gene forward by decades. Might this be what had happened - or could happen? He couldn't rule it out, but it seemed unlikely that Gilling would have sent him here if that were the case.

For the same reason, he could not -dare not- form any relationships, other than the most fleeting. A long-term partner would pick up on the fact that he didn't age... and besides, he already had a partner, even if they were now separated by nearly three centuries. He missed Vita more than he might have expected to, given that their relationship had been in difficulties for a several years. They had discussed staying together to give united support to Cassie as her health had begun to fail, but in every other way their marriage had been over.

He imagined Vita turning up at the hospital, her confusion at being left to deal with Cassie alone... what did she -would she- think had happened to him? Or would he be back before she even realised he had gone? There was so much he didn't know.

So here he was, feeling sicker by the minute as the bus grumbled its way through the snow-muffled streets. He should have stayed in Manchester, or at the very least in the hotel room for another twenty-four hours. But by early evening, feeling claustrophobic and unable to look at the same four walls any longer, Moran had bundled himself up against the chill and attended a recital at Saint Martin in the Fields, an Anglican church overlooking Trafalgar Square. By his time, the building would be a museum; seeing it used for its original purpose had been a temptation Moran couldn't resist, even though he didn't subscribe to any religion. The fresh air would clear his head, or so he had hoped.

Once the service ended, Moran had followed some of the congregation to a nearby public house. Feeling strangely uplifted by the service, he had consumed rather more alcohol than was sensible, given his health and the medication he had taken.

Sitting on a stool by himself at the end of the bar, he remembered Sanchez, and how the two of them would sometimes drink together after the successful conclusion of a case. How had Neil reacted when Moran didn't turn in for the next shift? Had his partner's own son -then aged seven- succumbed to the cancer pandemic? The thought pained Moran. He wasn't one to form close attachments, his institutionalized childhood making it difficult. Meeting Vita had been a revelation – she was one powerful woman, and she had made all the running. Moran – typical of his sex, he suspected- found it easier to acquiesce. When Cassie had been born his world had tipped on its axis – he would die for his daughter, pure and simple.

An elderly couple who had also been at the service acknowledged Moran with a smile and a nod as they made their leisurely way out of the bar. He returned the greeting with caution. Would they remember him? Did it matter?

With the day drawing to a close, his energy levels were beginning to dip – it was time he got back to the hotel. He stood up, leaning on the table for a moment to allow the dizziness to pass, then followed the elderly couple from the bar. Outside, the snow was coming down fast, and starting to settle in drifts. He saw the couple ahead of him, climbing aboard a double decker bus, and recognised the service number from the bus stop outside his hotel. Holding up his hand and forcing himself into a staggering jog, he made it onto the vehicle and fumbled for the correct coinage under the baleful eye of the driver. Someone wasn't happy to be working the evening shift...

When his timepiece told him that it was close to midnight, and they were still a few streets from the hotel, Moran's stomach began to churn – mixing alcohol with the medication had been a bad idea. He saw a young man with a small terrier on a leash stand up and press the 'stop' bell, and decided that it was time to get off. He could walk the rest of the way.

The fresh air was his undoing. Vomiting in the street had never been Moran's style - the last time had been the day of his arrival in the past – but to his shame, he couldn't help himself.

Feeling only marginally better once his stomach was empty, Moran set off for the hotel – his sense of direction, normally reliable, would get him there easily enough. As his head began to clear, he found himself walking slightly downhill alongside a park, sleet and snow pattering down the back of his neck. He began to shiver. He wondered if any drugstores might still be open – there was a pharmacy on the main road, and Moran decided to pay a visit. It wouldn't add much time to his journey, and he suspected a relapse was on the cards. He couldn't afford to be hospitalized, so his only recourse was self-medication.

At the junction of Primrose Hill Road and Regent's Park Road, Moran was relieved to see that he only needed to cross the road and he would be a hundred yards or so from the hotel. The pharmacy was only a little further along. A few feet in front of him he saw the young man and his dog who had got off the bus at the same time – they must have walked through the park.

A yellow gritting lorry rounded the bend on the other side of the road. It was travelling slowly and Moran would have plenty of time to get across. But as he approached the kerb, a searing pain shot through his scalp. Gilling's voice boomed inside his head:

'Alert- avoid- significant event!'.

An image burned bright on the inside of Moran's eyelids: Peter King. Disorientated, he stumbled, felt his foot slide from under him, and fell forwards.

His palms hit a mixture of ice, slush and tarmac. Instinctively, he rolled back in the direction he had come. He caught a flash of red as a vehicle flew past him, and a spray of icy slush hit him in the side of the face. An engine revved, then stopped abruptly, followed by a muffled thump. He lay winded for perhaps three seconds, then scrambled to his feet, tasting blood from a split lip.

'Bloody piss artist!' the young man pushed past Moran, and thrust something at him; a dog leash. Dazed, he took it. The terrier whined and jumped away from him as it tried to follow its master across the road.

Moran couldn't recall following the dog's owner, but he must have because here was the red car, its windscreen toppling onto the wet tarmac with a curiously insignificant tinkle of broken glass. Moran found himself staring into brown, sightless eyes, and a face he had seen before: older, it was true, and partially obscured by a full beard; but unmistakably the face of Peter King. Gilling's voice echoed in his mind, but the words were barely audible, drowned by the sound of his own blood as it roared in his ears. His vision blurred, and he bent double, his empty stomach clenching painfully.

'Jesus Christ...' Moran heard the young man retch, and then a shout from a different voice. He looked up. A middle-aged man was climbing down from the cab of the gritting lorry with which King's car had collided. He finished talking into a handset, flung it back into the cab and started towards Moran. 'Don't touch anything!' he yelled. 'I've called an ambulance!'

Moran heard the hiss of airbrakes as a bus shuddered to a stop behind him, and the clamour of shocked voices as the doors opened with a violent rush of air. He dropped the lead, turned and ran.

Moran spent that night in a homeless shelter, where in return for being robbed of his wallet as he (finally) slept, he managed to acquire another man's coat, and a flat cap which partially concealed his features and his silver hair. The coat stank, but the inner pocket yielded a twenty-pound note; enough for a coach ticket back to Manchester. He hadn't dared to return to his hotel – there had been too many witnesses, too many people who might give a description to the police, any one of which could lead to his apprehension. He would likely be required as a witness, at the very least.

* * *

Twenty-four hours later, Moran watched the winter landscape flash by as the coach rumbled towards Manchester. He would keep an even lower profile from now on; he would find a decent property in or near Manchester to serve as a permanent base – no more wandering the country as a casual laborer, living out of poky rooms and eating fast food. He would get himself a new set of identity papers, perhaps in Gilling's name (another signal, he hoped) and settle in for the long wait.

As a soldier, then as a detective, he was no stranger to unexpected -and occasionally violent- death; but his own part in the cessation of Peter King's life – and worse, that of his daughter, Moran had gathered from newspaper headlines on his way to the coach station – had shocked him, made him feel sick to his stomach, in fact. What events might the man's untimely death change? Would discovery of the gene therapy still unfold in the same way – or at least in a way that would allow him to save Cassie's life? Moran had no idea. He wondered if the ripples of King's death had impacted immediately… would people like Gilling (whom King's death would surely affect – no King, no time machine, surely) notice the change? Or would they be unaware that anything was different at all? Like everyone else, Moran was accustomed to living his life in a unilateral way. Birth, the succession of years from childhood to adulthood… death from old age, well that was something he and most people of his generation had yet to encounter. As part of the second generation since the Methuselah Program had begun, Moran had seen very few elderly people. There were some – people of intellectual brilliance who had undergone the therapy in their twilight years; but they were uncommon. He had been too young to understand the reasoning, but believed it had a lot to do with rising medical costs. Far better, they said, to use resources on those with something to offer society. He and Vita had often argued about it – as a lawyer, Vita held firm views which owed little to sentimentality and everything to the social value of each individual. 'Ask not what I can do for one, but what I can do for the majority.' Moran often asked himself if that might be what had happened to his own parents – were they elderly, or of unsound mind or body? His attempts to find out more about them had ended in disappointment. 'This record no longer exists in our database' - a phrase now indelibly engraved on his memory. An idea struck him – might he be able to research his family here? But he didn't know if his name had been changed... without a name, and at least some idea of a birth date, he had nothing... nothing other than his DNA, which although it might at some point be able to link him to his family, he could hardly share... or perhaps he did, perhaps he will – could he be the cause of it all? If the twenty-first century learned about the methuselah gene because they had *him*... he shook his head, earning himself a hard stare from the man seated next to him. He would look into it, at least.

He rubbed the skin inside his left wrist absently, where the transponder itched. Until King's death last night, it had given Moran no trouble. Now it had begun to irritate, and Moran found it hard to ignore. He had been subliminally aware of it since his arrival in 1979, but only as a small lump under the skin. Like all subcutaneous implants, it was powered by the electrical energy generated by the movement of his own muscles and, Moran now had to assume following the alert which had resulted in King's death, may have simply been waiting for a 'significant event' to trigger it. Now there was nothing except the irritation of a foreign body under the skin – the device seemed to be inert, his body already beginning to reject it. Moran could only assume that King's death had something to do with it – it was too co-incidental. He fingered the implant behind his right ear carefully – the stab of pain, the uncomfortable heat which had accompanied Gilling's warning, had been even worse than the first time, in seventy-nine. Now it felt as if the skin around the implant had become infected. If the implant was no longer working... dare he leave it in place? Dare he remove it? One thing was certain – he couldn't ask anyone else to do it.

6: MANCHESTER, 1991

The property was ripe for redevelopment, the estate agent told Moran. Built in the thirties by a wealthy industrialist, Helmshore Hall had been falling into disrepair since the eighties, when an elderly aunt had lived alone on the ground floor and eventually suffered a lonely death. Since then, the property had remained empty.

As the woman took him on an extensive tour of the house, Moran suppressed a shiver. That the building would survive several hundred years more, he knew, of course: Gilling had housed his company, Helmshore Inc., here, and it had been Moran's arrival point twelve years ago.

On his return to Manchester following the death of Peter King, Moran had immediately set about making enquiries about the property. Still empty, it would require 'considerable work' to make it habitable, the woman at the property agency told him, hence the low asking price. The idea that Moran's intervention might have even enabled Gilling to set up his company carried with it a delicious sense of irony. Suppose he was to raze it to the ground – how would that affect the timeline? Gilling might set up business in another city…it was worth considering. Moran nodded to himself, and the agent, misinterpreting, went in for the kill.

'Yes, it's amazing, isn't it? I'd buy it myself if I had the money. Will you be bringing your family here, Mr. Gilling?' She turned bright blue eyes on him, the pupils dilated. Was she coming onto him? Moran regretted letting slip that money wasn't a problem.

He took his time replying. It wasn't really any of her business, of course, but it wouldn't pay to alienate her. People tended to remember if they had been wronged, and he did not particularly want to be remembered at all, hence the use of Gilling's name for this purchase. He was already renting a poky two-bed apartment in the city itself, using his own name, and had concocted a story about staying with a friend (himself) whilst he looked for a property.

'Yes, eventually.' He paused. 'My daughter will love it.' The temptation to say 'would have loved it' was strong. She had to live – or what was this all for?

'Just the one?' She was disappointed, no mistaking it, but maintained the bright, professional smile.

He returned it, pushing his pain down. 'At the moment, yes. Perhaps later…' That would have to do. If you couldn't keep it true, keep it simple, that was the rule.

'Then it'll be perfect, Mr. Gilling.' She led him back down the wide, sweeping staircase and they stood for a moment in the granite-floored vestibule. Diffused spring sunlight made the upper walls and the stairwell glow, and Moran imagined childish laughter echoing in the empty space. Sorrow tightened his throat. He took a deep breath. 'Yes,' he said hoarsely. 'I believe it will.'

7: LONDON, 2010

'This is what you really want to do, is it, Em?' Her father's eyes glistened with tears.

Emma nodded. 'It is, Dad. I never knew Nathan, but I've seen what he means to you and Chloe. You know I've always loved science... I always got good marks in it, and when I saw that documentary about the little girl who has the same disease.... well, it just clicked. Are you okay with it?' Please be okay with it....

'You want to know if I'm okay ... Darling, it means more to me than I can say... and if that sounds like a cliché, well that's because it's true.' Tom stepped forward and drew Emma into his arms. She hugged him back, snuggling into his sweater just as she'd done when she was small. She loved the way her father smelled; mostly of his favourite cologne - he tried new ones from time to time, but always came back to the sandalwood fragrance she remembered from her childhood - and the tiniest hint of the cigarettes he couldn't quite give up, even though Mum nagged him.

To the world, he was Tom Morgan, successful actor - but to Emma and her half-sister Chloe, he was just plain old Dad. Some of the students in her first year at college had been all over her, wanting to meet 'Gideon'. He'd made that show more than twenty years ago, but it had become something of a cult classic. There'd been talk of a re-boot, but she knew her father hadn't been too keen at first. 'It was what it was,' he'd been quoted as saying in the press. 'I've moved on.' But Emma's desire to go to University had changed that – not that he'd said as much, but she had ears, and she knew he'd been in talks at the television centre. 'I'll pay for your course. I don't want you starting your working life in debt,' he had told her.

'So you'll be studying what, genetics?' He drew back and stared at Emma as if seeing her for the first time. As a grown-up, she hoped; he could be more than a bit over-protective at times. She nodded.

'Well, its molecular biology, but yes, eventually I'll be a geneticist. If I graduate – it's a tough course. Not everyone makes it.'

'You'll sail through it, Ems, I know you will. Your mam and I, we always said you were more intelligent than the two of us put together.'

Emma grinned. She loved that he called her mother 'Mam' sometimes – it sounded funny in his accent, which was, he'd once explained to her, mostly the product of drama school and a desire not to be pigeon-holed in his work. She liked how when he was upset, the accent he'd picked up at school in the north of England came out. 'Catterick with a smattering of Manchester', he called it. 'Mam' was his Welsh roots showing, because Grandpa Morgan used the same word, and so did her uncles. She had gone through a short phase in her early teens of wanting to marry a Welshman. And then she'd heard some wit talking about the Electra Complex (which suggested that girls wanted to marry their fathers) and had gone off the idea – because that would be too weird, wouldn't it?

'Thanks, Da.' She used the term unselfconsciously – long summer holidays spent with the family of one Uncle or another meant that she was comfortable with the terminology, even if she didn't often use it in London. 'I'd better tell Mum, or she'll feel left out.' She had never been able to call Eva 'Mam', though. Things were complicated with her mother.

'She's with a client at the moment – but it's getting late, I doubt she'll be much longer.' He smiled. 'Show me the website of this university, then.'

He'd missed the university interview trips because he'd been working away at the time. Some historical drama, she thought, but he didn't talk about his work much at home. Although she had been disappointed – her father was excellent company- Emma had hoped that sharing the experience might bring herself and her mother closer. At first it hadn't – but then they'd been to Manchester and suddenly her mother's whole demeanor had changed- she had been almost talkative. She'd told Emma that her first husband, Peter King, had graduated from UMIST. 'He was a very clever man – just not a very good husband.'

Then Emma had finally got to hear the whole story, and to understand why there had always been an odd tension between her mother and Grandpa Deacon at family gatherings, and why Aunt Jess –whom Emma had seen only a few times - had never been present at those gatherings, and had never been to their home. During her final months at college, Emma had persuaded her Grandfather to give her Jessica's phone number. They had met in the city before she left for University, and had hit it off straight away. Jess was brisk, outgoing, and passionate about her work as an investigative journalist, latterly specialising in features about women. She had warned Emma that her mother might not be too pleased that they were meeting.

'Your mother has lost or been betrayed by people she was close to, Emma. Her first husband, Peter, and her daughter, Amy, well you know how that happened. Then she found out about Peter and I – and if I could undo that one day, make it never happen, believe me, I would. It changed her.'

'Didn't she have any friends?'

Jess had shaken her head. 'She used to have a couple from school she kept up with, but mostly it was me and your mum. We were a real team. There were only two years between us, we were as close as sisters could be…I'd hoped that meeting your dad might soften her, but it never happened, though I know your grandpa tried to get her to change her mind. I don't suppose she ever will, now – your mum can be very stubborn.' Jess sighed. 'I really miss her.'

'That's so sad. I can't imagine falling out with Chloe like that….' Emma didn't see Chloe as often as she'd like – her outgoing half-

THE METHUSELAH PARADOX · 59

sister was a drama/voice coach in France, living with the most drop-dead gorgeous French guy. Cute as he was, Emma couldn't ever imagine a scenario where she might cheat on Chloe with Anton.

'I think it killed your mum, in a way. I was really worried about her until she met your father. I thought she would be okay, then.'

Emma wasn't sure if Jess knew that her sister had suffered from depression and insomnia for years...she didn't feel that it was her place to tell her.

Now Emma watched her father scroll through the University of Manchester website, and drew a deep breath, 'Dad, if I tell you something and ask you not to tell Mum, would you?'

Her father took his hand away from the mouse and looked at her. 'That rather depends on what you're going to tell me. You're not pregnant, are you?'

'That's not even funny.'

'It wasn't meant to be, sweetheart. It happens... Look, I know things aren't as they should be between you and your mother, but...' he sighed. 'I can't promise, Emmy. Do you still want to tell me?'

Emma took a deep breath. 'I've been seeing Aunt Jess. Just a couple of times so far. I really like her.'

Tom leaned back in the chair and blew out his cheeks. 'Well,' he said slowly, 'She is your Aunt...'

'Exactly. She didn't do anything to me, did she, so...Dad, she's lovely. And she misses Mum a lot, I can tell.'

Her father shook his head. 'I wish I could help with that, I really do. Sometimes I think your mother needs...'

'What do I need?' Eva's voice cut across the room like a whip, and Tom and Emma turned as one.

Eva stared at them. She seemed outwardly calm, her eyebrows raised in query and a half-smile on her lips; but Emma had caught the tiny tremor in her voice. How much had she overheard?

'... A holiday, Darling. Before Emmy goes off to Uni. We should all go away together. What do you say?'

Eva's eyes narrowed. Tom gazed at her, his eyebrows raised in a question, his expression one of puppyish hope. Despite the tension –

or perhaps because of it- Emma fought an urge to laugh aloud. Her father was so quick, but despite his undisputed skill as an actor, she didn't think this performance was convincing anyone.

Eva took a deep breath, and let it out slowly. 'What did you have in mind?'

She'd either fallen for it, Emma thought, or was putting on her own performance.

* * *

It was true, Eva knew: she *did* need a holiday. The trouble with that was that it meant spending time cooped up with your family, and it was then very easy for buried tensions to surface. Tom had learned – mostly- to keep clear of certain topics, and had a tendency to ignore what he knew he couldn't change; but Emma, with her curious nature and sometimes-blunt questions, wasn't blind. Eva suspected that her daughter knew that all wasn't well between her parents. She would be more surprised if she hadn't intuited it.

The four days spent visiting universities with Emma had been a revelation, and not for the first time, Eva regretted the opportunities she had already missed to get to know the young woman her daughter was fast becoming.

Inevitably, her mind turned to Amy. She would have been twenty-six now. Twenty-six! What would she be doing with her life, had she lived?

Eva set the timer on the oven and stepped over to the sink, gazing out at the darkened garden and blinking away sudden tears. She would never stop wondering. Most of the time, the pain was a distant tug of sadness; other times –like now- it felt as raw as if the accident had happened yesterday. Would it have helped if the police had ever been able to find the man who stepped out in front of their car that night? Eva didn't know, and would probably never know. She could perhaps make enquiries… She had considered it, several times.

Her memory of the man – silver hair, a square jaw- had not dimmed despite the intervening years –she felt sure that she would recognise him, even now. Why had he never come forward? He must have seen the news, had to have realised that people had died. How could he live with the knowledge? But even supposing he could be found –and she imagined the case file must have long ago been closed- what would facing him after all this time achieve? Would it give her closure, would it re-open wounds which had barely healed, despite the passing of time? What would she say to him? What could he possibly say to her? It wouldn't change what had already happened.

She knew that Tom had never been troubled by similar feelings about Nathan's death, but then he knew the cause; there was no mystery there, no itch needing to be scratched.

So, then. A family holiday, before Emma went off to University... would it be so bad? Assuming her daughter got a place, of course, but Eva didn't really have any concerns on that score. Emma had already had primary offers from two Universities; they were just waiting on her A Level results now. She was clever, articulate, and single-minded once she set her sights on something, Eva knew her daughter at least that well.

She wondered at the co-incidence of Emma choosing Manchester as her preference. It felt like a connection between Eva's old life and the one she had now, because Peter had been born and had studied there; and they had been travelling home from spending Christmas with his parents that night... the name of the City was synonymous in her mind with loss. She hadn't mentioned this to Emma, of course – it was clear that her daughter's heart was set on Manchester, and the course she would be taking was one of the best in the field. For a moment she wondered what Jess would make of it all – she would no doubt hear the news through their father. As far as Eva knew, Emma had not met her Aunt, apart from a handful of occasions as a small child. Wasn't Emma at all curious? Eva had occasionally wondered if she should perhaps tell Emma that she could see Jess if she wanted to, just so long as it wasn't on home ground, but had never quite found the right moment. Perhaps Emma had already taken matters into her own hands; or perhaps her father might have engineered something… Perhaps it was time to let the past go? But the very idea of approaching Jess now seemed impossible. Too much time had passed, and Jess had stopped trying to reach her years ago. No, it was safer to leave things as they were.

It had not escaped her notice that both her daughter and husband had started guiltily when Eva had entered the room. She had heard enough to know that they were talking about Jess. Were they planning something – a surprise meeting, perhaps? Tom wouldn't do that… or would he? How could she possibly ask him?

What had happened to her relationship with the man who had promised never to nag her about resuming her relationship with her sister? Who had reassured her that they were made for each other, and that Chloe would love a brother or sister? Another child wouldn't be replacing Amy, he had assured her… she would just be moving on with her life, as surely Amy would have wanted her to do? But Amy had only been six years old, she might have been jealous… Had she married Tom in haste? Sometimes Eva thought she might have done. But they had been happy, once, hadn't they?

That Tom was seeing other women, Eva was now almost certain, although at first she had dismissed her suspicions as leftover paranoia from what had happened between Peter and Jess. But his excuses were at times pathetically clumsy – so much for the actor. It was almost, she sometimes thought, as if he wanted her to know… perhaps he wanted to be challenged, so that he could tell her what a miserable, frigid bitch she had become. Those are your words, not his. What was the worst that could happen? It had already happened, in 1990. What could be any worse than that? Losing Emma? But Emma was now making her own way in the world, wasn't she… in a way, she was already lost.

But her marriage to Tom…Eva had had a sense of impending crisis for some time, and no idea what she might do about it. What did the future hold for them? Emma was not going to be moving back to London anytime soon, Eva knew - her room already seemed like a guest room now, even though she was still in residence; all her childhood toys had been packed away or passed on... it would always be Emma's room, but that was what children did – they grew up. Amy would have grown up and eventually moved away, had she lived... she might even have died in other circumstances. It was possible – similar things happened every day. There was no security, no safety – it was all down to chance, in the end.

Eva listened to Tom moving about upstairs, heard the rumble of his voice then Emma's laughter. Eva was not stupid - she had always known that keeping her distance, stopping herself from becoming too involved in Emma's life, had not, would never be, the answer. But she couldn't help herself, it seemed. Had it damaged her daughter? It didn't seem so, at least not that Eva could tell.

Eva had at least had her mother for her formative years – Margaret had already been sick with the disease that would ultimately take her life just as Eva was finishing school and looking forward to college. She had met Peter after her mother died. Then – two years later- she had married him, had become the wife of a scientist. They had lived in Farnborough for a while, and then Peter had received a job offer from a university department in London, doing work that he would never talk about. Would he still be alive if they had never met? Probably. Would she have ever met Tom, given birth to Emma? It was impossible to know for certain, but it was unlikely. Her mother had never met Eva's daughters. Sometimes the thought made Eva feel so down that she could barely drag herself from bed. The pills helped, but they couldn't change the past.

She flinched and quickly wiped her eyes as Tom knocked on the kitchen door. How long had he been standing there? 'What?'

'Sorry – I didn't mean to make you jump. Are you okay?'

Was his conscience pricking him? She nodded. Define okay. 'I'm okay.'

He looked relieved. 'I'm popping out for a bit – said I'd meet Dan down the Slug for a pint. You'll give the holiday some thought, won't you?'

Eva forced a smile. Was he really going for a drink with Dan, or was he seeing another woman? She couldn't ask. 'Of course. I said I would, didn't I?' She saw something flare in his eyes and instantly regretted her tone. 'I'll think about it, Tom, I promise.'

PART FOUR: 2018

8: MANCHESTER, SEPTEMBER

Moran grabbed the oak table for support, closed his eyes, and took a deep breath. When the sound of the blood roaring through his veins had faded somewhat, he forced himself to focus on the newspaper in front of him. A sob rose in his throat.

'*Cassie...?*' Of course, it couldn't be - his daughter wouldn't be born for another two hundred and thirty-six years. Moran touched the image gingerly, almost as if it might disappear and confirm a fear that had lately begun to take shape in his mind – that he was descending into madness; that his past – his future? - was nothing more than the figment of a damaged mind. No. It had happened, all of it. He might be lonely, he might be depressed – but he was quite sane.

But the image remained. Knowing it wasn't Cassie, Moran still let himself drink her in – the green eyes, glossy black hair (like his had once been) ... but where Cassie's locks had (once, before she became ill) been long and sleek, this young woman wore her hair in an unfamiliar, spiky style, surely only made possible by the rigorous application of some hair product or other. The arch of her eyebrows... always so expressive, just like Cassie's, giving away a hint of self-deprecation; it was obvious to Moran that she was unused to being photographed, and had felt self-conscious. The resemblance was breath-taking - it was, to all intents and purposes, an older version of Cassie. How was this possible? He took another deep breath, and forced himself to focus on the text covering the opposite page. His blood ran cold. *No.* This could *not* be right.

Our Life Expectancy in Her Hands, he read. *An exclusive interview with Geneticist Emma Morgan.* His mouth dry, he read on:

Doctor Emma Morgan is a remarkable young woman. Gaining a Ph.D. in Genetics at Manchester University earlier this year, twenty-five-year-old Emma is not your stereotypical scientist. She enjoys horse-riding, and admits to occasional recklessness in Role-playing Games. She is quiet, but has an infectious smile. She doesn't look at all like a typical boffin, I tell her.

Emma frowns. 'What is a 'boffin' anyway? Is there even such a thing as a 'typical boffin'?' She considers the matter. 'Actually, I do know the kind of person I think you mean, and I guess I've met a few of them...they're good, brilliant people, very focused on their work. My work is the most important thing in my life at the moment, so perhaps I am typical.'

What made Emma decide that she wanted to be, for want of a better term, a 'boffin' in the field of genetics?

'We're researchers – that's what we do. The reason I got into this field is...' she hesitates, but only for a moment. 'My parents were both married before. My father had a son who was born with a disease called Progeria, which meant that he aged too fast. He died following a stroke when he was three years old.'

'That's terrible', I can't help saying, even though I know the story well.

'Yes,' Emma nods. 'It was terrible for everyone. My father's marriage....' *She stops, as if realising she may have said too much.*

Emma's father is Tom Morgan, an actor perhaps best known for his role as Gideon in the television drama 'Gideon's Road', which has recently been revived after a hiatus of several years. It's perhaps unsurprising, then, that Emma chose the discipline of genetics.

'Unsurprising? I don't know. I just knew it was what I wanted to do.'

'Didn't your brother have a twin?' I ask.

Emma nods. 'My sister didn't have the faulty gene. Had they been identical twins, it might have been a different story. There are a few recorded cases of siblings being born with the condition.'

How can you possibly hope to identify and eradicate one faulty gene? I ask.

'That's what we're trying to find out at Xeon,' Emma says quietly, referencing the company who recently employed her. 'Until quite recently, it was thought to be a random mutation – which would, you're right, be very hard to pin down and eradicate. We now know that, in its most common form, it appears to be a random mutation. We are looking for indicators in the genetic makeup of the parents, related to the ratio of dominant and recessive genes.... How much do know about why and how we age?'

Not a lot, I confess. I know that once we pass child-bearing age, everything starts to go downhill. Built-in obsolescence.

'In very broad terms, that's right. There are certain groups of cells which shorten as we get older – we call them telomeres. What still isn't known is whether the shortening is the cause of ageing, or the result of it...and if they were short to begin with in the mutated cells, why did this happen; can we switch it off, or switch something else on, so that they don't shorten too soon? Which markers in the genetic makeup of each parent might combine to cause this mutation... should we therefore be treating the parents, or the child? So many factors could have a bearing, but if we can find the primary cause, and manipulate...'

Moran couldn't read any more. He knew precious little about his forebears thanks to the EMP attacks during the Eurasian Conflict, which had wiped out ninety percent of the world's digitally-held information; his parents had both died when he was very young, and he had been raised by the state. But Emma's similarity to Cassie couldn't be co-incidental – could it? Was Emma his target? What were the odds that the person he had been sent to eliminate might be related to him? More to the point, had Gilling known about it?

Moran had discovered that there were hundreds -perhaps thousands- of individual research projects looking at ageing and associated diseases all around the world, almost too many to count. It had been an uphill struggle to find and keep track of them all, and near impossible for Moran, no scientist, to know which of them might be the most advanced in its research. The only clue he had was Gilling's decision to send him to Manchester, implying that the breakthrough would come from someone working in that city. It couldn't be a co-incidence.

He'd had his eye on Manchester University's Genetics department, but they weren't hiring anyone with his career profile. Without an employee or student pass, there had been no way to get inside the building, or into the lecture rooms and laboratories without arousing suspicion. Now this. It was at once both exciting and terrible news.

The idea that one of his own ancestors might be responsible for his daughter's death -and billions more- made Moran feel sick to his stomach. But if it *was* true... perhaps, then, Gilling had known it all along? It might explain why he had chosen Moran, an ex-soldier turned police detective, instead of a scientist; a question Moran had asked himself many times. Moran's role was little more than that of a hired assassin. Whilst contrary to his nature he could have lived with that, to save Cassie... but this new discovery changed everything.

It seemed obvious now: Gilling must have known about the con-nection, and been prepared to sacrifice Cassie, and everyone in between her and Emma Morgan, including Moran himself. The re-semblance couldn't just be a co-incidence – could it? How could he prove it? Did he want to? Assuming he could prove a connection, what options did he have? If he did nothing, Cassie would die; if Emma Morgan did turn out to be the fulcrum on which the methuselah program rested, if they were directly related, and if he did what he had been sent here to do... Cassie would never be born, because *he* would never be born. It was the ultimate sacrifice... and he couldn't do it.

There had to be another way.

9: MANCHESTER, 17 SEPTEMBER

'I want my mum! Where's my Mum?'

His chest feels as if it is on fire, the stink of smoke in his mouth, up his nose, everywhere. He can't see his mum - there are people running out of the building, but she hasn't come out - why hadn't she come out with everyone else?

He feels the first tears spill over and looks down at his feet. His socks, the regulation grey, are black with soot and dirt. She'll be cross... where is she?

His father had eventually come for him, and taken him home. He had given him a bath, and tucked him up in bed with a hot water bottle, even though it was nearly summer, because he couldn't eat his tea, and couldn't stop shivering.

'I'm sorry, lad. Your mum won't be coming home.'

Hammond reached out into the darkness, cursing as his fumbling fingers nearly sent the lamp crashing to the floor. Yellow light flooded the room, and he fell back onto the pillows with a groan. The same dream still had the power to wake him every so often, the terror and misery as sharp as they had been in 1979, his cheeks always wet with both real and remembered tears. He wiped them away, sighed, and pushed the covers back. The bedside clock read 6:15: the alarm would go off in another fifteen minutes anyway. He turned it off and stumbled towards the bathroom.

* * *

Emma lay in the narrow bed and looked up at the grey sky, just visible through a tiny gap in the curtains. She had woken before the alarm, the tip of her nose and her left arm -which had been on top of the covers- icy cold. The heating hadn't come on, again – she would have to speak to the landlord about it. She'd had the same problem last winter, and the winter before... and it might be May, almost summer, but Manchester was so cold compared to London. Would she ever become acclimatized?

Emma didn't want to move out of this flat; she liked the independence, the way she could come and go as she pleased, not having to tiptoe around other people's feelings... But perhaps she and Simon *should* pool resources? He suggested it regularly, and it was becoming harder to ignore him. But if she gave in to what he called 'common sense', he would assume that she wanted to resume their relationship. She didn't have time -or the inclination- for a relationship with him, or with anyone else as it happened. They'd been there, done that as first year students, and it wasn't meant to be. Why couldn't he see that? So it was easier to stay put – wonky heating was easier to fix than a broken relationship, and it didn't affect her work.

She stretched, steeling herself for the dash to the thermostat and then a hot shower, her thoughts turning to the day ahead. Thinking about her work always calmed Emma, making her worries about how things were between herself and Simon seem irrelevant, unimportant.

The penultimate batch should be ready by the end of this week – and Archie was already putting the finishing touches on their feasibility study, leaving room for tweaking should the final results show any variances. She wasn't expecting them to; but you could never be certain until the last result was in. Hard data based on painstakingly slow research was the only proof that mattered, and it was the key to progress. Archie would hand in the feasibility study on the following Monday, when she would be on her way back up from London. The timing had been awkward, but Archie was happy to finish off, he insisted. Birthdays are important, he said. She thought that was rich, since he never seemed to celebrate his own.

They'd then have a week or two to plan the next phase, which would put them in a good position, even if they didn't get the 'green light' on the study, as her father called it. Then Emma would spend a week in France with Chloe, and would try not to think about anything to do with genetics.

It had been almost a year since she had last seen her half-sister, who was working as an English voice coach for drama students in Paris. She missed Chloe, and it would be good to think about something besides dominant and recessive genes, mutations, T-cells... When she returned, with any luck the board would have made their decision and (fingers crossed) the RCT – randomized control trial- could begin. What would she do if they turned the proposal down? The feasibility study showed that it could be done, she had at least a dozen families on board, and a dozen more willing to commit... they *had* to say 'yes'. If they didn't get the go ahead, would she go to Canada, take up SeaGene's offer? There had been too many sleepless nights already pondering that one, but yes, she would, if she had to. She owed it to Nathan's memory.

Stop putting it off. She threw back the duvet, jumped out of bed, and ran out into the narrow hall, where she twisted the thermostat all the way around, waiting until she heard the click and then the distant *whoomph* of the boiler kicking in. Then she ran into the bathroom, grabbing the dense cotton bathrobe from the bathroom door and wrapped it around herself. Roll on summer!

Rain pattered against the north-facing window, and Emma shivered as she waited for the water to run hot. It rained a lot in Manchester, but after eight years living in the city, she was used to that – it was the cold she didn't like. The weather today matched her mood – glum, maybe a bit anxious. Not about the work... there had still been no contact from either of her parents, and waiting for their reaction to Aunt Jess's interview was getting to her. She shouldn't have done it; why had she ever thought it would be a good idea?

It had been her aunt's suggestion – a features writer with a regular column in The Sunday Times, Jessica Deacon had been writing a series of features about influential women and had talked Emma into doing an interview. It had been published three weeks ago in one of the Sunday supplements, and Emma had been waiting for a phone call from one or other of her parents ever since. She ought to have warned them, perhaps even asked for permission to talk about Nathan and her mother's late first husband, who had also graduated from Manchester... but she had never found quite the right moment to pick up the phone. And then it had been too late.

Emma's mother Eva was an intensely private woman who disliked talking about the past, and ever since Emma could remember, had refused to have anything to do with her sister, Jess. What if Eva had asked her *not* to do the interview? Jess had been so enthusiastic. 'People need to know *why* your research is important, Emma – you're the human face – or one of them- of medical research. Whatever history your mother and I have between us is just that – history. It has nothing to do with this.'

So Emma had agreed, and they'd done the interview here in the flat. Jess had brought a photographer along, a briskly cheerful man in his mid-forties who worked quietly and left as soon as he'd got the shots he wanted, leaving the two women to talk.

Since the interview had appeared in print, her aunt - to Emma's profound relief - had not asked about her parents' reactions to it. Which was just as well, since Emma wouldn't have been able to lie and would have had to admit that she hadn't told them.... To be fair, Jess had urged her to do so, but knowing the troubled history between her mother and her aunt, Emma had taken the coward's way out.

Emma knew that Jess had once had a brief relationship with Eva's first husband, Peter King, which had only come to light after Peter had been killed in a road accident on New Year's Eve nineteen-ninety. Eva had found an incriminating note amongst his effects and the sisters, who up until that point had been very close, had not spoken since. The following year, Eva had met Tom, and Emma had been born the year after. Her father maintained that his wife had never fully recovered from the trauma of losing her first child; a little girl named Amy, who had died with her father in the accident. Had Emma not allowed herself to be swayed by her Aunt's enthusiasm, she would have known it was a bad idea to bring up the subject of Peter King's death at all. She should have asked Jess to cut the reference completely, because there was no way her parents *wouldn't* have seen the feature, and it was almost certain to upset her mother. So why hadn't Emma's parents been in touch? What was going on with them, that this hadn't even pinged on their radar? Or would she arrive home for her birthday weekend to a shit storm of upset and disapproval?

This wall of silence wasn't their style. Even her father - who regularly sent Emma cheery texts, sometimes including on-set snapshots of people he thought Emma might be impressed by (she invariably wasn't) - had been uncharacteristically quiet. At twenty-five (twenty-six this coming Saturday) Emma was no longer a child, but still the thought of upsetting either parent sent her into an agony of self-recrimination and doubt. Now this whole situation with the interview made her feel like a teenager all over again – she had ignored her instincts, allowed Jess to convince her that it would be all right, and she had been wrong, she was sure of it. There could be no other reasonable explanation for the sudden wall of silence.

Perhaps Canada would be a good idea...it was a shame she couldn't just fly out there now, but that would be cowardly, wouldn't it? The idea made her blush with embarrassment and self-loathing. No, she would just have to apologise and try to make it up to them, somehow... her dad would forgive her, she knew - if she could just nail this research, find a cure, he'd forgive her anything. But her mother, now that was an altogether different matter...

During the eight years that Emma been in Manchester, Eva and Tom Morgan's relationship had gone steadily downhill. Emma's last visit home had been full of uncomfortable silences and tension. Her father had been drinking more heavily than Emma ever remembered, and smoking more (on her previous visit, he had been vaping, and had declared that he was 'off the hard stuff' – it hadn't lasted for long.) His career was going well following the revival of 'Gideon's Road' (the science-fiction show that had made his name in the nineties) for a mini-series, which had become two; and there had recently been talk of another theatre stint in the West End in the run up to Christmas. But none of this seemed to be enough to keep him on an even keel in the face of his disintegrating marriage.

'You're better away from it, Em,' Chloe had told her over a crackly line. 'Why do you think I came to Paris? I love them both so much, but I can't be around them for too long.'

Chloe had spent part of her childhood with her mother, Alice; but by the time Tom had married Eva and Emma had come along, Chloe had been spending more time with her father – Alice couldn't cope with having a daily reminder of the twin she had lost, and had since entered into a relationship with another woman, with whom she ran a health food and 'holistic one-stop'. shop in Camden. The two girls were very close, and Emma missed her half-sister more than she missed anyone else, including her parents.

On her last visit, Emma had been surprised to find that her mother, had moved her office from the small back room to the larger front reception room – displacing her father's study first to the back room and then to the loft, which they'd had renovated so that it had proper access stairs, new flooring and a large dormer window; all paid for, she guessed, by his earnings from 'Gideon's Road'. Emma got the impression that her father spent most of whatever time he was home holed up in his new den. She had hardly seen her mother at all during the last few weeks of her visit, except at mealtimes - the genealogy consultancy was doing better than ever, Eva had explained quietly. 'People have a need to know their roots, and I can help them.'

Emma was happy for her, but as her mother's personal situation improved, so her father's seemed to be going the opposite way, for all his professional success. Why didn't they just sell the house and go their separate ways? She had fled back to Manchester and her research with relief.

10: MANCHESTER 20TH SEPTEMBER

'Well, this is an odd one, Doctor Morgan...' Archie scratched his head, and frowned at the print-outs he was holding. 'These results...'

Emma pulled a face. 'I do wish you'd call me Emma, Archie.' His formal manner made her feel uncomfortable, as did the way he would enquire solicitously every morning about her previous evening, as if her well-being was important to him. Well, perhaps it was – Simon often teased her about her 'fan club'. But if Archie wanted to ask her out, he was taking a long time about it. She desperately hoped he wouldn't – she didn't find him attractive, and she didn't want to hurt his feelings. But he was a *very* good lab assistant... if he were to ask her out and she refused (as she must), would he look for another post? He was so easily embarrassed... Archie was staring at her, waiting for her to pay attention.

'Sorry, I was miles away... what about them?'

'They don't make sense.' Archie put the clipboard on the desk, and pointed to a point half-way down the first sheet. 'Look.'

Emma picked up the report, stared at it, and then flipped to the second page, then the third. 'You're right. But I checked those myself... dammit, we'll have to run them again.'

'I'll get another batch out now.'

Emma sighed. 'Thanks... I don't understand how this could have happened...'

Archie turned away from the freezer, his face pale. 'I think we have a problem.'

Emma hurried over, and Archie pointed to the samples. The frost on the inside of the freezer looked smoother than it should be, indicating that a thaw had taken place. 'We've had a power failure,' he said.

'But the generator should have kicked in... no-one's said anything to you about it, have they?'

Archie shook his head. 'Not a word, Doctor Morgan. And we would have been told.'

Emma ran a hand through her short hair. 'So it can't be that. How could this happen? We're always *so* careful!'

This was bad news. None of the remaining blood samples they had painstakingly collected over the past month could be used; they would have to throw the whole lot out, and start again. With the study due in next Monday, they would be cutting it fine – and perhaps not all of the donors would be available... well, they would just have to make the best of it. This was her dream job, the project she had wanted to work on since starting her Ph.D. – no, before that, even.

'I've been thinking...' Archie ventured, the fingers of one hand playing with the cuff of his lab coat.

'About what?'

'Well, this...' he waved a hand at the freezer. 'I was in a bit earlier than normal this morning... I had to get mother ready for her hospital appointment, the transport was coming at eight... and since I was up... well, I saw that new security guard...he was coming along the corridor in a bit of a hurry. I didn't think anything of it at the time, but he could have come from here...'

Emma knew who Archie meant. He had pale green eyes and was very quiet, he didn't banter or offer cheery greetings like the man he'd replaced, who word had it had been mugged on his way home. She had caught him staring at her a couple of times, but he always looked away rather quickly. She hadn't given him much thought – why would she?

'And you think...?' Archie was what Simon called a conspiracy theorist, seeing threats where plainly there were none. Emma had learned to filter out his sometimes madcap theories because he was steady and reliable in every other way, and he was meticulous in his work.

Archie hesitated. 'I don't like to suggest... but what if he...I mean he has access....'

'Why on earth would he do such a thing?'

'I don't know...' Emma waited for him to come up with a theory. Do you think we should mention it to the head of security...?'

Well, that was a surprise. 'But if he didn't *do* anything, Archie... it's a serious accusation. Just because he .... we'd have to be sure. He could lose his job...besides, he would have been vetted. You don't just walk into a post without background checks.'

'I suppose you're right... please forget I said anything. I'll get in touch with the donors.'

Six hours later, with the first batch of new samples safely being processed under Archie's watchful eye, and another group of donors due to return the following morning, Emma stood up and stretched. It would be tight, but they might just do it.

'Well, I may as well stop for lunch...' Emma wanted to stay, oversee the rest of it herself - but she could rely on Archie, and she really did need to take a walk, get some fresh air; she had the big daddy of all tension headaches, and her neck and shoulders felt stiff. Hardly surprising.

'All right, Doctor... Emma. Enjoy your lunch. Although, it's actually nearer tea-time.'

Emma forced a smile. She knew Archie hadn't left the lab for a break either, but she would make sure he took one when she got back. And if the samples were ready, he might as well go home.

But a glance in her backpack as she headed down the stairs told her that she'd forgotten to bring her sandwich – it must be sitting in the fridge at home. It was turning out to be one of those days... Could she be bothered to go out to Greggs and get a hot, comforting pasty? There probably wouldn't be any left at this time of day. A

glance out of the window told her that it was still raining. Oh well...
She'd ring Clare, who was on her final year of her PhD and who often
skipped lunch – maybe they could go to Vasaio, it was just up the
road so they wouldn't get too wet.

'You look down, sweetie – what's wrong? Here, give me that.'
Clare took the tray from Emma and put it with her own on the vacant chair beside her.

Emma sighed, and stared at her salad. 'it's Archie...'

'Emma, you need to tell him you're really not interested.'

'It's not that.'

'Then what is it?'

Emma told her about the ruined batch, and Archie's suspicion that
one of the security guards might have been responsible. 'But I can't
see it – why would he do such a thing?' She lowered her voice. 'I
mean, he's a bit... well, I've caught him staring at me a couple of
times, but he always looks away.'

Clare shrugged. 'Well, maybe he fancies you.'

'I don't think so.' Emma wished she hadn't mentioned it now – everything came down to relationships with Clare. She was of the
opinion that if Emma sorted things out with Simon, Archie would
leave her alone, despite Emma assuring her that Archie didn't bother
her that much – he was always respectful, and never pushy, it just
wasn't in his nature.

'Your loss. Maybe I should check him out myself...'

Emma shrugged. 'Be my guest.' She sighed. 'Oh, perhaps this is
all just Archie being Archie – he suspects everyone, he thinks everyone is trying to steal our research...'

'Well, there you are, then.' Clare waggled her eyebrows. 'But if
someone did turn the freezer off, and this guy had the opportunity,
perhaps you should tell someone. They won't dismiss him if he
hasn't done anything, will they?'

'No, but it would be embarrassing...what would he think?'

'Well, maybe it might be for Archie. You don't have to back him
up, do you?'

11: MANCHESTER, 28TH SEPTEMBER

By working twelve hour shifts for five straight days, Emma and Archie had managed to source enough replacement samples to make up for the ruined batch, and Archie would be able to hand the study in on Monday as originally planned.

Emma, despite feeling that there was something odd about the guard's behavior, had managed to convince Archie not to say anything about the freezer incident to anyone. 'It might have been the cleaners,' she suggested, although she didn't believe it, and knew that Archie didn't, either.

But Archie's suspicions had been proved correct - three days later, Archie had noticed that the same guard was on duty again, and unknown to Emma, had done an all-nighter (earning himself a telling off from his mother, he later admitted to a bemused Emma) and had caught the man in the act. When the guard had tried to get away, Archie had thrown a small fire extinguisher at him, stunning him, and had turned the power back on before calling the second security guard, who had been at the other end of the building. The other guard's language had been 'extremely colourful', according to Archie, not least because he could have caved the man's skull in, instead of giving him a mild concussion. 'I always thought there was something off with Moran,' he said. 'And I'd never have had you down as a 'have a go hero' either,' he added to Archie, who had to be treated for shock.

James Moran had been summarily dismissed, of course – and although there had been talk of disciplinary action against Archie for throwing the fire extinguisher, Moran had not wanted to press charges. Apparently, he had even apologised for his actions. Emma, furious that Archie had been put in such a position, and at the risk to their work, had immediately been to see the head of department to find out if they knew why Moran had done it, if they knew who he was working for, and if the police were going to be involved. 'He might try it somewhere else.'

'I'll be meeting with the directors this afternoon,' Michael Draper had told her, 'But since no lasting damage was done, and Moran assured us that he was working alone, I think it unlikely they will want the publicity that police involvement might well bring. Something like this is likely to attract the media, unfortunately.'

Emma didn't agree that Moran should get off scott-free, but she knew if word got out that a company who held DNA samples had been targeted by one of their own employees, it would not do Xeon's reputation any good. Draper was either in the dark or unwilling to say what Moran's explanation might have been. 'He has problems,' was all he would tell her, 'not the least of which is that he'll find it hard to come by similar work. You are back on track? Then I think it's best we leave it at that.'

Archie was convinced that his theory that Moran had been working for a rival group trying to sabotage their study was accurate. 'I'm not sorry that I threw the extinguisher at him,' he said in a rare display of anger. Emma advised him to keep that to himself and insisted that he go home to recover.

But as infuriating as the whole Moran incident had been, at least they were now pretty much back on track. And she'd have something positive to tell her father tomorrow... because if someone else was working on the same angle and had been desperate enough to send someone like Moran to try to sabotage her work, that must mean they thought she was onto something... and they were, she could feel it. The randomized trial would clinch it – they had to get the go-ahead, they simply had to. She couldn't bear the thought of disappointing her father - he was counting on her to make Nathan's death mean something.

* * *

'Rats - I'd better get going or I'll miss that bus – are you quite sure you won't come, Archie?'

Archie looked alarmed, and shook his head. 'Oh no, I couldn't… but thank you all the same, Doctor Morgan. You have a good time, and I'll see you on Tuesday.' He turned back to his monitor, and began typing furiously. 'I'll make sure everything is secure before I leave,' he added, giving her a shy smile.

* * *

Emma's breath rose in a cloud in front of her face as she stepped out into the damp evening air. The weather had finally turned… and her duffle coat was still hanging in the lobby. She would definitely miss the bus if she went back for it now. She glanced at her watch and saw that she'd missed it anyway, which would mean a brisk half-hour walk to Simon's. Thank goodness the buses were regular and frequent - if she started now, she might be able to pick one up further on… if not, well at least she would be warm by the time she got to Furness Road. She was looking forward to the meal with Simon, Matt and Lili at one of their favourite haunts – Lazio's served the best Italian food in Manchester, and with the study safely back on track, Emma was ready to let her hair down. 'Best foot forward…' She set off at a fast walk.

Twenty minutes later, Emma paused at a cash machine and made a withdrawal. She felt hot and breathless, and was soaked through, and cross that she had forgotten to grab her coat. The rain had become heavier and the reflected glare from headlights more dazzling, causing her to squint, and her hair was plastered flat against her head. She must look a complete fright and would have to shower at

Simon's, even if it would make them a bit late – she couldn't go to her own birthday dinner looking like a drowned rat. To make it worse, the only buses she saw were nowhere near a bus stop.

Finally, she turned into the alleyway leading to the back entrance to Simon's flat. During the day, she could have simply walked through the shop – the proprietor didn't mind, although he would always try to sell her something- but it had shut almost an hour ago.

Simon lived in two small rooms (which Dickens might have described as 'mean' – and Emma often did) above a drugstore on Furness Road, because, he said, the rent was cheap. After a spate of robberies, the pharmacist had been desperate for some on-the-spot security, and as a result the rent was, according to Simon, 'a steal at fifty quid a week'. Emma wasn't so sure, because he didn't get much for his money, just a bed-come-sitting room, a tiny kitchenette, and a poky bathroom with a geriatric shower. The third room, always locked, functioned as a storeroom for the pharmacy. Emma couldn't have lived there – it felt claustrophobic to her, but Simon liked it. 'It doesn't take long to clean,' he said. She hoped the shower would be working… the thought of taking a cold shower was too much.

By the time Emma felt the presence behind her, it was too late to run, or even turn around - a gloved hand slid over her mouth, and a firm hand reached around to grip her right arm, pulling her tight against a solid body. Emma dropped her rucksack and with her free arm tugged at the hand covering her mouth, but her assailant was too strong. She tried to draw enough breath through her nostrils to scream, but the glove smelled of something that made her think fleetingly of hospitals: her head began to swim.

'Please don't struggle - I'm not going to hurt you, Emma.'

He knew her name! Her lips were tingling now, the smell/taste of the anesthetic overwhelming. She tried to turn her head away from the glove but the hand followed her movements. Emma felt the man's breath on her hair. She tried to pull free, but her limbs wouldn't obey. Who was he?

'I'm sorry…this is necessary.' His voice seemed to come from a long way away…

MANCHESTER, FRIDAY 28TH SEPTEMBER

'Matt – it's Simon - have you heard from Emma?'

The voice on the other end was indistinct; there was too much background noise. Simon made out '…don't tell me she's forgotten… I'm bloody starving!'

'Where are you, man?' He yelled into the receiver. This was all going tits up. Where was she? He glared at his watch, as if willing it to say something different.

'Pub… you know where we … get your arses over here, don't be pulling this crap.'

'I'm not pulling anything! Emma's not with you?'

Matt's voice suddenly gained clarity – he must have gone outside. 'No man, I told you – haven't seen hide nor hair. How can she be late to her own frigging party? Sod her, get yourself down here, now. She'll be along, you know what she's like.'

'I'm not coming without…' but Matt had gone, swallowed up in a guffaw of laughter and the clink of glasses as he went back inside. Matt could be a real pain sometimes, especially when he'd had a drink or two.

So where the hell had Emma got to? Sometimes she did forget the time, but this was late, even by her standards. She should have been here half an hour ago, latest. Surely she couldn't still be working….? Annoyed with Matt, and for Emma for being late to her own birthday gig, Simon rang the lab. She didn't like him ringing there, but sod it… To his surprise, someone picked up. Relief flooded him. She was there, she'd just forgotten the time, she was probably still engrossed because of the business with the guard; he knew it had put her back.

'Em? Have you forgotten?'

'Uh, no, it's not Doctor Morgan, this is Archibald Harrop. She isn't here. Who is this?'

'It's Simon – Emma's… oh, fuck, man, you know who I am! What time did she leave?' Simon had met Harrop a few times, and thought him a mummy's boy. That he had a crush on Emma was obvious, and amused Simon no end- she'd never look at Archie, not in a million years. He hoped.

'Oh. Oh, I see… well, Simon, she left about… yes, I'd say it must be at least fifty-five minutes ago.'

'An *hour ago*? Shit… Archie, d'you know how she was getting here? Was she walking, or getting the bus?' She must have missed the bus, but even so… she should be here by now.

'She intended to get the bus.' Archie's tone was disapproving – whether of the language or Simon's abbreviation of his name, Simon wasn't sure and didn't much care. 'But she was running a little late, she could have missed it,' Archie added. He sounded worried now.

'Okay, thanks…' Simon pressed the 'end call' button absentmindedly, churning over the possibilities. Maybe, as well as missing the bus, she'd forgotten something and had to go back to her flat… but he'd already tried her mobile, with no success. Could she have forgotten to charge it? That could be it… He thought about the incident with the guard, how Emma had told him that Archie threw a fire extinguisher at the guy to stop him running off. What if…no, that was stupid, surely he wouldn't … he'd have to be the first suspect on the list if anything happened to Emma, wouldn't he? But the thought wouldn't leave him. He paced the small room, his fingers making a roll-up almost without his being aware of it. He wasn't supposed to smoke in the flat, but the familiar ritual was comforting.

He'd spoken to Emma yesterday, and everything had seemed fine – she said she was over the business with the guard trying to sabotage her results, and was looking forward to a night out, then heading down to London to see her folks in the morning. He could believe that she might be late if she'd got so deeply into something that she couldn't tear herself away - but that wasn't it, at least not according to Archie. So, maybe there were family issues, a call whilst she was on route, maybe…could she have even got on the wrong bus? It happened – he'd done it himself once or twice, having been a bit under the weather, and had had a long walk back to his digs. Emma wouldn't have been drunk – she hardly drank at all- but she could have been thinking about her research… like many clever people (and Simon knew that he wasn't one of them) Emma often forgot the passage of time when she was thinking about work, it was her passion. Her only passion, sadly.

He fidgeted, and paced the room a few times. Sod it, Matt was right – there was no point waiting any longer. He'd go to the pub, meet up with the others. Hopefully Emma would be there, with an embarrassed explanation about getting the wrong bus or forgetting to bring her posh frock. If not… well, they'd think of something, between them. He shrugged into his coat, shoved the mobile and his wallet in his pocket, and headed for the door.

'No sign of Emma?' Lili Wu stood on her tiptoes to kiss Simon, and frowned. 'You did ring her, didn't you? I tried as well, but it went to voicemail.'

Simon rolled his eyes. 'of course I did – same thing. I called her at work and that useless tosser Harrop said she left ages ago… Shit. This isn't like her.' He scanned the crowd. 'Where's Matt?'

'Up at the bar. Oh come on, Simon – Emma's work has always been more important to her than we are. You know it.' Lili didn't seem too bothered. 'She'll turn up.'

Simon shook his head. 'Something's wrong.'

Lili caught Matt's eye across the floor, and smiled. 'We'll have to go after this round, or we'll lose the table.'

Matt shouldered his way through the crowd, cradling two glasses, and a packet of pork scratchings. 'Hey, Simon – so what've you done with Emma? You two had a row?'

'No, we bloody haven't. You know we're not together. Don't be a div, Matt.'

'Sorreee… have you tried her mobile?'

Simon sighed, nodded. 'Yeah, as I just told Lili. At least five times. It just goes to voicemail.…' He scanned the room again, but without any conviction. Fear made his mouth dry.

'Look, have a drink – maybe she just stopped off somewhere. She'll be here, man. Sit down, you can have my beer, I'll get another one…'

Twenty minutes went by. Their glasses were empty, and Simon decided that he couldn't go on to the restaurant without Emma.

'Look, you two go on, I'm going back to the flat. Maybe something's happened, maybe she's sick…' He'd check out Emma's place if she wasn't at his. Maybe she'd fallen on the stairs, passed out with some virus… a few days into fresher's week, one of the kids on his block had done just that, and had lain in the stairwell until the small hours, each of his friends thinking he was with them. He'd been carted off to hospital with meningitis, and never came back to resume his studies. Simon didn't think he'd died, but he didn't know for certain. He stood up, his legs shaking.

'You want us to come with you?' Finally, Lili looked worried.

'No, it's okay. I won't be long. I'll ring you when I get there, if….'

'Okay. Don't fret man, she'll be okay, you know Emma.' Matt pushed back his chair. 'Want us to order for you?'

Simon shook his head. 'I'll do it when I get back. Hopefully with Emma.'

He half-ran all the way back to the flat, arriving panting and sweat-soaked. If she was here, he'd need another shower before they set out. It was gone half-eight now, and would be getting on for nine by the time they got back to the restaurant … she had a key, she might have got soaked if she missed her bus, and be taking a shower…but the windows above were dark. Shit. He fumbled in his pocket for his keys, and his breath caught in his throat.

The sight of Emma's battered yellow rucksack lying a couple of feet from his doorstep turned Simon's bowels momentarily to water. Had it been there earlier? He hadn't noticed it on the way out, but then he hadn't been looking, had he? He had been focused on locking up and getting to the pub. He picked it up; it had been there for a while, and was soaked, having long ago lost any waterproofing it might have once had. Why would she have left it there? He stuck the key in the lock with trembling fingers, almost dropping them. Once inside, he put the rucksack on the table. On an impulse, he pulled out his mobile, and rang Emma's number again – the intro to the 'Blade Runner' theme rang out briefly from inside the rucksack and stopped – straight to voicemail again. Then he noticed a dark stain on the sodden fabric. Was that blood?

12: MANCHESTER, 28TH SEPTEMBER

Movement, and the sound of an engine, told Emma that she was in a moving vehicle. A soft fabric covered her eyes, but it wasn't very thick – she could see lights moving overhead. Her wrists and ankles were bound, and something soft had been tied across her mouth. Her head felt as if it was full of cotton wool; she felt sick. What if she were to vomit and choke? She drew her legs up, then kicked out at the door.

'We're almost there,' a man's voice said calmly, and she heard the soft tick-tick of the indicator as the car swung right, the movement threatening to tip her onto the floor. She struggled upright, her head swimming. The sudden exertion seemed to have pulled more of the drug into her bloodstream; she felt her mind grow fuggy again.

She woke up again with a jerk as the vehicle stopped, throwing her sideways against the seat. She heard the door open, and felt cool damp air rush in. The driver got out, and she heard his footsteps coming around the car. More cold air made her shiver as the door was pulled open, and strong hands helped her to her feet. Her captor untied the gag, then removed the blindfold. They were parked under an old carport, rain clattering onto the plastic roof above them. At first Emma didn't recognise her captor. As if he had realised her confusion, the man removed a dark wool cap to reveal silver hair. Moran. Of course, it had to be him. She swallowed.

'Why are you doing this?' her tongue felt thick, making her stumble over the words.

Moran held up a hand. 'All in good time. Please don't be frightened – I told you, I'm not going to hurt you.'

'They'll know it was you!' Emma tried to step away from him, but her wrists and ankles were still bound, and she stumbled. Moran reached out to steady her. She flinched. 'Let go of me!'

'Of course. One moment...' Moran bent down to untie the straps around her ankles. Emma tensed, readying herself to kick out, but he was too quick for her. He straightened up and offered his hand. Emma shook her head, but she could barely stand without swaying, the effects of the drug not quite dissipated. She cringed as he took her arm and steered her towards the house.

'I don't understand...what do you want?' He'd said he wasn't going to hurt her – but he'd drugged and kidnapped her...

'I'll explain everything soon. This way... please don't try to run – the sedative will soon wear off, but it wouldn't be a good idea.'

Emma walked on rubbery legs through the door Moran was holding open for her, and found herself standing in a tiled hallway. A wall light enabled her to see that it was a big house - the ceilings were higher even than those in her parent's Edwardian terrace, but here the décor was seriously dated. She shivered. What was he going to do? She remembered that he had apologised for what he'd done at the lab, and he hadn't pressed charges against Archie, she remembered.

'Do you live here?' Her voice sounded thin, and scared.

'Sometimes.' Moran led her along the hallway and into a small kitchen, the small size of which seemed wrong, given the rest of the house. He led her to a sturdy oak table and pulled out a chair, steering her gently into it.

'Why are you doing this? Please, I've done nothing to you, I don't understand why...'

'All in good time...' Moran took a glass phial from a small refrigerator and unwrapped a fresh syringe.

'Don't you come near me with that!' Emma tried to stand up, but her legs wouldn't obey her. Nausea bubbled in her throat, and she swallowed. If he was going to rape her, or kill her, why this charade?

'It will help to counter the effects of the sedative.' Moran pulled up Emma's sleeve. She tried to pull away, but her reactions were sluggish. 'Keep still, or it will hurt.' She froze, and he slid the needle into a vein, depressing the plunger. She shivered, but began to feel better almost immediately. He withdrew the needle and dabbed the tiny puncture wound with a small gauze pad. Then he pulled a small knife from his pocket and deftly snipped the plastic ties around her wrists. He slipped the knife back into his pocket.

Remember which pocket. 'I don't understand…' her throat was dry, and she couldn't finish the sentence.

'The sedative will have dehydrated you. Would you like a drink – tea, coffee, perhaps water?'

He was politeness itself. 'Water…please.' She rubbed her wrists, and licked her lips; she could taste blood where she must have bitten them. Would he use that knife on her if she tried to run? She watched him fetch a glass tumbler from an overhead cupboard and draw water from the tap, letting it run for a moment or two before filling the glass. He brought it back to the table and stepped away, as if sensing her need to keep some distance between them. She drank it quickly, and began to feel less headachy almost straight away.

'Why are you doing this?'

She was startled to see tears in his eyes. 'You sound just like …' he cleared his throat. 'Please believe me when I tell you that I am sorry this was necessary. You need to rest, then I'll tell you everything, I promise.'

13: MANCHESTER, 28TH SEPTEMBER

Hammond met his Sergeant on the steps leading into Police Headquarters, and turned to keep pace with him as they hurried to the car. Light reflected from ground water and the glass edifice behind them. 'Okay, what do we know?'

'It sounds like another abduction, a student who didn't turn up for a dinner with friends. Got a call from that Italian place up the Mile, Lazio's. Flynn's already on site – says a bloke called Simon Watkins reckons his girlfriend never turned up for her birthday bash. Name of Emma Morgan.'

Hammond groaned. 'It'll be a lover's tiff... why the hell have we been called out?'

Mortimer slipped the key into the ignition. 'The girl's father is Tom Morgan.' When Hammond didn't say anything, he added, 'Gideon's Road'? Don't you watch telly?'

'Not much, no'

'He's an actor, quite well-known – it follows the pattern...'

'Shit.'

Hammond and Mortimer had both worked on two recent kidnap cases, in which the children of wealthy celebrities had been taken for ransom. Neither man had been Senior Investigating Officer; that dubious honor had been Richard Adcock's ('Cocky' behind his back) and he hadn't been up to the job. One victim had been found dead, the other was still missing... Adcock's so-called 'Elite Kidnap Unit', formed to deal with missing people/runaways and abductions had been disbanded; with Adcock himself moved sideways (out of harm's way, as DCI Surridge had unexpectedly confided to Hammond) and Hammond was apparently considered a promising substitute, which was ironic since Hammond had also applied and been turned down in favour of Cocky.

'If Adcock had listened to you, Nicky Dew might still be alive,' Surridge had gone on to add. Surridge implied that if Hammond proved able to bring the next case – because they were all agreed that that there would be more- to a successful conclusion, he might get to head up the reformed unit after all. Hammond was not holding his breath.

* * *

'I'm Detective Inspector Hammond. What's your name, son?'

'Simon... Watkins...' Watkins was in his mid-to-late twenties, tall and lean with pale skin that looked as if it didn't get much sun. He fidgeted in his seat, running thin fingers through tight black curls. His nails were bitten almost to the quick, Hammond noticed. He could hear his team talking to the kidnap victim's other friends; one of them, young woman, was in tears.

The restaurant was only a quarter full: although it was a Friday evening Lazio's was known for keeping late hours, it seemed as if the appearance of the police had brought the night to an early close. Restaurant staff had begun clearing up, their voices and movements subdued. The manager, at first annoyed by the loss of revenue, was now covering it well, offering disappointed diners vouchers for a half-price meal on another date of their choice.

'So tell me what happened, Simon.'

'Emma was meant to be at mine for half-seven. When she hadn't showed for eight, I rang the lab and ...'

'The lab?'

Simon rolled his eyes. 'At Xeon, Brunswick Street. I told the woman on the phone…'

'Hang on – Emma's a student, isn't she?'

The young man shook his head. 'It's not part of the University, although they're kind of affiliated …she's post-grad, got her doctorate in genetics… anyway…'

'Flynn!' Hammond bawled across the suddenly quiet room. 'Who told you the girl was a student?'

Jonas Flynn hurried up; like many restaurants, the space between tables was minimal, the temperature higher than comfortable. The constable's dark face was shiny with sweat, his tie askew. 'Sorry Boss – info I got from the desk was a missing student.'

Hammond nodded, waved him away and turned back to the young man. 'She'd be what, twenty-three …?'

'She'll be twenty-six, tomorrow…' Watkins swallowed, tears welling in his eyes.

Hammond swore under his breath. The missing woman was technically an adult. If they had been dragged out for nothing more than a lover's tiff…but Watkins seemed genuinely worried, and the fact that the previous kidnap victims both had parents who were in the public eye was a similarity they couldn't ignore. Just because Emma Morgan was several years older than the last victim, didn't necessarily mean it wasn't the same gang. Maybe they'd decided to go for older targets.

'So, if Emma was meant to be here for half-seven, how come you waited so long to ring us?' In fact, as far as raising the alarm went, Watkins had done well – every hour counted.

'Well, when she didn't turn up I called the lab, I spoke to Archie, he's her…they work together. He said Emma left almost an hour earlier. She should have been at my place by then, even if she'd not caught the bus – but it was raining – why would she walk? She could have got a taxi… So we -me, Matt, Lili- went to the pub next door for a while – we'd agreed we would all meet there first. Maybe she got delayed – forgot something, went back to her digs, or she might've gone straight on… I thought, she'll turn up all out of breath like she usually does …' He was babbling now, desperate to get the words out. 'But she wasn't there.'

'So you thought you'd carry on partying without her?' Some friends, Hammond thought.

'It wasn't like that! We had a drink, waited for a bit, like Matt suggested - then when she still didn't turn up, I told the others to go on to Anzio's, and I went back to mine. I thought, maybe she got the wrong bus – I've done it, we all have – and maybe she's having a shower. Then I thought, if she wasn't at mine, I'd check out her place… but then I saw the bag. You know, her rucksack. She wouldn't have just left it in the street. She loves that bloody thing …'

'You're certain it belongs to Emma? Where exactly did you find it?' Something else Flynn had failed to pass on.

Watkins nodded. 'Yeah, it's Emma's…she's had it for years, keeps saying she's going to get a new one… I found it on the street, it was about two feet from my door, just lying there, like… as if she'd dropped it. It was wet. Well, it would be, wouldn't it, but I mean it was really wet, soaked.'

'It wasn't there when you left the building the first time?'

Watkins looked even more miserable. 'I don't know. It could've been… I didn't see it, but I was walking the other way then, and I wasn't looking…so… she must've got that far, mustn't she?'

'Where is the bag now?'

'It's still at mine – I took it indoors. Then I rang your lot, and came back here, just in case…'

The rain would likely have destroyed any useful evidence. 'We'll need it – and we'll need to take your prints – to eliminate you.'

'Should I not have touched it?' Watkins swallowed. 'I'm sorry…'

Hammond held up a calming hand. 'She's your girlfriend?' It was a shame that Watkins had touched the rucksack, but if his prints and the rain hadn't destroyed any evidence, they might still have something.

Simon flushed. 'No, no, I'm… no, we're not… we *were*…in our first year… now we're just friends. But she would've called, she *always* calls if she's going to be this late. Sometimes she forgets the time, we rib her about it... but this late, I knew it wasn't right. I should've rung you earlier, I know I should...' He looked at Hammond, shame and guilt written all over his face. '...it's just, we know what she's like. But she wouldn't just leave her bag like that.'

The lad still had feelings for her, no matter what he might claim, Hammond thought. 'Relax, Simon – you're doing all right, as it happens. Most people leave it a lot longer. Does she *have* a boyfriend?'

Simon flinched, then shook his head. 'No. I mean not that I know of– and I'd know, I think.' He swallowed. 'After I found the bag, before I came back here, I rang her dad, 'cause I thought... I wasn't thinking straight, really, but I thought maybe something had come up, family stuff, you know? Her mum, she's a bit flaky... but her dad said not.'

Hammond rubbed his temple, and wondered if he could cadge some paracetamol from someone. He hadn't been sleeping well, and the headache he'd started the day with had suddenly returned with reinforcements. 'Did you tell Emma's father that you found her rucksack?'

'No – I only told the woman on the phone. I thought it might upset him...Emma's parents, they....' He stopped, and shook his head. 'Doesn't matter.'

'Let me decide what matters, Simon.'

'Yeah, but it really doesn't – it wouldn't be them. They're in London. Look, can I go ...?' The young man's eyes flicked towards the 'Toilets' sign above a door just a few feet away; he looked decidedly green around the gills.

'Yeah, go on. When you come back, I'll get one of my colleagues to run you back to your place. We'll need the rucksack, and for you to come down to the station for your prints. Are you okay with that?' It didn't really matter whether he was or not, but Hammond's gut told him the boy wasn't involved. He hoped he was right.

Simon nodded, and shot off to the toilets like a greyhound out of the trap.

14: LONDON, 28TH SEPTEMBER

'Sorry, baby, I've got to go.' Dammit, where were his trousers?

Tina nodded. Her face was still puffy from sleep, a pillow crease bisecting one cheek.

Tom had woken with a start, his mobile buzzing from inside his jacket pocket, which was hanging over the dressing table mirror. It had been a long day – 4am alarm for a 6am shoot for pick up shots while the streets were quiet, and then the crowd scenes…there had been problems with the lighting rig and they hadn't finished until six-thirty. The idea of going home to his wife's accusatory silence had been distinctly unappealing, so he and Tina had grabbed a takeaway on the way back to her place at Devonshire Mews, and they'd made love almost perfunctorily before falling asleep. Then Simon had rung, and Tom's world had come crashing down around him.

'I hope your daughter is okay.' Tina blinked at him.

Tom managed a grimace that was about as far from a smile as you could get. 'Yeah, I hope so too. Go back to sleep - I'll call you, okay?' His heart was racing, and he felt sick. He had to get home before the police called there, because if Eva …

'Sure, whatever, darlin'…but I won't get back to sleep now.' She threw the covers back, and Tom turned away from the lithe figure that only a couple of hours ago had been entwined with his. If something had happened to Emma while they had been…

Tom hit the street running, wishing he'd bought the car, knowing he was probably way over the limit and that being done for drunk-driving wouldn't help. Within two blocks he'd found a cabbie, waved him down and promised the man forty quid if he could get him to Irene Road, Parsons Green, within ten minutes. The cabbie had pursed his lips when Tom gave him the address.

'I'll do me best.'

'Thanks, appreciate it if you would.'

He drummed nervous fingers on his knees, gnawed his lower lip, and sweated as the cab wove through the streets, thick with the usual traffic. His daughter, his Emmy. *Please let it be nothing, please let her be safe, a misunderstanding...* he knew it wouldn't be.

He hadn't wanted to take Simon's call too seriously at first; they'd had an argument, obviously, and she must have walked out in a huff; like him, she was quick to anger. But after he'd ended the call, he had sat with his pulse racing, and thought about it. She might duck out of a dinner date with Simon if they'd fallen out, but not her other friends, whose names he couldn't recall. Simon he knew, vaguely – he had been at University with Emma, Tom remembered– he thought they'd had a thing for a while during Emma's first year... were they still in a relationship? He didn't think so, but he didn't re-ally know the circles Emma moved in now that she had her own life, two hundred miles away... He played the conversation back in his mind. There had definitely been an edge to Simon's voice... But it hadn't been until Simon said he was going to call the police that it had sunk in – Emma was *missing*.

He stared at the crowds on the pavement as their progress was stalled by a red light. A young woman with the same hair colour and facial shape as his daughter leaned up on tiptoe to kiss the young man whose arm held her close as they walked in front of the cab, and Tom's stomach turned over. If Emmy was safe, he'd change, he really would – he'd dump Tina, make a real effort with Eva, cut back on the booze... *it's not about you, you selfish prat*. He fingered his mobile, willing Simon to call back with good news. The lights changed and they were moving again. Thank Christ for that...

'Here you are, sir. That'll be…'

Tom thrust two twenties at the man. 'Thanks, that's great, keep the change.'

'Are you sure…?' But Tom was out of the car and hurrying up the path, already pulling his keys from his pocket.

Eva's reading lamp was on in the back lounge, its soft light spilling out into the hallway. Tom dropped his keys onto the hall table and hurried towards the light. He could smell Tina on his skin - would Eva notice? He'd tell her the bad news, then have a shower, they had time for that, and Eva could pack a few things, then they'd jump in the car and go. He couldn't sit here while Christ knows what-all might be happening up there…

Eva was asleep in the recliner, her face turned towards him, a book open on her lap. He felt a pang of guilt. She still looked so young when she was sleeping, more like the woman he'd met twenty-seven years ago; the care lines smoothed out, her sad green eyes hidden behind long lashes which still made him want to kiss her and…how could he ever have thought Tina – or any of the others- could fill the gap? Even given how she was… Just how was he going to tell her that Emma was missing? He swallowed, and leaned down to touch his wife's arm.

'Eva… wake up, darling…' He hadn't called her that in a while.

'What? What? Oh, Tom…' she smiled up at him, and Tom's gut did another somersault. Then Eva frowned; her eyes clouded, and the shutters came down. The familiar lead weight settled in his chest.

'Hi. Sorry I'm late.' He had to wait until she was with it. The pills she relied on to function sometimes made her slow to wake. Had she been waiting up for him? It seemed unlikely. But what did he really know about anything to do with his wife's state of mind these days?

'What time is it? How long have I been asleep?'

Tom stepped away as Eva kicked the recliner back into place and stood up, stretching the stiffness out of her limbs. She was still trim, despite her mostly sedentary life-style. He felt desire rise in his loins, and felt ashamed. He raised his wrist and realised that he'd left his watch on Tina's bedside table.

'It's late…uh, getting on for ten, I think. I went for a bite to eat with the crew…I'm sorry.' He could feel his face burning with shame. How was it that he could stand on a stage, and essentially lie to a packed house - but put him in his own home, in front of the mother of his child, and he couldn't hide a damn thing from her? He never had been able to.

'I know I'm way later than I said, we had lighting problems…' *get on with it.* 'The thing is…'

She made to walk past him, stopped and sniffed. 'Have you been drinking? I thought you said you were working?'

Tom cursed silently. 'I was, then we had a meal, we… Look, that's not important. I had a call from…'

Eva leaned in close. 'Whose perfume is that?' She glared at him, wide awake now.

He hated himself for the lie, knew he wouldn't remember it, and would trip himself up again. He always did… 'There was some catch-up stuff… you know how it works…look, I know I need a shower, Evie, but I have to tell you…'

'Oh for God's sake - it's not as if I don't already *know*, Tom. But you don't have to rub my nose in it!'

'Eva, will you just shut up and *listen*?' Fear and guilt made him shout, and Eva flinched as if he'd struck her.

'Look, sorry, I didn't mean… the thing is…' he couldn't do it. But he had to, needed to say the unthinkable. 'I had a call from that boy, Simon…Darling, Emma is missing.' He held his breath, searching her face anxiously. She stared at him, uncomprehending.

'What?'

'Emma – she was meant to be meeting her friends for a meal, that Italian place she took us to when… it was a birthday thing… she didn't turn up.'

Eva swallowed, and shook her head – instant denial, her normal way of dealing with anything she didn't like. 'Who told you this?'

'I told you… Simon called me. You know Simon - you met him, last summer… summer before last, I don't know. They, he and Emma, they had a thing… look, he said he'd called, or he's going to call, the police. We should go up there, be on hand…' he felt sick, the takeaway sitting heavily in his stomach.

'The *police*?' Her eyes slid past him and down to the wet footprints on the carpet. 'Oh, for goodness sake, Tom, you've tracked muck in… I'll have to clean….'

Something snapped inside Tom. He grabbed Eva's arms, pulled her round to face him, and leaned in close, trying not to think about how frail she looked. She blinked at him, startled.

'Eva, our daughter has gone *missing* in Manchester. She didn't show up for a meal with her friends, who are fucking worried, as I am, as you *should* be. What's *wrong* with you?'

Eva's face crumpled as her body, until then stiff in his arms, sagged. 'I can't hear this Tom, I don't … she'll be okay, she'll be with…oh God, I can't…' She began to cry softly, her chin sinking until it almost touched her chest.

Tom took her into his arms, his own eyes tearing up, his heart pounding. The feel of her in his arms, her body against his – Christ, why was he such a bastard to her? All he'd ever wanted to do was make her happy…if he could take her to bed right now, maybe they could still reconnect… he pulled back, holding her at arm's length, disgusted by his body's betrayal.

'Maybe she *is* okay, darling, I'm sure she is – but if her friends don't know where she is, and they've called the police… something must be wrong. Look, let's try not to …' what, think the worst? What *else* were you supposed to think when someone tells you that your daughter is missing? He saw it all: the newsflash, a solemn-faced police spokesman, the headline banner rolling underneath his image as he told the nation, *'we are doing everything we can to locate this young woman. If you think you know or might have seen anything that could help us to find Emma Morgan, please call the number on your screens now…'*

Eva stared past him, her thoughts not on him, but on… Oh, Jesus. He could feel her trembling.

'Look, Eva, I need to shower. Pack a bag, we're going up there now, okay?' He didn't know what else to say to her. He knew exactly where her head was at this moment – New Year's Eve nineteen-ninety, the crash, the deaths of her first husband and daughter… He hadn't given a thought to Nathan. Should he have? He pulled in a breath and let go of her, stepping away, putting further distance between them. 'Did you hear me, Eva?'

She gave a little nod, her eyes slowly refocusing. 'I heard you. Yes. I'll pack.' She drew herself up, licked her lips and wiped her wet face with trembling fingers. She wouldn't look at him, and his heart sank. She was doing it again: pulling back, shutting him out. The news had chipped a hole in her armour, now she was plugging it up again. At least she was holding it together – for now. He had no idea what he would do if she became hysterical. He was usually good with women, wasn't he, with the emotional side of things; but since Emma had been born, Eva hadn't been herself. She'd suffered post-natal depression, then a nervous breakdown, and although she had seemed to recover from that, she had withdrawn from them both emotionally. He couldn't reach her… there were odd moments of warmth, as if she sometimes forgot; but they didn't last. She was not –and hadn't been for a long time – the woman he had married.

'Okay, good. I'll shower, grab a few things, won't take me long.'

15: MANCHESTER, 28TH SEPTEMBER

Archie Harrop's pale blue eyes were wide with anxiety as he eyed the two detectives standing on his doorstep. Hammond put him somewhere in his early thirties. He was dressed for bed, and wearing a dark maroon dressing gown similar to one Hammond's own father had once owned.

'Is this about Doctor Morgan?'

Hammond nodded. 'Yes, sir, it is. May we come in?'

Harrop glanced over his shoulder, his skinny body still blocking the doorway. 'My mother, she's… she's elderly, she doesn't sleep well, can we not…?'

Hammond grimaced. The tiny porch was in need of repair; while they had been standing there, rain had dripped down inside his collar and soaked his shirt. He thought longingly of his bed and the glass of single malt sitting on his coffee table that he'd abandoned when the call came. 'I'd rather not do this on the doorstep, Mr. Harrop – we'll be as quick as possible, but it's important that we talk to you *now*.'

Reluctantly, Harrop stepped backwards, allowing Hammond and Mortimer to step inside.

The house smelled like an old people's home; a faint whiff of urine and stale cabbage, with musty overtones of damp. The dated décor reinforced the impression. Harrop had no sooner shut the door behind them than the sound of a hand bell rang out.

'Archibald! Who is that at the door?' The voice was aged, female, and querulous.

'Excuse me, officers, my mother, I need to …' without waiting for a response, Harrop took off down the hallway, his slippers slapping against the worn linoleum, and disappeared into a room at the far end. Hammond heard the murmur of voices - Harrop and his mother, he assumed; hers questioning, his calming. After a couple of minutes, Harrop returned, closing the door softly behind him.

'I'm sorry – she gets frightened easily…and it's late… shall we go in here? Or would you like a coffee, or perhaps tea, we can use the kitchen… although it's next to Mother's room so perhaps not…' Harrop was nervous, and the skin on the back of Hammond's neck prickled.

'Here will do just fine,' Hammond told him, following the young man into a reception room that might have been his own grandmother's. 'We'd like to ask you a few questions, Mr. Harrop.'

Harrop sat down, as if expecting Hammond and Mortimer to do the same; when they didn't, he jumped up again.

'Of course. What do you want to know? He rang me first, you know.'

'Simon Watkins?'

'Simon. Yes, him.' He sniffed in a disapproving way. 'He told me that Emma hadn't arrived for their dinner date, and he seemed very concerned.'

His story tallied so far. 'When did you last see Emma, Mr. Harrop?'

'When she left work, at, um, well it would have been just before seven, I think… I told him, Simon, that she had been gone for almost an hour, so she would have left around seven o'clock.' He paused, and blinked. 'I think it was nearer six-fifty-five, actually. Yes, I'm sure it was.' He glanced down at his wrist, and seemed surprised to find that he wasn't wearing his watch.

'Does Emma normally work that late?'

Harrop nodded, and sat down suddenly, as if his legs would no longer support him. 'Well, sometimes we do – she's very dedicated, is Miss Morgan. I don't believe she meant to leave late tonight, but we had been trying to catch up after some samples were spoiled, and I suppose she forgot the time…' he swallowed, and looked at Hammond.

'I see. What about yourself, Mr. Harrop? Do you normally work on?'

Harrop nodded, then shook his head. 'Yes, again, sometimes – but not too often, because of mother…'

Hammond felt a moment of sympathy for the young man, and something else, which might have been envy. At least Harrop knew where his mother was.

'I see. Can you describe your relationship with Emma Morgan?'

Harrop blinked. 'Relationship? I don't have a *relationship* with Emma Morgan, Inspector. She's a work colleague, nothing more.' He blushed.

Interesting. Did Harrop also have feelings for Emma that were not being reciprocated?

'That's still a relationship – a professional one,' Hammond pointed out.

'Oh yes, I know, I mean of course, but I thought you might be inferring…' Harrop swallowed, squeezed his eyes shut for a moment and then opened them again. 'My apologies, I misunderstood. We work together – I'm a laboratory assistant, I assist Doctor Morgan in all aspects of her research.'

'You're older than she is,' Mortimer said suddenly. 'By what, ten, fifteen years?'

Harrop's eyes swiveled to him. 'Nine, actually.'

'Well, how come she's not your assistant, rather than the other way around? You must have graduated, right? Why do you play second fiddle?'

Easy, Hammond thought. He flicked a look at his sergeant, who didn't acknowledge it, but continued to look at Harrop, who looked indignant.

'It's not that unusual… but I've no desire to head a project, if you must know. I'm perfectly content to assist.' He paused, and then sighed, folding in on himself. 'If you must know, I had a nervous breakdown following my graduation. I don't take pressure well. So, I assist, rather than lead. I'm happier that way.'

Hammond let out a breath. It didn't mean Harrop wasn't a suspect, but on the face of it, he didn't seem capable of carrying out a kidnap – the planning, perhaps, but the subterfuge? Harrop seemed socially awkward, and Hammond couldn't see it. What would be the motive? Professional jealousy? Harrop claimed not. A thwarted attempt at a relationship with the younger woman, who, Hammond thought, perhaps didn't see Harrop as potential partner material? It seemed possible, if unlikely. But you never could tell…

'Okay, Mr. Harrop, that's fine, we're not here to judge, we just want to find Emma. What is she working on?'

Harrop brightened. 'A cure for Progeria.' He smiled proudly. 'It was her project, for her dissertation – and now she has been given a research position and funding at Xeon. We have just completed a feasibility study for a Randomized Control Trial, in order to…'

'What's 'Progeria'?' Mortimer interrupted.

Harrop nodded, as if expecting the question, and adopted a lecturing tone. 'There are several variants, but put simply, it is accelerated ageing - the result of a genetic mutation. Not always hereditary, but it can be. The sufferer ages eight times faster than their peers, leading to arterial scoliosis, stroke, arthritis, osteoporosis … most sufferers don't live beyond their teens or twenties, although with some strains, they can live into their mid-thirties. There are drugs which can help delay the symptoms, but Emma is looking beyond palliative care, for a way to stop the mutation occurring in the first place. It's a terrible disease.'

'I've never heard of it,' Hammond admitted.

'It's quite rare.'

'Why not research something that affects more people?' Mortimer asked. Hammond stared at him, and he shrugged. 'Just wondering.'

'Emma has a … a personal connection. Or at least, through her father, she does.'

'Tom Morgan? He's got it?'

Harrop shot Hammond a withering look. 'Of course he doesn't. I'm really not sure I should be telling you this…'

Hammond felt they were wasting time. 'Can I speak plainly here? We're trying to find out what happened to Emma, Archie – *nothing* is off limits, not if it could lead to her safe return.'

'Of course, Inspector. I'm sorry…you're right. Emma's father was married before. He and his first wife had twins, and one of the children, a son, had Progeria. The boy died when he was three years old, following a stroke.'

'Ah.'

'Yes. So you see… you have to find her, Inspector Hammond. The research *must* continue.' He frowned. 'There is one thing… we had an incident recently. One of the security guards tried to sabotage our work…'

16: LONDON, 28TH SEPTEMBER

Eva lay the small weekend case on the bed, and stared at it. What did she need? How long would they be away? A day? Two days? A week – longer? Think, Eva. Underwear. Jeans or skirt? Blouses or jumpers? It would be colder up there; everywhere was colder than London – jumpers then, jeans. Socks. She went to her sweater drawer and opened it.

'Eva – are you coming…? Bloody hell…'

Eva blinked, and found herself sitting on the bed, a pile of sweaters on her lap. The suitcase was still empty. Tom stood in the doorway. He didn't look happy.

'I'm sorry, I … I don't know what to pack, Tom. How long will we be there, where will we stay? I can't think…' She knew that her voice sounded dull, it was the pills; they sometimes made her slow. But she needed them…she had taken two more, on top of the ones she had taken earlier, and she probably should not have done. Tom would react badly, if he found out - he hated her medication with a passion, had accused her GP –she refused to go private, despite Tom's entreaties to do so - more than once of turning his wife into a zombie, that they didn't work.

Tom gently took the sweaters from her, put them on the bed, and hunkered down in front of Eva, resting on his heels, his hands on the bed either side of her. He was dressed, but his hair was still damp from the shower, sticking up in all directions. He looked as if he had been crying. She reached out a hand to smooth the hair down, but he caught it in mid-air and pressed his lips to her knuckles. His lips were cold. Shock, she supposed. Once, this might have been the prelude to lovemaking... but he hadn't been in her bed for months. She knew it was because he had someone else, and she had tried to convince herself that it was easier this way.

'Darling, I *know* this is hard for you. We just need enough for a couple of days, okay? We'll find out what the police know, book into a hotel and then we'll decide where to go from there.'

She struggled to hold onto her thoughts. 'But what if she comes home... and we're not *here*? She might have lost her key, she...'

'Then she'll go to your Dad's, won't she? Emma's an adult, Eva, she'll work it out.'

'And then... we can come home.' She didn't want to travel up to Manchester, in the car. It was dark, and the roads would be wet...

'Eva? Eva? Listen to me, darling.' He stood up, pulling her to her feet. She felt giddy, half of her mind pulling her back to that night... she couldn't do it. He'd have to go alone.

'I'm listening. Tom, we *can't* drive...'

'Yes, we can. We'll be okay. I know what you're afraid of, and it won't happen again, I promise. Look, if you want to, *you* can drive, okay?'

'No, Tom.' Now he was being unkind – he knew she wouldn't drive, at least not until the pills had worn off. 'The train would be safer...' that was laughable, wasn't it - she'd met Tom as a result of an underground train accident. Was there no corner of their lives that tragedy had not touched?

'Darling, it's too late, we won't get one now. The roads'll be clear, we can be there by three, four at the latest, if we start now. You can sleep on the way...'

There would be no convincing him.

'She *can't* be missing – it's a mistake. Who would take her, Tom? *Why*?' She imagined Emma crying and fighting as a faceless man grabbed her; saw her locked in a dark room, hands bound.... lying in the undergrowth somewhere, lifeless... with a supreme effort, Eva pulled herself back into the here and now. It hadn't happened, it *couldn't* happen.

Tom was talking, his grip on her hands too tight.

'We don't know that anyone *has*, Eva. She might've just decided not to go out ...maybe she had work to catch up on...' He was lying. She was sure she had heard him throwing up before taking a shower. What wasn't he telling her?

'Did she call you? She didn't call me; she hardly ever calls me. She's coming home tomorrow, Tom, we should be *here*...'

Tom sighed. 'You're not listening .... Simon was going to call the *police*, Eva. You know this is *serious*.'

Eva felt as if she didn't know anything; somehow, Emma had grown up without her noticing. One minute, her daughter had been at school, then she was going to college, finally university - and she hadn't ever really come back. She wouldn't now. But not like this, please, not like this... she was crying again, the tears running hot down her face.

'Why is this happening to us... haven't we been through enough?'

Tom sighed, and stepped away from her, and shook his head. 'When this is all over, we're going to get you some proper treatment. Ditch that useless quack...' He began opening drawers, pulling out underwear, tossing it all at the case on the bed. 'We need to get going.'

Eva took a deep breath. He was making a mess, pulling out all the wrong things. 'You're not helping, Tom. Stop it! I just need to clear my head...'

He turned, his colour high. 'Can't you do *anything* without those bloody pills, Eva? They've turned you into a... a *zombie*! When was the last time we even...?' he threw up his hands. 'Forget it, we don't have time for this... just pack a few things... I'll see you downstairs in five minutes, or I'm going without you.'

17: MANCHESTER, 28TH SEPTEMBER

Hammond's gaze swept across the incident room. He badly needed caffeine, and his mouth felt as if a small creature had laid down to die on his tongue. He'd found three paracetamol in his desk drawer and swallowed them dry. The machinery of a new investigation was gearing up; he felt the anticipation kick in as he watched his team, those who hadn't originally been on duty this weekend resigning themselves to the loss of whatever personal plans they might have had. Someone needed them; they'd chosen this job. Or perhaps it had chosen them.

A whiteboard stood in the centre of the room, a fuzzy snapshot of Emma Morgan taped to the middle. It wasn't the best, a hastily cropped image from a friend's Facebook page. They'd need to get a better picture from her employers or family as soon as possible.

'Anyone spoken to the parents, yet?' he asked the room.

Constable Lucy Rattigan pushed hair out of her eyes – with smudged eye make-up and her hair slowly coming unraveled in blonde ringlets that fell down her back, she looked as though she had been called from a hot date to be here.

'No answer from the house, Sir – we're trying the father's mobile, but it seems to be on voicemail. They must be on their way.'

'Well, what about other family, friends…? C'mon people…'

A thin young man with livid acne scars put his head around the door.

'Sir…DCI Surridge is here now…'

Hammond's heart sank. Great. 'Right, thanks, er…'

'Brown, sir, Tim Brown.'

'Tim, thank you.'

Brown hovered in the doorway.

'I'll be right up,' Hammond said.

'I'm sorry sir, I was told to bring you… in case you got distracted, sir.' Brown's face was bright red with embarrassment, his gaze flicking between Hammond and Rattigan. Hammond remembered hearing Rattigan complain that Brown wouldn't stop pestering her for a date. He wondered if he had got lucky… or perhaps unlucky, since they were all here…. He sighed, peeled his still sodden coat off and draped it over someone's chair.

'All right.' He turned to Mortimer. 'Find anyone who knows Emma Morgan - aunts, uncles, sisters, grandparents, call them, get the mother's mobile… you know what we need, Sergeant. I'll be ten minutes.'

'Yes, boss.'

'Ian. Sorry about Tim… but I know what you're like. So where are we at?'

DCI Alan Surridge was younger than Hammond by a decade; well-spoken, well-groomed – even at this ungodly hour– and privately educated; everything Hammond wasn't. Hammond couldn't decide how he felt about the man. He'd got on with Norton, still couldn't quite believe his former DCI was gone. Dropped dead in the middle of a game of squash with the Chief. Had it really only been three months?

'Just gearing up, Sir. Trying to get hold of the parents. Apparently they're on their way up from London. No sightings of the young woman as yet, but all the signs are pointing to abduction.' According to her friends, Emma Morgan was not the type to just up and leave them in the lurch, or her previously bereaved parents panicking as they imagined the worst. The rucksack was with forensics.

'It's Alan, Ian. The parents are on their way? Whose idea was that?'

'Theirs, it seems. The caller, a friend of the girl's, rang the father before he rang us, checking she hadn't already gone home for the weekend, I believe. Morgan told him he would be travelling up right away.'

'Hmm. This is Tom Morgan the actor, right?' Surridge had obviously had his ear to the ground.

Hammond nodded. 'Sir… Alan…I'll need…'

'I know what you're going to say, and no, I do *not* think we should involve anyone else from the old kidnap unit. Yourself and Mortimer have worked this kind of case before. We still don't know for certain it's the same people, though it seems likely, I'll grant you. No, it's with you, Ian – you've already got a good team, so use them. I have faith in you.'

'As you wish, sir…Alan.' dammit, he didn't want to be on first name terms with this fast track career man with his pressed suits and cut glass vowels, and he certainly didn't think his team deserved to have another department's work dumped on them. But a crime was a crime, he supposed…they had still to establish that one had taken place, but it was certainly looking that way. There'd been a small stain on the faded yellow rucksack which Watkins said he thought might be blood…Hammond hoped it wasn't.

'I want you to put out an appeal on the morning news,' Surridge continued, oblivious to Hammond's internal musings. 'Parents involved, do you think?'

Hammond hesitated. 'We have no reason to suspect it at the moment, sir – Alan. They live in London, and as I said, they're on their way. I'll check alibis, of course.'' He hesitated.

'Excellent.' Surridge talked as if he'd swallowed a handbook – *How to Command Effectively in as Few Words as Possible.*

'There was an incident with a security guard at the girl's employment a couple of weeks ago,' Hammond said. 'I've got someone trying to get hold of their HR manager, we'll get the details as soon as we can. Might be something, might be nothing.' Hammond's gut told him it was something, but Surridge had made it known that he didn't do gut feelings, so he kept it to himself.

'You know, sir, the husband might be good for the appeal – used to public speaking.'

Hammond hadn't been able to bring Tom Morgan's face to mind, but someone had found an image online; it would go up on the board beside his daughter's picture. Morgan's celebrity status would help to draw attention to the case – and it might be the reason his daughter was now missing. But first they had to establish that it was kidnap. If it followed the form of the previous abductions, police involvement was essential, they couldn't keep it quiet. Someone knew who the abductors were.

Surridge nodded. 'But you know as well as I do, the mother would be better, more emotional punch. Well, I'll leave that to your discretion. Make sure Family Liaison are assigned…'

Hammond rose, seeing his chance to escape. 'Will do, sir. Sorry…'

Surridge waved it off. 'Just keep me informed, Ian.'

18: THE M40, 28TH SEPTEMBER

'My father,' Eva said suddenly. 'I didn't ring him!'

Tom hadn't rung his family either. 'You probably should.' And so should he, but he couldn't imagine that conversation, didn't want to.

Eva fumbled around in her bag for a moment. 'My mobile – I left it charging...'

Tom dug inside his jacket, ignoring Eva's sharply indrawn breath as he took one hand off the steering wheel, and handed her his own. 'If the battery's low, there's a charger in the glove-box.'

Eva gasped. 'You've got messages, Tom!'

She held the mobile to her ear, and frowned. 'Nothing from Emma. A couple from someone called Tina...' she swallowed, shook her head. 'Oh, wait... can you put this on speaker?'

Tom thumbed a button on the steering stalk.

'Hold on, I'll start it again from the beginning...'

'... is DC Lucy Rattigan from Manchester CID. We're trying to call you in connection with your daughter, Emma Morgan. Would you please call me as soon as you get this? oh-one-six-one-seven, nine-three...'

'Shit! Ring her back!'

Eva fumbled with the phone, putting it back to her ear before realising she didn't need to.

'Manchester City Police, DC Rattigan. Mr. Morgan?' The woman's voice sounded loud, almost invasive, over the car's sound system, her accent pure Manchester. They could hear other voices in the background, phones ringing.

'Yes. Have you found my daughter?'

'Where are you, sir?'

'I'm on the motorway, about two hours from you... Have you found my daughter?' *Please, please....*

'Not yet, I'm afraid. Can I ask, do you have any current photographs of Emma with you?'

'Yes, yes – on my phone, plenty, why ...'

'We'd like to put out a television appeal, to catch the morning news. Can you make your way straight to Central Park, Newton Heath...?'

'I know it,' Tom said grimly.

'Then we'll see you soon, sir, but please drive with care.'

'Wait...do you know who took her?'

'We know very little at this stage - I just need you to concentrate on getting here safely. Is Mrs. Morgan with you?'

'Yes, but...'

'Then we will see you both when you get here, Mr. Morgan. Goodbye.'

Tom stared at the road ahead, chewing his lip. 'Bloody hell!'

'Tom, she's right, you should concentrate on the...'

Tom thumped the steering wheel. 'Don't tell me what I should and shouldn't be doing, Eva! This is my daughter, Emma, we're talking about!'

'She's my daughter too,' Eva said quietly.

'I know, I know, Evie, I'm sorry.' He reached across with his left hand to place it over hers, which were clenched into tight fists on her lap. She shook him off.

'Just drive, Tom, please...'

'Of course. Sorry.' She was right, he should concentrate – it wouldn't help if they both ended up in hospital.

'Eva, you really should call your father. You don't want him to find out from breakfast bloody TV.' He took a deep breath. 'And your sister.' It was time all that was put to bed. She'd need her family, especially if the bastard had...

'Dad can ring her.' She began punching numbers into the mobile.

Tom sighed. What would it take to reunite Eva with Jessica? Okay, so the woman had shagged Eva's first husband, but from what little he'd gleaned from awkward conversations with his father-in-law, the sister claimed it had only been the once. It would have been better had Eva never found out, but of course the idiot husband had to keep an incriminating letter...

'Dad, it's Eva. I'm sorry to wake you...no, everything's not all right.' She took a deep breath. 'Emma's gone missing. Yes, in Manchester. I don't know - we're on our way up now... I thought you should know, because it's going to be on the morning news... I don't know any more than that. Yes, yes, of course I will...no, I can't, will you...okay, thank you. Alright.'

'Dad is going to ring Jess,' Eva said. 'But she needn't think this changes anything.' Tears cascaded down her face.

'Isn't it time you let it go, Eva? I mean...for crying out loud, she's your sister...she's Emma's aunt...'

'It's not open for discussion, Tom. You *know* that. Especially after that thing in the magazine... how *could* she?'

Tom knew a lot of things, including the fact that the magazine interview didn't matter. Whatever happened after this, regardless of whether Emma was found safe or not... he couldn't go on like this. Only a few hours ago he'd sworn to give Tina up – but was there any point? Eva wouldn't accept his help in the past, she was unlikely to now. Could they ever repair their marriage, and did he really want to? Tina was good company in ways that Eva hadn't been for a long time; she made him laugh, and the sex was great... but did he want to live with her? He didn't know. But when all this was over... well, maybe then he would know what to do. Perhaps he would be better without either of them. He asked Eva to call his father's number.

'Dad? It's Tom. I'm sorry to call so late. I've got some bad news...'

19: MANCHESTER, 29TH SEPTEMBER

'The Morgans are here,' Rattigan put the phone down and stood up, stretching. 'Shall I bring them up?' She'd pinned her hair up and removed her make-up at some point during the evening, but now had grey smudges under her eyes and looked as though only sheer will-power was keeping her awake.

Casting aside his own fatigue, Hammond was already out of his chair and shrugging into his jacket. 'No, I'll do it. When does your shift end, Lucy?'

'Hour-and-a-half ago, sir.' Mortimer had caught an hour in one of the cells, Flynn was existing on coffee and adrenalin, apparently eager to make up for his earlier errors.

Hammond glanced at the wall clock: one-thirty-two. 'Then go home, get a couple of hours sleep. Things might kick off once the appeal's gone out. Thanks for staying on,' he added, and was rewarded by a tired smile.

'Thank you, sir. I'll just finish this and then I'll go.'

Hammond leaned over her shoulder, said quietly; 'I'm not bringing them up here, Constable – I'll see them downstairs. If you're so curious, you can sit in before you go home.'

Rattigan's grin turned into a yawn. 'Am I that obvious?'

Hammond nodded, but couldn't quite summon a smile. 'Yes.'

As he rode down in the lift with the newly energised Rattigan, Hammond reviewed what little he knew about Emma Morgan's parents, gleaned from Google and one old record sheet. The father, Tom Morgan, was an actor with a string of moderately successful stage and TV appearances (none of which Hammond could recall seeing) to his name, and one arrest for public affray thirty years ago, in Manchester as it happened: having just gone back to work on some short-lived drama series Hammond had never heard of, and evidently drowning his sorrows in a local pub following the death of his three-year-old son four months previously, Morgan had taken exception to a comment from a fellow patron. The other party had, on learning of the actor's loss, declined to press charges. That, and the fact that Morgan had just separated from his wife and had joint custody of the surviving twin, ensured that he was let off with a caution. Nothing since then (unless you counted a couple of tickets for speeding, five years apart) and nothing at all on the wife so far.

The desk sergeant had –wisely, Hammond thought, and made a mental note to thank the man properly later- already shown the Hammonds into a vacant interview room. Members of the public were normally asked to wait in reception, but although the late – or early, depending on how you looked at it- hour meant few punters, the father's celebrity made it a prudent move, if only for the wife's sake; she looked fragile, ready to lose it, Hammond thought as he stepped forward and introduced himself.

'I'm Detective Inspector Ian Hammond, and this is my colleague, Detective Constable Lucy Rattigan. Thank you for coming.'

Morgan had leaped to his feet as Hammond entered the room. He looked wired; a little taller than Hammond, and skinny with salt and pepper hair, he dressed well but had dark shadows under his eyes. His chin was fashionably unshaven and although his handshake was firm, his palms were slightly damp. Hammond could feel the man's nervous energy fizzing just under the surface.

'Thank you. This is my wife, Eva.' Morgan turned to his wife, who hadn't risen – she stared at Hammond with eyes devoid of hope. *She thinks her daughter is dead,* Hammond thought. He hoped she would be proven wrong.

'Good evening – or perhaps I should say good morning- Mrs. Hammond. I'm sorry that you both had such a long journey under the circumstances. We could have interviewed you in London, we did try to call...'

'We wanted to be here,' Morgan said, sitting back down beside his wife and taking her hand. She didn't look at him, and her eyes dropped from Hammond to her lap. *Something going on with those two,* Hammond thought.

'I understand. If your daughter is in some kind of trouble, might she not have travelled home early?' He wouldn't tell them about the abandoned rucksack just yet – or the possible bloodstain they'd found on it.

'She's due to – she was... coming home tomorrow – today,' Morgan said in an irritated tone. 'She would have called us if she was coming earlier – I always meet her from the train. Why would she run out on a dinner date with her friends?'

'Well, that's the sort of thing we would need to know, sir,' Hammond said. 'Look, you've come a long way, you must be tired – can we offer you something to drink - tea, or coffee?'

Morgan nodded. 'I'd kill for an Americano – black, please. Darling?'

Eva Morgan blinked. 'I'm sorry...?'

'Do you want tea or coffee? You should have something,' Morgan pressed when she remained quiet.

'I'm not thirsty, thank you.'

'She'll have tea, white, no sugar,' Morgan said. 'In fact, make it one sugar – for shock.'

Hammond watched Eva Morgan's face – not a flicker. Something definitely not right there.

'I'm not sure we run to an Americano, but the black coffee's not bad,' Rattigan said, and left the room.

'So, Mr. and Mrs. Morgan, can you think of any reason at all why your daughter might take off like this? Did she have any worries that you were aware of?'

'She has a name,' Eva Morgan said. 'Emma. Her name is Emma.' A single tear rolled down her face, but she appeared otherwise calm. Her pupils were huge – she was obviously on medication of some kind.

'Of course. Mrs. Morgan, is it possible that Emma...'

'I've already told you,' Morgan interrupted. 'She wouldn't. Someone must have taken her. Are you even looking?'

Hammond made himself count to ten before he replied.

'Yes, Mr. Morgan, we *are* looking. We have men searching the likely route that Emma would have taken from her workplace to Mr. Watkin's home, which is where we understand she was headed. We will also access CCTV footage of her journey. What do you either of you know about Simon Watkins?'

Morgan snorted. 'You can't suspect him? He was at University with Emma, he's harmless. He's a lazy sod, got a first class degree in computer science and now works in a bar and writes 'How To' guides from some kind of squat I believe... but he dotes on her. He'd never...' he shook his head. 'But you always suspect the people closest, don't you?' Something crossed his face – just a flicker- and Hammond filed it away for future reference.

'There's often a good reason for that, sir. Was Simon Watkins your daughter's boyfriend?' Morgan seemed to know as much about Simon Watkins as he did about Hammond's kitchen cupboard – they'd checked Watkins out and he was renting, not squatting.

Morgan laughed. 'No! Oh, he was a bit sweet on her for a while ... they might have had a thing in her first year. But no, not now, not as far as I'm aware. But I'm not there, so.... maybe.' He didn't look happy.

'Close to your daughter, are you, sir?'

Morgan glared at him. 'Yes, but not in the way you're inferring. Christ, I knew it would be like this...' he shook his head.

'With all due respect, Mr. Morgan, it isn't like *anything* at the moment,' Hammond told him. 'We are simply trying to establish what happened, who your daughter's friends and associates might be... any concerns she might have had that would explain her disappearance, or that we can rule out.' He didn't like Morgan, he decided. He seemed to think that he owned his wife – deciding what she would have to drink, answering for her- did he think he owned his daughter, too? They would have to separate them; the wife might have a very different tale to tell, once she was away from her husband. Was he a wife-beater? She didn't show any physical signs of it, but then the clever ones never left any marks...

Rattigan returned with the drinks, including a cappuccino for Hammond, and a tea for herself. Hammond nodded his thanks.

'DC Rattigan will sit in, if neither of you have any objection?'

Morgan shrugged, and thanked the sergeant for the coffee with a quick smile and a mouthed 'thank you'. His wife didn't appear to even notice.

'So what else are you doing to find my daughter?'

Again, the possessive. Hammond thought carefully before answering. 'We've spoken to Emma's colleague, Archie Harrop, whom we believe to be the last person to see her. We have officers out, speaking to anyone and everyone who might have come into contact with her recently. Can you think of anyone, or any reason, that someone might want to harm Emma?'

'Well, I don't imagine anyone has kidnapped her for ransom, do you? I mean, I'm not rich...'

'Perhaps not, sir, but some people might assume different. We have to look at all the possibilities. That's another reason it might have been better if you had remained in London.'

Morgan's eyes widened. 'I hadn't thought of that,' he admitted, and began to drum his fingers on his thigh. 'You think we should go back, then?'

'Well, you're here now. Is there anyone in London who can check your home for mail, or the telephone for messages?'

Morgan shook his head. 'The cleaner has a key, but she wouldn't...' he paused. 'My father-in-law lives in Putney, and Eva has a sister...' he touched his wife's arm. She flinched and slowly raised her eyes from her lap.

'Darling, could your father...?'

'He doesn't have a key,' she said quietly. 'And I'm not having Jessica in the house.'

So she had been listening, at least. 'Jessica?'

'My sister-in-law. She's... my wife and she are estranged. She won't have a key, either.'

'But she lives in London? Is she known to your daughter? Could Emma be with her, perhaps?'

'Well, it's possible – Jessica interviewed Emma - it was published two weeks ago, and upset my wife considerably. We don't have her number, but this is my father-in-law's...' Morgan said, and pulled his mobile phone from a pocket. It was the latest iPhone, Hammond noted. Well, it would be, wouldn't it? Morgan read out a London number, which Rattigan wrote down, and told them his father-in-law's name was George Deacon.

Eva Morgan gave her husband a sideways look and took a deep breath.

'She should have asked us first,' she said dully. 'About the interview.'

'Your daughter is technically an adult, Mrs. Morgan,' Hammond pointed out. 'What was the content of this interview?'

Morgan answered. 'It was a profile piece – women in science, that kind of thing. It named the company she works for, and had a full page portrait. Irresponsible, totally irresponsible.'

'Do you think Jessica might have harmed Emma?'

'Christ knows!' Morgan snapped. 'I mean, she has a successful career as a writer... but as far as we know, they barely know each other, at least they didn't until the interview...Why would she?'

'We're just floating possibilities, sir. Do you have a recent photograph of Emma?'

Morgan stood up and dug his wallet out. He pulled out several pictures, two passport sized, and three slightly larger. Emma was an attractive young woman with green eyes and black hair, an eye-catching combination.

'Take your pick.' Morgan's gaze stayed on the images as Hammond pulled them across the table. He tapped two – one a full face portrait, and another which was semi-profile.

'Has her hair style or colour changed since these were taken?'

Morgan shook his head. 'She keeps it short, can't be bothered with it, she says.' He smiled. 'She gets the colour from my father's side of the family.' He took the remaining pictures back and replaced them in his wallet with a careful tenderness that tugged something buried deep within Hammond's chest. Morgan loved his daughter; that much was clear. Did he love her too much? Hammond didn't think so, but you couldn't always tell. As for the mother...she seemed too quiet, almost completely withdrawn from what was going on around her. The shock of her daughter's sudden disappearance, or something more? He'd definitely have to get her away from her husband for a few minutes.

'We'd like to do a television appeal on the morning news,' he said. Despite Surridge's preference for using the mother, Hammond didn't think she'd be up to it. Morgan, however, would probably be perfect – perhaps too perfect. But as a 'face', someone the public knew, he would be an asset – he should be present, even if he remained silent.

'Do you think Emma is dead, Inspector?'

Eva Morgan's voice was so quiet that Hammond almost didn't hear her.

'We have no reason to think so at this stage, Mrs. Morgan.'

'But it's what usually happens, isn't it? I'm not stupid. I watch the news. You didn't find the last one, did you?'

Morgan was staring at his wife as if he'd never seen her before. 'Eva – Christ...' he turned to Hammond, his expression one of embarrassment. 'I'm sorry, I don't know where that came from...'

'It's a good point, actually,' Hammond conceded, and directed his answer to both of them. 'A kidnap case that one of our teams dealt with recently was, shall we say, mishandled. We don't intend to make the same mistake a second time.'

'I'm very glad to hear it,' Morgan said. His wife nodded slowly, her eyes meeting Hammond's. He remembered Surridge's advice. He should at least ask…

'Mrs. Morgan, would you be prepared to make a television appeal? We find that a mother's voice is often the best.'

'How can you ask that of her?' Morgan demanded. 'Can't you see, she's…?'

'I'll do it.'

'Darling, are you *sure*?'

Worried your wife will steal the limelight?

'Yes. I…yes, I'm sure, Inspector.'

Morgan schooled his face into a polite mask and gave a tight but not altogether convincing nod of agreement.

'Thank you, Mrs. Morgan.' Hammond stood up. 'Do you have somewhere to stay?'

Morgan shook his head. 'We didn't have time; we came straight here…' he looked exhausted. He had probably put in a full day's work before driving two hundred odd miles, Hammond thought, and made a mental note to speak to Traffic – Morgan must have broken speed limits to get them here as quickly as he had, but giving him a ticket would be like rubbing salt in a wound. At least it would put him out of the frame for the kidnap…he had never really been in it, but everyone close to Emma would have to be eliminated. He decided not to mention the rucksack for now. They already knew it was Emma's – Watkins had confirmed it- and the Morgans were alarmed enough.

'We usually suggest the Holiday Inn – it's not a bad price. Not sure you'd get in this late, mind…there are a couple of couches in the rest room…. Once you've done the appeal, we'll get someone to take you over to the hotel.'

'I've got a guest room…' Rattigan said, rather hesitantly.

'Oh that's fine, we don't want to put you out…' Tom Morgan began.

'It's fine, honestly. I can get you back here in time for the interview…Boss?'

Hammond nodded slowly. It was probably against regulations – they were always creating new ones, he couldn't keep up- but in the circumstances… and it would only be for a few hours. Perhaps Rattigan could get the wife on her own… He was pretty sure Rattigan was thinking the same thing.

'Sounds like a plan, Constable.' Something was definitely off with those two, and if Eva Morgan was going to talk to anyone, surely it would be another woman. He wouldn't tell Surridge if Rattigan didn't.

'Thank you,' Morgan said. He seemed at a loss for words, his anger dissipated in the face of unexpected kindness. His wife gave Rattigan a look of gratitude.

Yes, Hammond thought, and was glad he'd let Rattigan sit in.

20: 29TH SEPTEMBER 2:10AM

'Thank you for this, Sergeant Rattigan,' Morgan said as he and his wife followed the young constable down to the car park. 'You're very kind.'

'Please, call me Lucy. It really is no trouble. Your car will be safe here until the morning…' she yawned. 'Well, until later this morning, I mean. You made good time getting here.'

'I probably broke a few speed limits,' Tom admitted. 'I just wanted to be here, in case you found Emma and she needed us…' he fell silent.

Eva had remained silent throughout the whole exchange, but as they stepped out of the lift into the underground garage, she seemed to come back to life. While Tom went to their car – a top of the range Jeep with four-wheel drive, Lucy noted, hardly essential for London streets - to fetch the overnight bags, she turned to Rattigan.

'Do you think you will find her, Lucy?' She spoke quietly, almost as if she didn't want her husband to hear, and Rattigan thought quickly as she unlocked her car and slid the mess on the front passenger seat into an empty carrier bag and dumped it behind the driver's seat.

'Sorry about the mess.' She straightened up and attempted a reassuring smile. 'We're doing everything we can,' she said. 'But, you know, we were onto this within just a few hours – every minute counts, and normally we don't get called in until after people have been missing for a lot longer than that.' She walked around the car to open the boot as Tom returned, and he dropped two small overnight cases into it. Once they were all in the car, she continued.

'The first twenty-four hours in any investigation are crucial. We've got officers trawling through CCTV of the route Emma would most likely have taken from Xeon to her friend's house – it's on a bus route, with plenty of cameras. We'll find out where she was last seen, and anyone who came into contact with her on that route. Hopefully, they'll have something for us by the time the appeal goes out, and that will help enormously.' She twisted in her seat to smile at Eva. 'We're off to a good start, Mrs. Morgan.'

'I'm sorry I was a bit rude... earlier,' Tom, who had taken the front passenger seat, said as Rattigan took the car out onto the dark street. It had begun to rain again whilst they had been in the station, and the roads were slick and glassy with reflected light. 'I do know how it works, but when it's you that's involved, it... it feels different.'

'Please don't worry, Mr. Morgan. People react differently – I've seen much worse. You were upset, it was understandable.'

He nodded, said 'Please call me Tom,' and fell silent. Rattigan decided not to pump either parent for information on the journey. Despite the novelty of having a famous passenger, and one she had to admit she found physically attractive, she could feel her own tiredness beginning to kick back in. She should concentrate on the road, or she'd land them all in hospital.

When they reached Rattigan's home, she showed them the guest room, found clean towels and gave them a brief rundown of the ensuite shower and tea machine. She didn't think either of them were really taking it in, but Eva surprised her.

'Do you live here by yourself, Lucy?'

Rattigan nodded. 'My Grandmother used to run it as an occasional guest house. She died last year and left it to me,' she explained. 'I still have to pinch myself sometimes – it feels like I'm a guest in someone else's house most of the time.' What on earth was she talking about? All they'd be able to think about was their missing daughter – they wouldn't care about anything else. 'I'm sorry, I'm waffling a bit now – it's been a long day.'

'It's lovely, Lucy, and thank you so much for putting us up,' Eva said. Her face was very pale, and Rattigan wondered if the couple had eaten before travelling up. But if they hadn't, they surely wouldn't feel like it now, and even if they were hungry, Rattigan didn't feel up to cooking at this hour. She wanted her bed with a fervor she normally reserved for a good curry or a new lover.

'You're more than welcome.'

The smile Eva gave Rattigan didn't quite go all the way to her eyes, but it was a start, Rattigan thought. She knew Hammond would want her to bond with Eva – she had seen his expression back at the station and knew he thought something was amiss. She knew Tom Morgan from his TV work and had been unpleasantly surprised by the way he had continually spoken for his wife. Was he dominating her, or simply protecting her? Whatever Rattigan could find out, Hammond would welcome. But the couple were clearly exhausted by worry and the long journey; they needed to rest, and so did she.

'Would either of you like a hot drink before you settle in? I can do tea, coffee, cocoa, hot milk...' She could run to that, at least.

Morgan flicked a sly look her way. 'I don't suppose you have anything... stronger? I've a feeling that sleep won't come easy ...but if you haven't, it's fine, maybe a cocoa will do it.'

'I think I've got some scotch in the sideboard, or wine...if it hasn't turned. I don't tend to drink much at home.' Rattigan knew many of her colleagues did, some of them too much. She was determined not to go down the same path if she could help it.

'A scotch would be great, thank you.' Morgan had already shucked out of his jacket; now he sat on the bed, pulled off his boots and began rooting around in his overnight bag, pulling out shaving gear, making the small room his in a way that somehow –irrationally- got Rattigan's back up.

Rattigan turned to Eva as her husband began pulling off his shirt, apparently not at all fazed by Rattigan's presence. 'Mrs. Morgan, Eva, would you like anything?'

'Hot milk please, Lucy. Thank you.' This time the smile did reach her eyes.

Rattigan gave a reassuring smile and hurried from the room. To her surprise, Eva followed her downstairs.

'We don't expect you to wait on us,' she explained when they reached the kitchen. 'and please... don't give my husband too much scotch,' she added quietly. 'He...' she sighed. 'He drinks a little too much, and it makes him... tetchy.'

'Got you.' Rattigan put half a mug of milk into the microwave, then took the bottle of scotch which she had bought for Hammond as a Christmas gift and forgotten to give to him, and then been embarrassed to give it so late, and splashed two fingers into a tumbler. 'I don't think I've got any ice,' she apologised.

'A splash of water will be fine,' Eva said. 'We really appreciate this, Lucy. We left in such a hurry, we didn't even think to book a hotel...'

'It's really no trouble. I think we'll need to be back at the station for seven, because they'll want to do the broadcast live, to hit the breakfast audience. I'll wake you in...' she glanced at the kitchen clock and her heart sank. 'Four hours. Do you think you'll be able to sleep?'

'I don't know...I have pills, but if I take them now, I'll be too groggy...'

Rattigan filed that away. 'Maybe if you take half the dose...' Hammond would probably want her not to take them at all – an exhausted, frazzled and frightened mother would make more impact than a calm one, but the poor woman would clearly need something.

'Yes, maybe I'll do that. Thank you, Lucy.'

After Eva had gone back upstairs with their drinks, Rattigan made herself a small cocoa, locked the front door, flicked the lights off, and padded upstairs in the dark. She heard the soft murmur of voices in the guest room and sighed. It just went to show that fame and money was no guarantee of happiness or security.

21: 29TH SEPTEMBER, 7:25AM

'Are you sure you feel up to this, Evie? Maybe it would be better if I did it.'

Eva blinked in the harsh lights of the make-shift studio, which had been set up in what looked like a conference room on the station's third floor. She had been surprised by the number of journalists and television cameras present - but then Tom's face was moderately well known, and presumably the police had a press liaison officer who must have been busy. Bizarrely, she remembered a less-than-glowing review of one of Tom's TV dramas which had criticized his performance as the father of a missing boy, claiming he had cried 'crocodile tears' in a police appeal even though his character hadn't been responsible; she wondered if the man who had written that review was here now, waiting to evaluate Tom's performance in the theatre of real life. She shook her head.

'I'm fine, Tom. Let me do this for her, at least.'

Tom nodded and looked away, lips compressed. Eva sighed. Why did he always have to be in charge? Was he simply worried for her? Or put out because she would be taking the lime-light from him? No, that was unfair, she knew; Tom was generous to a fault with his colleagues, more often than not taking a back seat in interviews in order to give less well-known actors their chance in the limelight. And he had been a good father, when he was there; he still was. It was Eva who had been found wanting, and she needed this chance to make amends. If Emma came back safe and sound, things would be different. Maybe it wasn't too late. Last night she had even - whilst waiting for sleep that had finally come too late and too little - made a promise to a God she had told herself she no longer believed in, that if Emma came back safe, she would speak to Jess again. Emma needed a proper mother, and she also needed her Aunt. Eva had known for a long time that she had been wrong to shut Jess out of Emma's life, but it was hard to initiate contact after so long, hard to admit it to anyone but herself. An aunt was a window into your own mother's life before you were born, and Jess would have been –perhaps still could be- an opportunity for Emma to know a different side to her own mother, before life had changed her.

She was glad that she hadn't taken the sleeping pills after all – although exhaustion leant the whole experience a slightly surreal air, Eva felt sharper than she had done for a long time. Until this was over, she vowed, she would not take any more sleeping pills, no more of the anti-depressants which Tom claimed had turned her into a zombie. She wanted to have her wits about her when Emma was found and returned to them. A conviction that Emma would be found, **had** to be found, was replaced moments later by an almost overwhelming terror and the conviction that she wouldn't be found alive.

'Mrs. Morgan? Mrs. Morgan? I'm sorry, but we really need to…'

Eva snapped back into the here-and-now with a start. Everyone was looking at her. This was it; her debut on national television, millions of people out there eating breakfast, getting school lunch boxes ready, chasing kids out of their beds… except it was Saturday today, wasn't it? No school today. Would anyone be watching?

She nodded, cleared her throat, and waited for the red light to go green as she had been instructed. She glanced once at the sheet of paper she had been given, and lifted her eyes to the crowded room. She knew what she wanted to say: she didn't need a script.

'My daughter, Emma Morgan, is missing. She is twenty-six years old today. She left her place of work –Xeon Genetics on Brunswick

Street- at five to seven yesterday evening, but never made it to her friend's home on Furness Road, or to Anzio's Italian restaurant, where she was meeting her friends for a meal. Please watch the footage that will follow, and if you remember seeing Emma, or if you are one of the people shown on the film, please call Inspector Hammond's team on ....' She faltered, then remembered that the number would be scrolling slowly underneath her image as she spoke. '...the number below. I love my daughter, and I know she would not have chosen to disappear like this. Please help us to find her. Thank you.'

Beside her, Tom fidgeted, and cleared his throat. 'Please, help us,' he repeated, reaching for Eva's hand. His skin was cold, and slightly damp. *He's terrified.* Forgetting the camera, and the people around them, she turned to him. 'It will be all right, darling,' she said. 'They *will* find her – she'll come home.' She had to believe it; they both did.

Tom blinked away tears and pulled her into his arms. In front of them, cameras clicked and whirred, throats were cleared. Unseen hands guided them, hands still locked, out of the room. Voices began asking questions, and Eva heard Hammond's voice appealing for quiet before the door closed and left them standing in a narrow corridor. Rattigan and another woman Eva didn't recognise had ushered them out; now they stood politely to one side, waiting quietly as Tom and Eva composed themselves.

'I'm sorry,' Tom apologised to Rattigan. 'I don't know what...I just couldn't stand there and say nothing...'

'You did very well, both of you. I'm Amanda Carter,' the other woman said before Rattigan could reply, stepping forward to shake Tom and then Eva's hand. 'I'm your Family Liaison officer. It was inspired – that image will stay with the viewers, they'll want to help.'

'I didn't plan to do it,' Tom said sharply. 'But if helps, that's good.' He wiped the corner of one eye with a finger and took a deep breath. 'What happens now?'

Carter turned to Rattigan. 'Lucy, is there somewhere that Mr. and Mrs. Morgan and I could sit quietly, perhaps with a warm drink, and talk?'

'There's a little room just off the canteen,' Lucy said, trying not to show her annoyance at the way in which Carter was hinting that Lucy's presence was not required. In fact, she did have other duties, but she hadn't wanted to just dump the Morgans after the harrowing but necessary media circus, and she didn't care for Carter's slightly superior tone. 'In fact, if you could stand to eat something, why don't you have breakfast?' She addressed the last to Tom and Eva; they hadn't felt like eating earlier, they'd told her, but they should probably try to eat something now.

'Thank you Lucy, but I think just a drink will be fine – we really ought to sort out a hotel for tonight.' Eva seemed to have perked up since her husband's breakdown in front of the cameras. 'Will you be joining us?'

Rattigan saw that Eva didn't like Carter any more than she did. 'I wish I could. But I'm afraid I do need to re-join the investigation. I'll catch up with you later though.' When Eva nodded, Rattigan turned to Carter. 'You know the way to the canteen, don't you Amanda? I'll see you both later,' she smiled at Eva and Tom and hurried away before she was tempted to say something unprofessional.

Eva and Tom listened politely to everything that Amanda Carter had to say, then made their excuses, citing the need to find a hotel and try to catch up on some sleep. They refused Carter's offer of a lift, telling her that they had their own transport. If Carter was put out, she didn't show it. 'Of course,' she said smoothly, and gave them each a business card. 'I'm at your beck and call – if you have any concerns, remember anything that might help, or want to know what is happening, it's better that you come to me first, rather than take the detectives away from the investigation. Please try to avoid speaking to the press – they will hound you regardless, but I find a simple 'No comment' to be the best approach.'

'We understand, thank you,' Eva said quickly, just wanting Carter to go. The woman no doubt meant to be helpful, but she came across as patronising, and seemed slightly awed by Tom's celebrity status.

'Jesus, that woman...' Tom muttered as he drove them out of the car park.

'She's only doing her job, Tom.'

'Oh come off it! You dislike her as much as I do.'

'I don't much like her manner, no. But I suppose we don't get to choose. She talked a lot, but I'm still not entirely clear why we need her – I thought they only appoint Family Liaison when there is a...a death. We don't know if...' she couldn't finish.

'You're right. But don't you remember, darling, she said that they have a new directive. In cases like ours, they appoint Liaison right from the word go.'

"Cases like ours," Eva said. 'What does that even mean, Tom? There's been no ransom note, nothing to make the police think that she's been kidnapped, has there? Is it because of, well, because of who you are?'

Tom took a moment to reply. 'I don't know... I really bloody hope not. But do you remember that young woman who went missing in York a while ago? Nicolas Tindall's daughter? They never did find her, did they? And that other one...the one who... well, they're obviously trying to do better. I'm not complaining.'

'Well, you were, actually.' Eva could have bitten her tongue off. So much for putting aside their differences... 'Sorry. I don't like her, you're right.'

The Holiday Inn was easy to find, and while Tom parked the car, Eva went to the hotel's reception desk. She was nervous - they should have phoned ahead. Suppose they didn't have a room? The booking clerk gave her an odd look as she informed Eva that they did have a double room available, and asked her how long they would be staying.

'I don't know.' How could she know? Her brain refused to contemplate a time when they might go home. Tired but jittery, the idea that she might get any sleep at all seemed preposterous. She was saved from having to find a reply by Tom's arrival. The clerk clapped a hand to her mouth.

'Oh, I'm sorry,' she said to Eva. 'I *thought* you looked familiar – I saw you on TV this morning…how awful for you both. I'll make it an open-ended reservation; we do have someone else booked in this room for the end of the week but I can move them, I'm sure they won't mind …' She was helpfulness itself, taking their details quickly and efficiently.

'We don't need special treatment, we just want a room,' Tom muttered, but the young woman was on a mission, it seemed, and took their details with brisk efficiency, assuring them that it was no trouble at all.

'We don't normally let guests book in until two,' she said, 'but I know the room has already been cleaned and I can see the pair of you are dead on your feet…' she faltered, but recovered quickly and went on, 'If you'd like your meals in your room, so it's a bit more private, like, just ring down. I'll make a note on your booking so that everyone knows you're not to be disturbed, and anything we can do, anything at all, you've only to say. I hope they find your daughter, Mr. and Mrs. Morgan, I really do.'

When they were finally alone in the room, Eva dropped onto the couch and burst into tears.

'Oh God, Tom, they all think she's dead, don't they? I can see it in their eyes…I can't bear it.'

Tom dropped the bags on the bed and sat beside her. Placing his arms around her, he turned her gently to face him. 'We don't say that, ever! Let them think what they like, Eva. Loads of missing people *are* found, you know – but those don't get reported, because the press only likes a tragedy. In the mind of a journalist, death sells papers – 'happy ever after' doesn't, it never has. But we're not going to subscribe to that, okay?' He cupped her face in his hands and kissed her forehead. 'Now get some sleep, darling. You're as white as a sheet. Did you bring your pills?'

'I've decided I'm not going to take them anymore, Tom. I need to be alert, in case…' don't say it, don't think it. She sniffed, and drew a shuddering breath. 'What have we ever done to deserve this?'

'We've done nothing,' he said. 'You'll feel differently after you've rested.'

Eva nodded. Perhaps Tom was right. She let him help her out of her clothes, her limbs suddenly heavy with exhaustion, and sank onto the bed. Tom pulled the heavy blue curtains across the window, leaving a small corner lamp on. Within moments, sleep had pulled her into its depths.

22: 29TH SEPTEMBER, 8:00AM

The view from Emma's bedroom window looked out over empty fields. A line of trees was just about visible in the distance, shrouded in mist – a mile away, two miles? She never wore a wristwatch – they never worked longer than a few weeks. Apparently Grandma Deacon had been the same – so she had no sense of how long she had been unconscious in the car, or how far out of the city they had come. A long way, she thought, because it was so quiet here. Too quiet... she had woken with a gasp, feeling smothered, and she had been unable to go back to sleep. It had taken a while to realise that it was the silence – it felt suffocating, like a heavy blanket. She had turned the bedside light on and dozed fitfully, the kidnap replaying in her mind. Why had he done this? Was he going to hurt her?

Moran had refused to tell her anything last night. After muttering something about how difficult this all was for him (as if she was having a ball) he had become incommunicative.

'You need to rest,' he told her, 'and so do I. We'll talk in the morning.'

Moran had escorted Emma up a wide staircase to a room on the first floor, and locked her in. As prisons went, it was more than comfortable; its own small bathroom, a soft double bed, sturdy furniture and a deep pile carpet, all in white. But the windows were barred – there would be no getting out that way.

Moran had even provided a choice of pyjamas or nightdress, in several sizes. She had ignored them all, and kept her own clothes on, even her trainers.

Moran had obviously been planning this for a while, perhaps even before he had tampered with the samples... obviously, with a property this size, he wasn't really a security guard at all. But then she and Archie had worked that out already, hadn't they? She wondered what Simon, Lucy and Matt had done when she didn't turn up, would he call the police? He would worry, she knew – he might even have rung the lab, spoken to Archie. and what Archie would think when she didn't turn in for work on Tuesday she couldn't imagine. Would he suspect Moran? She was supposed to be getting a train to London today. Her parents would be worried sick when she didn't show. How dare Moran do this to them, to her?

She imagined her parents getting a phone call from the police – how would her mother cope with that? She might go to pieces; the way her father had once told Emma she had done soon after Emma had been born. Emma knew there had been another daughter, Amy, who had died with her father in a car accident, but her mother had never shared the details. Everything she knew about her mother's past, she had learned from her father and grandfather. Even Jess, who had grown up with Eva, had told Emma very little. She had hoped she and Jess might see more of each other; but Jess lived in London and was always busy, and Emma had not been down to London since before the interview.

A gentle tap on the door made her jump.

'Emma – are you awake? I have made breakfast, if you would like to come downstairs.'

'I'm awake.'

'Then I'll see you shortly.'

Emma heard the key turn in the lock. She waited a minute or two, then opened the door – the corridor was empty. He was very light on his feet – she hadn't heard him come up behind her outside Simon's either. She didn't want to eat his food, or sit across a table from him – but she *was* hungry, and she would need energy to escape.

The scene in the kitchen looked so normal that it felt surreal. If Emma shut her eyes, and ignored the silver hair, it could almost be her father at the stove, with his back to her, the smell of sizzling bacon making her mouth water. She hadn't eaten since lunchtime yesterday, she realised.

Moran turned. 'I do hope you aren't vegetarian...' he said, and Emma had an impression of sadness as he looked at her, quickly suppressed.

'No, I'm not. Look... this is... you can't just snatch someone off the street, then offer them breakfast as if nothing has happened! Are you some kind of... pervert?' She hadn't meant to say that, but it was too late to take it back now.

Moran looked shocked. 'No, that's not it at all!' He stood with his head bowed for a moment, then lifted bacon onto two plates, added scrambled egg, mushrooms, and grilled tomatoes. 'Please sit down.'

When he put the plates down on the table, Emma saw that Moran's hands were shaking. He was *nervous*. Was he afraid of her, or of what he was doing? The knowledge gave Emma a feeling of control that she hadn't had before. She took a deep breath and walked slowly to the table, and sat down. Moran sat opposite, and picked up his knife and fork.

'Please eat,' he said, as if it was the thing he wanted most in the world.

It felt like a weird nightmare, where surreal things feel ordinary, and vice versa. She was about to have breakfast with a man who last night had snatched her off the street, drugged her, and was now keeping her prisoner. Her friends would be worried by now, and her parents soon would be... she scanned the kitchen for any sign of keys, saw none. Well, he wasn't going to leave them lying around, was he? She picked up the cutlery on either side of her plate, and cut a corner of bacon. It was done just how she liked it – slightly crispy. Her stomach rumbled, and she began to eat, keeping her eyes on Moran as she did so.

Moran didn't seem to enjoy his breakfast – he ate mechanically, and without speaking, sometimes watching her watching him, at other times staring at his plate, deep in thought. How had he got hold of the sedative, and the syringes? Did he plan to ever let her go? He would go to prison if he was caught, she was sure. Maybe he was going to kill her, despite his promise that he wasn't going to hurt her.... how could he let her go? She knew who he was.

Finally, Emma couldn't take it anymore. She pushed her half-eaten breakfast away.

'Please, just tell me why you're doing this,' she said. 'Why did you pretend to be a security guard, why mess with my research, and why are you keeping me here?'

Moran poured them both a small cup of coffee -without asking if she wanted any- and stared at her as he sipped carefully at the steaming black liquid. He put his cup down carefully, shaking his head. 'You are so like my daughter...' he blinked. 'Let me clear this away,' he stood up and began to gather plates. Then I'll tell you everything.'

His daughter? Was that what she was – a surrogate daughter? 'Leave the dishes, just tell me what this is all about. Please?'

Moran nodded, and Emma thought he seemed almost relieved. She followed him out of the kitchen, across the hallway and into a large drawing room, where he went to stand by a large bay window. Sunlight streamed in, highlighting his silver hair. He glanced at her nervously; he seemed not to know how to begin.

'Why don't you just start at the beginning?' Emma sat in one of the armchairs. She didn't like how vulnerable it made her feel, but if it helped him to talk...

He nodded, and turned to face the window.

''The Methuselah program worked. I am living proof of it.'

'What is the 'Methuselah Program'?' She knew of the mythical 'Methuselah Gene'– everyone working in her field did. It was something of a holy grail for those amongst the scientific community who were searching for a cure for progeria. The genetic key to extending life... it hadn't been found yet, although an announcement four years ago from an international consortium of scientists had claimed that they were close.

'It will be the end result of a discovery made this year, in this city, Emma. Someone will discover a gene that will enable people to live for much longer than they do now. Hundreds of years, in fact.'

'You're talking about the 'Methuselah gene, then. I've heard of it. We're all looking for it…but no-one's found it yet.' He'd meddled with her research and kidnapped her for this? 'We're years away from…'

'You are closer to finding it than you think.'

She stared at him. 'What do you mean?' He couldn't mean her, personally… could he?

'How old do you think I am, Emma? Thirty, thirty-five, perhaps?'

Emma stared at him. 'Yes, something like that – but what has that got to do with…' The intensity of his gaze made her mouth go dry.

'I'm much, much older.'

'How much?' He couldn't be more than forty-five; even that would be pushing it. The silver hair was misleading, of course…

'You can treble it… and then double that. I'm two hundred and ten years old, Emma.' He said it quietly, but with absolute conviction.

'No way!' Emma found herself on her feet, her heart pounding. 'That's … that's impossible, you can't be… I don't believe you!' If someone had already made that connection, had found the so-called 'methuselah gene'… well, they wouldn't be able to keep it quiet for long - the whole scientific community would know about it by now. *She* would know about it. Her research might even be obsolete, if… It would be good, if it meant a cure for Progeria. It didn't matter if someone else discovered it, she told herself. But there had been no discovery… he was making it up, he had to be.

Moran continued to study her, his head titled slightly. There was a peculiar stillness about him; he seemed supremely comfortable in his own skin, appearing to have no desire to draw attention to himself. He just… *was*. Finally, he nodded, as if her reaction had been expected.

'I can prove it. Take a sample, run the test, Emma. The Methuselah Program has enabled - *will* enable- people to live for hundreds of years. But by the third generation the gene will mutate, causing cancers of the reproductive organs at puberty. My daughter Cassie is – she will be- thirteen when she dies.' He closed his eyes for a moment, as if in pain. 'We're talking about *billions* of people, Emma. Not just a few thousand... *extinction*. Think about that, please.'

Emma shook her head. 'I .... You're saying this has happened... *will* happen?'

Moran nodded. 'Yes. What reason would I have to lie?'

'I don't know.'

'So you understand...I need you to stop it, Emma.'

'Look, I can see that you've got...' *Problems* didn't even begin to cover it, did it? He had to be completely delusional. '...issues, Mister Moran, but I ...'

'You see nothing, Emma. Not yet.' Moran strode past her, heading for the door, and she flinched away from him. 'Come with me.'

Emma hesitated. But what else was she to do? So she followed Moran back into the kitchen, to a door set in the end wall. She hadn't noticed it earlier, and if she had, would probably have assumed it to be a pantry – but it led into a small lobby, barely big enough for two people, on the other side of which was another door. As Moran pressed a switch on the far wall, pushed the door open and stepped into the space beyond, Emma realised that they were now entering a small laboratory, protected from the kitchen by the makeshift airlock. The laboratory had evidently been put together in a hurry – wood shavings littered the floor, and some of the equipment still bore man-ufacturing and manufacturer's labels. An assortment of white lab coats sat, still in their packaging, under one counter. He had even fitted an air-conditioning unit: the temperature had begun to drop as soon as the lights came on, quickly raising goose-bumps on Emma's skin.

She wandered around the small room, recognizing equipment similar to what she and Archie used every day; a DNA sequencer, a StripSpin, a BioVac, a MinION; ChargeSwitch kits... even a GridION.... more than she would need for the simple test Moran had suggested. He stood quietly inside the door as Emma finished her inspection. He was serious; he really believed what he was saying. her thoughts whirling uncontrollably. 'Do you have every-thing you need?'

'I… it's more than enough. Do *you* use all this?' Why did he need her?

'No. I don't have the training. It's for you.'

'You can't keep me here.' He wasn't going to let her go.

'That's not my intention. I want you to take a sample of my DNA, Emma. I want you to examine it, and to tell me what you find. Then we can talk further.' He indicated a small desktop cabinet with a Per-spex door, behind which Emma saw syringes, ampules, and buccal swab kits. She could take a blood sample, or a swab - he'd thought of everything. But what would he do when the test came back normal? Because there was no way that he could be two centuries old, it was impossible. And if he was, there would be no way he would have been able to keep it quiet; people would have begun to notice that he wasn't ageing, it would be all over the scientific journals….it was completely ridiculous.

Okay, then. She took a deep breath, and removed a swab kit.

'Do you know how this works?'

Moran nodded, and pulled up a lab stool. Bits of polystyrene foam still clung to the metal legs, held there by static. He sat down.

Emma hesitated. She didn't really want to get close enough to him to use the swab. But, she reminded herself, he had shown no further signs of violence since abducting and sedating her- and had even apologised for his actions, assuring her that he had no wish to hurt her. 'Did you really think that destroying the blood samples would stop my research?'

His shoulders slumped. 'I believed it might be the better …option.'

She shook her head. 'Better than what? Archie and I, we're a team – we weren't going to just give up because of a few spoiled samples. Did you really think that we would?'

Moran shrugged. 'As I said… it seemed the better option.'

'And as I asked, better than *what*?'

Moran remained silent, averting his gaze.

Emma broke the seal, pulled out the swab stick and stepped closer. Moran stared at her for a moment, then shut his eyes and opened his mouth. She wiped the stick around the inside of his cheek -noting as she did so that his teeth appeared to be perfect- and then replaced the lid, sealing the sample safely in the phial.

'This won't show what you think it will.,' she said. She placed the phial into an empty rack. Then she walked slowly down the bench running along one wall, checking and then plugging each piece of equipment she intended to use into a buzz bar which had been hastily tacked to the wall. 'Did you build this yourself?'

'Yes. I've had time to learn many skills. Unfortunately, I am a master of none of them.'

Was he trying to be funny now? 'This will take a little while,' she said, dismissing him.

23: 29TH SEPTEMBER, 10:30AM

Vita, if you could see her… she's so like Cassie… Moran had needed to put some space between them last night. The urge to take Emma Morgan in his arms and hug her to him was inappropriate - she wasn't Cassie, no matter that they looked and sounded so alike, and such behavior would frighten and anger her – he needed her trust, and her goodwill. But everything about her reminded him of his daughter – her eyes, her voice, that little frown which told him she wasn't buying his explanation, even the way she moved – *this is how Cassie will look when she reaches her twenties, if she lives…*

If he and Emma *were* related, he couldn't possibly follow Gilling's instructions to 'terminate' her - it was out of the question. Had Gilling known? It might explain why he had chosen Moran – otherwise, why send him, why not send a scientist? The loss of so much virtual data during the Eurasian conflict had led to billions of records being lost… he may not have known…but if he had, it would make a warped kind of sense.

Moran had never -until now- been an assassin for hire. He had taken lives during his time in the military, of course, but that had been different, or so he had told himself.

Only his desperate need to save Cassie had kept Moran sane over four decades of being separated from her; four decades of wondering who he would have to kill to save her life, four decades of wondering if he would ever see her again.

But now he had seen Emma, and the fear that he had been set up - had never had any hope of saving Cassie – began to take hold. Now he could see it. Gilling had to have known, had always intended Moran to unwittingly erase his own bloodline from history, starting with the scientist responsible for the discovery of the Methuselah gene. For Emma and Cassie to be so very similar in looks, the blood-line had to be direct, didn't it? Emma might even be Moran's own great-grandmother. Nothing else made sense, did it?

Now he was running out of options. He could not kill Emma, so Cassie was doomed all over again. Unless he could convince Emma to stop her research... even supposing he could, would it be enough? She was just one scientist among many, all searching for the fountain of youth. If she didn't make the discovery, surely someone else would.

He paced the kitchen, pressing the heels of his hands into his eyes in a futile effort to stem the flow of tears. Cassie was going to die, no matter what he did. He had been stupid to believe anything else. And yet... how could he give up?

He had to try to convince Emma. If she were to accept his truth – *the* truth- she would surely agree that the program must never go ahead. She wanted to save lives – not take them. The only thing likely to convince her of the truth was running through his veins. She had to believe that he was telling the truth about his age, and he needed to know just how closely they might be related. If it turned out that they were not related after all... could he eliminate her then? Given that she so closely resembled Cassie? And if he were to do it, would it make any difference?

Fear of getting old, of dying, was an obsession with twenty-first century citizens. It was everywhere you looked – skin rejuvenation crèmes, plastic surgery, augmentation, reduction... this society valued youth and beauty because it was so precious; it could not be taken for granted. In Moran's own time, the reverse had begun to become true.

When the majority of the population had undergone some kind of gene therapy - either via in-utero surgery or from their parents, who had already been genetically modified- and almost everyone appeared to be in their prime, what was there left to aspire to? How could you tell a person's true age, know their life experience, the depth of their wisdom?

By Moran's time, there would be just a few corners of the world where the Methuselah Program hadn't been implemented for one reason or another; small, isolated communities, a drop in the ocean. It was from those communities that kidnap victims occasionally came; but like many secluded gene pools before them, exposure to the mainstream population carried a risk. The DNA of the offspring would not stay clean for long once exposed to the mainstream population.

Loading the Methuselah gene into an old and relatively harmless virus had ensured its spread far more effectively than anyone dared hope. Everyone caught head colds – and so everyone, eventually, would be exposed to the Methuselah gene.

There had been uproar, Moran knew from his schooling – those who serviced the health industry had seen their operating profits dwindle. The multi-billion pound industries who had until then survived on the back of society's longing to appear to be eternally young had began to disappear. Whole economies collapsed. All this would happen if Emma's research -and that of others- was allowed to continue.

Following his failure at Xeon, the idea of abduction and education had grown on Moran. He would need to keep Emma isolated until he could make her understand; could he recreate her lab at Helmshore? He certainly had room – the larder-come-storeroom off the kitchen would be big enough; all he would need to do to convert it would be to put up a false wall and a second door, to keep it well and truly away from kitchen contaminants; install a portable air-con and filter unit, and run some extra cabling in – he could do all that himself. Since arriving in 1979, he had worked as a builder, an electrician, a plumber... and having no family, he had put in long hours, made investments…. It had left him with a very healthy bank balance, and nothing to spend it on once Helmshore Hall had been made habitable.

So, following his dismissal from Xeon, Moran spent two days hunched over his computer, sourcing everything that his research efforts suggested he would need. He had paid over the odds for next-day delivery. Where items couldn't be delivered that quickly, he went without.

He was glad he had kept Gilling's identity – now, if it all went wrong, no one would associate deliveries to this address with James Moran – who as far as Xeon and the rest of the world knew, lived in a studio apartment on Aspin Lane. He was always careful to use false number plates whenever he travelled to and from Helmshore Hall – being a serving member of the EUPA for more than half his working life enabled him to think like a criminal, and the technology here was primitive, which made it easier for him – there was no biometric trail for each and every purchase. It was easy to disappear in the twenty-first century, simple to pretend to be someone else.

It had taken him another two days working round the clock to set everything up. Moran didn't know how to use most of the equipment, although he could take blood samples and knew how to store them –criminal elements would often remove or swap their biometric chips, so a blood test was the only way to identify someone with any certainty, and it was often quicker to run the test within the department than to wait for an outside agency.

Now, about to reveal his DNA to someone of this era for the first time, Moran began to feel afraid. It was make or break time, and Cassie's survival depended on what would happen next…

It was clear that Emma didn't want him in the lab while she worked, so Moran busied himself in the kitchen, trying to lose himself in mundane chores. Would she accept the evidence? She was a scientist – surely she would. But as just one researcher among many, how would she disseminate the information, and would anyone listen to her? Money talked - it always had, and it would be quite some time before the multiple consequences of a population who didn't age would hit home: youth, vitality and long life were the holy grail.

Something else had occurred to him; what if Moran himself had been the catalyst, his presence here setting everything in motion? He also began to consider the possibility that he might be insane, his thoughts and fears chasing each other around an ever- shrinking maze. Emma had to believe him. She *had* to agree that the Methuselah Program could not be allowed to happen. What would he do if she didn't?

As Emma worked, she heard the clatter of dishes in the kitchen. Why hadn't Moran approached her at work, and asked her to take a sample there? He could have even offered to be a donor, if he had wanted her to look at his DNA; they needed a control group, and many of the donors were students from the nearby university, plus a few members of the clerical staff at Xeon, in addition to samples from families affected by Progeria. Assuming that he was telling the truth about his age, they would have picked it up... but instead, he had made a feeble attempt to skew the results, and then he had kid-napped her, spinning her a ridiculous story about gene therapy gone mad and time-travel. He might not have used the words, but the way he had referred to everything in the future tense – 'the gene *will* be found', 'the Methuselah Program *will* be implemented'... it was obvious that Moran believed himself to have time-travelled.

When she had set the tests running and could do no more, Emma left the laboratory. The sequencing wouldn't take long, but she didn't want to stand over the equipment and wait. She wanted to talk to Moran again, to see if she could poke a hole or two in his ridiculous story. But the way he looked at her – he seemed almost to recognise her, talking about his daughter as if... her mind refused to make the connection, the answer remaining tantalizingly just out of reach. He was a parent, or so he claimed... Emma thought about her own, about what they must be going through, because they had to know she was missing by now. Her father would have called her to check that she had made her train -he always did- and when she hadn't picked up.... he would have definitely phoned the police when she didn't turn up. The police would speak to Xeon, and Archie, and they would soon find out about Moran's attempts to sabotage their work. They would find out where he lived... she just had to play for time. But he didn't seem to be in any particular hurry, did he? He'd marched her up to bed and then made breakfast as if he had all the time in the world.... She thought about Simon, Matt and Lili -what had *they* done when she didn't show last night? It seemed inconceivable that they might have just carried on without her. They would have gone looking for her, Simon would have eventually rung her parents... She felt a sudden surge of anger. How dare Moran do this to them?

Moran wasn't in the kitchen, and all the breakfast things had been cleared away- a dishwasher hummed softly under the counter. He had left her unsupervised – was he trusting her not to escape, or had he ensured that she couldn't?

Luckily she had been wearing trainers last night – stepping carefully so that they wouldn't squeak on the parquet flooring, Emma crossed the wide entrance hall to the front door, a massive treble-width affair that wouldn't have been out of place in a stately home. If he was in the lounge and should decide to come and look for her right now, there would be no way she could make it back to the kitchen without being seen, but she didn't care; anger and adrenalin made her hands shake.

But of course the door was locked, and Moran didn't have anything so predictable as a hall table and a bowl for his keys. Disappointed but undaunted, Emma made her way to the lounge, her steps faltering as it suddenly occurred to her that if she got away before the sequencing had finished, she wouldn't know the result. But that was stupid – she already knew what the results would be.

Moran was sitting in one of the armchairs by the window, his head bowed.

'The test is running. It'll take a while,' she said, walking towards him. 'Since you weren't exactly specific I've set up multiple...' she stopped. At the sound of her voice, Moran looked up, and it was obvious to Emma that he had been crying. He stood quickly, wiping his eyes with the back of his hand. He looked pale and worn, and older than she remembered him.

'I'm sorry.'

Emma hesitated, the angry rant she had prepared herself to deliver forgotten. 'Are you ill? Because I'm not a physician, Mr. Moran,' she said. 'If you need a Doctor...' It would explain a lot, she realised. A brain tumour, perhaps, causing hallucinations...

'No, no, I'm fine. Thank you for your concern.' He stood up, and walked over to the window, turning his back on her – to compose himself, she thought. 'This,' he continued, indicating the grounds beyond the house with a sweeping gesture, 'looks very different to how it will be in my time. By then, it will be surrounded by other buildings – all crammed together. There are very few trees.'

'You keep talking in future tense. Why?' Emma joined him at the window, keeping a few feet between them. Could she get him to open up, to admit that he was ill, that it was all a fantasy brought on by his condition?

'I was born in twenty-fifty-seven, Emma. I'm from your future.'

Her heart sank.

'There's no such thing as time-travel.'

'Not yet. But there will be.' He hesitated, then took a deep breath. 'Your mother's first husband, Peter King, was instrumental in the development of time travel technology. It came long after his lifetime, but his work... what he began was important.'

How did he know about Peter King? Emma took a step backwards. 'I know who he was... but he's dead. He died before I was born. How do you know about him?'

'What can you tell me about the man who tried to tamper with Emma Morgan's research?'

Antony Bremmer, CEO of Xeon Genetics, looked surprised, then annoyed. 'James Moran? Not a great deal, beyond the usual. We had to let him go, of course.'

Bremmer had not exactly been pleased to have Hammond turn up unannounced at his home just as he was about to leave for an early round of golf. He hadn't seen or heard the morning news, he told Hammond; 'I tend to ignore the media at the weekend,' he said, adding that until he had received a call from the security desk, he had not even been aware that one of his young employees was missing, feared kidnapped. He stood at the kitchen window, staring out over an immaculately manicured lawn, not looking at Hammond.

'So when you did find out, it didn't occur to you that the two events might be related?'

Bremmer nodded. 'Well, of course it did, the minute Jonathon told me – that was fifteen minutes ago, so… what can I say? The young woman hasn't even been gone twenty-four hours – how do you know she hasn't just…' he saw Hammond's impatience, and swallowed. 'But you'll have checked all that, of course…do you know yet what happened?'

'All I can tell you sir, is that Emma Morgan has disappeared in circumstances which lead us to fear for her safety.'

Bremmer shook his head. 'This is terrible. If anything has happened to her... she was a real find. Very bright, very committed. If we'd had any idea... the employment agency we use has let us down very badly, I don't mind telling you. We will be replacing them, of course....'

'So why didn't you report the sabotage to the police?'

'We did consider it. But some of the work we do at Xeon might be considered... sensitive. We don't need the kind of adverse publicity that taking it to the police could have attracted. People talk, Inspector, especially about things they don't fully understand... the media would have become involved. We are not 'playing God' or anything close to it, but there are people who accuse us of just that. Gene therapy is another tool in the medical arsenal, that's all.'

'Explain to me exactly what is it that your company does.' Hammond had been given a rundown of Emma's project by Harrop, but Xeon had more than two hundred employees – what did the rest of them do, he wondered?

'We give bright, enquiring minds with the appropriate skillset the opportunity to carry out vital research into genetic anomalies. Emma Morgan's project to find a cure for Progeria is just one of many fledgling gene therapies our employees are currently researching. Cancer, diabetes, certain blood disorders... and we are not the only company doing so. Are you certain it was Moran who...?'

'I'm afraid I can't tell you any more at this stage. Do you have internal CCTV of the laboratories?'

Bremmer looked annoyed. 'Yes, we do. There are cameras in the corridors leading to every laboratory, and motion sensors which are activated once the building is locked. But many of our people work odd hours, so...'

Hammond nodded. 'I'll have one of my team collect any footage you might have of the earlier incident, and for the last twenty-four hours.'

'That won't be a problem. The files are kept for three months, I believe. The wonders of digital technology – no physical storage space required.'

Hammond nodded his approval. 'As I understand it, Moran turned off the power to a storage unit, and ruined almost one hundred samples of blood. Are incidents like this… common?'

Bremmer looked surprised. 'No, not at all. Gene therapy does have its opponents, as I've already mentioned – but aside from a small street demonstration a few years ago, nothing like *this* has ever happened here before.'

This seemed slightly at odds with Bremmer's earlier claim that they had wanted to avoid unnecessary publicity for fear of a public backlash, but Hammond let it lie for now. 'So it could be industrial espionage.'

Bremmer shrugged. 'Who can tell, Inspector? Background checks were done, of course – but that doesn't mean Moran couldn't have been working for someone in the community.' Bremer opened his laptop, a top-of-the-range MacBook. 'I asked my assistant to get a copy of his employment file sent over from Centra Employment when this breach occurred… if you will just give me a moment, I'll see if it has arrived…' Bremmer opened a laptop sitting on the breakfast bar, and began tapping keys.

'Had he worked for this particular agency before?'

'That, I couldn't tell you. Here.' Bremer turned the laptop around, so that Hammond could see the screen - Moran's bio, work record, home address and an image which had clearly been used for his security badge. Suddenly Hammond was eight years old again. *Woolworths.* He drew in a sharp breath, tasting bitter smoke on his tongue. *'Have you seen my mum?'*

'Do you know him?'

Hammond ignored Bremmer. It was hard to take his eyes off the screen. *It can't be the same man. It looks like him…* but he would have been too young in 'seventy-nine… yet the resemblance was striking. A father, or uncle, perhaps?

'Inspector?' Bremmer was staring at him, a frown creasing his tanned face.

'I'll need a copy of this.' He felt breathless, as if he had been running, his heart beating too fast. He had to pull himself together, now. And he couldn't bring this to the table – Surridge would pull him off the case if he suspected any hint of personal involvement, no question. But it *couldn't* be the same man, so there was nothing to worry about, was there?

'Of course. So... you know him, then?'

'I'm sorry, Mr. Bremmer, I really can't say too much at this stage. You've been very helpful.' He wanted to get out of Bremmer's house. He needed time to process what he had just seen.

'It's no trouble at all.' Bremmer's fingers resumed their dance across the keyboard, then he closed the lid down. 'I'll just go and retrieve your print...'

Hammond took a moment in the car before starting the engine. His hands were shaking, and he felt sick. He picked up the sheet of paper again and stared at the face of James Moran. Green eyes, silver hair.... A face he hadn't seen since the 8th of May, nineteen-seventy-nine, and had only glimpsed in snatches of nightmare memories since.... except it couldn't be him. *Get a grip.* He put the sheet back down on the empty passenger seat and took a deep breath.

A coincidence? It had to be – the man he had seen when he was a child must be all of... well, if he had been, say, in his thirties then, and that was pushing it, because Hammond remembered him as older... he would be in his seventies or eighties, now, maybe much older. Moran's file gave his age as thirty-five. Granted, adults often seem older than they really are to a child... So why did he feel as if someone had just walked over his grave?

'Is this Detective Inspector Ian Hammond?'

The voice was hoarse; clearly that of a smoker, it almost certainly belonged to an older man. The accent was measured, local, but slightly diluted.

'It is. Who is this?'

'Name's Tony Clarke, ex-job. Saw your appeal, and there was something on the CCTV footage … rang a bell.' There was a pause for breath. 'Interested?'

'Of course. Where were you working out of, Tony?'

'Same as you, for the first few years – the old site, mind. Then I moved down to London, met the wife, ended up staying until she passed. Now I'm back up, living with my niece. This might relate to a case I worked on in London, in nineteen-ninety.'

Hammond sat up straighter in his chair. 'Related? How?'

'Your man matches a photo-fit that I'm looking at right now.'

The hairs on the back of Hammond's neck stood on end. He'd *known* there was something… 'Okay, you've got my attention, Tony. Can you come to the station?'

'Love to – but these days I'm pretty much housebound…'

Clarke lived in a small wheelchair-friendly annex attached to a smart detached property on the Hopcroft estate, West Didsbury; it was a home where at least one inhabitant had to be a good wage-earner, although no doubt Clarke's police pension helped. The door was answered by a slim, dark-haired woman in her mid-forties. She smiled when she saw Hammond. 'You must be Inspector Hammond. I'm Alison, Tony's niece. Please come in.' As she led Hammond through the house, Alison explained that her uncle had suffered a stroke two years ago, and that he'd sold his house in London to pay for the annex. 'He recovered his speech, but not the use of his legs. He's alright up top, though.' she tapped the side of her head to emphasize the point.

Clarke was a well-built man in his late sixties, with greying hair and piercing blue eyes. He maneuvered his wheelchair until he was in front of Hammond, and held out a big hand. 'Hello, Inspector Hammond. Thank you for coming.'

'It's my pleasure, and please, it's Ian.'

'Grand. I'm Tony, then. Before we start, would you like a drink? Tea, coffee, or something stronger?' He indicated a small sideboard, on which sat a bottle of ten-year-old Laphroaig. Hammond gave a little sigh.

'If I wasn't on duty… I'd better stick to coffee. Black, one sugar, thanks.'

He waited patiently while Clarke made the drinks, maneuvering his wheelchair around the specially-designed kitchenette with ease; he'd have been a force to be reckoned with in his prime, Hammond thought. The man must be six-five in his stockinged feet. He resisted the temptation to check his watch; you didn't hurry some people, and Clarke was one of them.

'There you go, lad. Right, I can tell you're itching to see what I've got, so…' Clarke led him through to a light and airy living room overlooking a long, narrow garden which dropped away to overlook playing fields and a small copse of trees. A pair of binoculars sat on top of a notebook on a low window ledge, beside a top-of-the-range camera. A book about bird identification sat beside them. Once Clarke had watched criminals, now he watched birds instead, it seemed. Once they were seated, Hammond on an old but serviceable sofa opposite Clarke, the older man pulled a sheet of paper from a grey cardboard wallet sitting on a table beside his chair, and slid it across a coffee table whose legs had been extended to accommodate the wheelchair.

Hammond picked up the photo-fit. It showed a man in his mid-thirties, with wide-set green eyes and silver hair. Moran again. *But it can't be.*

'You never got a name?' Hammond said, for something to say while he collected his thoughts. He wasn't about to share the events of seventy-nine with Clarke, not when his own team weren't in on it; he wanted to see what else Clarke might have before telling him anything at all.

'You recognise him, I can tell. We never had a name, though - this is a witness description of a man we believed to be responsible for the death of a father and daughter in an RTA in 'ninety. It's all there in the file…'

'I've seen his face before, yes.'

'Just as well I rang, then.' Clarke's eyes twinkled – he knew he was onto something. 'Your CCTV wasn't up to much, but I reckon he might be one of the people on it – he wasn't more than a minute or two behind your misper, was he?'

Hammond nodded. They'd spotted the figure's proximity to Emma, but he had been wearing a beanie and a scarf around his neck, and his head had been angled away from the cameras. The images were still being cleaned up, but Clarke's photo-fit bore a striking resemblance to Moran's Xeon ID. It couldn't be the same man, of course – maybe it was his father…?

'So what's his connection, with the Morgans, Tony?'

Clarke shook his head. 'What do you know of Eva Morgan's history?'

Hammond began to find Clarke's habit of answering a question with a question irritating, but he pushed it down – the guy was ex-job, he probably couldn't help it. 'Not a great deal as yet. We've yet to interview other members of the family.' Where was this going?

Clarke's eyes lit up. 'Then you're going to find this very interesting.'

'I certainly hope so.' Hammond took a sip of his coffee in an attempt to disguise his growing impatience.

'You'll be aware that Mrs. Morgan had another daughter?'

'No, that information hasn't come to light.' He wanted to shake the information out of Clarke – didn't he realise that every minute, every second, could make a difference? Maybe the stroke had done more than knacker the man's legs, despite his niece's claim that he was *all right up top*. 'But there does seem to be some trauma in the background… Mrs. Morgan is…she seems fragile.'

'Is she, poor lass? I'm not surprised.' Clarke settled back in his chair with the air of someone who liked to tell a good story. 'On New Year's Eve, nineteen-ninety, this man' – Clarke indicated the photo-fit with a bony finger- 'stepped out in front of a car at the junction of Regent's Park Road and Primrose Hill, and caused the driver, Eva King's –as was- first husband to swerve. King- and the couple's six-year-old daughter, name of Amy, were killed. Him outright, the kiddie died a few hours later, never woke up. He – your man's doppelganger – did a runner. We were never able to find him, despite half a dozen eye-witnesses, one of whom gave us this likeness.'

Hammond picked up the photo-fit again. 'Was it deliberate?'

'The main witness didn't think so. He said the man might have had a few, he seemed a bit unsteady on his feet. But for whatever reason, he didn't stay around to help – he just buggered off, quick as you bloody like. We put it down to shock, but he never did come forward. Never did find him.'

Hammond was disappointed. He'd hoped Clarke might at least have a name. But the man in the photo-fit was indeed Moran's double … it was a connection. The sooner he talked to Eva Morgan, the better.

Clarke cleared his throat. 'Worth the trip, was it?'

Hammond allowed himself a smile. 'It certainly was. Thank you.' He stood up, and leaned down to shake Clarke's hand. 'I appreciate it.' He picked up the photo-fit. 'Can I take this?'

Clarke thrust the grey folder at him.

'Take the whole lot,' he said. 'Copies of my interview notes with the witnesses, and with Mrs. King. That little girl's death stuck with me... I've been waiting for the chance to make use of that file for twenty-eight years.'

Hammond had decided to go straight to the Morgans' hotel, since it was on his way.

'Oh my God…' Eva took the photo-fit and Moran's Xeon ID from Hammond, and sat down on the double bed, her face drained of colour.

'Who is he?' Tom demanded, taking the images from her and waving them at Hammond. 'Is *this* the bastard who's got my daughter?'

Hammond held up a cautionary hand. 'We can't be sure, yet. But it's very likely. A man fitting his description recently attempted to sabotage Emma's work.' He'd had a call from Rattigan as he was driving – Moran's name appeared to be as false as his employment record, which might just scupper Hammond's fledgling theory about a family connection.

'But this photo-fit…it's dated nineteen-*ninety* - that *can't* be right.' Tom didn't appear to have heard Hammond, but Eva put a hand to her mouth.

'Is he… violent?'

Hammond hesitated. 'We have no reason to believe so at this stage. He has no criminal record.' *He's got no bloody records at all.*

Eva held out her hand for the images, and Tom gave them back to her. He made to put an arm around her shoulders, but she flinched at his touch, so he quickly removed it and instead sat down next to her on the bed.

'You know who he is, don't you, Eva?' Hammond had seen the flash of recognition in her eyes.

Eva spoke softly, her focus on something only she could see. Her first family, Hammond guessed. 'Yes. He... he was there when Peter and Amy....' She shuddered, and dropped the photographs on the bed, pushing them away.

Tom stared from one to the other. 'Hang on... this is a police photo-fit, right? Are you saying this guy caused the accident in 'ninety, and now he's kidnapped our daughter?' He stood up and began to pace the hotel room, his voice rising. 'That's just.... but,' he lunged forward and stabbed a finger at the photo-fit, 'look at him. He's not a day over forty... it can't be the same man.'

'We think they may be related. Eva, can you think of any reason why this man, or perhaps someone related to him, might want to cause the deaths of your late husband and daughter, or want to harm Emma?'

'I thought what happened then was an accident?' Tom interrupted.

Hammond glanced irritably at Morgan, but kept his eyes on Eva as he spoke. 'The investigating officers at the time didn't have any reason to think it *wasn't* an accident. The man who caused your husband's car to crash could have had many reasons for fleeing the scene. One of the witnesses reported that might have been drunk. Do you know him in any other context, Mrs. Morgan?'

'What are you trying to imply?'

Hammond glared at Morgan. 'Mr. Morgan, please be quiet, or I will have to ask you to leave the room – I'm talking to your wife, not you.'

Morgan glowered at him, but kept his mouth shut.

Eva shook her head. 'No, of course I don't know him. I'd never seen him before that night. I wasn't much help putting the image together, Inspector –I saw him step out in front of the car, but it happened so quickly – he was there in the road, Peter swerved... then I woke up in hospital.' Eva Morgan's eyes had lost focus as she relived the memory. 'But someone else saw… someone walking their dog I think…. I remember that when they showed me this picture, I remembered him – I was certain then, and I'm certain now. It *was* him. This…' her hand hovered over Moran's ID photo as if she couldn't bear to touch it. '…it *looks* like him… but as Tom said, how can it be? He'd have to be… well, he would be in his seventies, at least.' She shivered. 'Will you have to publicize what happened in nineteen-ninety…?'

Hammond nodded. 'It's likely that we'll want to mention it, yes. Someone might remember something.'

Eva nodded. Tom Morgan looked as if he might be on the verge of protesting, but then he seemed to think better of it.

Hammond gathered up the photographs. 'I'm sorry if this has opened old wounds… it may be relevant, even if we can't yet see how.'

27: 29TH SEPTEMBER, 10.15AM

'I caused Peter King's death.' Moran spoke quietly, with the same conviction he'd shown when talking about his age.

'I'm sorry?' He would have been around twelve years old in nineteen-ninety, Emma calculated. Her father had told her about her mother's first husband and daughter, who had died in a road accident on New Year's Eve that year. Emma knew that a man had stepped out into the road, causing Peter King to swerve, and the car to overturn. A *man*, not a child.

'I caused Peter King's death…and his daughter's. I was in the wrong place, at the wrong time… your mother remarried, didn't she? You are the result… and so it began.' He began to pace in front of the window, a muscle ticking in his jaw.

The atmosphere in the room had changed. Was he going to become violent? Adrenalin flooded her bloodstream.

'How do you *know* all this? Where *what* began?' She took a deep breath and exhaled slowly, forcing herself to calm down. 'Look, my parents must be *frantic* by now – I'm supposed to be meeting them this morning, my father will have tried to call me…and I was meant to meet my friends for dinner last night – they'll all be wondering where I am … can I at least let them know that I'm safe?' She wanted to remind him that he'd promised not to hurt her; but if he was as delusional as he seemed, could she trust him?

Moran stopped pacing and turned to look at her.

'You promised me that you didn't want to hurt me. Well, knowing that the people I care about will be worried about me is hurting me.'

Moran frowned. 'If the police have been involved, then they may be waiting for a call – they'll try to trace it. I'm sorry … this is too important, Emma. Once we have the results, and you understand why I am doing this, then …'

'Well then, I'm not going to analyse anything for you. You can do it yourself.' This had to be something personal – if he knew that much about her mother's first marriage and how it had ended… She folded her arms, not wanting him to see how much her hands were shaking.

'I don't have the training, not for that.' He swallowed. 'Please, Emma, this is so important. It is not a game.'

'No, it's not. So if you want my help… let me tell my family that I'm safe. Then I'll help you.'

Moran was silent for what felt like an age. Eventually he nodded; slowly, reluctantly.

'Agreed. But you must say just enough to reassure them. I can't have the police tracing the call.'

Emma nodded. She couldn't tell them anything useful, like where she was being held, because she didn't know. But she could at least tell them she was alive, and well. It wouldn't stop them worrying, of course, but it was something. It would have to do for now.

Moran pulled a mobile from his pocket. 'Give me the number.'

'It would be easier if I did it.' He wouldn't let her, she realised – in case she rang the police instead. Sure enough, he told her, 'No.' So she gave him her parent's landline, and his fingers flew over the keypad. He listened for a moment, and then held the phone close to her ear, so that she couldn't see the screen. 'Be quick,' he said as she heard her father's voice say '…leave a message' and the beep. Her heart sank. They weren't at home.

'Mum, Dad, it's Emma – I'm okay, Moran hasn't hurt me, I'm …'

Moran snatched the mobile away and switched it off. Then he removed the back, slid the battery out, and put everything back in his pocket. 'Using my name won't help them to find you,' he said quietly.

Emma's spirits sank. Of course the police would suspect him, after the sabotage. They might not know about this place – either it didn't belong to him, or he had bought it in a different name. Perhaps 'James Moran' wasn't his real name. She swallowed tears. She wasn't going to let him intimidate her.

'So I have kept my part of our agreement – your parents will soon know that you are unharmed. We should get to work. Once you have the results, I will need you to stop looking for the Methuselah gene.'

'You want me stop my research? Seriously? I've worked hard for this - no way!'

Moran held up a calming hand. 'Emma, if I could show you… you have no idea what you'll be unleashing. My daughter, she…look, if you continue this research, billions of people *will* die. Do you want that on your conscience?'

Suddenly it wasn't about her own safety, or her parents' fear.

'Of course not! But … this therapy, if I, if we can unlock the key, it will save lives…but you're not a scientist. How do you know?'

'Because I have seen the future. I *am* the future, Emma.'

There it was again – time travel. He surely couldn't expect her to believe him? Play along… the police will find him, there would be a paper trail, even if he did use a false name… and there would be CCTV… 'Okay… say I do this, say I believe you…if I stop… but other people are working on this, all around the world. You can't… you can't just put the genie back in the bottle! And suppose I refuse… what will you do? Will you kill me? Will you kill them all?'

'I don't know that I could do that… but perhaps. If that's what it takes.'

'You don't look like a killer to me.' It was true. He had drugged her, kidnapped her – and then apologised. She had seen him crying. He was delusional – he had to be- but he didn't seem… what, evil, bad? People were a mess of contradictions, but Emma realised that she was no longer afraid of James Moran. He needed help. Perhaps he had a brain tumour…she could run a test for cancer markers. He wasn't a scientist; he wouldn't know; she could tell him the buccal swab wasn't enough…

'I'm not,' he sighed. 'But to save my daughter, to save Cassie… I *will* do what it takes.'

28: 29TH SEPTEMBER, 1.55PM

In the hotel restaurant, Tom and Eva sat at a table in a secluded corner, nursing coffees. Eva had wanted to eat lunch in their room, but Tom couldn't settle; he felt cooped up and wanted distraction from his own dark thoughts. Where was Emma now, and what might that bastard Moran be doing to her? It was getting to the point where he couldn't stand to look at Eva, seeing his own fear and misery reflected in her face. They had picked at their food, the waitress collecting their plates with a sympathetic smile. Tom wanted to shout at the world: *my daughter is not dead, don't give up on her!* But if he started shouting, he might not be able to stop. So he tried to contain his fear, feeling it bubble and coil in his guts like a live thing as it tried to consume him.

The family Liaison woman had caught up with them just as they were finishing their meal. She started to tell them about the new leads, but since they'd had already had the news from Hammond about the photo-fit, Tom told her –rather rudely- to go away. She took it gracefully, reiterating that she was there for their benefit, on-one else's.

Once Carter had gone, Eva pushed her cup away, and stood up. 'You shouldn't have done that, Tom. She was only trying to do her job. I'm going back up.'

Lost for a comeback, Tom watched his wife walk away. He knew she disliked the woman as much as he did, but what good would it do to remind her of the fact? The lack of news was getting to them both, it was probably an excuse to get some time alone. How did it come to this? They were neither of them strangers to loss. When they first met, she was still grieving for the husband and daughter she'd lost little over a year ago, and he had been trying to put the death of Nathan four years earlier behind him. Now as then, Eva looked dreadful: her eyes were puffy and red-rimmed, her hair dull and un-kempt, and too thin; like him, she had barely touched her meal, but he had polished off two thirds of a bottle of wine. If the worst was to happen, and Emma never came home, could he honestly bring him-self to leave her? What would become of her if he did? He suddenly longed –with a passion so deep that it made his chest ache- to hold his wife tightly and –somehow, he would damn well find a way-make everything alright again. Where would they be now if they hadn't happened to be on the same tube train that day? Would she have found someone else – would he? He thought he would almost certainly have someone, but Eva… he doubted it. He'd saved her then. He could, he wanted, to do it again. But did she want him to?

Tom had long suspected that Eva had accepted his marriage pro-posal not because she loved him, but because she needed to forget the past. Hadn't there been an element of that for him, too? But if they hadn't met, there would be no Emma, and he could never regret her – the only good thing to come out of the whole mess their lives had become. His clever, beautiful Emma. If anything were to happen to her…

'Excuse me…it's Tom, isn't it?'

Oh Jesus, not here… expecting to see nervous hands clutching a napkin she wanted him to autograph, Tom quickly wiped his eyes and looked up to see a woman standing behind the chair Eva had just vacated. She was not holding a napkin, but she did look nervous, and oddly familiar: a riot of highlighted copper curls framed a face which reminded him of Eva. She smiled nervously, leaning forward to extend an elegant hand, and finally he recognised her: the wicked sister, Jessica. He'd met her only once, at some family event or other – a pub garden party for his father-in-law's seventieth, that was it. Eva had insisted they leave immediately, but after a hurried and emotional conversation with her father, Jessica had been the one to leave. He stood up.

'Jessica?' They shook hands, her grip surprisingly firm.

'I wasn't sure you would remember me. I'm so terribly sorry to hear about Emma, I can't believe it... Is Eva around?'

He indicated that she should sit down. 'She's gone back to our room.' He badly wanted to have a go at her about the interview, but it was clear from Jessica's reddened eyes that she was also suffering, maybe even blamed herself for leading the kidnapper to her niece, and what was done, was done. He sighed. 'Give her five minutes,' he said. 'Then it's Room three one three.'

Jessica nodded, and sat down. 'You must blame me.'

'The thought had crossed my mind,' he might as well be honest.

'You and me both. How is Eva taking it? Not the interview, because I can well imagine, but ...'

'Not well, as you might expect.'

'Look, do you mind if I go up right away? I really need to see her...'

Tom nodded, and watched his sister-in-law walk away. For a moment he considered following his sister-in-law, but really, what could he do? He'd just be in the way. No, what he needed was to find a bar and get very, very drunk.

29: 29TH SEPTEMBER, 6:15PM

'Oh, it's you.' Harrop was wearing his coat; a dated mackintosh which had seen better days. Hammond wondered if he was going out or had just come in. 'Do you have any news?'

'As a matter of fact, I do, but I think it's something you already know. May I come in?'

Harrop nodded, a frown puckering his brow. 'You're lucky to catch us in, Inspector – mother and I have only just come back from...' he faltered. 'What do you mean? What do I know?'

'About Moran.'

'Oh. Well, yes, I did tell you about him, you'll remember. He was fired for tampering with our research.'

Hammond nodded. 'What would you say if I told you that James Moran - or someone who looks just like him - was involved in a death in Emma's family in nineteen-ninety? Or that the address he gave his employers was false?' He wouldn't normally divulge such information to a potential -if unlikely- suspect, but this case was turning out to be anything but 'normal'.

Harrop looked shocked. 'I can't say it comes as a surprise to hear about his address – but the other... I would say it's impossible. Moran is maybe ten years older than me – he would have been... well, hardly a teenager....' His eyes widened. 'Ah. You think...'

'Is it at all possible that someone might already have found a cure for Progeria, Archie?' The question had seemed to pop into Hammond's head out of nowhere, but he realised as he said it that it was a logical -if unlikely- conclusion. Was Harrop's surprise because he wouldn't have expected Hammond to arrive at it, or because he had been caught out?

Harrop shook his head. 'Absolutely not. One day we hope it *will* be possible to slow ageing, as you must realise – it's the focus of our research. But we have a long way to go … are you *serious*?'

'We have to explore every possible avenue of enquiry. And it would make sense, wouldn't it?' Well, if you could imagine someone being retrospectively 'de-aged'… 'When did you discover the cure?'

'We haven't. With respect, you are no scientist, Inspector. You can have no real conception of the amount of work involved, the thousands of DNA samples, the hours and hours of waiting for results, interpreting them… What brought you to this ridiculous conclusion?' Two bright red spots had appeared on Harrop's cheeks.

'You're the only one who saw him in the lab, Archie – we only have your word for it. Either he was never there, or you- or he- have tampered with the CCTV footage. The second time, you lay in wait, assaulted him as he made his rounds, and then raised the alarm. Did you want the glory for yourself, Archie? Or did Emma find out that you and Moran were working for someone else?' The lack of CCTV coverage had been a disappointment. Someone had overwritten the footage from both days when Moran was supposed to have tampered with samples. The first set had obviously been Moran's doing, but the second… Moran had been marched out of the building following his second attempt, no way could he have got access. So it was either staff incompetence, or someone else had been involved.

Harrop drew himself up, his voice shaking with anger as he spoke. 'You're insane! I wouldn't… how would *I* tamper with CCTV footage? I not only don't have access to it, but I wouldn't know *how* to alter it! I can assure you that I am not working for anyone else, nor am I in cahoots with that man! How d-dare you!' he stuttered, blinking furiously as tears filled his eyes. He reached out a hand to

steady himself against the stair bannister, and shook his head, vehemently. 'I *love* my work, Inspector. I would never do anything –
anything- to compromise that. And you'll not be able to prove otherwise.'

Eva stared at her reflection in the mirror. She hadn't made it up to their room – feeling nauseous as she walked away from Tom, she had ducked into the Ladies in the lobby, and had taken a few minutes to calm herself down. She had managed not to lose her lunch, but it had been touch and go.

She looked old, she realised. When did *that* happen? In her mind, she was still the young widow who had examined herself in another mirror twenty-five years ago, and wondered what Peter had found in her sister that he hadn't been able to find in her. She had been so angry with him… Not just for dying and leaving her, or for steering their car into a bollard and killing their daughter… but for leaving behind evidence which revealed their marriage had been a lie. She would have preferred not to know. If only he hadn't kept that note… she had often wondered, if she hadn't found it, would Jess have ever said anything? Their relationship would surely have been damaged just the same…She still missed Jess, the closeness with someone who remembered their childhood, the shared references. Without Jess, Eva found it hard to remember her life before she had met Peter. It was almost as if part of her life had died with Peter and Amy, wiped away in one fell swoop the moment she found the note…

And now here she was, right back where she had been then – facing the loss of another daughter, wondering who she had married

... She had long suspected that Tom was seeing other women, but had felt unable to confront him about it. Would she cope if he left her? She was frightened to find out. She wasn't a good wife to him, she knew that: they should never have married, she had realised it almost when Emma was born. They had been good for each other at first, each knowing what the other had been through. But it was too much sorrow to contain. When Emma had been born, Eva had been so afraid to get close to her. If anything happened... and now it had.

Eva remembered the press conference, and Tom's body shaking against hers, his broken sobs. That awful family liaison woman thought he was *acting*! At that moment, she had allowed herself to believe that it might be all right...*they* might be alright. Emma would come back; they would be a family again... now she knew that she had been wrong. They were both too damaged to pick up the pieces, even if Emma was found safe.

Eva took a deep breath, turned the tap, and splashed cold water on her face. She had felt in control during the Appeal – but hours had passed and now the fear was constant, dominating her thoughts, sapping her energy. She had dealt with it by holding on tightly to her emotions and reactions, as if that alone might be enough to bring Emma back; *don't let anyone see how afraid you are*... but it wasn't working. The terror was starting to drown everything –and accompanying it, a simmering anger. Anger at the world, herself, and everyone in it. Everything Tom said seemed shallow, self-serving, or mean-spirited. She'd barely been able to look at him as they picked at their food, or as he had earlier prowled around their room. He'd wanted to go out, it was obvious. He wanted to run away, pretend this wasn't happening. But wasn't that what she had been doing all those years? Using the pills to distance herself from the memories, from the reality that her marriage was broken and she couldn't even tell her daughter that she loved her? Had she really neglected Emma? Perhaps she had. She had given her daughter everything she could – except, perhaps, herself.

She'd had a few counselling sessions, after Emma turned fourteen and an almighty row had ensued when apparently Eva had failed to remember the name of Emma's best school friend. Not her *best* friend (that would be Chloe, her half-sister), but the girl she walked to school with, and with whom she later fell out with over a boy…and whose name she still couldn't remember… Claire, was it? The bereavement counsellor Tom had insisted she see had gently suggested that Eva was afraid to connect with Emma because she secretly feared that she might lose her as she had lost Amy – she was trying to protect herself. Well Eva had managed to work that out by herself, thank you very much; it was hardly rocket science. She had refused to go to the second appointment, and her relationship with Tom had gone steadily downhill. Emma, quiet and studious, had simply got on with her studies, and had stopped bringing friends home. 'They only want to be friends because of who my dad is, anyway,' she'd told them. 'I don't need those kind of friends.' Thank God Chloe had been there for most of Emma's childhood. But now Chloe was in France, and Emma… would she become someone else that Eva couldn't bear to think about?

It still hurt to think about Amy, of course it did; and she still couldn't bear to talk about her with anyone. Reading about the accident in the interview… even if Emma had been led by her aunt, Jess should have known better than to bring it up. Why had she been so cruel?

Eva badly wanted to take one of her tranquilizers. She had come to rely on them more and more, just to get her through each day. They didn't make her forget, but they put a buffer between Eva and the pain, gave it a soft edge, and made it possible for her to function. When her GP questioned the long-term usage and suggested that she might like to try reducing the dose, or to try something less 'habit-forming' (he meant addictive) Eva had simply moved to another practice. Tom disapproved – although at first he'd been sympathetic. 'Whatever gets you through the day, baby,' he'd said. But then, when she began to cry off going to red-carpet functions, where he'd wanted his wife on his arm but she had been consumed by the fear that someone might mention the accident, or that something might happen to Emma whilst they were out - he had been less understanding. He had managed to move on from Nathan's death – why couldn't she do the same?

'They're interested in *me*, not in what happened to *you* before we even met,' he'd told her once, spiteful in his anger. After that, she'd refused to go to any more events with him. After a while, he stopped asking, and began taking pretty co-stars, or going alone. Eva had been relieved. Was that when the affairs had started? Probably. Perhaps it was her fault...but what did it matter now?

She patted her face dry with a tissue because the paper towel dispenser had run out, and delving into her handbag for lipstick discovered that she hadn't packed any.

She had always known that coming off the pills would be hard. She had only missed a couple of doses, but she hadn't been prepared for the confusion or the constant, dragging fear. But she *would* get through this – she had been through much worse, after all. And the police thought Emma was still alive – or at least, that's what they were telling her. She had to cling to that hope, because without it...

A young woman in a hotel uniform ran into the room, hurling herself into a cubicle with loud desperation. Eva heard the sound of retching. *Your life is going to change in ways you can't even imagine ... you'll live in constant terror...* but not everyone lived liked that, did they?

She should apologise to Tom for walking out on him – he was suffering too, and even if it made him uncomfortable company, they should try to give each other strength, at least until Emma was found. After that...she would apologise to him. Women were always the peace-makers, after all.

She took a deep breath, ran her fingers through her hair – *it needs washing, how could I not notice?* – and headed back to the restaurant. Tom was still sitting at the table, but there was a woman standing behind Eva's seat, talking to Tom. It seemed their conversation had run its course, and the woman turned and began to walk away from him. *Jess.*

Her sister hadn't changed much – a little thicker around the waist, perhaps – but still the tousle-haired, confident character she had always been. As her eyes met Eva's across the room, Jess's hand flew to her mouth. Her face fluttering with emotion, she strode forward to envelope Eva in a hug.

'Eva, oh my God, look at you... I've missed you *so* much...'

Without conscious thought, Eva relaxed into the hug, over-whelmed.

31:29TH SEPTEMBER, 2:30PM

Tom stepped out into cold drizzle. He'd left his jacket back at the hotel, but hadn't wanted to follow the two women up to their room to retrieve it – let them catch up, reconcile their differences.

He had slept badly last night, despite the night-cap. It would have been better to go back to the room and take a nap, except now it was out of bounds. He would stick to his original plan, then.

It had begun raining again, and by the time he found a bar that didn't seem too busy or too noisy, Tom was soaked to the skin. The walk had given him time to think; now that Jess had shown up, Eva might well withdraw from him completely. Or maybe Jess would talk some sense into her, get her to stop taking those damn pills… it all hinged on Emma's safe return, of course. What would he do if she didn't? Find whoever was responsible and kill him… *don't be ridiculous. You're an actor, not James bloody Bond....*

The barman recognised Tom, but in deference to his haggard countenance –and probably because he'd seen the news - waved away the five-pound note Tom tried to give him. 'This one's on the house, mate.'

Tom nodded his thanks and took his pint and whisky chaser – well, he wasn't going to be driving anywhere anytime soon- to a corner table. Out of habit, he put his mobile on the table. It was dead – he'd forgotten to put it on charge. What if Emma had tried to contact him? Or her kidnapper? Then they'd probably have called the house…had the police tapped the phone like they'd said they would? Or would the kidnapper try to call Eva's mobile? Emma would have to be alive, wouldn't she, to give him the number… maybe they should have stayed in London after all. The barman walked past, holding two empty glasses.

'Excuse me, do you have a mobile charger I could borrow, or a payphone?' He hadn't noticed one, but then he hadn't been looking.

'Payphone doesn't work, mate, but you can have a lend of me charger, no worries. I'll get it for you. iPhone, is it?' He eyed Tom's phone.

Tom nodded, and within a couple of minutes the man returned with a black connector and lead. 'It's not kosher, like, but it works well enough. Just leave it on the bar when you're done.'

'Thanks, appreciate it.'

There was a socket in the wall near his table, and although the lead was barely long enough for Tom to be able to hold the phone on his lap, the charger seemed to be working. By the time he had finished his first pint and started on a second (which he paid for), he was able to turn the phone on. He scrolled through a seemingly endless stream of texts, mostly messages of support from people he'd worked with over the years, and one from his agent, which simply said 'CALL ME'. He cursed – he had missed an important meeting with Clara: he had planned to see her and then meet Emma off the train this afternoon… He let the phone charge for a minute or so longer, then removed the lead and tapped out Clara's short code.

'Tom, my dear, how are you doing? How is Eva holding up?' Clara's broad Glaswegian accent made Tom yearn for normality. He had to swallow before he could speak.

'Not great, Clara, not great. Listen, I'm sorry about…'

'Ach, don't be daft, Tom – as if I'd expect you to remember with this going on! Look, I've had the contract back from the theatre, but I've spoken to them this morning and they're willing to hold until, well, for a wee while yet. So don't worry about a thing. I've also spoken to Donald about the ADR on Monday - that can wait too. Do the police have any leads?'

'If they have, they haven't told me,' he said. 'I've been wondering if I should come back down, in case the kidnapper tries to get in touch, or Emma does…I don't know what to do, Clara. We've got this Family Liaison woman, but she's a pain in the arse…'

'Tom, listen to me. The police are on your side – I'm sure if they wanted you at home, they'd have told you so - they've probably got people watching the place. As for Family Liaison – if you don't like the one you're assigned, can you not ask for another? Come on Tom, don't be a victim here.'

Tom choked back a sob. 'Clara, why the fuck didn't I marry you instead?' They'd had a brief 'thing' while he was still married to but not getting on with Alice, but even though he and Clara were strictly business- only now, Tom sometimes still wondered.

'Because I'm not the marrying kind, and because you love your wife. Take care, Tom, and I'll see you when Emma's back safe and sound.' In typical blunt Clara fashion, she ended the call.

Blinking away tears, Tom quickly scrolled through the rest of the messages, his pulse racing as he looked for Emma's name – but there was nothing.

One pint turned into four, one short into three, almost without him realising it. He got up to return the charger and the barman, thinking he was about to order another drink, shook his head. 'I think you've had enough, man, don't you? I mean, it's your money, but…'

'You're so right,' Tom mumbled. He *had* intended to have another, but as if the barman's words had flicked a switch, now the thought turned his stomach. He handed over the charger. 'Thanks for this.' Aware that the man was watching him, he stumbled into the gents, and threw up into the urinal. A tattooed man came out of one of the cubicles and spat at Tom's feet.

'Look at the state of yous,' he said in a broad Tyneside brogue. 'Probly did ha y'self, I know ya sort.' He sniffed and turned away to wash his hands. Tom flew at him, propelled by rage and alcohol. The big man swore and stepped out of the way. Caught off-balance, Tom crashed to the floor, the side of his head catching the edge of the urinal.

Tom woke to find himself being hauled to his feet. His hands had been cuffed. He could feel a lump on the left side of his forehead. Bile rose up his throat and the uniformed coppers stepped back smartly as he gagged and retched, bringing up beer and bile in a foul-smelling watery stream.

When he had finished, the coppers helped him to his feet.

'Can't you take these bloody things off?' He needed to wipe his mouth, couldn't they see that?

'I'm sorry, sir – it's for your own good.'

Tom swallowed, gagged and spat, aiming at the urinal. 'Well at least…my face…?'

The younger of the two men pulled a length of paper towel from the dispenser and without comment roughly wiped the worst of the mess from Tom's chin. As they hustled him through the main bar, the publican caught his eye and raised his hands in an apologetic shrug.

'Yeah, fuck you,' Tom mumbled, and immediately felt ashamed. Of course the man would call the police; what else could he do? 'Sorry,' he managed, but they were half-way through the door and he knew the man hadn't heard him. His head throbbed with each step, and the daylight hurt his eyes. He blinked and stumbled as he was marched across the pavement to a waiting patrol car. There was no sign of the tattooed man.

'Where's the other guy?'

'Says you attacked him, sir, he was only defending himself. He'll be making a proper statement, don't you worry. Mind your head, now.'

Tom found himself being folded into the car, a beefy hand pressing on the top of his head – it hurt.

'Bullshit… he started it.' Oh for Christ's sake, now he sounded like a petulant child.

'Yes, and you finished it, sir.'

'Tom... what were you *thinking*? Look at your face...'

Well, at least it had got a reaction. Tom shrugged. He'd been given a cup of cheap, bitter coffee soon after being relieved of his personal belongings and belt, and shut in a cell. He had promptly vomited the coffee up again, further staining his still-damp shirt. The hangover from hell was making an early entrance. He wanted to die.

'I think we should get him back to the hotel, Eva, get him showered and let him sleep it off.'

Tom turned to stare at his sister-in-law and found himself sitting on the floor. 'Who the hell asked for *your* opinion?' He scrambled back to his feet, shrugging off Jess's offer of a hand. Eva looked dismayed.

'Tom, stop it – you're still drunk. I know you're upset, but there's no need to be rude to Jess, she's here to help.'

Well, that was a turn-up for the books.

As they made their way out to the lobby, Hammond stepped out of the lift. The look he gave Tom spoke volumes.

'Can I have a word?'

Tom swallowed and nodded. A dressing down from Hammond he did *not* need... but the Detective's outstretched arm encompassed them all. *Self-absorbed twat...*

'This way.' Hammond led them to a small interview room. When they were all seated, he eyed Tom. 'Not a smart move, Mr. Morgan, but perhaps understandable in the circumstances. The man you assaulted won't be pressing charges, and nor will we, but best leave the booze alone, eh? Now, I've some news.'

'You've found her?' Eva grabbed Jessica's hand. Jessica's, not *his*, Tom noted sourly, still smarting over Hammond's remark.

The detective shook his head. 'I'm afraid not. But a call *was* made to your home landline this morning.' He slotted a cassette into the recording machine and hit the 'play' button.

'Mum, Dad, it's Emma – I'm okay, Moran hasn't hurt me, I...'

The call ended abruptly.

Eva began to sob. Jessica put an arm around her shoulders.

'What the fuck…?' Tom stared at Hammond. '*When* was this?' He couldn't get his head around it – she had sounded so… normal. Nervous, perhaps, a little upset, but compared to what they'd been going through…anger rose, then fell, and relief overwhelmed him. He blinked away a tear. Emmy was alive… thank Christ.

'About four hours ago,' Hammond told him. 'We couldn't get a trace, unfortunately; it's a pay-as-you-go, unregistered mobile, and the call wasn't quite long enough for us to get a fix. He knows what he's doing. But at least we know she's alive, and who's took her.' He allowed that to settle. 'How did she sound to you?'

Tom swallowed, his thoughts clearing. 'She sounded… nervous, but… well, okay, actually…. What are you suggesting? That she had something to do with… no! She's a good girl, she wouldn't put us through this…!'

'To be honest, I'm not sure, it may be nothing… but we would have expected your daughter to sound more distressed. Sometimes we don't know people as well as we think we do.' Hammond turned to Eva. 'Mrs. Morgan , how did Emma sound to you?'

Eva sucked in a breath and let it out. 'I don't know…' she swallowed. 'I'm not as close to her as Tom is. If he thinks she sounded normal, then …'

'You might not want to hear this, Eva,'' Jessica said quietly, 'but if it's something to do with her research… I think that Emma could be quite capable of anything. She is *very* driven.'

Tom stared at his sister-in-law. He wanted to see her as an interloper; how dare she insinuate that she knew Emma better than her parents did? But if she had a different kind of connection with Emma, maybe they could use that…he turned to Hammond, who was observing them closely. 'Can we make another appeal?'

Hammond nodded. 'Would you be willing to go in front of the cameras, Miss Deacon?'

Jess nodded. 'I'll do anything it takes, Inspector.' She turned back to Eva. 'I didn't mean that as a betrayal, Eva. I just think maybe I saw a different side to Emma than she shows to either of you.' She looked at Tom. 'She wouldn't deliberately hurt you, of that I'm certain.'

32: 30TH SEPTEMBER, 7.45AM

Jess had been shocked by her sister's appearance; the TV appeal had not prepared her for the reality of Eva's ashen skin or her bloodshot eyes, or the way she moved carefully, as if confined by her fear. She felt nothing but anger towards her brother-in-law. Why the hell wasn't he looking after his wife? Emma had implied that all wasn't well between her parents, and here was the proof. He was a self-obsessed, arrogant...but he *was* Emma's father, she reminded herself, and Emma loved him. He couldn't help being a vain idiot. She couldn't for the life of her imagine what Eva had seen in him... she knew the story of how they had met on the tube train, how Tom had looked after Eva when she suffered a concussion, and how their shared experience of losing a child must have seemed like common ground... they had been two damaged people looking for solace, and presumably they both believed they had found it in each other, at least to begin with. Now though...but that was none of her business, was it?

Hammond's suggestion that Emma might in fact be involved in her own disappearance was disturbing, but Jess had glimpsed the steely resolve in her niece to find a cure for the terrible disease that killed the half-brother she never met, and knew that Hammond was an intuitive investigator, a good judge of people. Eva and Tom wouldn't want to believe it, but Jess knew just how driven Emma really was. But could she be complicit in her own disappearance? It was a bit of a leap, to be fair – Emma *was* a very self-possessed young woman, and could simply have chosen to ignore her fear. But the incident at the lab, Moran's attempt to sabotage Emma's work, and now her kidnap – it didn't *feel* like the kind of scenario which would lead to her niece's body being found in woodland days later, of that Jess was sure. Emma may not have chosen to disappear, but she did sound as if she was dealing with it.

A fake kidnap attempt, taking her away from her laboratory and everything she had worked so hard to achieve, would at best hinder Emma's research, and would almost certainly damage her credibility if it ever got out. It simply didn't make sense. But there *was* a connection there…even if Jess couldn't see yet what it was.

Hammond had told her that they were looking at the deaths of Eva's first husband and daughter as well, because the same man, or perhaps someone related to him, might be involved. Jess had immediately sensed a story, and then felt ashamed – this was *family*; her niece's life could be on the line. How could she even consider making money from it? But she had good investigative skills. Her unique insider's perspective might help, and her judgement wasn't clouded the way Tom and Eva's must be. She knew Hammond's core team was quite small, even if extra help *had* been drafted in. But her suggestion that she do some digging on Moran had been met with a warning not to get involved.

'We don't know if he's working alone or if he could be working for someone else,' Hammond told her. 'It's best if you leave the investigating to us.'

The cleaned-up CCTV footage had finally come back, and Hammond had told them that they were confident that the figure which appeared to be following Emma was indeed Moran – even though they still couldn't make out his features, the forensics team had calculated that his height and build were a match for his employment file at Xeon. With a link between Moran and the family now likely, and her kidnapper's identity confirmed by Emma herself, any other perpetrator seemed unlikely. Eva had told Jess that she didn't know

Moran, but Jess wondered if anyone else had noticed the likeness: Eva, Emma and Moran all had green eyes. It might mean something, it might not, but if it did, Jess didn't like the implications. She hadn't spoken to Eva since early 'ninety-one. How much could someone change over time? Had Eva's continued refusal to speak to Jess been partly down to guilt? If she'd had an affair with Moran's father, could Moran actually be *younger* than his records suggested? Could he even be Eva's son, Emma's brother? How far back could this go, and if it had happened before Peter King died – which obviously it had to have done- then how had she, Jess, not known about it? Until the mistake with Peter – and that's what it had been, a mistake, never-to-be-repeated, and she had told him that – she and Eva had been close. Or so Jess had always believed…

'This needs to be an appeal to the kidnapper,' Hammond insisted, 'Not to Emma. If she is involved, we need to prove it, and we don't want to give them a reason to run. I'm not altogether convinced that she is – the call *was* cut short, so I think it's safe to assume that Moran hadn't expected her to identify him.'

'Do you think naming him has put her in danger?'

Hammond frowned. 'We've no reason to think so. He clearly has an agenda of some kind – first he tries to sabotage her research, and when that doesn't work, he kidnaps her. He needs her for something, and whatever it is, he may have communicated that to her, and for whatever reason, she is okay with it.'

'She just wanted to let Eva and Tom know that she was safe…'

'Yes, it looks very much like it. Moran may have allowed the call… or he may not have. But all this is speculation. We need to find the facts.'

'I think it has everything to do with Emma's research, Inspector.' Jess could not, would not, voice her suspicions about Emma's paternity. If she and Moran *were* related, that was for forensics to prove. Eva was either keeping a very big secret from everyone, including her husband, or there was no blood connection, it was just a coincidence.

But what Emma was researching amounted to a 'cure for old age' – it had tremendous implications. Already two of the national dailies had picked up the story: 'Scientist working on old age cure disappears', 'Genetics Researcher Vanishes, Parents Fear' … and there would be more, she knew, as the media machine geared up.

When her father had rung her to give her the bad news and to warn her about the TV appeal, Jess did at first wonder if Emma had simply taken off – perhaps Eva and Tom had reacted badly to the interview, and she had needed time to think… but that hadn't been the case, because apparently Emma hadn't even spoken to them about it, not even to forewarn them, even though she had promised Jess that she would. How much did Emma know about Moran, and he about her, before the interview had brought Emma into the spotlight?

Watching the playback of her appeal later, Jess cringed. Did she look too polished, somehow too unaffected by the fact that her niece was missing, presumed kidnapped? But no, it was there – the slight tremor in her voice, the pauses between words so that she could compose herself. They had sat Eva next to her, Tom next to his wife, and the inhalations of breath, the tiny sob from her sister as Jess had fallen silent, had made it hard to maintain her poise. She hoped she had come across as quietly desperate.

'This is an appeal to whoever has taken my niece, Emma Morgan,' Jess stared directly into the camera. They had agreed not to name Moran on the appeal for now. His appearance was distinctive enough, and they didn't want to spook Moran into fleeing with Emma in tow, or worse. Moran would know that they now knew who had taken Emma – if he'd wanted to hide his identity, why risk the sabotage? – and would, Hammond hoped, realise that they were trying for a good outcome.

'Emma is an educated young woman with a bright future ahead of her, and the work she is doing will benefit people who are sick with a disease called Progeria. Please let her get back to that work, and to her family, who miss her very much. Thank you.'

'You did very well,' Hammond told her just before she, Eva and Tom left for the hotel. 'If you should hear anything from Emma, you'll let us know immediately.' It wasn't a question.

'Right, what have we got?' Hammond looked around at his assembled team. They were all dog-tired now, with just a few hours' sleep between them. The second television appeals had yielded nothing as yet, and he was beginning to feel as desperate as Emma Morgan's family.

'I saw Emma's grandfather this morning,' Rattigan said. She had just returned from London, a four-hour round trip with barely an hour in the capital itself, and longed for a shower and her bed. 'He hasn't heard from her since her last trip home, doesn't really know too much about her life in Manchester, and reading between the lines, I think he blames his daughter for not caring enough. He didn't seem to understand why Emma had to go all the way to Manchester to study.' She smothered a yawn with her hand. 'I'd planned to visit the husband's family in Wales tomorrow…'

Hammond nodded. 'Good. But I don't think they are likely to be involved - give it to one of the locals, Rattigan - I think you'll be more useful here. Joe, what else did you get from the Xeon staff?'

Constable Joe Mortimer flipped open his notebook. 'Nothing new – like I said earlier, some of the early job references Moran gave … most of the companies don't exist anymore. The ones that are do, well, I haven't found anything much earlier than Ninety-three, mostly casual labour, cash-in-hand, so the records aren't that good.

He's got one main account, a couple of grand in it, hasn't been touched since the day of Emma's disappearance, a savings account with a couple of hundred grand in it.' But Joe found something....'

Mortimer cleared his throat. 'We got a call from an estate agent about half an hour ago. Says she sold a property to someone fitting Moran's description twenty-five years ago, but she's not sure about the name, thinks it might have been different. It's been archived, but she's going to try and find the paperwork for us.'

'Twenty-five years ago? He'd have still been in his teens. Is that why she remembers him?'

Mortimer shrugged. 'She didn't say so – just that it was a big sale, a place out at Rosendale. Helmshore Hall.'

How would someone in their teens be able to afford a property like that? More and more it was pointing to two people, maybe a father and son.

Maisie Dunstable raised a hand, then stood up. 'Deepak and I have been checking Ancestors United,' she said, naming a popular genealogy website, 'and there are about 570 entries for 'James Moran' listed in roughly the right time-frame. Haven't found our man yet.'

A chubby man at the back of the room pushed his chair back. 'Constable Learner, on loan from Hyde. There's no school record either... nothing that fits our suspect, at least.'

'Good work.' Hammond addressed them all, pointing to various members of the team: 'Joe, call Angela Foley, warn her that we'll be wanting a search warrant. While we wait for the Rossendale address, someone get on Google Street View and see if you can find Helmshore Hall. Once we've got the warrant, we'll go in. The rest of you, as soon as we have the intel, and especially if the name it comes up is different to what we already have, I want us to drop the search for Moran and look into the new name. Family, employers, inside-bloody-leg measurement. If James Moran *is* a legend, then maybe he bought Helmshore Hall using his real name – assuming it is him, of course. This could be the break we're looking for.' He grinned at them, his fatigue fading. 'While we're waiting, I'm going to talk to Surridge.'

Hammond hadn't returned from Surridge's office more than five minutes when Mortimer poked his head around the door.

'We've got the address, sir – and we should have the warrant any minute now. The name Moran used was James Gilling.'

34: 30TH SEPTEMBER, 3.00PM

Emma turned away from the monitor, a frown creasing her brow. Moran had seemed relieved when she told him that the samples from the swab hadn't been enough, and had readily agreed to let her take a blood sample.

In truth, the swab had been enough to prove that he had told the truth about his age, but not enough for the additional tests she wanted to run without warning him. The results had been astounding.

The first and second set of test results *hadn't* been wrong. Moran had all the markers of someone of an extremely advanced age, just as he had claimed: just without the physical infirmities. But it wasn't that which had set her pulse racing; looking from one DNA code to the other – and even with the evidence in front of her - Emma couldn't quite get her head around what the images were telling her: that she and Moran were *related*. It also told her that there were no cancer markers, lending credence to his claim that the mutation hadn't occurred until his daughter's generation. Her reaction to the confirmation that the elusive Methuselah gene *did* exist had surprised her – fear. She should be happy – it meant that Progeria could now be cured. She tried to picture her father's face as she gave him the news, and a sob rose in her throat. How could she celebrate, knowing what she now knew about where her research would ulti-mately lead?

'Emma?'

Instinctively, her hand flew to the button on the lower right of the screen, plunging it into darkness. She needed time to process it all…. Moran was every bit as old as he claimed to be. It didn't mean that he mightn't be delusional, but the evidence was there for all to see. Could he even be telling the truth about having time-travelled? It was too much, all at once; she couldn't cope with him right now.

'I… I need more time….'

Moran came to stand beside her, his hand hovering over the mon-itor's power button. Then he pressed it, and they stared at the test results together, in silence.

'Explain these to me, please.'

Emma shook her head. 'It's… I don't know what to say. Your bloods tell me that you *are* much older than you appear to be.' She smiled weakly. 'I should be glad, shouldn't I? It means that the gene does exist, the therapy works… no evidence of cancer. I'd need to do more detailed tests to see if there is any sign of imminent mutation… but then, there's this…' she pointed to two genetic 'bar codes', one displayed above the other where she had split the screen to show both, enabling her to compare them. 'This is yours…'

Moran touched the screen, indicating the second chart. 'And this…I can see that it's slightly different. Is it yours…?' His voice was quiet, almost a whisper.

She swallowed. 'Yes. I wanted to make sure that the machines were properly calibrated. I'm familiar with my own DNA sequence, so….'

'Emma…'

She held one hand up, stalling him. 'I need to run more tests to be absolutely certain, but…' she swallowed. '…you and I would appear to be related.' Moran didn't say anything, but his face fell. 'You knew this already, didn't you?'

He nodded. 'Not for certain. But I suspected it, because when I saw your photograph… you are so *very* like my daughter, Cassie,

Emma. I didn't believe it, at first. I didn't want to, because that would mean… I won't be able to save Cassie, not by following my original mission. There's more at work here than … I think *you* are the reason I'm here.'

Emma gave a shaky laugh. 'Well, if you've really come from my future, then I think you mean the other way around … that doesn't mean I believe your story about time-travel.' Even if it was the only explanation that made any sense.

'Emma, I *am* from your future. I was sent here to prevent the gene therapy from ever being developed.' An expression Emma couldn't read passed across his face and was gone.

'By using violence.'

'Yes, if it proves necessary.'

'But how can you know for certain that *I* found – will find- the gene?' She shook her head. 'As I said before, a *lot* of people are working on this, it isn't just me.'

'But you are somehow pivotal, Emma. It's too much of a coincidence. Think about it – I saved the life of Peter King in nineteen-seventy-nine…'

'Hang on – I thought you said you caused his death – in nineteen-ninety?'

Moran ran a hand through his hair. 'Yes, that too. Please listen.'

She nodded. 'Okay. So…'

'I first arrived here -from your future- in nineteen-seventy-nine. At first I thought it was a mistake. You've heard of the department store fire in Manchester, in May of that year?'

'No…maybe…' A distant memory struggled to surface, something her father had once said… 'Was it… Woolworths?'

'Yes. I encountered Peter King in the store, and realised who he was -one of the men whose work would result in the time travel technology which brought me here. I got him out of the building. Then I didn't see him again until nineteen-ninety. I had no idea he was in London. I don't know how it works, but something…fate, if you like to give it a name, threw us together again, and he -and his daughter-died. When I saw his body in the car, I… panicked. I came back to

Manchester. I knew that I had to wait until science had progressed sufficiently for work to begin on what would eventually become the Methuselah Program. It was the only real lead I had, that it would happen in Manchester. How many research programs looking to cure Progeria are being carried out in Manchester, Emma?'

Emma felt the blood drain from her face.

'I'm not sure – but Xeon is the biggest employer of bio-technicians in the city…'

If Moran had not caused King's death then she, Emma, might never have been born at all…

'So now you see, Emma. It all comes back to you.'

'I can't … this is crazy. Does my mother know?'

'No.'

'You'll have to tell her.'

'What purpose would it serve? I'm trapped here, Emma – I can't change what has already happened now, only what *will* happen – and I'm not even sure of that. You're still here, aren't you?' He shook his head. 'And I have just told you everything. If I hadn't, perhaps you would never …I just don't know, anymore.'

'You can't go back… to the future?'

Moran shook his head. 'No.' he sighed. 'I believe that the man who sent me here may have intended for me to wipe out my blood-line. If he had confided in me…'

'You wouldn't have done it.'

'Of course not. I'm doing this to save my daughter – not wipe her out of existence.' He sighed. 'He should have sent someone else.'

'Well, I'm glad he didn't,' Emma shocked herself by saying.

Moran looked surprised. 'Do you mean that?'

'Yes. Because now that I know…perhaps we can still save Cassie…' She wasn't afraid of Moran anymore, Emma realised. He was just a pawn in someone else's agenda, an agenda with which, she realised, she could not in all honesty disagree, even if she didn't agree with the method. If the gene therapy was given to everyone, not just those in real need …. It would be wrong. The population would expand beyond the planet's capacity to feed it, society would surely break down... she didn't want to imagine that kind of future for her children, grandchildren... her mind shied away from the obvious question.

'I only wanted to cure Progeria,' she told him. 'But I can see how the commercial applications would be irresistible to business ....'

'But finite. At the moment, your health industry is massive. All that, it will disappear.'

It was an interesting use of the possessive – 'your', not 'our'. Moran didn't belong here anymore than she might belong in his future.

'I can't imagine the strain on food resources...overcrowding....'

Moran nodded. 'And when the pandemic began, it caused panic. And crime... everyone wanted a cure, and they wanted to have healthy children... I was a soldier. I was drafted into the EUPA – United England Police Authority' and discovered that I was good at it.'

'The cancer pandemic ... it would be nature's attempt to redress the balance.'

Moran nodded. 'I believe so. Cancer had been all but eradicated... but the Methuselah gene mutated, and found a way to bring it back...'

Emma shook her head. 'It's incredible. Horrible.' She touched the screen, ran her finger across Moran's 'bar code'. 'And it's all my fault...'

'Only in so far as you made the original discovery, Emma. I do not believe, now that I have spoken to you, that you were directly responsible for the Methuselah Program.'

'If I have *anything* to do with it, that makes me responsible.' She closed her eyes and took a long breath. 'How can I stop it? If *I* don't find the gene...someone else will.'

'Yes, that seems fairly certain. So we have to make sure that you do, but that somehow, the therapy is never distributed to the general population.'

'Everyone will want it, though. Money talks, and not every scientist has a moral compass.' She fell silent, and Moran waited. 'We would need to encode a limiter of some kind… I'd have to patent it …'

'I can't be involved, Emma. I don't have the scientific knowledge, for one thing.'

Emma stared at him. 'And the second?'

Moran shook his head. 'I don't think the… for want of a better term… 'time stream', or whatever you want to call it, would allow me…this is not part of my past.'

'You're talking about cause and effect…but how do you know… oh, I see. It would be a paradox. You couldn't kill me because if you had, you wouldn't have been born and in that case you wouldn't have been able to travel back in time to kill me… so the man who sent you back, got it wrong. You were never going to be able to kill me, were you?'

Moran swallowed. 'Even if I had not realised our connection… I don't know, Emma. As I said before, if it was the only way to save Cassie…'

'But it isn't, it can't be. Because if you kill me, you … I was going to say, you would never be born. But it depends – if the bloodline is direct, then I don't think you could. If it isn't…' but it *had* to be a direct link, didn't it? Emma was her mother's only surviving daughter, so for herself and Moran to be related…. she would need to test her mother, too, and her father, to be absolutely certain. Could she ever tell them? She didn't know, didn't want to think about it. She already had a sample of her father's blood back at the lab, Emma remembered – as Nathan's father, he had been only too happy to help. Alice, Nathan's mother, had not, which meant that she hadn't been able to use her father's sample for the work she'd done so far. How would he react if he were to discover her kidnapper was related to them by blood?

'So you can't be more of a part of changing your past than you already are, because…' she sighed. 'You need a quantum physicist to explain this, I can't get my head around it. But if you were born thirty-nine years from now… you must be my *grandson*.' Emma stared at him. Who would his father be – someone she already knew, or someone she had yet to meet? Suppose, armed with this knowledge, she were to choose the wrong man? The permutations – and the possible consequences- were overwhelming.

'You see how dangerous this is.' Moran was ahead of her. 'My being here, us talking like this…'

'…it could affect who I meet, who becomes your father…' She could do a paternity test, check Moran's DNA against every man she knew, every man she met from now on… but what kind of relationship would that be? *I need to take a sample of your blood. You and I have to have a child together…* what kind of person would she become? 'I almost wish you hadn't told me.'

'I agree. It is a terribly responsibility, and I am sorry. Emma, I need to leave. You know what's at stake now – you don't need me.'

'But…' she had gone from fearing Moran to… what? Believing him, accepting his story because science had proven beyond doubt that they were related? Further tests wouldn't prove anything. Who could she tell? No-one. Could she do it alone?

'I'm right. Think about it, Emma. How *can* I be here?' He was already withdrawing, moving away from her.

'Wait… how do you know that there might not be *more* than one possible future? Maybe there's one where you stayed here, one where you will help me!' She was clutching at straws, could see that he saw it too.

Moran shook his head. 'I can't explain it. But something tells me that it would be the wrong course of action to take.'

'I shouldn't even know this…now that I know, how can I…'

'This is what I have had to face every single day since I arrived,' Moran said. 'Not knowing if anything I might do, the smallest thing, could have terrible consequences … a man who should have been born might not be, someone might die who should have lived… I believe it's called the 'butterfly effect'.

Emma nodded, miserable. 'What can you tell me about your parents? Since I know some of it, I think I need to know as much as possible…' Or would it simply make things worse?

'I don't remember them,' Moran told her. 'My father -also a James-died aged ninety-three, on active service, when I was two years old. My mother – Laura- died from complications during childbirth – she was thirty-five. I was brought up by the state. The data was stored digitally, you see, and a number of EMP weapon strikes during the Eurasian conflict wiped out billions of records. When I... left, the database was still being repaired – it is, it will be, a huge task. All I know is that they -we- lived in London, and the dates that they died. I have no photographs.'

Emma felt sick. Her son, or her daughter, would live in London. 'Your father was *eighty-nine*? So he had the therapy...?' That would mean it couldn't be him – he would be in alive now, and in his fifties. She knew, from Moran's stricken expression, that he had already worked it out, had probably done so many years ago. 'You were looking for your father in nineteen-ninety, weren't you?'

'Yes. I didn't find him. Both my parents had the therapy, or so I was told. They were the first generation.'

'They didn't waste much time rolling it out.' This was horrendous. Moran seemed certain that Emma would not have been involved in the Methuselah Program – but if her own child, his mother, was among the first generation to receive the therapy, then Emma had to have been involved... Well, she would make sure that no child of hers received the therapy.... even if it cost her everything.

'The thing is... I can't just stop the research, James.' It felt right to use his name now. 'Xeon have invested in this, they've invested in me. They could just put someone in over me...' She would have to be careful, she realised. 'No one must know about you. I can't use your samples... not if you have to stay hidden...' Because if other re-searchers were to gain access to his DNA, how would she explain it, or him? Even now, there was a risk that someone else might be on the verge of finding the gene... of undoing Moran's past, altering their shared future. It might be enough to change the future, but if no-one knew what she now knew...

'I think you should go back work, Emma. You know what will happen ... it's up to you, now, what you will do when you find it. But I cannot be here.'

He was right. 'What will *you* do?'

'First of all, I have to get rid of all this.' He looked around the laboratory. 'If anyone were to find out that you were ever here...if it was thought that you were complicit...'

'Let me help you.'

He shook his head. 'No. You need to leave. Can you lie about me, Emma? Tell them that I was confused, that I thought you might be my daughter...?'

'If the police catch up with you...'

'I will claim the very same thing. But I don't intend to be found.'

Will we meet again?' There had been a finality to Moran's statement that Emma wasn't sure she liked. 'You won't do anything... stupid?'

He allowed a brief smile to crease his lips. 'Define 'stupid'. I will only do what is necessary to keep our secret,' he added. 'It's better that I don't tell you – you won't have to lie when the police question you, as they will.'

Having removed the blindfold, Moran left Emma outside a Mac-Donald's on the Rochdale Road. He was wearing a flat cap and dark glasses, and it would be difficult for anyone who might have seen them to give an accurate description of him. There was a phone box across the road, and she had assured him that she would place a reverse charges call to her parents from there. 'I'll be all right,' she said. He nodded, touched her hand briefly, and got back in the car. Emma felt bereft as she watched the tail lights disappear. He had removed the number plates, she noticed, and hoped he wouldn't get picked up for it. She was sure she would never see him again. *My grandson.*

Twenty-four hours ago, she couldn't have imagined wanting to reassure Moran... Perhaps he *was* delusional, and she had just been taken for a fool - but better that than being responsible for the extinction of the human race. The tiny flash drive that he had given her

-containing all the test results and his genetic code - sat tucked into her pocket. She wrenched the phone box door open, wrinkling her nose at the stink of urine in the enclosed space, and picked up the handset.

'I'd like to place a reverse charges call, please.' She recited her father's mobile number, thankful that she had a good memory for numbers, and waited anxiously for the call to connect.

'Mr. Tom Morgan? I have a reverse charges call for you – are you willing to accept it? It's your daughter, sir.'

'Emma? Christ, yes, put her through – thank you – Emma? Are you all right?' Her father started to cry, bringing a lump to Emma's throat.

'Yes, I'm all right, Dad. Please don't be upset, honestly I'm OK...he let me go...I'm in a phone box on the Rochdale road, near Mac-Donald's...can you come and get me?'

35: 30TH SEPTEMBER, 5.45PM

It took Moran twice as long to get back to Rosendale as it had to reach the city outskirts, thanks to the post-shopping traffic heading out of Manchester.

What Moran hadn't told Emma was that the moment she had started to believe him, and to ask sensible questions rather than facetious ones, he had begun to feel unwell. At first, he had dismissed it as a reaction to nearly four decades of being alone with his secret; the sheer relief of being able to talk about it was, without a doubt, immense. But by the time they had agreed what was to be done, he had begun to realise that it was more than relief. The changes were not psychological, they were physical; an unfamiliar ache in his joints, a sick, empty feeling in his stomach, a loosening of sinew and ligament... as if he had begun to blur at the edges. He had muttered some excuse about needing a moment, and had fled to the bathroom. There, the evidence was, if underwhelming to anyone else, obvious to him: tiny lines around his eyes which hadn't been there before, a slight -very slight- loosening of the skin around the jowls. He was ageing.

The shock must have shown on his face, because when he rejoined Emma, she gave him a long, hard stare, and asked him what was wrong. She had gone very quickly from being a frightened captive to a willing co-conspirator. She 'had his back', as Sanchez would have said. He brushed it off, telling her that he hadn't been sleeping well, a perfectly plausible explanation.

Sanchez – Moran hadn't thought about his colleague in a long time. How had Neil reacted to his partner's sudden disappearance? Or, thanks to the vagaries of time travel, would he have even been aware of Moran's departure? Would time have healed around him? Moran had no idea.

But never mind Sanchez. Should he tell Emma that if his physical symptoms of decline were anything to go by -and they must be, surely? – then she would make it work? She would, he was now convinced, find a way to stop the gene from being used to extend life for the majority. He decided against it. Emma was a research scientist first and foremost – she needed to find out for herself. He didn't think that the certain knowledge of her success would affect how she might approach the problem, but it was better not to risk it.

Suddenly, Moran could think about nothing but Cassie. He would die here, he now realised, and he would never see her again. That knowledge hurt. He wondered how long it would take... in the meantime, he had to do whatever he could to hide the truth of his existence from anyone who might come looking. His makeshift lab must not be found, nor any trace of Emma's presence there. But he might not have time to move the equipment out before he became too infirm, and once Emma spoke to the police, they wouldn't simply stop looking for him. She didn't know the location of the house – and had agreed to be blindfolded for part of the way back, so that she couldn't tell the police anything about where she had been kept. But if they took her shoes and compared soil samples, they might eventually find out where she had been. Would they bother, since she had reappeared safe and well? He couldn't afford to take the risk.

Moran remembered meeting Gilling here for the first time. The building would still be standing three hundred years from now – could he change that, should he? If he were to destroy the bricks and mortar here and now, how would he ever travel back in time? Perhaps events would rearrange themselves... perhaps they wouldn't. If Emma was going to succeed in reverse-engineering the gene therapy before it had even been created, then there would be no need for Gilling's time machine... but if there was no machine, how would Moran get here in the first place to tell Emma about it, give her the information she would need to make the change? It was all too confusing. Moran thought he could feel his mental abilities declining. He had to do this now, while he still could.

They could see the glow above the tree tops even before they'd left the main road.

'Shit! Call the bloody fire brigade!' Hammond swallowed his Chinese supper back down with considerable effort. If Emma Morgan was still in there....

The lower floors of the old house had been gutted by the fire. It had started in the kitchen, and had been fueled by some kind of accelerant; the stench of it was everywhere.

'There was a vehicle here recently,' one of the fire fighters called to another. The carport roof had gone, but the man had noticed oil stains on the floor.

'Boss! Boss!' Mortimer hurried across the drive, in his haste splattering water from the fire hoses up his trouser legs. He stopped in front of Hammond, a grin splitting his dark face from ear to ear. 'Emma's okay, she's alive!'

Hammond felt almost light-headed with relief. 'Jesus...'

'Morgan rang. Moran let her go. Left her by a phone box on the Rochdale Road.'

'Thank Christ for that, Joe, thank Christ for that...' Hammond clapped his sergeant on the shoulder. 'We'll leave these boys to it, I need to speak to her.'

The experience might be over for Emma and her family, but for Hammond and his men, the hard work would continue: now he had to catch the bastard.

37: 30TH SEPTEMBER, 8:15PM

Emma's father had insisted on taking her to the hospital to get her checked over, despite her protests that she was unhurt; and now she found herself in a curtained-off cubicle in the assessment ward. It had taken an age to get this far, and she had yet to be pronounced fit or otherwise by a Doctor. Her repeated claims that she hadn't been hurt had been waved away.

'I'm not taking any chances, Emma. You could have been drugged, anything… I want to make sure.' There was to be no arguing with him.

Her mother had sat in the back seat with Emma, holding her hand the entire way. She had repeatedly apologised for being a poor mother, until Emma began to feel annoyed. 'You're not a bad mother, please stop saying that.'

True to his word, her father had called the police, and they had arrived moments after Tom Morgan had executed an illegal U-Turn and headed back into the city at speed. They'd had what amounted to a police escort to the hospital, and they hadn't been happy. 'If he thinks I'm stopping…'

Emma had heard part of a conversation between her father and the man now sitting across from her: Inspector Hammond. Harsh words had been exchanged between the two men in the corridor, and the nursing staff had asked them to 'take it outside'.

Hammond seemed to be furious that her father hadn't waited for the police, that he might have caused the loss of valuable forensic evidence by his actions: her father was equally convinced that getting his daughter to a hospital had been the priority.

Her parents had now gone for a coffee, leaving Emma alone with the detective, who had been warned by a harassed-looking nurse that he would have to leave when the Doctor arrived.

Detective Inspector Hammond looked as if he might have slept in his suit. He was a tall man, probably in his mid-forties, Emma guessed, and seemed impatient to get on with the conversation.

'How are you feeling, Emma?'

She didn't have to think about it. 'Tired,' she said. 'Relieved.' *Keep it simple, stick as closely to the truth as you can,* Moran had advised her. She could do that. Besides, it wasn't a lie – she did feel tired. She was also anxious to get back to the lab and resume work, suddenly consumed by the fear that someone else would discover the Methuselah gene while she sat around in hospital.

Hammond nodded. 'I won't keep you long. I need to ask you, Emma, is this man who abducted you?' He pulled a photograph from his jacket pocket, and Emma recognised Moran.

She gave a small nod.

'Yes – he works, worked, I mean, at Xeon. He was on Security. James Moran.' He would have been their first -perhaps their only- suspect. If only he had come to her first, instead of trying to wreck her results...

'Do you know why he kidnapped you?'

'He said I reminded him of his daughter.' She sighed. 'I felt sorry for him, in the end.'

Hammond's eyebrows shot up. 'His daughter?'

They knew he didn't have a daughter. At least, not here, not now. 'He didn't say, exactly...' she needed to be careful, not get too elaborate. *Keep it simple.* 'I got the feeling she was ill, that she might even have died.' Should she give them the name? What harm could it do? 'He called her Cassie.'

Hammond scribbled something in a tiny notebook.

'Did you know James Moran before you met him at Xeon?'

'No – of course not. He was just a security guard.' Was she being too defensive?

'He never approached you, prior to tampering with your research?'

'No.'

'Do you know why he tried to spoil your samples?'

'No.' She knew that having asked a few control questions, Hammond might spot the lie. She hoped he was as tired as he looked, and might miss it. 'I assumed… well, I thought she might have had a genetic condition…that perhaps he thought science had failed her. But he didn't say.'

'And you didn't ask?'

Emma shook her head. 'No.'

'Might he have seen the interview in the Sunday Supplement?'

So he knew about that. Well, he would, wouldn't he? 'He said he saw it, yes – and that I reminded him of his daughter.'

'So he took a job at Xeon because you looked like his daughter?'

Emma shrugged. 'I suppose so. But if he is recently bereaved…'

'I don't think he is, Emma. But we'll come back to that. So talk me through it.'

Emma recounted her experience – how Moran had come up behind her and sedated her, how she had woken up in his car (at which point he interrupted to ask if she could tell him anything about the car to help his colleagues identify it – she was able to tell him 'no' truthfully, because Moran had blindfolded her both times they had used the car; all she could tell him was that it was silver or grey and had four doors) and been escorted blindfold into the house. She described the house as briefly as she could, telling him that it seemed old, and was quite big, that it was out of the city. She could see that he believed this.

'So… he drugged you, took you to his house, and then…what?'

Emma shook her head. 'I don't know what to tell you, Inspector Hammond. He locked me in a bedroom overnight, and made me breakfast the next morning. He kept apologising. He told me that he had a daughter and that something was wrong with her. He didn't say as much, but I think she died. And then he let me go. That's it.'

'So why did he vandalize your work, Emma? Surely he must have talked about that?'

Emma closed her eyes. She couldn't cope with this – he would wear her down, get her to say more than she wanted to. Keeping her eyes closed, she shook her head.

'No. I'm sorry, but he didn't. I thought he would... I asked him, but he wouldn't tell me. I can't really tell you anything else.' She closed her eyes. 'Please, it's been... I'm tired.'

The click-clack of the curtain being pulled open made Emma open her eyes. Hammond stood as a young woman in a white coat advanced to Emma's side.

'I'm afraid you'll have to leave now, Inspector. I'm not happy that you were allowed in at all.'

Hammond nodded with good grace, pulling a card from his pocket and placing it on the bedside table.

'Of course. Emma, I will need to speak to you again. Goodnight.' He struggled for a moment with the curtain, then he was gone.

'Hello Emma, I'm Lisa Bale. You could have rung for help; we'd have got shot of him for you. He shouldn't have been here.'

'I didn't think to...'

'How are you feeling?' Bale's eyes – a vivid blue, seeming to miss nothing- quickly scanned Emma's chart. There couldn't be much on it, Emma thought – she'd had her blood pressure taken, been asked a few questions about when she last ate or drank and if she was on any medication.

'I'm okay, a bit tired... I'm not even sure why my father...he was just being cautious, I suppose.'

Bale smiled. 'Yes, I'm sure he was. Well as far as I can see, and from your notes here, there would seem to be no reason for us to keep you here. Is there anything you want to tell me...? We can offer counselling, you know.'

'No, I don't need... he didn't ... nothing like that.' Emma hesitated. She didn't want to mention being sedated, in case Bale decided to keep her in for tests. It had worn off, in any case, so what would be the point? 'He thought I was someone else,' she added. 'That's all.'

Bale made a note on the clipboard. 'I'll arrange for your discharge. If you would just wait here, someone will come for you shortly. Are your parents still here?'

Emma nodded. 'Yes, they just went to get coffee…'

'Good. You don't appear to be suffering from shock, but it could manifest itself later. I'll make sure you're given a leaflet to take home, and if you or your parents are at all worried, just follow the instructions. You take care now.' Bale gave Emma a tight smile and then she was gone. Had she believed Emma? Well, it hardly mattered, did it?

Hammond nodded to the Morgans, who were heading back down the corridor. Morgan was clearly still smarting from their earlier encounter.

'Have you found him yet - the security guard?'

Hammond shook his head. 'Not yet. I will need to speak to your daughter again,' he addressed them both. 'Will you be taking Emma back to London?' It would be the kind of thing Morgan would do, he thought; keeping control. But Hammond had questions – he had to find out what Emma knew about her kidnapper, and he had yet to tell her about the fire at the Rossendale house. It was where she had been kept, he was certain. Forensics might not be able to verify it, but some of the upper rooms were partially intact – she might recognise them.

'I don't know – we haven't talked about it yet.' Morgan frowned at him. 'We're just glad to have her back, Inspector.'

'Of course you are. Well, please don't leave without letting me know, will you?' Hammond left Morgan standing in the corridor, heard a muttered, 'For fuck's sake…' as he walked away.

Something about Emma's story didn't add up. Granted, by her own admission she hadn't been hurt, but for someone who had been snatched in what would be a shocking manner for most people, then held captive for twenty-four hours, she was far too composed, her answers too pat, and he was certain she had been lying about some-

thing. He would have expected her to be more distressed, still frightened by her experience - not evasive. Moran's personnel records
hadn't mentioned a daughter – either he had lied to his employers, or
to Emma. Or, quite probably, to both of everyone.

Hammond was now convinced that there was a connection, somewhere, to the family. It was too much of a coincidence that Peter King
had been studying at UMIST in 1979 when a newspaper photo had
shown someone who was a dead ringer for Moran in a crowd of on-
lookers at the Woolworth's fire; someone he himself had recognised.
Too much of a coincidence that Moran -or someone looking very like
him- had been photo-fitted as the man responsible for the accident
which had killed King and his daughter, Emma's half-sister, eleven
years later. Now Moran had snatched Eva's second daughter off the
street. Why? What linked them? And how the hell did Moran get to
look so young, if it had really been him in 'seventy-nine and 'ninety?
Something about the whole case was making the hairs on the back of
Hammond's neck stand to attention.

PART FIVE

38: 1ST OCTOBER 2018

'Hello – I called earlier, I'm Jessica Deacon?'

The plump, middle-aged woman who had opened the door looked flustered. 'Oh yes, my father did tell me that you'd called. I'm Alison, please come in. I hope you don't mind, but I wonder if you'd mind not staying too long. Only Dad had a bit of a funny turn this morning - the Doctor has been, and he's due to come back again shortly after his rounds. He wants Dad admitted to hospital, but he won't hear of it.'

Jessica's heart sank. 'I'm very sorry to hear that, and of course I'll make it quick, if you're quite sure …?' She hoped it had nothing to do with their conversation – the retired detective had sounded fine on the phone, if a little tired. He had seemed keen to meet her once he knew who she was.

Alison nodded. 'I tried to persuade him to cancel you, but he wouldn't hear of it.'

* * *

Tony Clarke looked like an ex-copper, Jess thought, even diminished by age and frailty. She hadn't liked to ask what was wrong with him, but seeing him, she knew immediately – his position in the wheelchair, the slight droop at the corner of his mouth, the way only one eye seemed to fix on her as she entered the room, all pointed to a stroke at some point in the past. But his voice, when he spoke, was clear enough, and not a lot different to how he'd sounded on the phone.

'You'll be the lassie who rang earlier – Miss Deacon? You'll excuse me if I don't get up… my legs aren't what they were.'

He had old-fashioned manners, too, and a dry wit.

'Of course, please call me Jess.'

He inclined his head, and waved vaguely in the direction of a comfy-looking armchair.

'Aye. Will you take a cup of tea, Jess?'

'That's very kind of you, but I'll make this as short as I can, your daughter told me you haven't been well.'

He sighed. 'True enough. You're the Aunt, aren't you? I saw you on television.'

Jess nodded. Had he forgotten the reason for her visit? 'You won't have heard yet, I don't suppose, but my niece has been found.'

He seemed to perk up. 'That's grand news. She's all right?'

'She's okay, yes.' Clarke looked ill, so she hurried on. 'I wanted to talk to you about your link to the kidnapper, James Moran.'

He frowned. 'My only link, lass, and my failing, is that I didn't find him in 1990. James Moran… so that's his name?' He must have seen the appeal; they'd mentioned Moran's name in the latest one. He had forgotten. Jess realised she ought not to be here – Clarke was clearly far from well.

'Yes, apparently so. He was a security guard at the same research company where my niece works. The man who died in nineteen ninety, Peter King, was Eva's first husband. He studied at the same University.'

'Aye, I told the Inspector it looked like the same man.' His eyes closed for a few moments, and Jess wondered if he was growing bored with the conversation. She pulled the iPad from her bag, and having called up the image she had saved earlier, passed it across to him. It had taken hours of staring at microfiche images until her eyes blurred, but she had found it.

'But I found this, as well.'

He held it at arm's length and studied the screen. His hand shook quite noticeably, and Jess held the iPad for him.

'Well I'll be damned. I remember that well, the Woolworth's fire. Does Inspector Hammond know about this?'

'I don't know,' she confessed. 'I will show him when I next see him. But I remembered Peter talking about that fire, and how he was warned before anyone else knew.' She hesitated, not wanting to tell this essentially good man that she had committed adultery with her own sister's husband. Clarke gave her a lopsided smile, and Jess knew that somehow, he'd worked it out. In spite of his failure to find Moran, he'd have been a good detective. He knew people.

'I'll not judge you, lass. You do know it's not me you should be telling this to, don't you?'

She nodded. 'I'll tell Inspector Hammond, I promise. What do you think is going on, Mr. Clarke?'

He shook his head. 'I've no idea, lass. That's why I called…' he hesitated. 'How did you find me, if you've not spoken to him about this?'

'I'm a journalist, it's what I do. I dig around in other people's pasts, make connections. I was trying to find a common link… it can't be co-incidence, can it?'

'I can see you'll not let it go. But if you take my advice, you'll leave it to the police. I take it they've not got this Moran in custody, then?'

'Not as far as I've heard. I'd just found this,' she closed the iPad and put it back in her bag, 'when Eva called me with the news.'

'You haven't seen your niece yet?'

'No. I didn't want to be in the way.' She took a deep breath. I feel partly responsible. I interviewed her, you see. Her picture was in the magazine just weeks before he took her.' She shivered.

Clarke smiled wanly. 'Seems to me, the link is with your sister, the lass's mother.' He closed his eyes, and Jess realised that it was her signal to leave.

'I'm sure you're right, Mr. Clarke. I'm really sorry to have bothered you.' She stood up, and Clarke roused himself enough to shake her hand; it trembled in her grip, and Jess felt a rush of warmth for the old man, and sorrow that he should be so reduced. 'Thank you so much for your time.'

Clarke nodded, but his thoughts had already turned inward. 'Nice to meet you, lass. Take care, now.' He closed his eyes again.

Jess found Clarke's daughter in the hallway – she had just opened the door to a harried-looking middle-aged man with a black case.

'Thank you so much for letting me see him,' she said quickly to Alison, and saw a look of irritation cross the Doctor's face. 'I think he's sleeping now. I hope he'll be okay.'

Alison managed a worried smile. 'So do I.' she turned to her visitor, who was already making his way along the hall. 'I'll be with you in moment, Doctor.' Then to Jess, 'I hope your niece turns up safe and sound.'

Jess could see that Alison was anxious to get back to her father, so she didn't update her. Her father could do that later, she hoped.

39: 5TH OCTOBER

'Morning, boss.'

Mortimer, staring glumly at his monitor, sounded as flat as Hammond felt. He dumped his jacket over the back of his chair, and went back out to the main incident room. The investigation was winding down: half the desks were empty, with many of the drafted officers now returned to their original duties. The phones were mostly silent, and despite the safe recovery of the kidnap victim, the whole room had a defeated air. Moran hadn't been seen on any CCTV in the city since the night of the kidnap, and there had been no activity on either of his bank accounts. Fire investigators had combed through the wreckage of the house, but as Hammond had half-expected, they hadn't found any human remains. Moran must have dumped Emma first and then gone back to set the fire, but with no sightings of his vehicle on the route between either of his homes and Emma's flat, there was no way to tell where he might have gone after that. He had simply vanished.

Emma had been discharged from hospital the same evening. Her parents were on their way back to London, but according to Family Liaison, had tried to persuade their daughter to go back with them for a while, to recover. Emma had refused, saying that she was anxious to resume her work. Hammond had yet to speak to her a second time; it would have to happen soon. He was still convinced that she was protecting Moran, but couldn't fathom out why.

The Morgans had called at the station yesterday afternoon to tell him they were returning home and to ask if there was any further progress in the search for Moran. Hammond told them they were following a few leads – not strictly true, they'd been drawing blanks for days- and asked them how they thought their daughter was coping following her ordeal.

'She's behaving almost as if nothing has happened,' Tom Morgan said. Clearly, he was worried. His wife agreed.

'I think she may be in denial,' Eva said, and in answer to her husband's muttered 'Well, you'd know all about that, wouldn't you?' had shot him a venomous look, and gone on to say that she had asked Emma if Moran had made inappropriate advances. Emma had told her that 'no, it was nothing like that.'

'You mean, did the bastard rape her?' Tom snapped. 'Why the hell would she keep quiet about it if he had?'

'Your daughter was offered counselling, and she did agree to let our forensics team take various samples from her,' Hammond told them. 'Not that kind,' he added, seeing Morgan blanch. 'Blood tests showed nothing untoward, a few traces of sedative, which fits with what she told us. Emma insisted that Moran didn't sexually or otherwise abuse her. She maintains that he is a bereaved parent who was, as she puts it, 'confused.' I have to tell you both now, I believe that your daughter is lying. But I can't for the life of me imagine why.'

'You can't seriously think she planned all this?'

'No, Mr. Morgan, I don't… but, according to a psychologist who has seen her file, there are indications that she may have come to empathize with Moran. At first we wondered if it might be something to do with her research – but Emma is sticking to her story that they didn't talk about it, so unless we find him…' He felt embarrassed by his failure to give them answers. As for his own questions… they too, remained unanswered. Had it really been the same man he saw on the day his mother had disappeared? It seemed to be altogether too much of a coincidence.

'But you will keep looking?' Eva seemed clearer-headed than at any time since Hammond had met her. It seemed clear from her attitude towards her husband that their marriage was almost certainly over. Hammond thought that at least something positive had come out of the whole affair, although it was clear that Morgan didn't share this view. He was a shadow of the man he had been; clearly he had managed to get some sleep since his daughter had been found, but his eyes were haunted; he seemed somehow smaller, less sure of himself.

'I'm still looking, Mrs. Morgan.'

'If you find him, what will he get?' Morgan fretted. 'You will find him, won't you? This day and age...'

'Moran's picture has been circulated to every police authority, and if he tries to access his bank account, or to leave the country, we'll be alerted. He's laying low.' Hammond didn't mind telling them this; it was better not to give them false hope of a conviction. He knew the idea that their daughter's kidnapper was still at large worried them – it worried him, too. 'As for what he'll get if we catch him ... For kidnap, false imprisonment? Hard to say, but he probably wouldn't be inside for long, if he behaved himself. He might even end up in a psychiatric unit.'

Morgan snorted. 'Emma told us some sob story about a dead daughter...' he fell silent.

'Grief can make us do strange things, inspector, can't it?' Eva was looking at Hammond as she spoke, but he knew the remark was aimed at her husband.

Hammond had finally managed to get a formal interview with Eva Morgan without her husband being present, but she had been unable to shed any light on why Moran had been so disastrously involved in her life. She seemed convinced that it must be the same man, but couldn't imagine why he hadn't changed, or why would have targeted only people close to her. Her main concern seemed to be that left on the loose, Moran might try again. Hammond sympathized, but told Eva he thought it was unlikely, since Moran had let

Emma go. He had advised the Morgans to check their home security nonetheless, and had suggested to both Emma and Xeon that they should increase theirs.

Now, looking around at the case board, Hammond chewed his bottom lip as he stared at the photographs and the lines and notes linking them. He had to be missing something... He marched back to his office, grabbed his jacket, and told Mortimer he was going out for a bit.

40: 5TH OCTOBER

Archie had been almost in tears; he had been so pleased to see her. He even forgot to call her 'Doctor Morgan'.

'Emma! Oh my goodness…how are you? Were you hurt? I wasn't expecting …' He might have seen the small item about her safe return on the evening news, Emma thought, but it had been very brief. Had she died, it would have been all over the front pages of the tabloids.

'I'm okay, Archie, thank you – really, don't look at me like that… shall we get on, then?'

She had been back at work for four days, but was having difficulty concentrating. She would come to from long minutes spent in deep thought, to find Archie standing beside her with a worried look on his face.

Somehow, her initial determination to work through the data (at home, on a new laptop she had purchased specifically for the purpose) Moran had provided had dissipated. Copying files without Archie noticing, transferring it all to the new laptop, and working long into the night, then working normal hours at the lab, was taking a toll. And weirdly, even though she had only known him for two days, she missed Moran.

Where was he? Without his presence, the whole story was starting to seem just that – a story she might have imagined. Only her parents' continued presence in Manchester and the data on the laptop were proof it had ever happened.

Had she felt a familial connection with Moran, once the connection had been revealed? She had tried to imagine telling her father that his own great-grandson had travelled back in time to kidnap her. It wouldn't go down well. What would her mother say to the news that Moran, her own flesh-and-blood, had caused the death of her first husband and daughter? Her parents wouldn't believe her, they would assume she had either been brainwashed by Moran or -more likely- was having some kind of breakdown. She could forget telling any of it to D.I. Hammond too – people like Hammond dealt in facts, hard evidence. The data on her laptop was the only proof, and that could be made to vanish. It wasn't verifiable without Moran, and if he was found…

She often thought about Cassie, about how Cassie would so closely resemble her great-great grandmother. About whether she might survive the cancer. It was the only thing which kept her going. *Think about Cassie…*

She knew that Archie was worried about her – or perhaps about the research trials, which pretty much meant the same thing. Suppose she gave it all up – walked away? Would Archie and others like him stumble on the gene? As she had told Moran, it was entirely possible – if the gene was there to be discovered, someone would, eventually. Without Moran to confide in, to share her doubts, Emma was coming adrift. Could she trust Archie with what she knew? She couldn't risk it.

Moran hadn't seemed well the last time she had seen him. Might this mean that she would be successful? If she could only see him again, find out for sure…if he had begun to age, then she would know that success was around the corner. Odd that now she equated success with finding the gene and tempering its' affect.

She hadn't heard from Simon either, apart from his first visit, when in direct contrast to his concern during their phone conversation he become angry when she refused to take time off to get over her ordeal. It was clear that he didn't understand her, would never understand her. She had stared at him so hard – trying to imagine him as Moran's grandfather, that he had cut short his visit, unable to bear her scrutiny. The others – Matt, Lucy- had called round, but it was clear that they didn't know what to make of her refusal to talk about her experience, or of her wish to return to work so soon. There had been no invitations to recreate the birthday dinner she had missed, thanks to Moran; whatever cards and gifts might have been coming her way had also failed to materialise. Not that she was worried about those, but the loss of faith their absence seemed to indicate stung her. Would they have preferred that she'd been raped, or murdered, or beaten up? She couldn't talk to them about it without inventing a story, because obviously she could never tell them the truth. Quite apart from the possible consequences of telling anyone, if they didn't think she was mad, they would assume she was lying. All she had now, it seemed, was Archie's quiet loyalty, and her work.

She was not sleeping well, either. Her feelings seemed to see-saw; could she still find a cure for progeria without causing the pandemic of Moran's time? She would never be able to explain it to her father. He was counting on her to make Nathan's death mean something; how could she let him down by walking away from the lab, or sabotaging her own work in a way that no-one would discover? It was impossible. She had almost called him a couple of times, to tell him she was having doubts…but picturing the look on his face, his hurt … she couldn't do it to him. She needed to see Moran again, but unless he got in touch, it wasn't going to happen. Had he returned to his own time? She hoped so, and also hoped not…

Her parents were still troubled – not just about Emma's kidnap, but by their disintegrating marriage. Eva had taken Emma for lunch the previous day, and in addition to apologising -again- for being a bad mother for most of Emma's life – an apology Emma was quick to assure her wasn't necessary- had told her daughter that she didn't think the marriage was going to survive.

'We married each other for all the wrong reasons, I can see that now. But I don't regret it, because if we hadn't, I wouldn't have you.'

Emma was less moved by this news than she might have been be-fore meeting Moran – his guilt over the death of her mother's first husband and child had only been assuaged (and then not com-pletely) by the fact of Emma's own existence – an existence which had put his daughter's life at risk. But, like Eva, he couldn't un-wish his own daughter's existence…family was family, after all.

A week and a half after returning to the lab, Emma couldn't stand it any longer.

'Do you ever think we should be working on something else, Archie? Something that affects more people, like cancer?'

Archie put down the pipet he was holding and stared at her. 'No,' he said, and frowned. 'I'm worried about you, Emma – you haven't been yourself since you came back.'

Emma closed her eyes and sighed. 'I know, and I'm sorry. I seem to have lost my focus…' She hesitated. 'When I was locked up in that house, I got to thinking…' was she really going to say it?

'Thinking what?'

'If we succeed in helping Progeria patients to live longer with gene therapy…'

'Please God,' Archie said vehemently,

'Well, yes. But just suppose everyone else wants it? You know, if everyone decides they want to live longer?'

Archie stared at her. 'It won't work like that.'

'But what if it does? It would be the biggest news since…'

Archie reached for his mouse, clicked it, and came to stand beside Emma. 'Emma, is something wrong? Are you having second thoughts?'

Yes, I am, Emma wanted to say. *If only you knew….* She shrugged. 'No…but sometimes I wonder…what if we have no say in it?'

'I think you should take some time off,' Archie declared. Since she had come back to work, Archie had seemed different, too – more as-sertive. He had told her that he was thinking of having his mother put into a nursing home, and hadn't seemed at all apologetic about it, which she was sure the old Archie would have done. She was glad for him; perhaps now he could begin to live his own life, rather than the one he had been living with his mother. If a little voice inside Emma's head whispered that perhaps he was hoping to share his home with someone else, and that someone might be her, she chose to ignore it. She was not –never had been- romantically interested in Archie. And yet…Archie had never submitted his own blood for the trials, and she could hardly ask him to now, but what if he was the one? The weight of what she knew was becoming heavier with each passing day. She was, quite simply, terrified of doing the wrong thing.

'I can't…' what would she do with herself all day? She couldn't impose on her parents, who had their own problems. Simon wasn't talking to her, and Matt and Lilli… she had no idea what Matt and Lilli were doing, she realised.

'Emma, my dear…' – that was his mother talking, she thought- '… your work is, um, suffering at the moment, don't you think? I really do think you should have gone home with your parents for a short break – they'll understand,' he waved his arms, encompassing the lab and, by extension, Xeon. 'You've been through a traumatic experience, you need to rest and recover yourself.'

Emma thought that perhaps he was right – but if she stayed in her digs, she would end up going into the lab anyway, because that was what she did, who she was… the flat was a place to sleep and eat and study, nothing more. She wanted to see Moran again. She *needed* to see him. Well then, perhaps she would go looking for him. She knew something the police didn't – that Moran's father was somewhere in London.

'Perhaps you're right, Archie – I can't seem to stop thinking about it …'

'Do you know where he is?'

The question took her by surprise. 'You mean Moran? No! Of course not? Why would I?'

Archie frowned. 'I don't know… it was just something that occurred to me. Did he ever tell you why he tampered with the samples? I've been wondering about that.'

If there was ever a time to tell Archie, this was it – but Emma couldn't bring herself to do it.

'No,' she said. 'Well, that is, not in so many words. I think he had some idea that I could cure his daughter, he said she was sick... but he also said I reminded him of her... I don't know. He was *very* confused.' Had she laid it on too thick?

'I thought you said his daughter was dead? How could you possibly cure her – and what of?' Archie's tone had changed. *He knows I'm lying. Just like Inspector Hammond....* Even her parents thought she was holding something back, didn't they?

'Emma, if there's anything you want to tell us...' her mother had said just before taking her leave. From being a mother who kept her distance, Eva now seemed to want to make up for lost time.

'Do you know what, Archie...? I think you're right. I *do* need to rest... I can't focus anymore. Would you mind? Just carry on with the trial... I'm sorry, you know what to do.'

Archie's face –and his tone- softened. 'Of course, Emma. I think you're wise – it has obviously affected you. You can trust me; I will continue the work.'

Emma closed her computer down and gathered her bag and coat, and left Archie to it. Outside, she was met with warm spring sunshine, and as she stood wondering where to go, felt a weight lift from her shoulders. She would find Moran, and once she had spoken to him, she would feel better.

41: 13TH NOVEMBER, 8.30AM

'I don't get it, sir.'

Hammond looked up to see Rattigan standing in the doorway of his office. She was frowning.

'You don't get what?' He rolled his head, trying to ease the stiffness in his neck, and heard cartilage creaking. He was getting old.

'Moran. Gilling. Whoever he really is. How did he just disappear? He hasn't been near his flat, his second home's been trashed by the fire; his bank accounts haven't been touched. What's he living on? I just think we're missing something. Sir.'

Hammond waved a hand at the chair on the other side of his desk, and Rattigan sat down. She had her notebook with her, a sign that she had been reviewing the case, probably.

'Topped himself, perhaps.' Their failure to apprehend Moran left a bitter taste in Hammond's mouth, and not just because of his connection to his mother's disappearance – if it had even been him, which he felt certain it had. He still hadn't been able to work out Moran's motivation. Why take the girl, and then let her go again? There was no sexual motive (or so Emma claimed, and why would she lie?), no ransom demand… Moran, whoever he really was, had deliberately torched his own home, and gone on the run. Why? What was he hiding? None of it made any sense. Whatever the link back to the mother's past might be, she wasn't saying. He was either the man who had destroyed her first family or closely related to him, and he'd had a go at Eva's second daughter decades later... if she did know anything, why wouldn't she say? If they had been able to recover any forensic evidence at either location, he could have requested samples from Emma and Eva, to see if they were related... but the flat had been clean, suspiciously so. No hairs, no fingerprints, no lip prints on a used cup...no nothing. And the upper rooms at the Hall had yielded nothing either, except a few hairs which proved Emma had been kept there. For a builder-come-security guard, Moran knew a lot about forensic footprints... just who the hell was he?

With no new leads, and Emma returned safe and well, the investigation was slowly winding down – other cases were cutting into their day. The whiteboard had been pushed to one side, soon they would have to wipe it and use it for another case. He knew that some of the team were already beginning to wonder why he was preserving it.

Surridge had been relieved by the daughter's safe return, and apart from a brief flurry of interest by the tabloid media when news of the failure to apprehend the kidnapper had been admitted, the nation had lost any interest it might have had. Morgan was apparently well into rehearsals for a play, and Hammond had no idea what Eva Morgan was doing; instigating divorce proceedings, if she had any sense. The Aunt had, it seemed, refused to capitalise on the drama – despite Hammond's hope that she might stick around for a while, Jessica Deacon had gone back to London, and had not returned his call. He'd warned her off, and she had listened. It was all bloody frustrating.

'Maybe. I know we've been over this a thousand times, sir, but do you think she was involved all along – Emma, I mean? She was that quick to drop charges...'

Hammond sighed. 'Christ knows... she was definitely hiding *something*. Look, Lucy – we're going to be putting this one on the back-burner soon.'

Rattigan nodded. 'I know. But it's bothering me, sir. I can't help thinking there's more going on here than we've seen. Mrs. Morgan's first husband…her daughters. I mean…. how *can* it be the same guy? He'd be an old man by now, wouldn't he? I'd like to speak to Tony Clarke again – maybe the Aunt… would you mind?'

Hammond hesitated. Surridge would probably do his nut, but it was surely worth a punt… 'I can give you a couple of days; but if you don't come up with anything…will that do you?' He liked Rattigan – she'd go far, he thought, and he was happy to help her on her way. Rattigan's grin made him feel old, and tired.

'Thank you, sir. You won't regret it.'

Hammond hoped she was right.

'DC Rattigan, Manchester CID. May I speak to Tony Clarke, please?'

The voice on the other end of the line was quietly apologetic, muted by grief. 'I'm very sorry – my father passed away almost a week ago.'

Damn! 'I'm very sorry for your loss – I won't disturb you any further, Miss Clarke.'

That left the Aunt, and perhaps Eva Morgan. She'd established a rapport with Eva, hadn't she? Perhaps she would also speak to Eva's first mother- in-law – Barbara King hadn't been interviewed, it hadn't been deemed necessary – a mistake, Rattigan was now convinced. Maybe she was clutching at straws, but Barbara King was local, so she could pop in on her before she got the mid-morning train to London. She'd need to call in at home first, pack a small overnight bag…

'Mrs. King? I'm Detective Constable Lucy Rattigan. May I come in, please?'

The elderly woman who stood in the doorway of the modest terrace in Gledhill Road was silver-haired, stooped and thin, and looked as if a puff of wind might knock her over. Rattigan had been surprised to discover that Mrs. King wasn't on the phone – wasn't everyone, these days? Maybe she had a mobile… people could -and often did- surprise you.

'What's it about? Only I've got my dinner on…'

'I'm sorry – I won't keep you a moment. Please…?'

'Come on then, lass. Shut door behind you.'

'You're not local, are you?'

Barbara King chuckled softly. 'No – I grew up in Stokesley. Always meant to go back there… but you know how it is.'

Rattigan wasn't sure she did, having lived in the city all her life, but nodded anyway as the old woman led her down a dark hallway to a small kitchen at the back of the house. A tin of vegetable broth sat on the counter, an empty pan on the electric hob. Rattigan's stomach rumbled.

'I were just looking for a tin-opener… I'm always putting things down and forgetting where they are…ah, there you are.' The old woman tugged open a drawer and drew out a butterfly- style opener - just like the one which had lived in the kitchen drawer in Rattigan's childhood home – and fumbled with it.

'Here, let me…' Rattigan gently took the can opener from Barbara King's arthritic fingers and fastened it onto the rim of the can. The device had seen better days and it took two circuits before the top of the can came away.

'Thank you love – it's always a bit of a struggle.'

'You need a new can-opener, Mrs. King. Tell you what, why don't you sit yourself down and I'll see to this while we talk – would that be all right?' She wondered if this was to be the woman's main meal of the day. Judging from the bony wrists and the over-prominent cheekbones, she thought it might be, and hoped Mrs. King didn't think her patronising. To her relief, the woman didn't seem to.

'That'd be grand. What is it you want to talk to me about? I'm not in trouble, am I?' Smiling, Mrs. King moved stiffly to the kitchen table, where a single setting looked as if it was never moved, and eased herself into the only chair, which creaked as she lowered her tiny frame onto it. Like everything in the room, it had seen better days.

Rattigan put the hotplate on, and turned so that she could stir the broth and see Mrs. King at the same time.

'You're not in any trouble, I promise. I'm sorry to bring this up after so long…'

'It'll be about my Peter, then.' She smiled sadly. 'It were the only time police ever crossed our doorstep.'

'Yes, it is, and I'm really sorry. Are you okay to talk about it?'

Mrs. King nodded stiffly. 'Though I don't know what I can tell you, lass. It were a long time ago, now.' She coughed, and Rattigan averted her eyes as a handkerchief appeared from the woman's sleeve, just in time to receive the phlegmy result.

'I wondered if anyone had ever come back to you about the man who caused the accident which took your son and your grand-daughter's lives.'

'Him that were on the telly t'other day?' Barbara King shook her head. 'No. They never caught him.' She sniffed. 'Must be his son, by the looks of him. I'm glad the lass is safe.'

Rattigan felt a tingle of excitement – here was someone else who'd seen a link. 'Well, perhaps…so he wasn't someone your son knew?'

'Not as far as I know, love. But he were in the paper after that fire.'

'Fire?'

'Yes, lass – Woolworths, it was, nineteen-seventy-something… nine. It were my birthday. I nearly lost him then, you see.'

'How do you mean?' Rattigan knew about the Piccadilly Street Woolworths fire – anyone who lived in Manchester did. Her mother knew someone who lost a brother.

'Careful lass – you'll burn it…'

Rattigan turned back to the stove, but the damage had been done. 'I'm so sorry – it's spoiled.'

'I don't mind – better than when there is none, is what I say.'

An idea came to Rattigan. 'Look, I couldn't eat this, and you shouldn't have to.' She glanced at her watch – she h still had ninety minutes before her train. 'Tell you what, why don't I nip down to the chippy – I haven't had my lunch yet. It'll be my treat. Cod and chips?'

'I couldn't let you do that…' but the woman's eyes had brightened.

'It's no trouble – like I said, I haven't eaten either, so….' She turned the stove off and smiled at Mrs. King. 'I'll be five minutes.'

'All right, love. Thank you.'

Rattigan was relieved to see no queue at the chippy. If she hurried, she could still make her train, easy. She hadn't wanted to cut the conversation short – sometimes interviewees would change their minds if you didn't seize the moment, but she didn't think Mrs. King would. She was obviously living on her own and seemed happy to talk about her long-dead son – and she was definitely in need of a good square meal.

'That smells good,' Mrs. King said as she let Rattigan back in and shuffled back to the kitchen. 'I've set you a place, but I couldn't manage the extra chair, I'm sorry, lass.'

'That's fine – I'll perch on this.' Rattigan had noticed a battered kitchen stool in the corner under the counter and pulled it out, depositing a pile of old newspapers on the floor.

They ate straight from the cartons – 'saves washing up' as Mrs. King noted- and Rattigan let the woman eat for several minutes before broaching the subject of her son again.

'So was Peter hurt in the fire?'

Mrs. King shook her head. 'No – he weren't inside by then. He said it were very odd… I still remember it, because as my late husband John - God rest his soul- said, fancy that man saving Peter, only to see him off all those years later.'

'What do you mean? Who saved him?' Rattigan put her fork down, her mind racing. Was the old lady talking about Moran?

'I don't think we ever knew his name, but I saw the appeal… Eva's daughter… I was going to give her a ring, but I couldn't find my old address book.…and she'll have moved, I thought…. It couldn't be *him*, of course, but he reminded me of the man in the paper, the one John recognised.'

'So what happened?'

'It were a while before he told us – not until Amy – God rest her soul- was born, and he got some kind of promotion at work…he said the promotion was all down to him, this man who'd saved his life.

He told Peter something... Peter would never say what it was, but he changed his university course after that.'

'So how did he save Peter? He rescued him from the fire?' Rattigan glanced quickly at her watch.

'Well, Peter had gone to get my birthday card, when this fella turned up and grabbed him. Took him right out onto street, just before the fire took hold.... Saved his life, because if Peter had been inside... there was a little lad lost his mum, and of course he wasn't the only one. At least we had Peter for a while longer...'

'Did you tell the police about this after the accident, when they released the photo-fit?'

'No, because right after we saw it, my husband had his stroke...he were poorly for months before he went, couldn't even make it to Peter and Amy's funeral... It went clean out of my mind...I'm sorry.'

'Please don't be. I'm sure it wouldn't have made any difference.' Rattigan didn't know any such thing, of course, but nothing would be gained from burdening Mrs. King with guilt. 'You had enough on your plate.'

'Aye, I did. So... Eva's lass is all right, is she?'

Rattigan nodded, her thoughts far away. The connection went even further back than they'd thought. Hammond needed to know about this...

'I'll make us a brew, you'll have one before you go?'

Rattigan shook her head. 'No, I'm fine, thanks...' It couldn't be a co-incidence, could it? She stood up. 'You've been very helpful Mrs. King, but I really have to get going – I've a train to catch, I daren't miss it.'

The old woman smiled. 'You youngsters, always dashing about... well, thank you for my dinner, love – it's been a while. There used to be a young lass two doors down who'd look in and bring me a supper from time to time. She's moved now – and I don't get out so much these days.' She put out a hand as Rattigan made to pick up the carton. 'Would you mind leaving it, lass? I can eat it tomorrow. Unless you were planning to eat it on the train, like.'

Rattigan shook her head. She'd actually been about to bin it. 'No, I wasn't. Thank you for talking to me, Mrs. King. I hope it hasn't upset you.'

'No, love, it hasn't – to tell the truth, it's nice to talk about my men-folk to anyone who'll listen. Anytime you're passing …' she smiled, and Rattigan knew the old lady wasn't really expecting her to call again. Well, maybe she'd surprise her. *Don't get involved*, Hammond had warned her often enough, quickly surmising that his DC was a sucker for a sad story. But what she did in her spare time was her own business, wasn't it? She wouldn't make promises she might not be able to keep, however. She returned the smile, and knew that Barbara King understood the rules of the game.

'Well you never know. Take care, Mrs. King.'

She barely made it to the platform in time – throwing herself into her seat, Rattigan remembered that she hadn't put the stool back, and felt guilty as she imagined the old woman struggling to slide it back under the counter. Well, maybe there was her reason to go back…

As soon as she'd recovered her breath, and as the train began pulling out of the station, she called Hammond.

He was in the canteen – she could hear the clink of cutlery and the sound of conversation around him.

'Sir, did you know that someone resembling James Moran saved Peter King from the fire at Woolworths in 'seventy-nine?'

There was a brief silence, broken by someone close to Hammond saying '…so I said to her, what d'you fucking expect…?'

'Hang on, Lucy – let me find somewhere quieter. I'll call you back.'

She imagined him hurrying along the corridor to the Gents' – the Gents loos or the fire escape were the favoured place for a call if you took one in the station canteen - and hoped the signal wouldn't drop before he got back to her. The phone began to vibrate and she stabbed 'answer' and put it to her ear. Hammond was already talking:

'Now, what was that about Peter King and Woolworths?'

'He was there, sir – with Moran, or someone who looked like him, when the fire broke out. Moran – or whoever he was- saved his life, she reckons it was the same man seen in London when her son died, her husband recognised him. Mrs. King reckons the man told King something that made him change his University course. Apparently his photo – the man, not King's- was in the newspaper after the fire – it might be possible to find it, see if it the same man … it's weird, isn't it, sir – it can't be a coincidence, can it?'

'Good work, Lucy,' Hammond said after a long moment, during which Rattigan quickly pulled the phone away from her ear to check that she still had a connection. She had the strangest feeling that her news hadn't been news at all to the DI. 'And you could be right – I'll get it looked into. Where are you now?'

There was something he wasn't telling her; she was sure of it. 'On the train, sir. Oh, I called the Clarke residence – the daughter says her father passed away. I wasn't sure if you knew.'

'No, I didn't.' There was another pause. So you're going to talk to the Aunt now?'

'I thought I would, yes – and Mrs. Morgan, too.' Rattigan wondered if Jessica Deacon also knew about the man who had saved Peter King's life. She would have said, surely, if she knew there was a connection? She could imagine Hammond nodding, his habitual frown.

'Well, keep me posted, Constable.'

'I will…' But he'd already gone, and as Rattigan made to put the mobile back in her pocket, she saw 'no signal'. She settled back for the three-hour journey, her mind sifting through the facts as they knew them, trying to fit the new information into the picture.

Hammond had mooted early on that he thought there was something about Eva Morgan's response to her daughter's kidnap that felt 'off' to him, but he hadn't been specific. Had Peter confided in his wife about what happened at Woolworths' in 'seventy-nine, or just his mother? But if he had, why would Eva not have said? Could Moran be an ex, out for some kind of twisted revenge, and if so, for what? King's fling with his wife's sister? But the age was all off – no way could the man who had kidnapped Emma be the one who saved Peter King, or who might have caused his death eleven years later.

They had been over and over this, what were they missing? It had to be Moran's father, or some other close relative. They had to find the newspaper photo of the man King claimed had saved him, the one that John King had recognised from the photo-fit in 1990, shocking him so much that he had suffered a stroke. Only then would they see if the likeness was familial, see if the connection really existed. Jessica Deacon, as a journalist, would probably be able to find newspaper archives a lot quicker than CID, Rattigan thought.

The really interesting thing about James Moran though, was that according to official records, he barely existed before the early eighties. Oh, he had two bank accounts, and he had a flat on Aspinal lane in that name, plus the house out at Rossendale in the name of Gilling- but they'd found no birth records for either name which made any sense. 'James Moran' appeared to be a legend, and not a very well-constructed one at that, as did 'James Gilling'.

So who was the man in the newspaper photo from 1979, and in the photo-fit from 1990? That they looked like the same man was obvious, but there was no way that could work - unless he had a time machine.

'What the hell do *you* want?'

Rattigan blinked, and her mouth snapped shut, shocked by the change in Tom Morgan's appearance. He might have been stressed out the first time she had met him, frantic with worry over his daughter's disappearance and ready to have a go at anyone or anything he thought might delay her safe return, but at least he had shown some semblance of keeping himself together. It had been his wife who had been almost in pieces. Now he stood blinking in the doorway of his smart London home, a shadow of the man he had been four weeks ago. He hadn't shaved in a while, his hair was uncombed, and he stank of booze and stale cigarette smoke.

Caught on the back foot, Rattigan had to clear her throat before answering; she had expected Eva to answer the door, hadn't even expected that Tom would be home; he was meant to be in rehearsals for his next play, wasn't he? Or so she had read in one of the dailies.

'I wondered if I might have a word with your wife, Mr. Morgan.' He didn't respond, 'May I come in, please?'

He stared at her for a long moment, then abruptly stood back, waving her in with exaggerated and unsteady movements.

'You can come in, but as for speaking to my wife…' he snorted, and stumbled away from Rattigan, down the tiled hall and into a large kitchen. Rattigan shut the door and followed him, wrinkling her nose. He hadn't showered in a day or two, and the house smelt stale, unaired. A prickle of apprehension ran down her spine.

'What do you mean? Sir, is your wife here?'

Morgan stood at the kitchen sink, his focus on the darkness of the garden beyond it. He sighed, and turned to face Rattigan, leaning back against the sink. He looked dreadful, a man without an anchor. His daughter was safe, but still in Manchester, out of his influence, and it looked as though his wife had left him. Clearly the safety of his daughter or his success were not enough to keep him on an even keel.

'Look around you - what do *you* think? Hmm?'

Rattigan remained in the doorway, remembering his arrest for drunk and disorderly behavior in a pub twenty-five years before, and the assault charge which had been dropped only a few weeks ago.

'Do you know where she is?'

He shrugged. 'Not with me. Not in my bed. Not in my house. Our house…' he blinked, and Rattigan realised that he was close to tears.

'I'm sorry for your trouble, Mr. Morgan. Really I am. But I would like to speak to your wife, do you have…'

'So would I, darling, so would I…' he interrupted, and stumbled away from her, through an open doorway into what looked like a utility area beyond. A moment later Rattigan heard the unmistakable sound of retching, then a toilet flushing. By the time Morgan returned a few minutes later, she had leafed through the dog-eared calendar and ascertained that Eva Morgan –if indeed it was she who kept the calendar updated – might not have been here for a week or more.

'I'm sorry. Caught me at a bad moment. Not that I have many good ones…. Coffee, tea?'

Rattigan hesitated. It was Eva Morgan she had come to see… what could Eva's second husband tell her about events in 1990? But as he stared at her, Rattigan realised that Tom Morgan was as much a victim of events in Manchester as his daughter and wife. His and Eva's marriage, already on a rocky footing, had not survived the kidnap –or even the safe return- of their daughter. She could give him five minutes, couldn't she?

'A coffee would be nice, thanks.'

Morgan set about making their drinks, appearing to feel no need to fill the silence with small talk. Rattigan pulled out a chair and prepared to sit at the heavy oak table, but Morgan, carrying both mugs, walked past her and back out into the hall.

'Not here, it's a tip.'

Rattigan couldn't argue with that; the kitchen bin overflowed with takeaway cartons, a pile of unwashed crockery littered the draining board and the table; the room stank of neglect.

The large sitting room Morgan led her into was only marginally better. A pillow at one end of the expensive leather couch spoke of sleepless nights, cups and plates sat on the hearth and the coffee table; a cracked television screen spoke of anger and frustration.

'What a lovely room,' she said. Cleaned up, she knew it would be; lined with bookshelves, paintings and family photographs, the design led the eye naturally to a large patio door which looked out onto the same garden overlooked by the kitchen window, albeit hidden in darkness. An ancient tabby cat lying on a discarded sweater under a radiator opened one eye, yawned, and went back to sleep. She wondered who had fed it when the Morgans were in Manchester.

'Thanks. Means bugger all, though, I can tell you, when you've no one to share it with.'

She hoped he wasn't going to get maudlin on her.

'I'm sorry, sir. So do you know where your wife is?'

Morgan took a long swallow of his coffee before answering. 'She's at her sister's. Don't know the address, offhand, but I'm sure you can find out.' He stared at her. 'Have you found him yet?'

Rattigan took a sip from the mug. Dow Egbert, the expensive stuff; she'd seen the jar. Well, he'd hardly be drinking Lidl's basic, would he?

'No, sir. That's part of why I'm here…'

'Your boss doesn't like me, does he?'

Rattigan didn't see what that had to do with finding the man who had abducted his daughter. But perhaps Morgan was used to being liked, maybe he found rejection hard to take – he must do, if his reaction to his wife leaving him was any indication.

'He's a copper, Mr. Morgan. It's not his job to like people, just to get to the truth.'

Morgan laughed. 'He's got you well trained. Are you two, you know…?' He winced, and shook his head. 'Sorry. Forget I said that. None of my business.'

Rattigan took a deep breath. She didn't fancy Hammond, but people sometimes mistook her enthusiasm for the job and devotion to her boss as something more.

'I'm really sorry about your situation, sir. Something like this, its… well it's hard on everyone. Harder still if there's a death.'

'Hah, I take your point. I know we're lucky, compared to some, Sergeant… as for this…' - he waved a hand, encompassing the room and by extension, the deserted house – 'well, it's been on the cards for a while. So,' he took a deep breath, and sat up a little straighter in his seat. '… you haven't found him. But you've got a new lead of some sort, something you want to ask my wife about?'

'I wouldn't say we've had any new leads, sir, but there's a couple of things that have been bugging us…me.' She put the mug down, and got out her notebook. 'This man who stepped out in front of your wife's car in 1990… did you get the feeling your wife was holding something back, sir? Like, maybe she knew him from before?'

Morgan sighed. 'She used to have nightmares about him, Sergeant Rattigan. For years. Probably still does. He caused the death of her little girl… of course she bloody knew him from before!'

Rattigan didn't flinch. 'I don't mean that, sir – I meant, did you ever get the impression that she might have known him before that… before the accident?'

'Well, I wouldn't know, would I – I met Eva in ninety-one. She didn't talk about it much, then… or at all, really. But after we married, when Emma was born… she'd have nightmares, as I said…

she'd wake up crying and screaming...sometimes she'd talk in her sleep.' He shook his head. 'She never got over losing Amy. Finding out that her husband had been shagging her sister... it was the icing on the cake. She probably won't ever get over it; I see that now. I haven't exactly helped.'

'You lost a child, didn't you, sir – your son...?'

He stiffened, then let his shoulders slump. 'Yes. He had a condition called Progeria – he was just three but he had the physiology of an eighty-year old. Look, you must know all this – it has nothing to do with what happened to Emma...'

Rattigan's pulse quickened as an idea began to form.

'Maybe not... but doesn't it strike you as a bit odd that this man, this James Moran – or whoever he really is- was interested in your daughter's field of study?' she hesitated. She didn't know if Hammond had told Morgan about the lab in the burned out house. Couldn't see what harm it would do to mention it now, even if he hadn't. 'You know that he had a makeshift lab in his home?'

Morgan started at her, his brows lifting in surprise, then dropping into a frown. 'No, I didn't... what does that mean, exactly? Do you think he was working for a rival company?'

'We're not sure, to be honest. But something about what she was working on must have drawn Moran to her...' She knew Hammond had been thinking along the same lines; but neither of them could quite see the connection. 'And then there was her first husband – he met Moran...'

'*What*?' Morgan tensed. 'Is that true? When... who told you that?'

'Just this morning, as it happens... I spoke to Peter's mother.' Rattigan knew Hammond might chew her out for divulging sensitive information, but what if Morgan knew something he didn't even know that he knew? It had to be worth a punt.

'Christ, is she still alive? What's her name...?'

'Barbara. Barbara King. Obviously...' She'd been about to warn him off harassing Mrs. King, but surely even he couldn't be that insensitive?

Morgan nodded, and ran a hand over his face. Rattigan heard the rasp of stubble against skin. 'Barbara, that's right… I remember now, she came to our wedding. She wanted to come. Eva wasn't keen, but her father thought it was a good thing, he thought it might give the poor woman something…some kind of closure maybe… I don't know. The husband was ill, he couldn't come. I don't know if it helped her, or not…Christ…how is she?'

Well that was something – Morgan was showing thought for somebody outside himself and his own misery… 'She's old, she's on her own… she has tinned soup for lunch.' A more different life to Morgan's Rattigan couldn't imagine, and felt a surge of anger at his self-indulgent wallowing. If his wife had left him, it probably had more to do with his drinking and womanizing than with anything that had happened to his daughter.

Almost as if he'd read her mind, Morgan's gaze darted about the room before coming back to her. 'I'm sorry…'

Rattigan decided to deliberately appear to misunderstand him. 'Sorry for what, sir, if you don't mind me asking? Only, it weren't… wasn't your fault her son died, was it?' thinking about Barbara King had thrown Rattigan back into the vernacular of her childhood. Morgan didn't appear to notice.

'No, of course it wasn't. But if he hadn't died, I probably wouldn't have met Eva… and I wouldn't… *we* wouldn't, have Emma…' he swallowed, and closed his eyes for a moment. 'You know how we met, don't you?'

Rattigan shook her head, giving him his head to talk. You never knew… she resisted the temptation to check her watch. If he didn't know anything that would help them, she could be wasting her time. It was getting late, and she felt tired and headachy. She'd booked into the hotel – wincing at London prices- and come straight out to Morgan's place. She hadn't eaten since half a fish dinner at Mrs. King's. But she'd led him down this conversational path; the least she could do was hear him out.

'I don't, sir. Is it relevant?'

Morgan looked at her. 'Probably not....' He stood up. 'Look, you caught me at a bad time...I wouldn't expect you to understand, but despite what you or your boss might think, I do love my wife. All this, it's, well, it knocked the stuffing out of me, that's all.' The coffee had finally begun to sober him up, and he was embarrassed. Rattigan decided to cut him some slack, but it was obvious that he didn't know anything useful.

'I understand, sir. Look, I really should be going... Thank you for the coffee.'

'No problem. I'll show you out...' he stopped, and turned to look at her. 'How'd you get here? Drive?'

Rattigan shook her head. If he was going to offer her a lift, he could forget it – he had to be way over the limit. 'No, sir - train, then taxi.'

'Jesus. Your boss sign off on that?'

'Well, he knows I'm here ....' Not that it was any of his business.

Morgan smiled. 'Probably don't get down here much, do you? Ever been before?'

Rattigan wasn't sure she liked where this might be going. 'A few times. I can't say as I'd like to live here, mind...'

'Where are you staying? Don't tell me it's a Travelodge...?'

'No, sir, it isn't.' She had no intention of telling him.

He shook his head ruefully. 'Look, Sergeant Rattigan...' he swallowed, and ploughed on, undaunted. 'As you can see, I've not been dealing with this very well...I apologise if I was in any way rude to you earlier. Can we start over? Have you eaten?'

She sighed inwardly. Men, they were all the same, weren't they? 'I'll be heading back to my hotel for supper now, sir. I suggest you fix yourself a meal, it might help to soak up the alcohol.' *And freshen up,* she wanted to add. Even disheveled and unwashed, the man had a magnetism about him that Rattigan could see women falling for. But not her, not now.

Morgan nodded, in no way abashed. 'I could do that. I was actually going to suggest going out for a meal...I'd pay, and for the taxi. Less for your boss to complain about. What do you say?' he hesitated. 'This isn't some cheap pick up line, if that's what you're thinking. You have to be what, a couple of years older than my daughter. I could just... I could do with the company, with doing something normal...'

'I appreciate the offer, sir, really I do. But I don't think it would be a good idea, do you?'

Morgan shrugged, trying to pretend he didn't mind, wasn't hurt. 'You're probably right. Look, I really don't have my sister-in-law's address, but my father-in-law will. Do you want his number?'

Rattigan nodded. She could call the station, get it from CID, but it would cost nothing to let Morgan feel he'd been useful in some way. 'That would be very helpful sir, thank you.'

'Good. And its Tom, please...at least let me call you a taxi.' He put his coffee cup down on the hall table and pulled a mobile out of his pocket. She wrote down the number he rattled off, and when he held out his hand, smiled at him and shook it. To her relief, he didn't hold onto it for any longer than was necessary.

'Thank you for the number. And I'll be fine – I'll walk up to the main road and call the firm I used before– it'll make it a bit cheaper.' Why was she even explaining herself to him?

'Okay, I know when I'm not wanted. Seriously, thank you for coming –I appreciate the wakeup call, Lucy.' He opened the door, and stood back.

She walked up the path, her cheeks flaming, and was glad it was dark and that he couldn't see her face. He'd remembered her name all along. But then he was an actor, wasn't he – they had to remember lines, stage directions... she knew he was standing in the open doorway, watching her leave, but she wasn't going to look back. She might feel sorry for him, but she wasn't about to become another notch on his belt.

43: 14TH NOVEMBER 9:30AM

'Hello, Sergeant Rattigan. You'd better come in.'

Rattigan stepped into the small entrance hall. 'I'm glad I found you, Mrs. Morgan. I was also hoping speak to your sister, Jessica, is she here?'

'Please, call me Eva. I'm afraid she isn't – she told me that you would be calling, and had hoped to be here, but she was called into the office an hour ago. I'm not sure how long she might be.'

Rattigan was disappointed. Was it a coincidence, or a fabrication on Jessica's part? But Rattigan hadn't divulged anything during the short conversation she had with the journalist on her way back to the hotel, and Jessica wasn't exactly under suspicion. She would keep.

Unlike her husband, Eva Morgan looked better than the last time Rattigan had seen her. She seemed calm and looked well-groomed, her sleek black bob topping an attractive ensemble of a black knee-length skirt and a soft cashmere sweater in a pale green, which emphasized her eye colour. Black court shoes clicked confidently on the wooden floor as she led Rattigan into a large, high-ceilinged kitchen.

The morning had dawned bright and crisp, an antidote to a night of broken sleep, thanks to the noisy life next to her hotel room and the thoughts churning around her head. Situated in an unremarkable mid-terrace in an endless street of similar houses in the suburb of Turnham Green, it had taken Rattigan an hour by tube and then a good thirty-minute walk to find Jessica Deacon's home.; but now she was knackered. She'd eaten a very unsatisfactory burger from a take-away and had gone to bed feeling tired, the greasy food sitting uneasily on her stomach. The hotel breakfast had restored her, but now the long walk in bright sunshine had brought last night's travel headache back. She was relieved when Eva offered her a drink.

'I'd love a cup of tea – one sugar, a mugful if you have it. It's a bit of a hike from the tube, isn't it?'

'You didn't get the bus?'

Rattigan hadn't even thought of that, and filed it away for the return journey she didn't even want to contemplate yet. 'I didn't know there was one, but it was such a lovely morning…' she followed Eva into the kitchen.

'There's a stop just across the road, you'll want the 12A going back.' Eva filled the kettle, switched it on, fetched mugs and smiled at her guest. She seemed quite at home in her sister's house, a woman she hadn't spoken too for the best part of three decades. 'I've got to know the bus routes quite well,' she added. 'At the moment most of the documentation I need for my work is still at Irene Road.'

'Thank you, I'll remember that.'

'I understand that you spoke to my father this morning.'

Rattigan had quite a long chat with George Deacon before setting out – like many of his generation, he was an early riser and had not been at all fazed by Rattigan's seven-thirty am call. He confided in her that he had been somewhat upset his granddaughter hadn't come 'home' after her ordeal; he very much wanted to see her, but 'couldn't take the travelling.' He was a Londoner through-and-through. Rattigan wondered when Eva had decided she didn't want to sound like her father, and why.

'Yes, mainly to get your sister's address, since your husband didn't seem to know it. I didn't realise you and your husband had separated. I'm sorry.' She didn't actually care one way or the other, but it felt like the right thing to say.

Eva waved Rattigan's apology away. She seemed almost like another person: but perhaps she was just more like herself than she'd been in Manchester. That she wasn't taking whatever medication she had been on then, was obvious.

'So am I. But things hadn't been right for a long time. So, what can I help you with, Constable Rattigan?'

Eva might seem outwardly relaxed, but now Rattigan saw tension in the way she smoothed her skirt, fiddled with her gold bracelet, and kept checking the kettle.

'I just wanted to follow up on a few things we talked about before… about James Moran, and what happened in nineteen-ninety. I know we've asked you this before, but are you certain that you didn't know him before the accident at all?' The kettle came to the boil and turned itself off in the sudden silence.

'Just let me make these – we'll take them through to the lounge, it's more comfortable.'

'Of course.' Was Eva buying time to get her story straight?

The walls of Jessica Deacon's lounge were covered by art deco prints; magazines lay in organised piles around the room, and a floor-to-ceiling shelf groaned with books on every conceivable subject.

As they sat – Eva in an armchair to the left of the fireplace, Rattigan in another one opposite to it, Rattigan followed Eva's glance to a professionally-framed black and white photograph sitting on the mantelpiece. It was a family portrait: Eva being hugged by a dark-haired, bearded man with a wide, toothy grin, and a little girl in Eva's arms of no more than three with blond curls and the same wide-set eyes as her mother. They were all wearing winter clothing, and the little girl was throwing a handful of autumn leaves into the air. Rattigan wondered who had taken the photograph, and whether it was a reminder for Jessica of her betrayal or a reminder of happier times? Probably both.

'My sister took the picture…' Eva explained. 'Amy was three years old.'

Rattigan nodded. 'She was very pretty.' What else could she say? She ploughed on.

'So… James Moran, Eva. Were you telling the truth when you told Inspector Hammond that you had no knowledge of him prior to the accident in nineteen-ninety?'

Eva nodded. 'Yes, I was. Why would you think otherwise?'

'Because it seems too coincidental, Eva. First, James Moran is present – and according to witnesses was very probably the cause - at the accident which killed your husband and daughter…and then, twenty-eight years later, he tries to sabotage your daughter's work, and then kidnaps her. You know that Emma is claiming that he mistook her for his daughter… a daughter we have been unable to trace…?'

Eva's eyes widened, and she put her coffee cup on the occasional table beside her chair with a clatter, spilling some of the contents. 'Do you think this man is Emma's *father*? You do, don't you? Well he isn't - Tom is Emma's father. Do a paternity test if you don't believe me!' She shook her head. 'Why would he say such a thing?'

'We don't know, Eva. He did recant it, apparently – it's why he let Emma go, he told her that he'd made a mistake. But have you noticed that your daughter and James Moran both have green eyes? It may be that a paternity test would prove him wrong, if we can find him.' Rattigan wasn't at all sure they would have grounds for such a test – Emma hadn't been murdered, after all – she had been set free to go about her business. Perhaps there was nothing more to it than that – a case of mistaken identity. But Rattigan didn't think so, and she knew Hammond didn't, either. And what if Moran decided that someone else looked like his imaginary daughter?

Eva nodded. 'Yes…I did notice it, when Inspector Hammond showed me his security identification. As I expect you know -or you wouldn't be asking- Green eyes are quite rare, per head of population. But I promise you, there is no *way* that Emma could possibly be his daughter. I hope you haven't said this to my husband?' The idea seemed to distress her.

'No, we haven't, and I apologise if the suggestion upsets you. But it's rare for someone to do what Moran -or someone who may be related to him- did, targeting you and your family in this way, unless there is *some* connection…do you see what I'm saying?'

Eva looked down at her hands, fingering her wedding ring.

'I used to dream about… a man,' she said suddenly. 'After… the accident. I don't know who he was, not for sure, I never saw his face. But I felt as if I should know him…it wasn't Peter, and of course it wasn't Tom, because I didn't meet him until a year after it happened. I used to think it was the man who stepped out in front of the car… now, I don't know. I saw the photo-fit, Lucy, and I agree that it does look like the man who took Emma - but it's quite impossible for it to *be* him, isn't it?' She took a deep breath then let it out slowly, as if letting the pain of the memory go, but carefully, in case it might still overwhelm her even after all this time. 'Have you ever lost anyone close to you, Lucy?'

Rattigan nodded. 'My dad… ten years ago. He was ill, and it was very quick, in the end.'

Eva nodded. 'Then you know. But unless you've lost a child…'

Rattigan shook her head.

'There's a hole there…' Eva put a hand to her breast, above her heart. 'It never quite goes away. Whatever else you do, whoever you meet, whoever you might fall in love with, however many children you might go on to have…you can never forget, and you can never replace the child you lost. You will always wonder… 'what if'? Birthdays are the worst. Amy would have been thirty-one years old, Lucy. She might have been a mother herself…' she swallowed. 'I love Emma. I have found it hard to show, and harder perhaps to admit to myself that I was afraid I might lose her, too. It felt safer not to get too close… When she disappeared, I thought…well, you can imagine. So when he…when that man let her go, whoever he is, I made the decision that my life was going to be different. No more living in the past, letting fear of what might not ever happen rule my life.' She grimaced, a not-quite-smile. 'If James Moran *was* Emma's father, or if I knew him, I would tell you. But he isn't, and I don't. So I'm sorry, I don't think I can help you.'

'Did you know that Peter knew Moran?'

The colour drained from Eva's face. 'What? No, no, I didn't – where did you hear that?'

'From his mother, Barbara King. I spoke to her yesterday. She asked after you,' Rattigan added.

Eva's lips twisted, her chin wobbling as she tried to control her emotions. 'Barbara...I haven't spoken to her for a very long time. I couldn't... how is she?'

'She's doing okay. She knew she lost her husband?'

Eva pulled a small cotton handkerchief from her sleeve and blew her nose. 'No, I didn't. She came when Tom and I got married, and I knew he was ill then, we were all surprised she came. I'm sorry to hear that. I should have...' she sighed. 'It's water under the bridge now. So how did Peter know him? Are you sure it wasn't Moran's father? Because for Peter to know the man who took Emma... well, we've been over that already.'

'To be honest, Eva, we don't know *who* it was. But Mrs. King told me that a man resembling James Moran saved her son from the Woolworth's fire in 'seventy-nine. And we have another witness who can place him there, too. His photo was in a newspaper at the time. If we can find it...'

Eva began to cry, silently at first, then deep, racking sobs. 'Who are these men? Why are they doing this...?'

'That's what we're trying to find out, Eva. Emma was returned unharmed, but Moran is still out there, and we can't be sure he won't take someone else. It appears to be personal to your family, but we don't know that for sure. If we could just pin down the connection...'

'Does Emma know? I begged her to come back with me, at least for a while, at least until he was caught... but she refused to come. I know her work is important to her, but she's important to us! I know Inspector Hammond thought she might be complicit, but I can't imagine why she would do something like that...'

'I don't know, but I doubt it.' Would Hammond have told Emma? She doubted it.

'When are you going back? I'll come with you.' Eva stood up. 'It won't take me a moment to pack a bag. And I must tell my sister.'

44: NOVEMBER 14TH, 7:00PM

Fourteen days ago, Moran had abandoned the car on a run-down council estate – knowing it would soon be stripped and probably burned out- and under cover of darkness had raided a clothes bank. His appearance now gave him the appearance of someone who was what he had been for the last month and a half: homeless. He had shaved his head before leaving the house for the last time, dropping the cuttings into a puddle of accelerant, but now his hair was begging to grow through again – he was keeping it covered with a woolen cap. He had continued to age, but not so that he would be unrecognizable - he couldn't relax just yet.

Moran estimated that he was ageing at the rate of one decade for each month. If his lifespan was now normal, he would probably have less than six months to live. The police would be looking for a man in his forties – very soon, he would be invisible to them. In the meantime, it would probably have been prudent to leave the area. But Emma was his only family now – he couldn't bear the idea that he might be unable to make his way back to the city, that he might lose her. He had considered going to London to look for his father, but what would be the point? He could hardly introduce himself. And he had to know what progress Emma was making. He would give it another month, and then try to make contact. It would be safe enough to wait for her near the Xeon building - no one would look twice at an old man…if he knew things were going well, could see it in her eyes, he could die content, if not happy.

A gaggle of young men surged past him, laughing and leaping about with the energy of youth, fueled by alcohol. One of them swiped at Moran's head, whipping the cap off.

'Thanks Granddad – just what I need!' Hollering and whooping, they ran off down the road, taking it in turns to put the cap on before dropping it in the gutter. Moran muttered, like the old man he was rapidly becoming. Well, if they thought he was a grandfather…. he wondered if he ever would be.

Moran knew that he would never see Cassie again. That he was going to die here, trapped in his own past, homeless and unknown by all but a few, was a price worth paying for his daughter's life…. He stumbled, his foot catching on the uneven pavement, and so did not see the patrol car drive slowly past and stop, or the two uniformed men look at each other and get out of the car, heading across the pavement in his direction.

As Moran reached for the door of the homeless shelter, his hands were pulled behind him. He cried out in pain as newly arthritic joints protested.

'James Moran, I'm arresting you for the abduction and false imprisonment of Emma Morgan…'

'Hold up, Dave – are you sure this is him? Looks like his dad…'

Hands fumbled in Moran's pockets, pulling something out. As the second officer pulled him away from the door to allow a sickly man Moran knew as Rafferty to exit the building, Moran saw what the young man had pulled from his pocket – a tattered magazine clipping. It was the only thing he had saved from the house – Emma's portrait, from her aunt's interview. He'd kept it because it reminded him of Cassie, and it had been a mistake.

The man's lips tightened. 'It's him.'

45: NOVEMBER 14TH, 7.30PM

'Boss, you'll never guess who uniform just picked up!' Flynn could barely contain his excitement.

Juggling the mobile and his coat, Hammond dropped the warm fish supper onto his kitchen table and transferred the phone to his right hand.

'Surprise me.'

'Only James bloody Moran. But boss...he's not looking in great shape.'

'Bloody hell. I'll be there in five.'

He stared at the fish supper. 'Sod it.' He snatched it up and headed for the door.

Hammond nodded at the constable standing in the corridor outside interview room one.

'OK, Bob.' He'd got chip grease on his tie, he realised as he pulled it into shape. Bob Jenks tactfully avoided looking at it, but Hammond didn't care. They'd got Moran!

PC Jenks shut the door behind him, leaving Hammond and Flynn alone with the room's occupant.

Hammond put two cups of coffee down on the table, took the file he'd clamped under one arm and put it down beside the two paper cups. He unbuttoned his jacket, and sat down. He stared at Moran for a few moments, sizing him up as Flynn broke the seal on two cassette tapes. A shiver ran down Hammond's spine: the man sitting across the table was recognizably James Moran, but he looked older than his Xeon ID. How was that possible? This man had to be in his mid-fifties at least, with a compact, stocky build. His silver hair was close-cropped. Ex-military, perhaps. His eyes, a vivid green, were wide-set and although blood-shot, stared steadily back at Hammond. Hammond had the unsettling notion that Moran knew the drill, might even have been arrested before. He nodded at Flynn. 'Let's crack on.'

'Interview tape one, 14th November, twenty eighteen, time is twenty-oh-five. Present are myself, Detective Sergeant Joseph Flynn and Detective Inspector Ian Hammond, and the interview subject – would you state your name for the tape, please sir?'

'James Moran.'

'So… James Moran – is that even your real name?' Hammond pushed one of the paper cups across the table to Moran, who didn't even glance at it, but continued to regard Hammond.

'It is.' Moran's eyes flicked to Flynn, to Hammond's coffee, and finally to the cup in front of him. One corner of his mouth twitched – in amusement?

Hammond suddenly felt eight years old again; a child, patronised by an adult intent on other purposes. He cleared his throat.

'Well, that's strange, because we've got no record of *you*. James *Arthur* Moran died in nineteen-seventy-four. Funny, that, don't you reckon?'

Moran cocked his head on one side. 'Have we met before, Inspector Hammond?'

Something cold slid down Hammond's back; sweat. The fish supper he'd eaten on the drive to the station sat uneasily in his stomach. 'I'm asking the questions.'

Moran nodded, as if he expected nothing else.

'So why don't you tell me the truth, Moran? Starting with why you abducted Emma Morgan, why you've been targeting her family…your connection to Peter King.'

Moran stared at Hammond for a moment, then his eyes slid down to the cup in front of him. 'Thank you,' he said, and drained the contents in one go. 'If I were to tell you the truth, Inspector, you wouldn't believe me.'

'Let me be the judge of that.' Hammond opened the folder, removed Clarke's photo-fit of Moran and slid it across the table. Moran's eyes flicked down to the image, and back to Hammond. Waiting for the question.

'DI Hammond is showing the suspect a photo-fit image, evidence number EM two-one-a.' Constable Flynn said for the tape.

'Is this you?'

Moran inclined his head.

'For the tape, please.'

'It would appear to be a passable representation of my face, yes.'

Hammond took a deep breath.

'So tell me what happened on the night of the thirty-first of December, nineteen-ninety.'

'I have been arrested for the abduction and false imprisonment of Emma Morgan,' Moran said calmly. 'This is not relevant.'

'Peter King, the man who died that night, and his daughter, are related to Emma Morgan – King was her mother's first husband. The little girl who also died in the crash would have been Emma Morgan's half-sister.'

'Again, how is this relevant?' Moran shifted in his chair, wincing.

'That photo-fit was assembled twenty-eight years ago. You must have been, what, thirty-five, maybe forty years old? If it isn't you, who is it - your father, an uncle?'

'No comment.'

'All right, then – let's talk about nineteen seventy-nine, shall we?'

Moran couldn't hide his shock. Hammond felt a stab of satisfaction, and didn't give Moran time to reply. 'Who was it that saved Peter King from the Woolworth's? We know that someone who looked just like you was there. So… I'll ask you - who was Eva King to you then, and who are Eva Morgan – and her daughter Emma – to you now?'

Moran closed his eyes. A muscle in his jaw jumped. 'It was a mistake, Inspector. I was in the wrong place at the wrong time.' He opened his eyes again. 'I very much regret the deaths of Mrs. King's husband and her daughter.'

Well, at least he'd dropped the 'no comment' routine. 'Did you *know* that Emma Morgan's mother was Peter King's widow when you took her?'

Something flickered across Moran's face. He closed his eyes, as if in pain. 'I did not.'

'But you knew before I mentioned it just now. Who told you?'

'It isn't relevant.' Moran had closed his eyes again.

'Did you and Eva Morgan have a relationship?'

Again Moran looked surprised, his eyes flicking open. 'No, we did not, Inspector.'

'I think you did. Perhaps you wanted to get her husband out of the way, and perhaps she found out what you'd done, and rejected you. So you took her daughter away.'

Moran snorted. 'Speculation and fantasy. I had no reason – *have* no reason – to harm either Emma Morgan *or* her mother.'

'You caused the death of her husband, and her little girl. A case of mistaken identity? Twice? You must think I was born yesterday, Moran. You thought Emma was your daughter, Cassie, didn't you? Who, I'm telling you now, we haven't found hide nor hair of – she doesn't exist.'

Moran's eyes narrowed. 'Emma told you…. No matter. Yes, that *is* what I am asking you to believe.'

'So it's all one big, *amazing* co-incidence that someone who looks just like you saves Peter King's life in nineteen-seventy-nine, causes his -and his six-year-old daughter's- death in nineteen-ninety, and then abducts his widow's second daughter two months ago?' Hammond leant back in his chair. *Keep calm.*

'I have explained the mistake, and apologised. Does Miss Morgan wish to press charges?'

'Don't get smart with me. Answer the question. Who *were* those men? What's this all about, Moran? Or whatever your name really is.'

'There is no need to bully me, Inspector. I can only tell you what happened, and how very much I regret it. The deaths of Mr. King and his daughter *were* an accident, as the police report and the witnesses will confirm... and the abduction of Emma Morgan was ... as she has told you, and as I have now confirmed... a simple case of mistaken identity.'

'So you want me to believe that it was you in nineteen-ninety? Got a painting in your attic, have you?'

Moran frowned, as if he didn't get the reference.

'I can't tell you what you want to know, Inspector Hammond.'

Moran was good at this. Hammond's frustration grew. He knew his anger was starting to get the better of him. He should stop the interview now, have Moran banged up in a cell overnight, and tackle him in the morning.

'I think you can, you just won't. Who are you protecting? Who the hell *are* you, 'James Moran'? And *don't* tell me that's your real name, because we both know it isn't. Why did you try -and fail, I might add- to sabotage Emma Morgan's work before you decided to abduct her? Your C.V. is full of holes... but it's pretty obvious from the property you torched that you're no security guard. Who are you working for?'

'I'm not working for anyone.'

Hammond suddenly reached across the table. 'Interview paused at...' he glanced at his watch 'Eight fifteen. Let's talk about nineteen-seventy-nine again. Was that you?'

'I have already explained...'

'No, you haven't. I was there too, you know.'

Moran stared at him. Was it fear that Hammond could see in his eyes?

'Explain.'

Cheeky bastard. 'I *saw* you. In the store, frog-marching Peter King out, just before the fire. You nearly knocked me over, Moran. I was eight years old, and I lost my *mother* that day.'

Moran's face had paled. He stared at Hammond, his eyes narrowing.

Got him. 'It *was* you, wasn't it? I don't know how it could be, but it was. You spoke to me. I asked you if you'd seen my mother, and you told me you hadn't.'

Now Moran closed his eyes, as if trying to recall the memory. When he opened them again, he looked sad. 'Yes. I do remember you. And I can't tell you any more now than I could then.'

'But you saw her? You *saw* my mother?'

'Boss….?'

Hammond had forgotten Flynn's presence. 'As you were, Sergeant. I'll explain later.' He stared at Moran.

'I did, yes.'

'Then why did you tell me you hadn't?'

'Because it wouldn't have changed the outcome.'

'What *outcome*? What do you mean?' Hammond stood up, his chair teetering on two legs before falling back down with a clatter.

'I couldn't interfere. And that's all I can tell you, because it's all I know.'

'You're lying.' He was so close… Moran knew, he had to. Why wouldn't he just… 'Why are you lying?'

'I'm sorry, Inspector. That is all I can tell you.'

'Bullshit!' Hammond stood up and made for the door. He heard Flynn turn the tape machine back on.

'DI Hammond is leaving the room. Interview terminated at eight-sixteen. Boss, are you coming back…?'

Hammond barely made it to the Gents in time.

46: NOVEMBER 15TH 08:30 AM

'What's going on, Hammond?'

Gone was Surridge's easy-going manner. His lanky frame seemed to fill Hammond's office, and the DI had to fight a compulsion to offer the Chief Inspector his own chair. He stood, nonetheless, putting them on equal footing. 'Sir. We now have Emma Morgan's kidnapper in custody.'

'I'm well aware of that, Hammond. What I'm not clear on is why I had to hear it second hand, from idle chatter on the stairs.'

Hammond uttered silent thanks to Flynn – at least he'd kept quiet about Hammond losing it. But he had broken the rules, turning the tape off. Flynn would be questioned about it, and he might not be prepared to lie outright.

'Apologies, sir, my error. Traffic brought him in last night – he'd been living in a shelter for the homeless. I conducted a preliminary interview which I'll be resuming shortly…' The truth was, he hadn't given it a thought … he'd slept -briefly- in the office, reviewing the case files, preparing himself for another session with Moran. He felt – and looked- like shit, he knew.

Surridge wasn't happy. 'Are you all right, Ian?'

'Yes, sir. I had a dodgy take-away last night…'

'I've done my share of overnighters in the office, Ian – when you've got a murderer on the loose, it's par for the course. But Moran let Emma Morgan go…and I hear that she doesn't want to press charges… we may, of course, but it's hardly cause for sleeping in the office, is it? Or is there something that you haven't told me?'

If ever there was a time to confess the link to his own personal circumstances, this would be it. But the words wouldn't come. He didn't want to be taken off the case, not yet. He shook his head. 'No, sir. A lapse of judgement on my part, perhaps…' he was floundering.

'You don't want too many of those on your record, Ian.' Abruptly, Surridge seemed to lose interest in the conversation. He turned away, putting a hand on the door he had pulled shut only minutes before. 'Keep me informed, won't you? But if you haven't already, start assigning your team to other cases… the Didsbury hit and run, for instance. It's the fifth this year…' He opened the door, his grey eyes boring into Hammond's.

'Yes sir, of course.' Hammond had never fancied himself a 'yes' man, and Surridge knew he wasn't one. But the Chief Inspector merely nodded. 'Good.' He turned and walked away.

Hammond flopped back into his chair. Glancing at his watch, he saw that it was eight-thirty. He'd find Flynn, thank him for his discretion, and see if he wanted to sit in on the next interview. His mobile buzzed, sliding across the desk. He snatched it up.

'Lucy.' She didn't know they had Moran – he'd completely forgotten to call her.

'Morning, sir. I should be with you by early afternoon, I reckon.'

'Fine. But you didn't ring just to tell me that… but I've got some news, anyway. We've got Moran.'

'Really? Bloody hell, sir! What's he said?'

'Not much, yet – acknowledges he was in Woolworths in 'seventy-nine, says the deaths of King and his daughter death was an 'accident' – and maintains that he thought Emma was his daughter. How'd it go with Eva Morgan?'

'Erm… she's with me now, sir. Not *with* me, with me… I'm in the loo on the train. But Mrs. Morgan and her sister are travelling back with me. Neither of them admit to knowing that Peter had earlier contact with… whoever it was, and I believe them. Sir… I suggested to Eva Morgan that Moran might be Emma's father... she wasn't best pleased, denied it outright. I said I thought that a paternity test, if we find Moran, might prove he was mistaken... or, you know, otherwise. I didn't say that, but... Well, I just thought you should know, sir, in case...Do you want me to tell her that we've got him?'

'No – let's keep it to ourselves until they get here, shall we? What about the father?'

'I don't know if Eva has spoken to him – they've separated, but she seemed pretty upset when she thought we might have talked about Emma's parentage to him. I didn't, sir – I only thought of it when I was talking to her.'

'Christ, Lucy, you've been stirring it up a bit, haven't you?'

'Sorry sir. I just thought it might startle some birds out of the trees, as my dad used to say.'

Hammond felt his mouth curve into a smile. 'It's a good thought, but I wish you'd run it by me first. Never mind- do you believe her about Emma's father?'

'I don't know, sir. Maybe. So you don't know yet if there's Moran family involvement?'

'Nope. But there's something a bit odd going on with Moran... looks like he's aged ten years since his Xeon ID photo. I'm guessing they wouldn't Photoshop their security guard IDs, so I'm not sure what the hell is going on with him.'

'Sounds weird, sir. I'll have to go, someone's banging on the door...'

Hammond pondered the legitimacy of a paternity test to prove -or disprove- that Moran might be Emma's father. He didn't think they'd have justification for it, in the circumstances... but if they did the test and it proved that Emma and Moran *were* related... well, that would be interesting, wouldn't it? It might bolster Hammond's somewhat shaky theory that Moran and Eva might have had a relationship... maybe Moran had had his sights on Eva even when she was married to King? Except Rattigan believed Eva's claim that she didn't know him before nineteen-ninety...

47: 15TH NOVEMBER 10:00AM

Hammond eyed Moran across the table. After his conversation with Rattigan, he had changed his mind about having another go at Moran right away. He'd been home, had shaved, showered, and put on fresh clothes. Apart from a stiff neck, where he'd slept awkwardly at his desk, he felt close to normal, but jittery. Moran had to know something more about his mother, and his claim that he had been at all three events couldn't be true, even if Hammond felt convinced that the man sitting across the table was the same man his eight-year-old-self had encountered. Never had he felt so convinced that something so impossible was the truth; it went against everything he believed in as a detective: the facts were king, if they didn't stack up, nothing could be proved.

He should have waited, yesterday – let Moran cool his heels overnight, instead of wading in and having a go at him, letting his frustration and his need get the better of him… now he was on the back foot, and Moran knew it. Hammond had revealed his hand, and Moran was probably just going to keep denying everything. They could get him on abduction and false imprisonment, even without Emma's agreement. His defense would probably get him a reduced sentence, citing diminished responsibility, the balance of his mind being disturbed by the death of a daughter they couldn't prove even existed.... Perhaps he should just be content with that, stop chasing after the rest of it.

'Mr. Moran. James. I will ask you again: why did you abduct Emma Morgan from the corner of Rusholme Street on the 28th September, twenty-eighteen?'

Moran stared at him. He frowned. 'I have already told you – I thought she was my daughter.'

'You don't *have* a daughter.'

Morgan compressed his lips. 'No comment.'

'Okay.... Let's move on. Why did you torch your own home? What were you trying to hide?'

'I can't answer your questions, Inspector.'

'Are you working for someone else? Is that it? A rival research company?'

'I am not working for anyone else.'

'I think that Emma Morgan is your daughter. I think you had an affair with Eva Morgan, and Emma is the result.'

Moran's eyes widened in alarm. 'That is not true.'

'It *is*. I can see it in your eyes.' Now who was on the back foot?

'You see nothing, Inspector Hammond. Emma Morgan is *not* my daughter.' But Moran looked worried. Hammond decided to press home his advantage.

'What if we were to do a paternity test?' Beside Hammond, Flynn fidgeted – Hammond had briefly appraised him of Rattigan's news, and of his theory that Eva Morgan and James Moran – or someone related to him- had been in a relationship, but Flynn, perhaps understandably, hadn't seemed altogether convinced.

Moran shook his head. 'I am *not* Emma Morgan's father, Inspector. You are disrespecting her parents by even suggesting such a thing.'

'*Then tell me what it was all about*! Come on, Moran, help me out, here! What was, is, the man in Woolworths in 'seventy-nine to you, and why do you say that the deaths of Mrs. Morgan's first husband and daughter in 'nineteen-ninety were 'an accident'? Why did you sabotage Emma Morgan's work and then kidnap her? What is it about her work that so disturbs you?' It was a stab in the dark... but Moran was unbending.

'I can neither confirm nor deny anything. I have said all I am going to say.'

'What was the *point* of it all? Tell me that!'

'There *is* no point, Inspector. No point at all. Whatever happens to me now, whatever you or your justice system might do to me...it can't change what has happened, what *will* happen. I'm part of it... I always was, I just didn't see it.' Moran sat back in his chair. He seemed tired, as if the words had taken something out of him.

'Boss...' Flynn saw Hammond's hand reaching for the tape machine.

'Yes, yes... Mr. Moran, I am going to recommend you for psychiatric evaluation. What d'you say to that?'

Hammond's finger hovered over the recording machine. His whole body was shaking, and both Moran and Flynn must be able to see it. I need to calm it down... but he couldn't. Somehow, it was all tied up, wasn't it – Moran, the Morgans, Peter King, his mother...but how? He couldn't see it... nausea bubbled in his gut.

Moran shrugged. 'I have nothing more to say, Inspector. You must do as you see fit.' He turned tired eyes to Flynn. 'May I go back to my cell now?'

'Interview terminated at ten-twenty-two.' Flynn got the words out just before Hammond pressed the switch. He glanced at Hammond, then went to the door and summoned the duty sergeant. Hammond also stood up, and leaned over the table. He knew his behavioiur was unprofessional, but suddenly he didn't care.

'This isn't over, Moran. You might be trying to pass yourself off as delusional, but I'll have the truth from you.'

On the stairs, Flynn cleared his throat. 'You really think he's bonkers, sir?'

Hammond thought about reprimanding his Sergeant, reminding him that 'bonkers' wasn't exactly politically correct for what might be

Moran's problem, but decided that after his own behavior, he'd be better not to throw stones.

'No, Flynn, I bloody don't. I think he's very smart, and he's got some game plan, some agenda... I just wish I bloody knew what it was.'

48: NOVEMBER 15TH 11:00AM

The cell Moran had spent the night in had no natural daylight. The polished steel door, with its round observation port, reminded him of the UEPA cells, and the last interview he had conducted before Gilling had changed his life forever. He thought about the last time he had seen Cassie, and about how he now knew that he would never see her again. Reluctantly, he thought about the detective who had just interviewed him. That he was the adult version of the small boy he had met in nineteen-seventy-nine, Moran had no doubt. He wished he could give Ian Hammond the closure he so clearly needed, but he genuinely didn't know what might have happened to Hammond's mother; he only knew that she had fallen on the stairs because of him. If her body had never been recovered, then she must still be alive somewhere, but perhaps with no memory of the son she had inadvertently abandoned. It was his fault, he knew without a doubt, but what good could that knowledge possibly do for Hammond?

He had slept very little the previous night, and now that Moran saw just how close Hammond was to uncovering the truth about his relationship to Emma Morgan, fear for Cassie's life had returned tenfold. Because if Hammond were to follow through on his threat to run a paternity test, it could, very likely would, ruin everything. It wouldn't show Hammond what he was expecting, but it would expose *a* familial link between himself and Emma, and how could that be explained? He couldn't simply pass himself off as a previously-unknown relative on Eva's side, because of course his DNA would also show Tom Morgan as a close match. That in itself would raise questions that would be impossible to answer without revealing everything he had tried so hard to keep secret. And then, there was the matter of his own rapidly advancing age, and his DNA, which contained the coveted Methuselah gene. The gene would become public knowledge, and Emma's attempts to limit its use would come to nothing. Unless… could Emma could find a way to use his deterioration to demonstrate that the gene therapy couldn't, *mustn't* be used…? He was no scientist, but if anyone would be able to work out a way… he had to speak to her again, or find a way to get word to her… he lay down on the thin mattress, wincing as his rapidly ageing body protested. Would he have time?

49: NOVEMBER 15TH 2:30PM

'Mum? What's wrong? Is it Dad?'

'Darling – has no one told you?' There was noise in the background – voices, a garbled announcement; she could barely hear what Eva was saying. Cold fear settled somewhere in her chest.

'What? Have I been told what, Mum? What's happening? Is Dad…?' Emma had tried to push her concern for her father's state of mind to the back of her own, but now it returned.

'It's not about your father. Inspector Hammond hasn't told you?'

'Told me *what*, Mum?' Relief came out as frustration. Why couldn't she just *say*?

'They've got him – the man who took you. James Moran.'

Emma stood up, her workstation stool scraping on the lab floor. She could sense Archie's concerned glance, but didn't have time to worry about him. Moran, arrested?

'When? Is he all …' She bit the words off – her reaction was all wrong. She should be relieved, not concerned for Moran. 'I mean, how and when?'

There was a short pause. 'I don't know the details, darling. But Jess and I are on the train – we'll be with you in a few hours. It's over, you're …'

Emma's mobile bleeped, signifying a lost connection. She hit speed dial, but got only voicemail. 'Mum, please ring me back!' She waited, starting at the mobile, willing it to ring, but it remained silent. She had to hope that her mother might not have heard her properly...

If Moran was in custody, how long would it be before he found himself in the health system? Despite the finality of their parting, Emma had thought about him almost constantly – he was her grandson, and since last seeing him, Emma had slowly come to accept it, no matter how impossible it seemed. She had felt the connection even before he had made himself known to her, hadn't she? She'd thought his interest in her was the usual... but now, with hindsight, she realised that he had been waiting, perhaps trying to work out if she was his grandmother, and, probably, wrestling with his conscience and his orders, which she had been horrified to learn had been to *kill* her if she proved to be the one to find the elusive Methuselah gene. He wasn't a bad man, just someone caught in an impossible situation. She had come to hope that she would be able to contact him at some point, see him again. Surely he would stick around to see how she was getting on? Evidently he had, and the police had caught up with him. Without thinking about it, Emma tapped out her father's speed dial. Just when she thought it would go to voicemail, he picked up.

'Em? What's wrong?'

He sounded dreadful – his voice was hoarse, as if he'd been shouting, or perhaps crying. She imagined him unshaven, perhaps with a hangover... oh Dad, what's happening to you?

'Nothing's wrong...' she began. 'Actually, something has happened – they've, the police, I mean, they've got Moran.' Her mother hadn't mentioned her father; she was coming up with Jessica. Did Dad even know? And how much did Jess know, how much would she work out? It was all going horribly wrong, and even though she couldn't – wouldn't- tell him about his grandson, Emma's need to speak to the parent with whom she was closest was impossible to ignore.

'Jesus, really? Well, that's great! Has he talked? Said why he did it? Bloody hell...'

'I don't know any of that, Dad, I just got a call…' better not say she heard it from her mother.

She could hear scuffling sounds. 'I'm coming up, darling. Have you told your mother?'

Well, it would come out, wouldn't it? 'She told me, Dad. Look, I don't think you need to… aren't you working?' she wanted to see him, of course she did – but it was too much, with Mum and Jess rocking up as well. She just wanted to hear his voice. She needed to have no distractions, to think about what to do next…she had to protect Moran's secret, and, she realised, her own, at least for now.

Her father made a scornful, dismissive sound. 'Don't be silly, of *course* I'm coming! The police might want to interview you again – your mother and I should be there. I'll see you soon, darling. Love you.'

Emma stared at her mobile. She wasn't a child anymore: they didn't need to protect her … but how would she feel if it was her daughter? Probably much the way she was feeling about Moran, she realised. She pushed the phone into her pocket, and grabbed her coat and rucksack.

50: NOVEMBER 15TH 3:30PM

The lab hadn't been the same without Emma. But at the same time, it had begun to feel liberating for Archie to be left to his own devices. No-one could be sure when she might return, or even if. The Department head had suggested Archie put everything on hold until her return, but Archie preferred to carry on working. He knew Emma would be pleased if he kept the work going, and he had to believe that she would return. He could prep the samples, run them through the first test, he had explained to Andy Jeevan - at least he would be able to winnow out the ones they couldn't use... Jeevan had looked at Archie with respect. If Emma didn't come back... well, he hadn't wanted to think about that, but perhaps he was now ready to run a project...? He and Emma had worked together on this, after all...

Now Emma was back, and Archie told himself he was pleased; and he was. He was glad she was safe, and he had quickly pushed aside any feelings of regret that he wouldn't now get a chance to prove himself after all. But something was wrong – Something about Emma seemed different. He told himself that of course it would take time for her to recover from her traumatic experience at the hands of James Moran. She hadn't told him much about what had happened, only that Moran hadn't hurt her, he'd just thought she was someone else, and that she'd felt sorry for him.,

Archie found that hard to believe. He had read the newspapers, of course – but they weren't saying much, either. That the police hadn't made an arrest worried Archie. So Moran had let her go (she said) but what was to stop him changing his mind and coming for her again?

So Archie had made a point of leaving the lab at the same time as Emma for the first few days after her return, which hadn't pleased his mother, and made Archie feel guilty about leaving her for so long when Emma worked late – but really, he'd done a lot for his mother, hadn't he; in a way he had put his own life on hold to take care of her. He didn't regret it, or resent her, but now it was his turn to have some of his own time. He had even said as much, and that hadn't gone down well at all. Even though it had taken him slightly out of his way, Archie had walked part of the way home with her (at least as far as the last bus stop he could reasonably use) until Emma had firmly told him she was grateful, but she really didn't need a body-guard. He stopped doing it after that, but it didn't stop him worrying. Whatever had happened to Emma during her two days of captivity, it had certainly affected her ability to work. Where once she had been eager to get on, and had been incredibly focused, now she seemed listless, and easily distracted. If Archie hadn't known better, he would have said she seemed frightened... which since Moran was still at large, made sense. He worried that she might even be heading for a nervous breakdown (he knew the signs, after all). He had seen her sitting motionless at her workstation, apparently in deep -and if her frown was anything to go by, troubled- thought for minutes at a time. She had become secretive, too – more than once she had turned her screen off or quickly clicked away from whatever she had been working on when Archie came to talk to her. What was she hiding? Damn James Moran – he had spoiled everything, hadn't he? Had he said something to Emma which gave her doubts about the work she was doing? He *had* tried to sabotage it, after all... Then another idea insinuated itself into Archie's troubled mind: he didn't *want* to be-lieve that Emma might be working with Moran, as Hammond had suggested Archie himself might be (the very idea still made him angry), but if she *was*, well, mightn't she behave in just this way? No, he couldn't believe that of her. All the same, Emma's behavior was making him feel very uneasy. An hour ago she had taken a call from her mother and had left the office without so much as a word to him. Almost as if he wasn't there. He tried not to mind, put it down to Moran, and continued with his work.

He had prepped another two dozen slides when he came across one which didn't have the same reference label as the others. He couldn't recall seeing it before, but the label bore Emma's handwriting, so that in itself wasn't unusual. What was unusual, however, was that instead of being cross-matched to another slide, it referenced a document number. It was also undated, which was unusual; it meant that there was no way to tell when it might have come in, even which group it belonged to. The document code told him that it would be found on Emma's computer, so he quickly jotted the code down and tucked the sticky note in his lab coat pocket, his heart pounding.

He had just put the slide back where he'd found it, when he heard the outer door slam. Through the window, he saw Emma hang up her rucksack and take a fresh lab coat from the shelf. She looked anxious.

'Emma - what's wrong? Has something happened?'

Emma jumped, and stared at him like a startled rabbit.

'The police have got James Moran in custody.'

'Really? That's good news. Isn't it?' Why didn't she look pleased? The hair on the back of Archie's neck prickled. 'Emma, what's wrong?'

'Nothing's wrong, Archie. I just… I thought I would feel different about it, that's all.' She heaved a sigh. 'And my parents are on their way.' She dropped onto her chair, and put her hands over her face with a deep sigh.

'Well… that's good too, isn't it – at least you know you're safe now, he won't come after you again…perhaps we'll find out why he did it. And I'm sure that your parents are worried about how this might affect you.' But Emma didn't seem happy or even reassured.

Emma touched her mousepad, and her computer login screen came back up. She became brisk and business-like, briskly tapping in her password. Almost like her old self. Almost. 'I don't want to talk about it, Archie. Let's just carry on, shall we?'

The phone on Archie's desk rang. Grateful for the distraction, he grabbed it.

'Oh. Yes…all right, I'll tell her.' He put his hand over the mouthpiece. 'Emma – the police are downstairs. They want to come up.' He didn't want them here; it was too much of an intrusion. But if he was bothered, Emma looked positively terrified.

'Tell them I'll come down.' Emma hurried from the room. Archie stared after her.

51: NOVEMBER 15TH 3:40PM

'Hello, Inspector. How can I help you?'

Hammond hadn't waited for the desk to confirm that it was okay to go up to the lab – he had made for the stairs, flashing his police badge, and met with no resistance. Emma had been coming out of the lab as he rounded the corner, and had stepped in front of the door, her body language defensive. That and the pitch of her voice told Hammond that she was worried, perhaps even frightened. That she knew Moran was in custody was obvious.

'Miss Morgan, Emma – I thought you should hear it from me. We've got Moran in custody…'

Emma ought to be pleased…but she didn't look it.

'I know; my mother called me.'

'Then you may appreciate that in light of things James Moran has said, that I need to ask you some more questions. Is here a good place, or…?' Behind Emma, Hammond could see Archie Harrop through the interior window. He was pretending to be busy, but kept shooting glances at them, clearly concerned by Hammond's presence. Were they both in on it? He had decided that timid Archie Harrop wouldn't be involved in whatever the hell was going on, but people could surprise you…

'No… I mean, here's not a good place…we're working, Inspector Hammond. Can we talk outside?'

Either she hadn't been outside lately or didn't care that it was raining heavily. Hammond could see her mind scrabbling, but for what? She was no doubt wondering what Moran had said… he would keep her guessing, then, just say enough to feed her anxiety.

'The station might be the best place, Emma – away from your colleagues. You're not under arrest,' he added, when alarm flared in her eyes. 'Moran has made certain claims… we need to check them out.' He watched her face pale, saw her swallow, and felt the thrill of satisfaction. She did know more than she'd told them so far, and now she was about to be called on it.

'Okay. Can I get my bag? And I need to tell Archie…'

Hammond nodded. 'Of course.'

He watched as Emma went back into the lab, saw Harrop's face fall as he absorbed the news. Something about his reaction struck Hammond as off: he seemed almost relieved, and anxious for her to leave. What the hell was going on there? Should he bring Harrop in as well? He had no grounds, he realised. Not yet…

Emma followed him to the car, where Mortimer sat behind the wheel, looking bored. Glancing back up at the window of the lab, Hammond hesitated. Harrop might even now be destroying evidence, he fretted. But evidence of what? His gut told him that Harrop wasn't involved – his distress at her disappearance had been real. He got into the car, and as Mortimer pulled out into traffic, twisted in his seat to address Emma.

'Sorry to hear about your parents.' He said as she stared at him from her seat behind Mortimer.

Emma shrugged, the studied casualness of the movement at odds with the anxiety radiating off her in waves. 'They haven't got on for a long time.'

'So what made you decide to study genetics? Your half-brother?'

She looked startled at the sudden change of subject, but nodded, her fingers playing with the strap on her backpack. She'd got herself a replacement, he noticed, in dark green. It enhanced the colour of her eyes.

'Yes. I've always known about him… Dad doesn't talk about him, really, he never did like to be reminded, I think. But he's got this photo… him and Alice and Chloe … Nathan's last Christmas…it always fascinated me, when I was younger. Nathan looked so different – when I was very small, I used to think he was a little gnome, or an elf….' She paused. 'Kids can be so cruel, Inspector. Chloe told me it was hard sometimes, at school. Most of the kids were alright, but you'd always get the odd one or two… I wish I'd known him.' She looked genuinely sad.

'Didn't your parents meet after your father's first marriage broke up?'

Mortimer gave Hammond a swift sideways look; he had no doubt heard about his boss's meltdown in the interview, and was probably wondering where Hammond was going with this.

'As far as I know,' Emma said quietly, and Hammond wondered if the family ever talked about anything personal. That she didn't seem sure seemed… wrong, somehow. Don't all parents tell their kids 'the story of how we met'? His own parents had known each other as kids at school; they'd been friends and then teenage sweethearts. But Ray Hammond stopped talking about his wife after she vanished; the young Hammond had found it confusing. He hadn't wanted to forget his mother, but any mention of her within his father's hearing had earned him a cuff round the ear, or worse. He soon learned not to talk about her, but he never stopped missing her. When his aunt had finally confessed to Hammond that her sister had been planning to leave her husband that day, taking Ian with her to Coventry, he realised that he wasn't surprised, that somewhere deep inside himself he realised, as he grew older, that he had seen things as a small boy that hadn't made sense then, but which did through the filter of almost-adulthood. He hadn't visited his father in two years. But now that Ray Hammond didn't recognise his only son any more, was there any point? Hammond had often thought he ought to hate his father for what he'd done; but he had spent his whole childhood in ignorance, and parental love didn't just disappear overnight. Now, Hammond knew that he didn't love his father anymore; but he did respect that, at least in the beginning, Ray and Dorothy Hammond must have loved one another.

Jerked from his thoughts by the truncated squeal of a siren as a patrol car shot past them at speed in the opposite direction, Hammond saw with a flood of relief that they were pulling into police HQ. He realised that in the ensuing silence, Emma had been watching him.

52: NOVEMBER 15TH, 4:15PM

Archie gave it a few minutes after Emma and Hammond's departure before approaching her computer. He had noticed almost right away that she had forgotten to log out; confirmation (as if he'd needed it) that she had been worried by Hammond's appearance. She had seemed anxious to get the detective away from the lab – but Hammond likely wouldn't understand anything he might see, so why was she so jittery? He glanced up at the door; no-one would disturb him, he was almost certain, but the knowledge of what he was about to do still made him nervous. He sat down, and took a deep breath. It was probably nothing to worry about, but he and Emma were of one mind when it came to the project: the work was their priority. *You can do this.*

Emma's hard drive was organised neatly into folders and sub-folders, and sub-folders under those. Fishing the note from his pocket, he entered the code he had copied from the slide into the search box, and it took him straight to the matching folder.

It quickly became clear to him that two samples had been analyzed and cross-checked, which was normal: where there was a relationship between two or more samples, they would usually be logged in pairs or as part of a group, denoting that they might belong either to a sibling, a husband and wife, or other family member. The final suffix indicated the degree of familial removal, but only a further search of a separate database would link the sample to a named research subject, whose details were held in a protected file on a removable disk which was updated weekly and always kept off-site, in order to protect the subject's identity in the unlikely event of a security breach. One record carried the same code number as the slide Archie had seen earlier; the data underneath it made Archie lose his breath for a moment. The T-cell count didn't make sense, it was way off… if these readings were correct, the individual was much older than even their eldest test subject – in fact, and he did a quick calculation to check, this person was *impossibly* old. A result like this simply couldn't exist, so what was it doing here? Archie scrolled down to the second record, his heart thumping uncomfortably in his chest.

'Emma…what are you doing…?' Archie knew Emma's sample code, just as he knew his own, off by heart. Occasionally they would include their own records as a way of double-checking that the machines were properly calibrated – if the readings came up differently to what was on file, it could mean that the machines needed to be reset and the samples run again. This was definitely Emma's DNA, there could be no doubt. What worried him, however, was that there was clearly a familial relationship between Emma and the owner of the first sample – who was, if the readings were to be believed, older than any human who had so far ever lived. The level of remove suggested… No, this couldn't be right… Archie stared at the screen, his thoughts scattering like frightened mice, refusing to be pinned down. Where did Emma get this sample, assuming it wasn't faked? If it was a fake -and really, it couldn't be anything else, could it? - who would do such a thing, and why? He backed out of the file without saving it, and saw that the last time it had been amended was yesterday evening, at five minutes and two seconds past nine. He had left Emma still working and gone home at six-fifteen; she had seemed relieved to see him go. So that she could do… what?… with this file? Falsify the results? Why would she do such a thing? If it was what it looked like, it could end her career…

'Emma, what are you involved in?' He clicked back into the folder and stared at the file again, feeling sick. He should save a copy of this, he knew, but he didn't want to look too closely at why, not yet. To expose her – or save her? A hurried search of their small stationery supplies cupboard revealed the box to be empty, and he groaned. Just a few days ago, there had been at least half-a-dozen discs in it; they wouldn't have used them all, surely? He knew he hadn't, if Emma had been working around the clock... what was she doing with them? Copying their data to pass on, to Moran, maybe? It would make sense. The very idea was a betrayal of their shared goal, and hurtful in the extreme. He had trusted her, and had believed -until now- that she trusted him. Whatever her reasons for doing this, she had not seen fit to share them with him. So had Emma found the fabled 'Methuselah gene', and kept the discovery from him? Or had she simply wanted to verify her findings before telling him? No – they had always shared every result, every success or failure or misstep, as it happened. This, the ... holy grail, if he could believe the evidence of his own eyes... it would have -should have- been a cause for much celebration. Instead, he had found it hidden away, like a dirty secret.... He shook his head. No, it was impossible – it had to be faked. They were nowhere near finding it yet, as he had told Inspector Hammond. By the end of the trial period, they *might* have a lead... it was by no means certain the gene even existed, despite the optimism of an international consortium four years earlier. He hurried back to Emma's computer, and stared once more at what was beginning to look more and more like a betrayal.

He couldn't save a copy, so he did the next best thing: he took several screen prints, capturing all the salient data, printed them out, then deleted the images without saving them. Then he folded the printed pages and put them in his pocket. Well, *he* could keep secrets, too.

He didn't plan to share this with anyone else, at least not yet. Not only did it have the potential to destroy their friendship, but he without knowing the full story, Archie was reluctant to take it further. He would have to tell her he had seen it, see how she reacted. The idea of having such a conversation terrified him, but he couldn't just ignore this, could he?

He exited out of the file, making sure not to save it, so that Emma would not know he had seen it. Would she remember that she hadn't logged out of her PC? But of course, it wouldn't matter – left logged in and idle, the computer would automatically log her out after ten minutes had elapsed. If he hadn't noticed that she'd left it on, he would never have found it, would probably have put the stray sample down to a recording error and (perhaps) thought no more about it. Except that wasn't his way, it never had been. He would have had to ask her about it, at some point. Would she lie to him?

Archie returned to his workstation, but realised that he couldn't just resume work as if nothing had happened. This was too big. It had to be connected with Moran, didn't it? Emma had seemed different since her kidnap, and now he knew why. How could she do this? How *dare* she? The sudden surge of anger surprised Archie, and frightened him. He looked around him, at the lab he had shared with Emma for the last year. Had it really been such a short time? His work had always given a meaning and a rhythm to his days, but until he had been partnered with Emma Morgan, he had been going through the motions, always aware that he wasn't fulfilling the ambition he'd once had, before his breakdown. Emma had rekindled the spark; he had even begun to think he might, once their work was complete -if it ever was- be able to pick up where he left off with his own abandoned PhD… Now, he wasn't so sure. An uncertain future loomed ahead of him. A sudden urge to be away from the lab seized him. He couldn't go home – his mother would want to know what was wrong, if he was ill – but he couldn't stay here, not while this awful secret was hanging over him.

So he logged out of his own computer, tidied his desk -which was always tidy anyway, and gave a last look around the lab before shutting the door behind him. He took the printouts from his lab coat, dumping the coat in the laundry bin, and quickly slipped the printouts into his knapsack. The sight of it reassured him, but only for a moment. It had been his father's before him and his grandfather's before that – a small canvas hold-all designed to hold a WWII respirator, it was the perfect size for his sandwiches and flask. It reminded him of his father, who had died suddenly of an aneurism when Archie was eleven years old. Pulling on his coat, Archie picked up the knapsack again, locked the door behind him and made his way down to the security desk. Handing over the lab keys, Archie was reminded of the times he had given them to James Moran. Could the blood sample be his? The thought stopped him in his tracks, and he only realised that he was still standing at the desk when the guard cleared his throat.

'Goodnight, sir,' the man said quietly, a trace of amusement in his tone. It told Archie that the man was used to the sometimes peculiar ways of academics. Unlike Moran, he exhibited no real interest in what Archie might do all day. He was there to provide security, and look after the keys. Moran had seemed a bit too... engaged, Archie suddenly realised. He hadn't thought too much of it at the time, because some people were like that; interested in the people they met. Not that Moran had ever wanted to chat – but he had asked where Archie worked the first time they met, and on several occasions when he and Emma had left the building together, he had sensed a quickening in Moran's manner. At the time, Archie had put it down to the fact that Emma was an attractive young woman; Moran's apparent interest in her had bothered him more than slightly, but it wasn't as if he had any claim on her. He had told himself that he just thought she could do better ... but that in any case, it was none of his business what she did in her own time. If only he had listened to his feelings, warned her about Moran. But what would he have said, and just suppose she had already been colluding with him at that point? He realised he was still standing in front of the security desk, and blushed.

'I'm sorry,' he said, embarrassed and irritated with himself for feeling that way at the same time. 'I was miles away... Goodnight.' He hurried out of the building, aware of the guard's amused gaze following him. Outside, it was raining, a bite in the air which threatened sleet, or perhaps worse. A young couple ran past him, laughing, and he heard '...Costa!' He would break the habit of a lifetime and make use of one of the city's many coffee bars, he decided; he'd find a quiet corner (if there was such a thing to be had) and think about what to do next.

53: NOVEMBER 15TH

'I want to see him.'

'Eva, I don't think that's a good idea. Let me at least speak to my boss…'

Eva shook her head. 'I need to know, Lucy – if it's him.'

Eva seemed calm, but as they had neared Manchester, she had become quieter and more withdrawn, as if proximity to the place where her daughter had been kidnapped was turning her back into the person she had been then.

'I really don't think Inspector Hammond will sanction it, Eva.'

Eva shook her head. 'I want to ask him one question, that's all. Please?'

Rattigan stared at her. 'Well…. I can't authorise it, I'm afraid - I'd have to clear it with Inspector Hammond, as I said. Look, why don't you get yourselves booked into a hotel?'

The news from Eva – following a short but heated call Eva had taken from her husband - that Tom Morgan was also heading their way concerned Rattigan. He had a history of violence – no way would he ever be allowed access to Moran, no matter how much stink he might kick up. Rattigan didn't believe that Eva should have access, either. Any questions they wanted to ask Moran could come through Hammond, and he would only pass on what he thought was appropriate.

'She's right, Eva. You -or Tom- probably won't be allowed to see him.'

Jessica had been very quiet during the journey; almost monosyllabic; she seemed to be deep in thought for much of the time, and Rattigan suspected the journalist was still blaming herself for bringing Moran to Emma's door. As well she might, Rattigan thought. But if all the connections stacked up, it wouldn't have made any difference if she hadn't – Moran, and his relations, if that's what they were, seemed to have an agenda. They would almost certainly have found Emma eventually...

The train's intercom crackled into life, announcing their arrival at Manchester Piccadilly.

54: NOVEMBER 15, 4:35PM

'Emma, you are not under caution, but this interview *is* being recorded. Are you okay with that?'

Emma Morgan nodded. She was nervous; she had hardly spoken a word since leaving the car. In Rattigan's absence, Hammond had asked a female constable, Zara Sedghi, to sit in. There'd been an odd little moment when Emma had recognised Zara; her brother, Jaz, had been a student at the same University, and had dated one of Emma's housemates in her second year. Once they'd got the awkward chit-chat out of the way, Hammond had quickly reassumed control.

'When asked why he had abducted you, James Moran stated that he made a mistake. He also claimed to have made a mistake in December nineteen-ninety, in London. Do you know what he meant by that, Emma?' He wanted to see just how much she really knew about James Moran, and if that meant misleading her a little, well as long as he didn't lie to her…

Emma's response was immediate, and unconvincing. 'No. How could I know? I hadn't even been born. He, he just told me that I reminded him of his daughter…'

Hammond pushed Clarke's photo-fit across the table to her, and saw her eyes widen. 'He claimed first of all that he was there when your mother's first husband and daughter died, and then seemed to change his mind. Did he say anything to you about it?'

Emma shook her head, but she kept her eyes on the photograph, not looking at him. 'I don't know anything about that,' she said, too quickly. 'As I told you before, Mr. Moran thought I was his daughter. That's all the explanation he ever gave.' She looked at Hammond then, but quickly dropped her gaze back to the image. 'It couldn't be him, could it, though – he's too young.'

Was this the time to tell her that James Moran seemed to have aged almost a decade in a few weeks? He decided to keep that back for now. It seemed improbable even though he had seen it with his own eyes.

'You see, Emma, there are too many connections between James Moran and your family, whether you know it or not. And I think you do know… don't you?'

'I don't know what you're talking about.' Emma shrugged, her eyes sliding away from him, to the fingers twisting in her lap.

'Look, we know he tried to sabotage your work. We also know that he has a connection – a very tenuous one, I have to say- to your mother's first husband, Peter King. We have information which leads us to believe that either James Moran, or a close relative, may have saved Peter King's life in the Woolworths' fire in nineteen-seventy-nine.'

Emma laughed nervously. 'I don't believe you.' But it was obvious to Hammond that she did; that she already knew.

'Yes, you do. Because Moran told you the same thing, didn't he?'

'No.' Again the shake of her head, avoiding his eyes.

Hammond sighed. 'Look, as it stands, Emma, we can charge James Moran with common assault and kidnapping. We don't need your permission for either. But if there's something you're not telling me…something that links him to your family, some… mitigating, shall we say, fact… like, he's your father…'

Emma flinched as if he'd struck her.

'Don't be ridiculous! That's not true!'

She was scared, Hammond saw. 'Then what is he to you, Emma?'

She stared at him, changing her tactics, trying to convince him of the lie. 'He's no-one! I had never met him until he came to work at Xeon, and that's the truth, Inspector!'

It was probably the only truth she had given him.

'Look, Emma… it seems pretty obvious to me that, for whatever reason, you're protecting James Moran. Now, if there's some awkward family secret about to come out in the open, something that's changed what you thought you knew about your family, maybe even yourself, I get that you'd maybe want to deny it. But we can do a paternity test, you know. Well, of course you'd know,' he said, his pulse quickening. The look on her face told him he was on the right track. 'You've already done one, haven't you?'

'No, you don't know what you're talking about,' she whispered. 'You have no idea…'

'Then tell me, Emma. Whoever or whatever James Moran is to you, I can tell that you're concerned about him, about what happens to him. I'm right, aren't I?' she remained silent. 'If you don't want to see him go to prison on charges of abduction and false imprisonment, Emma, please, tell me what you know. We're not in the business of locking up innocent people.' He didn't think James Moran was innocent, but clearly there was something going on here, and whether Emma liked it or not, Moran's actions were criminal offenses.

'I can't.' She was fighting tears now. He thought she wouldn't be able to hold out on him for much longer, but the knowledge didn't bring him any satisfaction.

'Look. Obstructing a police enquiry…pretending to be the victim of a kidnapping…wasting police time, they're all chargeable offences, Emma. There's no walking away from this.'

'I can't tell you anything, Inspector. I'm sorry.' Emma looked down at her lap, fingers twisting around themselves in a gesture which reminded Hammond of her mother. He sighed.

'Thank you for your time, Emma. Interview terminated…' He stood up. 'Constable Sedghi will see that you get back to…' he glanced at his watch, 'your lab, or to your home if you prefer.' He pulled a card from his pocket, and slid it across the table. 'If you decide that you want to tell me what you know, give me a call. We may want to do that paternity test, Emma.'

'You don't have grounds,' she said.

'Don't I?' Hammond opened the door and walked away.

Back in CID, he saw Rattigan's coat lying across her chair, and Rattigan herself was turning away from his closed office door. She looked relieved to see him. 'Boss? I need to talk to you.'

'Come in, Lucy.' He opened the door, waving her in ahead of him, and shut it behind them. If Rattigan thought it unusual, she gave no sign. Closed doors were normally reserved for bollockings.

'I've threatened them both with a paternity test.' No point beating about the bush – the parents would be descending on them all too soon, Hammond had no doubt.

'So you think Moran is Emma's father...?'

'I don't know what to think, but it's about the only thing that makes sense, isn't it?'

Rattigan frowned. 'But what's the link between all that, and Moran's... I don't know, father, uncle, whatever... in 'seventy-nine? Eva and King didn't even know each other then...he was a student. We're missing something, sir.'

'I know we're bloody missing something, Lucy!' He sighed. 'I'm sorry. Look, I know we are... but they're not saying. If Moran did somehow commit murder eleven years later, and made it seem like an accident...'

'It can't have been him, sir. Can it?'

Hammond shrugged. 'To be honest, I don't know anymore. Look, Lucy, I'm going to share something with you now, and I don't want it going any further...' it was all on tape, now, of course. Unless he was going to somehow tamper with the tape – an action which would lose him his career- it was going to come out. 'at least, not for now.'

'Sir...?'

'The reason this case has got under my skin, Lucy, is because I've seen James Moran before.' Committed now, he took a deep breath, and ploughed on. 'When I saw his Xeon ID, Lucy… you maybe don't know that my mother disappeared in the Woolworths fire of 'seventy-nine…'

'No sir, I didn't. I'm so sorry.'

'So am I. But the thing is, Moran – or his father or his bloody Uncle, whoever he is- was there…' Rattigan nodded. '…and so was I, Lucy.'

Rattigan sat up straighter in her chair. 'You were? Were you hurt?'

'No, not… no. But I remember Moran. Or whoever he is/was. I saw him grab Peter King, walk him out of that building, just before the fire took hold.'

'Bloody hell, sir…'

'And then I saw him again, outside, afterwards. I was looking for my mother…and he stopped to talk to me. I asked him if he'd seen her, and he said he hadn't.' Hammond swallowed. 'I asked him about it, Lucy, and he said… he said he couldn't change what happened. He knows something, he knows what happened to her, I'm sure of it… but he won't tell me.' His hands were shaking. 'Don't tell me I should have declared an interest the moment I knew - I know I should have. But Surridge would have taken me off the case, and I want to find out, Lucy. If he knows…'

'No-one will hear it from me, sir.'

'Thank you. But I don't want you to compromise yourself. I shouldn't have told you.'

'Told me what, sir?'

Hammond couldn't quite manage a smile. 'Well, I've already put my foot in it – it's all on tape. So…'

'You don't know that the DCI will take you off, sir.'

'No, I don't – but he's a stickler for the rules. I'm not putting any bets on him letting me stay. So I wanted you to know… just in case.' He put his hands on his desk, palms pressed against the surface. 'I don't mind telling you, Lucy, I'm stumped. Moran's not talking,

Emma's not talking… I'm not sure we have grounds for the test, but if I can prove that Moran deliberately targeted Peter King, and that Emma is his daughter… it might be enough to put him away. I just need to make that connection…'

'Because why would Moran, or his father… okay so it can't have been Moran in seventy-nine, we know that, right? He wouldn't have been old enough. He wouldn't even have been old enough to fit the photo-fit in nineteen-eighty, would he? So whoever that man was, or men… it must be Moran's father. So…'

'Hang on, hang on… Moran's father saves King from the fire. Then, for some reason, either he, or his son, brother, whatever, causes King's death eleven years later. Let's say it's the same man, okay – it could be, the photo-fit is only an impression, he could've been older. So Moran's father, for some reason we don't yet know, caused King's death. Then *his* son, the James Moran we know, somehow finds out about it, and…'

'…has a relationship with Eva King sometime soon after her husband's death, resulting in the birth of Emma…'

'Who either doesn't know that Moran is her father, or is concealing the fact, perhaps because she's afraid of Tom Morgan's reaction…' he shook his head. 'It works…but where's the motive?'

'Perhaps there isn't one, sir. Perhaps Moran just happened to meet Eva – he might not have known about…'

'…and maybe when he did realise, he couldn't stay with her… maybe his father was still alive… but that won't work, because we've found no records for 'James Moran' that match the dates, even if they're father and son, or uncle and brother… the paternity test is the key, I'm convinced of it. Unlock that, and the rest…' Hammond stood up. 'I'm going to see Surridge,' he said. 'I won't be mentioning you know what…'

'Good luck, sir. What do you want me to tell the parents, by the way? Eva Morgan is asking to see Moran… I told her it was unlikely.'

Hammond paused, his hand on the door knob. 'Did you? Maybe we might all learn something…'

'Yes, sir,' Rattigan said, her tone telling him she wasn't so sure it was a good idea. 'I imagine Tom Morgan might want to see him, as well.'

Hammond's mouth curved into a tight grin. 'Now that *wouldn't* be advisable...'

'No, sir. It wouldn't.'

55: NOVEMBER 15TH, 5:45PM

A uniformed officer with bad skin and worse breath had come to fetch him from his cell, waking him from a fitful doze. Moran was tempted to overpower him as the handcuffs went on, but dismissed the thought almost immediately. He doubted that he would have the strength, and as for getting out of the building, and away to somewhere they wouldn't find him... the security was too good, CCTV cameras were everywhere, keypads on all the doors... he was trapped.

'Where are you taking me?' If they had come to take a blood sample for the paternity test Hammond had threatened, all was lost.

'Interview Room,' the officer told him. 'You've got a visitor, chum.'

Emma? He had told her not to try to find him, but if she knew he had been arrested...no, she must realise the risk. Who, then?

It was another twenty minutes before Hammond appeared. Behind him, Moran could see a young female with tight blond curls, the lanyard hanging from her neck identifying her as a police officer. And behind her, a woman he hadn't seen for twenty-eight years: a woman he had seen in Peter King's car as it had shot past him, not realising their connection; the woman whose daughter he had abducted. His Great-grandmother.

Eva Morgan stood framed in the doorway, her face pale.

'Mrs. Morgan…' the name felt awkward on his tongue.

Eva stepped forward, and the female detective followed suit. Hammond stepped past them, positioning himself between them. 'Turn the tape on, please,' he instructed the uniformed office.

'Mrs. Morgan, are you able to formally identify this man, known to us as James Moran, as the same man present on the night of 31st December, nineteen-ninety?'

Eva Morgan nodded. 'It's him,' she said.

Moran thought she might collapse; her complexion was paper white, her pupils dilated, her hands clenched tightly. He bowed his head, heard Hammond's snort of disgust, and ignored it. *Don't think about him.* What should he say to her?

'I am so very, very sorry for your loss, Mrs. Morgan.' Even the name…he should have seen it – his own a corruption of hers, thanks to corrupted data files. He had to give her more – could not let her go with a simple apology, no matter how heartfelt. 'It was never my intention to cause your husband or your daughter's deaths, you must believe me. I was ill… in the wrong place, at the wrong time… it was an accident.' He wanted to tell her that he hadn't known who she was, who her daughter would become, but of course, he couldn't.

'*My daughter*… she was *six years old*! They said you ran away… and you might have *saved* her…' she was crying openly now, tears streaming down her face. Hammond was staring at him, his jaw clenched.

No, I couldn't. Was that true? He had no idea of the extent of the little girl's injuries, had not even realised she was in the car. He was no doctor…What had happened couldn't be undone. Not even if he could somehow get back to his own time, and return here to try again, he realised. Because Cassie was meant to live. Was her life worth all those his presence had shattered? Yes - because he would be saving not just Cassie, but billions more…in the war against mass human extinction, Peter King, his daughter, and Inspector Hammond's mother were collateral damage. But he could never tell them.

'I had no idea she was in the car. I *am* sorry.'

Eva drew a shuddering breath – she wasn't finished. 'I wish I could believe that. Why did you kidnap Emma? What is she to you? What have we ever done to you?'

What could he possibly say to her? How could he explain?

'She reminded me of someone I once knew….' It was close enough to the truth, and it would have to do. He heard a sound from Hammond and turned his way, saw pity and something else on the detective's face: anger, and frustration. His lips moved, and Moran heard the words 'paternity test'. The rest was garbled, drowned out by the sudden and deafening sound of his own blood roaring in his ears. He felt dizzy, his breath suddenly coming hard, as if all the oxygen had been sucked from the room. His vision began to grey out.

'Call the duty medic!' Hammond's voice, suddenly clear, sounded far away. The detective was kneeling beside him, leaning over him; Moran couldn't remember falling.

Hammond's face receded to a pinprick and winked out.

'Dad!' Emma flew into her father's arms.

'Darling… How've you been?' Tom released his daughter and took a step backwards into the narrow hallway, holding her at arm's length as he took in her reddened eyes, the too-thin face.

'What's wrong?'

'They've got him in a cell, Dad.'

'Yeah, I heard. About bloody time! Now we can all relax! Can I come in, then?'

Emma stood back and her father stepped past her, into the entrance hall. He dropped a small hold-all on the floor and pulled her back into his arms.

'You look tired, darling. Are you okay?'

Emma pulled out of his embrace, and led the way into the small lounge. Tom followed.

'Dad, I…' she bit her lip, and wrapped her arms around herself, a habit she'd had since she was a little girl.

'What's wrong, darling? This is *good* news – why are you behaving as if … oh Jesus, tell me it's not that – not you and *him*? Christ, Emma – he's what, thirty-nine, forty? He could be your father, for fuck's sake!' He began to pace the small room. 'Tell me that's not it!'

Emma glared at him. 'No, Dad – that's *not* what… we aren't – how can you even *think* that?' She pushed past him and into the lounge. 'I don't know what to do, Dad.'

'What do you mean?'

'Moran told me things…'

'What things? Tell me, darling. We can sort it out, whatever it is.'

She shook her head. 'No, we can't, Dad. I can't.'

'Darling, you're not making any sense. What can't you do, what the hell did he say to you? Is it your work? Is that it?'

She nodded. 'I can't tell you, you wouldn't understand.'

'You don't know until you try.'

'No, I can't. I promised…'

'Help me to understand, Em. I want to help, but if you don't tell me…'

Emma shook her head. 'You wouldn't believe me, Dad.' She wiped her eyes with the heel of her hand. 'Inspector Hammond – he doesn't believe me, either…but I can't tell you. I really can't.'

'Yes, you can. Otherwise… how can I help? Does Moran want you to stop your research? Is that it?'

She nodded. 'He knows things about it…' she sat down, then jumped up again, and began pacing. 'Progeria is a terrible disease Dad – you *know* this. But the research I'm doing…it's not the right way to cure it.'

'But you were so certain it was, Emma – what's changed? What did Moran say to you?'

'I can't tell you. Not because… oh, this is awful, I don't know what I can tell you that won't…I just know that gene therapy is not the right way, not for this. Because, what if I – or someone else- finds the… finds a way to… it could cause, it will cause, worse problems. Genes can be switched on and off, Dad, but they can also mutate…'

'Yes, I know – it's what caused Nathan to born the way he was.'

She nodded. 'If I find a way to stop people being born with Progeria, it could lead to other… worse mutations in generations to come.'

'Well, isn't that why you and what-his-name are doing all these blind trials? Not that I really understand…it's all you've ever wanted to do, Emmy. But if it's making you ill…you don't have to do it for me, darling. If it's too much…'

Emma looked disappointed, as if he had somehow missed her point. But then she nodded, and sighed. 'I don't know that it's too much… exactly… I just need to think of another way…to get the same result.' She wiped her eyes. 'Look, I don't expect you to understand, Dad. But I want to go to the station. I need to speak to him…'

'You want to speak to *him* – Moran?' Tom couldn't believe what he was hearing. She was having a breakdown: that had to be it. The trauma of the kidnap…Moran had done this to her. 'No way, Emma. I won't let you put yourself through that.'

'I'm not a child anymore! I love you Dad, but you're such a control freak – I'm twenty-five, for God's sake! I have my own life, I don't need you to tell me what you will and won't *let* me do. I just wanted… I *needed* someone to talk to, someone who might understand…' she rubbed her eyes again, her movements quick and furious. 'I'm going to the station, Dad. You can stay here, or do what you want, but I'm going.' She pulled a mobile out of her pocket, and tapped a number. 'Hello – I'd like a taxi, please, from 221 Oldham Street, to the police station at… yes, how soon? Morgan. Thank you.' She looked at her father. 'They'll be here in five minutes, I'm going to wait on the street.' She grabbed her jacket and a backpack he hadn't seen before from the back of the sofa, and headed for the front door.

'Hang on, Emma – of course I'll come with you.'

She nodded. 'Thanks. But no interfering, Dad.'

'I promise.'

57: NOVEMBER 15TH, 6:00PM

An ambulance passed their taxi on the way into the station car park. Morgan recognised Hammond and his female Sergeant in the unmarked car following it, blue lights flashing from the grill.

'Some poor bugger's felt the wrong side of the cosh,' the taxi driver muttered, as Emma rummaged around in her back pack and pulled out a small purse. Her eyes followed the direction of her father's gaze.

'Darling – that was…'

'I saw him. It wasn't him I came to see, Dad.'

As they approached the station entrance, Eva walked out. She threw her arms around Emma, completely ignoring Tom.

'Hello, darling. How are you?'

'I'm okay. I came to see if I could talk to Mr. Moran. Are you okay, Mum?'

Eva nodded, and finally let Emma go. 'Yes, I'm all right. But you won't be able to talk to Mr. Moran – he just collapsed. They've taken him to hospital, and Inspector Hammond has gone too.'

'Good bloody riddance to him,' he added.

Emma looked upset. 'But I need to see him…!'

'I don't think it will be possible….' Eva's gaze settled on Tom. 'Hello, Tom – how have you been?'

'As if you care...' Tom snapped. 'Shit, I'm sorry... let's just get out of this damn place, shall we? Where are you staying?'

Their taxi driver, who had been taking a call and hadn't yet moved on, was being hailed by their daughter. Eva shook her head, and hurried down to the taxi. Tom matched her step for step. She kept her face averted, her body language rejecting him.

'I'm at the Holiday Inn. I've booked a single,' she said absently. 'Emma, wait...'

'Okay...well, that's good... Eva, we really need to talk.' Tom tried to grab her arm, but she twisted away, coming to a stop as the taxi pulled away with Emma on board.

'Not *now*, Tom! Where is she going? *Emma!*'

Tom sprinted after the taxi, but he was too slow. A police van tooted as he came to a stop in its path. He ignored it, turning to Eva with his arms outstretched in disbelief.

'What the fuck was all that about? Eva?'

She already had her mobile out, but after a few moments dropped it back into her bag, and turned on her heel, heading back into the station. 'The battery's flat...'

'Wait up...Jesus, Eva, what the hell is going on with the pair of you?'

'I'm going to the hospital, Tom. I don't know what's happening, but it's all to do with him.'

He ran around her, blocking her path, pulling his own mobile from his pocket. 'Okay, okay...I've got a taxi number here some-where....' He was forced to move as two uniformed officers came out of the station.

'Is everything all right, madam?' The thicker set of the two men stared at Tom, and frowned. Clearly he thought he knew him from somewhere, but had not yet made the connection. Or maybe it was because he was trying to accost his own wife... Tom sighed and stepped away, thumbing at the screen on his mobile. 'Come on...'

Eva nodded at the man who had spoken. 'Yes, we're fine, thank you – just trying to get a taxi to the hospital....'

'Hello? Yeah, the police station on Northampton Road, to… Eva, which hospital?'

'The General, I think they said…'

'The General. How long? OK, OK, that'll do –we'll be out front. Name's Morgan.' He put the mobile back in his pocket and heaved a sigh.

'Very good, Ma'am.' The two cops walked past them, the thicker set man still frowning at Tom.

'He was there, Tom – when Peter and Amy died. He apologised, said it was an accident. I think he might have known Peter…'

Tom snorted. 'Seriously? What, this is all some kind of vendetta? For what?'

'I don't know, Tom.' She hesitated. 'Inspector Hammond wants to do a… a paternity test. He thinks Emma is Moran's daughter.'

'What?'

'Don't shout, Tom. Hammond thinks…'

'I heard you – I just didn't believe … you are kidding me, right?'

'No, Tom. He's got it all wrong. But…'

'But what, Eva? Oh, please don't tell me…'

'I don't have anything to tell you, Tom. Emma *is* your daughter; you know she is. But there is a likeness…I didn't see it before. And Moran thought she was his, didn't he – he says it's why he took her…'

'Bollocks. Taxi's here.' Tom jogged down the steps, away from her, carrying his indignation like a banner. 'I don't want to talk about it here,' he said as the taxi moved off. 'But if there's anything in it, Eva… Jesus Christ…'

Eva remained tight-lipped throughout the journey. Tom sat angled away from her, his eyes staring out at but not seeing the streets roll past. What the hell was going on?

The acne-scarred young man in the white coat stepped in front of Hammond and held up a hand. 'I'm sorry, sir, you can't go in there.'

'Hammond, CID. Police business.' He flashed his badge, for the third time in almost as many minutes. Everything was conspiring against him today, and he was bloody sick of it.

'Well, unless you're family… what's he done - stolen an invalid carriage?'

Hammond glared at him. 'Don't get smart with me, lad.'

'I'm sorry, Inspector. But you'll have to wait until they've finished. And then only if the doctors say it's okay. You *can* wait here, though.' He pushed through the door.

'If he's qualified, I'd be bloody surprised,' Hammond fumed.

'What did he mean sir, about the invalid carriage?' Rattigan was frowning.

'Not a bloody clue. God, I hate hospitals…'

'Did you see who was in that taxi we passed on the way out?'

Hammond nodded, and looked glumly at the plastic chairs lining the small waiting area. His arse ached at the very thought of spending any time on them. 'Happy bloody families.'

'Sir… if Moran dies…'

'Of course he's not going to bloody die, Rattigan!' He hoped it was true.

'I don't know sir… he looked pretty sick to me.'

Rattigan's first sight of James Moran in the flesh – as opposed to the CCTV footage and his Xeon security pass – had been a surprise, although she couldn't have said what she might have been expecting. Someone younger, certainly. She wondered if they had got the wrong man, but didn't dare voice the thought. Hammond had been surprised too, she thought – and he had seen Moran only a few hours earlier.

Whilst the medics worked on Moran, and Hammond paced and grumbled at everyone, Eva had asked Rattigan if her DI had grounds for the paternity test. 'What would it prove?' she wanted to know. 'I know that Moran isn't Emma's father, and he let her go… why does he want to do this?'

'I can't discuss that with you, Eva, I'm very sorry. I'm sure he has his reasons.'

'Sir… are you really going to push for the paternity test?'

'Yes, I am. Do you think I'm wrong?'

Rattigan was shocked. Hammond had never solicited her opinion like that before: he was her superior, with more years' experience by a long mile.

'I don't know, sir. But if you think he murdered Peter King…'

'I don't know what I think until I see the proof,' Hammond grunted. 'But something's got to give pretty soon…' before I get taken off the case, he meant. Before Surridge told them to drop it as a waste of police time and resources.

After about twenty minutes, the same white-coated individual who had barred their entry came out again. 'Not yet,' he said, and hurried away.

'I *could* just barge in there…' Hammond was tired, and fed up with the whole bloody case.

'You *could*, sir…' She knew he wouldn't.

'Look, I need the loo…I'll be back in five.'

Rattigan watched Hammond hurry away. She wasn't sure why he'd even bothered to come to the hospital – Moran wasn't going anywhere, and it certainly didn't seem as if he was a threat to anyone. She got that Hammond thought Moran had been in Woollies when his mum had gone missing, but it couldn't have been him. If Moran didn't make it – and Rattigan knew enough of medical terminology to realise that he was a very sick man – then the case would be closed, end of.

A nurse with bright yellow hair pushed the door open and peered out at Rattigan.

'Are you his grand-daughter? He's a bit confused, but he's been asking for you …you can go in now. But just for a few minutes, mind -he'll be going down to x-ray as soon as that porter gets his arse into gear…' she gave Rattigan a sympathetic smile, not having noticed her police ID.

Rattigan stared at her. She'd got the wrong person, obviously, but it was a way in… Hammond would be pleased. If they let him in as well, that is.

'Thanks,' she said, and pushed through the doors. Behind her, she heard Hammond's query – he must have turned back – and the nurse asking Hammond if he was family, heard his voice raised in exasperation.

At first she couldn't see Moran – the tiny assessment ward consisted of just half a dozen beds, all with their curtains drawn. Then a face appeared at the far end of the room, a junior doctor who looked as if he could use a good night's sleep.

'Ah… you must be Mr. Moran's…'

'How is he?' Rattigan interrupted – she didn't want to lie to the bloke, but if he'd had made assumptions about who she was…

He shook his head. 'We're sending him down for an x-ray, but I don't want to raise your hopes. He should really be in palliative care…his notes say that he was in police custody…?' Clearly he found the idea shocking.

'Yes, apparently,' Rattigan said, and hoped he wouldn't notice her police ID just yet. What was going on? 'Palliative' implied something terminal…. were they even talking about the same man?

'Well, it's none of my business…I'll leave you alone, then.' He gave her a tired smile and went to the next bed.

Rattigan pulled the curtain aside and stepped inside.

The elderly man lying in the bed bore little resemblance to the one who had apologised to Eva Morgan back at the station. They'd got confused, must have sent her to the wrong bed… but then the old man opened his eyes, and Rattigan saw with a shock that it *was* Moran – the green eyes, even faded by age, were the only spot of colour on his pallid skin. His lips moved, but no sound came out.

'Mr. Moran?' Rattigan felt sick. This… whatever it was… it just wasn't possible. They must have switched… but how? Moran had to have been under constant medical supervision since collapsing in the interview room, there wouldn't have been an opportunity…She watched the old man's papery eyelids flutter and close. He raised a skeletal hand, let it fall. That he recognised her, she had no doubt.

She heard Hammond's voice, and another. 'I just need a minute, mate, alright?'

'I've got my orders, he's to go down to x-ray… you can ride with us if you like, but I'm taking him and that's that.'

The curtain flew back, the noise making the figure on the bed flinch.

'Wondered where you'd got to… hang on, is this a bloody *joke*?'

Hammond glared at Rattigan. 'You've got the wrong bed, Sergeant…oh, fucking hell…'

At the sound of Hammond's voice, Moran's eyes had flown open. He was trying to say something, shaking his head back and forth.

'Sir… it *is* him, I don't know how, but…'

Hammond elbowed her to one side, shaking his head, and leaned over the bed, ignoring the porter, who tutted.

'Where's your son? How did you do this? Bloody hell…!'

Moran had grabbed Hammond's sleeve, his mouth working. Rattigan could hear fluid bubbling in his chest as he fought for breath.

'Look, I told you, he's to go to X-ray. Get out of the way, man!' The porter had followed Hammond, and released the brakes at the foot of the bed. Now he marched around to the other side, deftly unclipping the breathing tube and plugging it into the cylinder he'd brought with him, which he lifted from its trolley and placed on a rack under the bed. Then he unclipped the IV, dropped it onto the covers, and pushed the bed forward.

Hammond had no choice but to step away, and Moran's fingers lost their grip as the porter pulled the bed away, flicking the curtains aside with practiced ease.

'Sir…'

Hammond shook his head – his face was almost as grey as Moran's had been. 'I did not just see that…' he muttered, and strode past her, after the porter.

'Sir, we can't…'

When they reached the lift, the porter shook his head as the doors opened. 'You're not coming in, man,' he told Hammond. 'You're up-setting him. Take the stairs, okay?' He blocked Hammond's access with his body, and short of physically assaulting him, there was nothing Hammond could do. He swore, and headed for the stairs, Rattigan trailing in his wake. She'd never seen him like this – but then it wasn't every day your suspect appeared to have aged fifty years in as many minutes, was it?

'Which bloody floor, Rattigan?' Hammond seemed possessed, barging down the stairs at breakneck speed; Rattigan was younger and undoubtedly fitter, but she was having a hard time keeping up.

'I don't know – Sir – *Ian!*' She had never used his first name before – he was the boss, it had never felt right.

Hammond stopped suddenly, so that she almost ran into him. He stared at her, panting. '*What?*'

Rattigan took a deep breath, and put a hand on his arm. 'Sir – that *was* Moran, wasn't it?'

He sagged against the wall, and wiped sweat from his brow with a sleeve. 'I…' he shook his head. 'Christ knows… it looked like him, yeah, but there's no way… how the *hell* did he make the bloody switch? He couldn't have made a phone call, they must have been waiting...' he shook his head again, and began jogging down the stairs. Rattigan followed, her voice echoing in the empty stairwell.

'Sir, I know you've got previous with him... or ... his father, who-ever... But ...he *knew* me, he *recognised* me. How could he, if it's not him? But how...?' Family likeness was one thing, but she'd seen recognition in the old man's eyes. It had been no act.

'Christ knows... this is a nightmare, Lucy, a bloody nightmare...'

59: NOVEMBER 15TH, 6:40PM

Emma stood behind the old man, and tried not to glare at his back. If he'd only hurry up…

'Can I help you, love?'

Emma dashed to the second reception position as the woman settled herself behind her monitor. 'Sorry love, you know how it is…'

Emma didn't know, and she didn't particularly care. She'd rehearsed this in the taxi, muttering under her breath until the cabbie, perhaps peeved because she'd ignored all his attempts at conversation, had slid the little dividing panel shut.

'I'm looking for my…father… James Moran? He was brought in a little while ago…'

'Hang on pet… here we are, he was in Purple, Assessment… no, wait, he's just gone down to X-ray, but they've assigned him to Geriatric ward three. It'd probably be best if you go up and wait on the ward, they'll probably not be long, not this time of day… it's on the third floor, pet, follow the red corridor until you get to blue, then it's all the way to the end and first right. You can't miss it. …' she stared at the monitor, and frowned. 'Hang on love - did you say your *father*? Then I've got the wrong…'

Emma didn't hear her; she was already feet away and moving fast, her trainers slapping the floor as she ran. The woman shrugged, and turned to the young woman with the bulging figure of advanced pregnancy and a toddler on what was left of her hip. 'You can't tell 'em, can you… now how can I help you, pet?'

'Tom, promise me you'll stay calm?'

Tom's left leg jiggled up and down as he scanned the road ahead, looking past the back of the cabbie's head as if he was driving them, searching for a break in the traffic. He pointed.

'*There*, man – go for it!'

'Look, man, I won't tell you again – put your belt on, or I'm stopping this bloody taxi right now and you can walk, okay?'

'Yes, he will, I'm very sorry…' Eva tugged Tom back into his seat, and grumbling, he fastened the belt.

'Tom, if you cause a scene…'

'Oh for God's sake, Eva - Someone's playing a weird, sick game - what else can it be? Whatever he's doing, it stops now. Oh, thank Christ for that!'

The taxi surged forward, almost throwing Tom and Eva from their seats, and slid into the hospital grounds.

'This must be a mistake…' Emma turned to a passing nurse. 'This isn't…'

'Sorry, love – you'll need to go back to the desk if they've sent you to the wrong ward. I can't stop…'

Emma turned back to the bed. The elderly man had his eyes shut, but it couldn't be Moran… could it? She moved closer, not wanting to disturb him. The wispy hair was short, the nose… she was about to turn away when the man blinked, and for a moment she caught a glimpse of pale green eyes.

'James…?' It felt odd to use his given name, but it got a reaction; the rheumy eyes opened again, and peered at her. The wizened face grimaced and the lips, tinged with blue, stretched in a rough approximation of a smile. Then Moran's eyes closed again.

Emma fumbled for the visitor's chair and sank into it, her mind whirling. She had told him that she believe him, had told herself that she did – but seeing the proof, the human reality, right in front of her… it had worked, would work. Whatever she was doing, or was not doing…the methuselah program had never been put into action, this proved it … didn't it?

'Emma?'

Inspector Hammond and the female detective whose name Emma couldn't remember were heading towards her, followed by the same nurse who had given Emma the brush-off just moments earlier. The nurse was trying to head them off.

'I'm sorry, Sir, Madam, two visitors per bed only…'

'Well, he's a popular gentleman… down red to the end, first right on blue, then it's on your left. You can't miss it, Mr. Morgan. Family, is he?' The receptionist smiled at him, clearly a fan.

'Thank you,' Eva said, and took Tom's arm, a warning. She knew that look.

'Jesus…' Tom muttered as soon as they were out of earshot.

'It must have been Emma who asked for him. The police will probably be here, so please promise me you'll stay calm?'

'Yes, yes… I just want this whole bloody thing… whatever it is, to be over…'

Eva struggled to keep up with her husband's long strides as they turned into a corridor which had a blue stripe running along both walls.

'Emma!'

Their daughter wasn't alone. Hammond and Rattigan hovered nearby. Hammond looked like shit, Tom thought, with some satisfaction. A harassed-looking nurse saw them, did a double-take, and threw her hands up.

'If you're with this lot, you can't go in, he's only just come back from Radiology!' She hurried away.

'Mum, Dad…' Emma had been crying. 'I've *seen* him…'

'Is he dead, then? Good bloody riddance.'

'No, he's not dead yet, Mr. Morgan.' Hammond looked tired, and uncomfortable. 'But I don't reckon he's long for this world. He…' he shrugged. 'I don't know that they'll let you see him, being as you're not family...'

'What DI Hammond is trying to say,' Rattigan said, 'Is that the person they've got in there,' she jerked a thumb at the ward door , 'is a very old man. I don't think he's going to make it.'

'Not you as well – look, it'll be his father, his bloody grandfather, won't it...?' Tom looked from one to the other; Hammond, Rattigan, and his wife and daughter.

'Yeah, you go on thinking that, Dad.' Emma stood up. She turned to Hammond. 'I think you should leave, Inspector.' He raised his eyebrows but remained where he was. 'What are you going to do – take him back to the station, lock him up? He's dying, you said as much. What would be the point? And besides, how will you explain it? 'The suspect got away, so we're going to lock up his grandfather instead?''

'I won't be able to charge him, as well you know, Miss Morgan. But I can't just close the case...'

'Why not?'

Rattigan stepped forward. 'Emma – look, obviously we don't know why you're so protective of Moran, especially after what he did. But we've got procedures. As Inspector Hammond just said, we can't just leave things as they are... it doesn't work like that.'

'Well, it should! How can you...'

The sound of running feet interrupted her, and the ward door flew open. A young, white-coated woman stared at them. 'Could you move out of the way please?' She flung the door wide as the spotty-face lad Hammond had had a run-in with earlier hurtled past, followed by a man and a woman in white coats, wheeling a small trolley. The doors swung shut behind them.

'Well, that's that, then...' Tom grabbed his daughter's hand. 'Look, I don't know what this man is to you, baby, but we shouldn't be here. We're *not* his fucking family, and I for one have had quite enough of this whole bloody thing! Please, come home with us, darling – the research can wait, it'll still be there for you when you've recovered...'

She slapped his hand away. 'You don't understand... I want to talk to him ...'

'Darling, you need help. It's not your fault...'

'Mum, for goodness sake, tell him, please...I'm not a child, when is he going to realise?'

'Tom, shut up!' Eva took Emma's hand. 'Darling, I don't know what has passed between you and Mr. Moran, but you can't do anything here.' She looked at Hammond. 'If he survives, then I'm sure Inspector Hammond will allow you to speak to him...won't you, Inspector?'

Hammond shrugged. 'Be my guest.'

Eva looked momentarily nonplussed. 'Thank you. You don't need us for the moment?'

Hammond shook his head wearily. 'No, we've got your number, if ...' he looked completely out of his depth, far more upset than a policeman who might have lost a suspect had any right to look, surely?

Emma cleared her throat. 'Whatever you're all thinking went on between James Moran and me, you're almost certainly wrong. He isn't my father, and he didn't rape or otherwise hurt me. I don't want any charges to be brought.' She turned to her parents. 'And I'm not going anywhere, but I'd like you to leave me alone for a while, please, if you don't mind?'

Tom Morgan opened his mouth, then shut it again when his wife glared at him. 'Okay. Whatever you want, Emma.'

Eva smiled at her daughter. 'I hope you'll come and talk to us when this is all over, darling?'

Emma nodded. 'Of course I will, Mum.'

Hammond and Rattigan watched the Morgans walk away.

Emma glanced at the ward door. 'I need to make a phone call,' she said after a moment. 'Are you staying?'

Hammond nodded. 'For a while,' he said. 'Do you mind?'

Emma looked surprised, and then she managed a half-smile. 'No. I won't be long.'

She hurried down the corridor, in the opposite direction that her parents had taken.

* * *

'Is there much point waiting?' Rattigan nodded at the closed doors. 'I mean, even if he pulls through… can we actually charge *him* with anything?'

'No bloody point at all, Lucy.' As he stood up, the door opened, and the woman who had come out earlier scanned the corridor, clearly surprised to see it empty apart from the two detectives. 'Ah. Are you the family…?'

Hammond stood up. 'No, we're not family. A case of mistaken identity.'

'Is he…?' Rattigan had to know.

The woman hesitated, then nodded quickly. 'He didn't make it.' she went back inside.

'Well then,' Hammond said, and started walking. 'Time for a pint, I'd say…what a waste of bloody time that was.'

Rattigan wasn't shocked, but she was surprised. Hammond wasn't callous, or even a bad loser, as a rule, but Moran had clearly rattled him.

'You're not waiting to speak to Emma, sir?'

'She doesn't need us hanging around.'

Rattigan agreed with him. 'Do you really think it was him? You know, when your mum…'

He didn't slow down, didn't look at her. 'Don't know. But I don't want to talk about it, Rattigan.'

He would, she thought. Get a couple or five pints down his neck, he might get it off his chest. But did she really want to know?

60: NOVEMBER 16TH

'Hello, Archie.'

'Miss Morgan.'

'So…I promised you an explanation.'

Archie nodded. 'Yes, you did. But before you say anything, I wanted to tell you… I'm thinking about putting my mother in a nursing home.'

Emma tried not to let her surprise show. 'I'm sure that's the best thing. She'll get the care she needs.'

'Yes. I said there was something I wanted to tell you, too.'

Emma had called Archie from the hospital and told him that she had something very important to tell him. She had realised, as she stood looking at her parents, and at the two Detectives, all of whom had their own theories about James Moran, about who he was and why he had done the things he did, that the only person who might truly understand her dilemma -and the science behind it- was Archie. He was every bit as committed to their work, and he would understand the potential hazards as Moran had -in layman's terms- haltingly attempted to explain to her. Her parents and the police would never understand. They were not stupid, but their strengths and talents lay in altogether different directions. And she knew that Archie was fiercely loyal.

'I think I should speak first.'

Archie nodded. 'All right.'

Emma took a deep breath. She had thought long and hard about what she would tell Archie, and how she would tell him, but it really came down to this – how much did he need to know in order to accept that they needed to revise their project – and more importantly, to agree to help her? And the answer was: pretty much everything.

'James Moran was, will be, my grandson.'

Archie became very still. He frowned. Then, to Emma's surprise, he smiled.

'Well, that explains a lot, Miss… Emma.'

'It does?' She found herself smiling back, a weight lifted from her shoulders.

Archie nodded. He had been holding a few folded sheets of paper. Now he unfolded them, and laid them out on the desk, smoothing them flat. 'I found something,' he said. 'A slide…and because I found the slide… I went looking for these.' He pushed them across the desk towards Emma, and watched her eyes widen and twin red spots appear on her cheeks.

'I'm so sorry that I kept this from you, Archie. But I think you understand why I had to be careful.'

'Oh yes.' He fiddled with his cuffs. 'When I realised what it meant, I didn't know what to think at first. All along, I didn't believe what Inspector Hammond was trying to suggest…but when I found this… I wondered, for a while. But I couldn't believe it of you.'

'Thank you. I didn't want to believe what James was trying to tell me. How could I? I told him that it was science-fiction. But he asked me to take samples, and when I saw the results… well, how could I dismiss it?'

'How indeed. The same conclusion I came to. Who else knows… about your relationship to Mr. Moran, I mean?'

Emma frowned. 'The policeman – he suspected. I'm not sure how he worked it out, but somehow he did. He was going to do a paternity test, Archie. If I tell you that when I saw James in the hospital, he had aged… he looked as if he was a hundred years old, more. He told me…' she swallowed, finding it hard to credit even though she had seen the evidence. 'He said he was two hundred and ten years old, Archie. I called him a liar, I told him -not in so many words- that he was delusional. And he never got angry, never threatened me, never hurt me... he sedated me, he said, because he didn't want a scene, didn't want to be caught before he could tell me...'

'Time travel...' Archie shook his head. 'I find that harder to believe than that there really is a longevity gene...did he explain how it worked?'

'No. He was no scientist, Archie. He told me he used to be a soldier, then he became a policeman - a detective, like Hammond, I think. He... I don't think he chose to do this, but reading between the lines, I think the people who sent him used his daughter, Cassie, as leverage. She was dying – they told him that if he took this assignment, he would change history, and Cassie would live. Then he got trapped here. He was sent to kill whoever found the Methuselah Gene, Archie. He didn't know at first that it was me, or that we were related, until he saw my photo in Aunt Jessica's article. Then he realised...'

'That he couldn't kill you, because it would mean he would never be born... that's a paradox. You've seen the 'Terminator' films...? Oh, well. You can't go back and kill your grandfather, because if you do, you will never exist so couldn't travel backwards in time in the first place...'

'I didn't know you liked science-fiction, Archie.'

'If you don't mind me saying... there's quite a lot you don't know about me,' Archie said, and blushed.

'Ditto,' Emma said, more to ease his embarrassment than anything else, but it was true, wasn't it?

'So... I could tell you everything he told me... which actually wasn't very much, just the important things.'

'As in...?'

'The gene wasn't just given to people with Progeria. It was delivered, via the common cold virus, to the general population.'

Archie looked troubled. 'Which would mean overcrowding, breakdown of … well, many elements. Food production would be stretched to the limit, housing… the mind boggles.'

'Yes, that's what he said. But that's not the worst part. And it means a wonderful thing is just around the corner Archie…and if we don't change what happens, something terrible.'

'Now you're teasing me.'

'A cure for cancer. Isn't that terrific?'

'What was the terrible thing?'

'The gene mutated in the third generation. They only had to deliver it once – Moran's parents were treated, they passed the ability to live longer to him, and he passed it to his daughter. But nature – and I think this is what happened, will happen, Archie- nature found a way to correct the unnatural balance. Cancer came back – and it was triggered – will be triggered- by puberty. So…'

'Another generation and no-one is being born.'

Emma nodded. 'That's what James Moran told me, Archie. But he aged more than a hundred years in just a few weeks, Archie – and at the end, it was so fast… Mum saw him at the station and he was in his fifties, sixties maybe… when I saw him in the hospital, he was much, much older. You had to see it to believe it.'

'Your parents saw him? The police, and the hospital staff? Emma, if they did…'

'Inspector Hammond, one of his colleagues and I were the only ones to see the change take place,' Emma told him. 'The hospital staff only saw him as an elderly man. My parents didn't see him at the end – but they must know something odd was going on. They might ask, and to be honest, I haven't worked out what I'm going to tell them, yet. I think my father believes I'm having some kind of nervous breakdown. My mother… well, she saw him when her husband and daughter died in nineteen-ninety…' Archie's eyebrows rose, and Emma realised there was still a lot she hadn't told him. 'I'll tell you all about it, I promise. But now… well, I need to rethink everything, Archie, do you see? Because James died the way he did, it must mean that I will be successful, that the gene doesn't get rolled out to ev-

324 · EJ JACKSON

eryone… but how I'm going to make sure of that, I don't know, because we aren't the only ones looking for the secret to longer life, are
we? If I try to think about what might still happen…I worry that I
won't be able to stop it.'

Archie leaned forward. 'Emma, I think you can do it. I know you
can. You know something that almost no-one else knows yet. I don't
always agree with it, but well, what if we were to patent the gene
once we find it, and then put a universal ban on its use? And, you can
do it because, well, you've got me.' He grinned, and Emma realised
that she had never seen him do that before - until now. A wide open,
honest-to-God grin. It changed his whole face.

'Well then,' she couldn't help grinning back, 'That's all right,
then… thank you for believing in me, Archie. It means a lot to me, really.'

'That's okay. We should shake on it.' Archie stood up, and offered
Emma his hand. Bemused, she stood, and took it. Archie shook it
twice, solemnly, and then he grinned at her again. She liked it.

'Shall we get to work, then?'

'Yes, let's. But first, I need a really strong – and I mean strong –
coffee. I'll pop down to Costa and get some. What would you like?'

'Whatever you're having, Emma, will be fine.'

'Great. Then we'll talk this through…I won't be long.'

Archie waited until the door had closed behind Emma, and then
he punched the air triumphantly, not once, not twice, but three times.
Then he settled himself at his desk, still smiling.

61: 20TH NOVEMBER

'Are you ready, sir?'

Hammond quickly slid the copy photograph of Moran under his keyboard, then thought better of it and pulled it out again, slipping it into his jacket pocket. He knew Rattigan had seen, and decided he didn't care.

'As ready as I'll ever be.' He stood up, pushing the chair away from him, and flicked the lamp off. The main office was in semi-darkness – a rare and welcome moment, one to be savoured, made the most of.

Rattigan had told Hammond that a date had stood her up – that the table was booked, and she had a hankering for a curry. All on the Q.T. of course – no-one in CID had any idea that the two of them were going out for a meal. It wasn't exactly a lie, and nor was it a date – Rattigan had booked the table for herself and Tim Brown, but Tim had cried off, citing a family crisis. Rattigan didn't believe him, but decided she didn't actually mind. She'd yet to get even one pint down her boss's neck, and the whole of CID knew something was up with their D.I. Only Rattigan knew -or thought she knew- why. It was a shame to waste the booking, she'd told him rather off-handedly. If he didn't fancy it, she probably had a girlfriend who would. He hadn't taken much convincing, but told her to keep it quiet. 'Because you know this lot…'

Rattigan knew them, alright.

She waited until the first course came before raising the subject that had clearly been foremost on Hammond's mind since Moran's death, and never far from her own.

'So... boss, Ian...if you don't mind me asking... was it really Moran you saw in seventy-nine? I mean, you were so young...'

Hammond sighed. 'I don't know, Lucy. I thought it was... I was -am- convinced of it. He even bloody referred to it, the first time I got him in the interview room. Surridge would've had me off the cast that bloody fast... no-one ever transcribed that tape, thank God. I don't know how it was him... but it was.' He took a long pull from his glass of Cobra, and shook his head. 'What did you make of it all?'

Rattigan took her time. 'I don't know, and that's the honest truth. I mean... it's too fantastic for words, isn't it... if one man could really live that long... Emma knows, doesn't she, but she's not saying...'

'No, she's not. But it doesn't matter – case closed.'

'Do you think he had something to do with your mother's disappearance?' There, she'd said it. It sounded almost as stupid as it had when the idea first occurred to her, but something shifted in Hammond's eyes.

'That's what I keep coming back to,' he admitted. 'Look,' he jabbed the table with his forefinger to emphasise each point. 'Say Moran *was* there in seventy-nine, and say he did save Peter King...'

'King's mother is certain that someone did,' Rattigan pointed out.

Hammond nodded. 'And say he was there again in ninety, and caused King's death – for whatever reason, or maybe it was just an accident, as he claims. That's weird enough on its own, right? But then, then he decides to kidnap Emma Morgan. What's the one element linking both people?'

'Eva Morgan.'

'Right. I keep coming back to her. And Emma Morgan was really worried about that paternity test.'

Rattigan nodded.

'I did some research of my own, Lucy, and guess what I found? Green eyes aren't that common. They make up something like two per cent of the population at any given moment. So, what are the odds, eh?' He sat back in his chair and pushed the remains of his starter away. 'I know it's a bloody cliché, but I don't believe in coincidence. Let's say it's nothing more complicated than some long-standing family feud, passed from father to son to grandson… how come we haven't found any trace of them?' He drained his glass, putting it back on the table with a thump. 'As for what any of it means for me, how it might help me find out what happened to my mother…damn it, I should've pressed him harder on it. Now I'll never bloody know, will I?'

Rattigan took a sip of her own beer. 'What will you do now?'

'What can I do? Case bloody closed.' He groaned. 'I'm going to be like Clarke, still mulling it over when I'm in my dotage…'

'You could talk to Emma Morgan again. I think she and Moran talked about a lot more than she's told us.'

'Yeah, I could. But it would look like harassment – that bloody father of hers, he'd be on it like a rash. Surridge would throw the book at me.'

'Maybe I could…'

Hammond stared at her. 'No. You don't need that kind of crap on your record, Lucy.'

'I won't get it, if I don't make it official,' Rattigan said slowly, an idea coalescing in her mind as she spoke. 'I'm not that much older – three years, tops. If I can find out where she hangs out after work, bump into her by chance…it'll take time, and it might not give us anything. But it's worth a punt, don't you think?'

'Maybe…no. It's too risky. She mentions it to her father, and he'll see right through it, I know his type.'

'Well, if she does, and he kicks up a fuss, I'll back off. Surridge can't tell me where to go when I'm off duty, can he?'

Hammond shook his head. 'I don't know, Lucy… this is my problem, not yours. Why are you so interested?' He frowned. 'Look , if it's… this can't go anywhere…' he faltered.

Rattigan felt herself blush. 'God, sir, it's not…it's nothing like that, I promise.' Was it, though? She'd been relieved when Tim cried off, hadn't she – and quick to think of Hammond. But she didn't fancy him. He must be almost ten years older... that was nothing, of course. One of her cousins had married a man sixteen years her senior, they still had a long and happy marriage – a miracle, these days- and three children to prove it. 'I'm sorry, I didn't mean that to sound... it's just, well it's obviously bugging you, and it bothers me, too. I like a mystery, don't you?' She sounded unconvincing, even to her own ears.

To her surprise, Hammond grinned. 'You're a piss-poor liar, Sergeant.'

'You mean Constable.' Let him think what he liked. She wasn't going home with anyone tonight.

'Well, yeah, at the moment. But if you put in for it...you should, you know.'

Rattigan had thought about it. Quite a lot. 'Maybe I will, then.' The force frowned on personal relationships between members of the same team, but if she got transferred... no, it was all moving way too fast. She liked Hammond, but she didn't fancy him...did she?

'Good.' He eyed his plate.

'Aren't you going to eat that... sir?' Her own plate was empty, and Rattigan couldn't remember eating it.

'Do you know, I think I will....' he pulled the plate towards him, and the waiter who had been heading their way veered off towards another table.

'Do you fancy another beer?' Rattigan couldn't hide her smile.

Hammond nodded. 'Go on, then.'

EPILOGUE

'James…James, wake up…'

Vita's voice had once been so clear in his dreams, becoming less so with the passage of time. But now she was beside him, the clipped, precise sound of her Scandinavian roots bringing a rush of warmth to his soul. For just a fleeting moment, he heard the echo of another voice; but the face it conjured up wasn't Vita…wide-set green eyes, yes, but something about the hair… something was wrong.

'…Mother?' He lunged from sleep with a gasp, as if breaking the surface of water, voices and half-remembered images clinging to him like droplets and running away as fast as he could pursue them.

'You were dreaming…'

He turned. The face next to his on the bolster was familiar, so dear to him – and unexpected. He forced a smile, and found that it came quite naturally.

'Vita…I was… I thought…' he found tears in his eyes without quite knowing why. What was wrong with him?

'You were crying for your mother… but it's okay…it's the anniversary, so it's only natural, after all.'

He sat up. Weak winter sunlight filtered through the blinds of their bedroom. He always dreamed of his mother when it got close to the anniversary of her passing. He had never known her, didn't even have a photograph of her, but it had become something of a habit, a way to mark the passing years. Now she had a face…

So what else could be troubling him? The room looked just as he remembered it, Cassie's Persian cat stretching on the chair, chirruping his usual subdued greeting. A shiver ran down his spine. Something felt odd, out of kilter – Cassie. What was it about Cassie that he couldn't quite remember…? It was gone. A bad dream, then. Nothing more.

Vita dropped a quick kiss on his shoulder, and slid elegantly from the bed. Santo got stiffly to his feet, yawning and stretching the age from his bones. How many cats had shared their short lives with them…? It was so hard to keep count…it wasn't something he'd given much thought to. Why now, then?

'I'd better let him out… come along, Santo…You'll be along for breakfast, James…'

No answer was required of him, it seemed. Moran watched his wife exit the room, her figure still trim, and felt a sudden, almost overwhelming relief. He was exactly where he ought to be…. yet something nagged at the edge of his memory…a dream he couldn't recall, a lingering feeling of regret…even as he turned his attention to it, the fragile memory slipped further away.

Moran flung back the covers, and headed for the shower. As he had done yesterday, and would do again tomorrow. Why did that simple thought fill him with such pleasure, as if he might lose it?

As he pulled on a shirt, Moran's cell chimed. He picked it up; he didn't recognise the number, but thought he should.

'Gilling here. We have need of you, James.'

A wave of anger took him by surprise, so that his fingers fumbled with the device. *Gilling….?*

'It's… my mother's memorial today.' Why did he feel such fury? It was there, part of the dream…unattainable.

'Yes, yes…of course, I forgot. Please forgive me. Tomorrow, then.'

He put the mobile down, feeling uneasy. Gilling had forgotten… but so had he, almost. There was something, he was sure of it. He finished dressing, his stomach a tight ball of dread.

The kitchen was bright with reflected sunlight. Moran took his place at the breakfast bar, and sniffed appreciatively, tried to put aside the nameless fear.

'Who was that? Oh, tell me it wasn't *Gilling*?' Vita set the coffee pot on the table between them, frowning.

It seemed important that he maintain normality, whatever that might be. 'He forgot. It's sorted.' He hesitated. 'Cassie …?' His pulse began to race. That was it…something to do with Cassie. And Gilling…

'She'll be there, James. You spoke to her yourself last night – don't you remember? What is wrong with you today? You are not yourself. It's Gilling, isn't it? What did he say?'

He shook his head. 'Nothing. He forgot the date. He apologised for disturbing me.'

'You must tell him, James. Tomorrow. We can't go on like this – each time you come back, you seem further away from me… from us. You promised…'

Moran's throat felt tight; he had to clear it before he could speak. 'Let's not talk about him. Not today. Today is for *us*.' He smiled at his wife. This was their time. As for tomorrow… He would not think about it. There would be another mission, he thought; it would be dangerous… despite his promise to Vita, he knew he would not tell Gilling that he wanted to quit. Even if he couldn't remember why he should.

He took a sip of coffee – strong and black, just how he liked it. Cassie was alive! The thought came from nowhere; and with it, a surge of relief which made him feel dizzy. He blinked, confused. Of *course* she was alive – why on earth would he think otherwise? A memory flickered behind his eyes: a darkened hospital room, his throat tight with tears. A figure on the bed that he couldn't quite see, but felt he should know… a nightmare, nothing more, surely?

The familiar signature tune of Morning Local pushed the shadows away, and he stared at the hologram.

'This morning, sources report that a fuel pipe ruptured in the Piccadilly Development. Fortunately, no lives were lost, but the building will be uninhabitable for some time. Sources at the fire department say…'

Moran's stomach knotted. He remembered acrid smoke, sirens, and screams… and a small boy, his face streaked with soot and tears.

'Have you seen my mum?'

ABOUT THE AUTHOR

EJ Jackson is the author of 'The Journey & Other Short Stories' and 'The Methuselah Paradox'.

A native of Hampshire, Elaine has loved science fiction for as long as she can remember. 'Star Trek', 'Doctor Who' and 'Captain Scarlet' were early and enduring favourites, later joined by such stalwarts as 'Blake's 7' and 'The Hitch Hiker's Guide to the Galaxy' - in 1980 Elaine founded the official appreciation society for the series, ZZ9, which still has a healthy membership.

Elaine's next project is to adapt 'The Methuselah Paradox' for the stage, and a follow-up novel also featuring D.I. Hammond. She is also developing a graphic novel and a short animated science fiction film, titled 'Minding Mama'. You can find out more on: the website: www.mindingmama.org

Elaine is an avid reader, and enjoys TV, movies and going to the theatre. She lives in Surrey with her husband and son.

Keep up to date with new projects here:

www.ejjackson.org

or follow Elaine on Twitter:

https://twitter.com/ElaineJackson12